Danielle Steel is a descendant of the Löwenbräu beer barons. Her mother is Portuguese and her father is German. Their common language is French, although they all speak eight languages. Danielle's father's family, the prominent banking and brewing clan, has always lived in Munich and the family seat was a moated castle in Bavaria, Kaltenberg. Her mother's family were diplomats and her maternal grandfather was a Portuguese diplomat assigned to the United States for a number of years.

American-born, Danielle lived in Paris for most of her childhood. At the age of 20 she went to New York and started working for 'Supergirls', a before-its-time public relations firm run by women who organised parties for Wall Street brokerage houses and designed PR campaigns for major firms. When the recession hit, the firm went out of business and Danielle 'retired' to write her first book, *Going Home*.

Danielle has established herself as a writer of extraordinary scope. She has set her various novels all over the world, from China to New York to San Francisco, in time-frames spanning 1860 to the present. She has received critical acclaim for her elaborate plots and meticulous research, and has brought vividly to life a broad range of very different characters.

Also by Danielle Steel in Sphere Books:

The Ring
DANIELLE STEEL

SPHERE BOOKS LIMITED

A SPHERE BOOK

First published in Great Britain by Hodder & Stoughton Ltd 1980
Published by Sphere Books Ltd 1981
Reprinted 1981 (twice), 1983 (three times), 1984, 1985 (three times),
1986 (twice), 1987, 1988, 1989 (twice), 1990

Printed and bound in Great Britain by
BPCC Hazell Books
Aylesbury, Bucks, England
Member of BPCC Ltd.

ISBN 0 7221 8179 5

Sphere Books Ltd
A Division of
Macdonald & Co (Publishers) Ltd
Orbit House, 1 New Fetter Lane, London EC4A 1AR
A member of Maxwell Macmillan Pergamon Publishing Corporation

To Omi

Love
d.s.

Book One

KASSANDRA

Chapter 1

Kassandra von Gotthard sat peacefully at the edge of the lake in the Charlottenburger park, watching the water ripple slowly away from the pebble she had just thrown. The long, graceful fingers held another small smooth stone, poised for a moment, and then threw it aimlessly into the water once again. It was a hot, sunny day at the end of the summer and her golden strawberry hair fell in one long, smooth wave to her shoulders, pushed away from her face on one side with a single ivory comb. The line of the comb in the smooth golden hair was as perfect and graceful as everything else about her face. Her eyes were enormous and almond shaped, of the same rich blue as the bank of flowers behind her in the park. They were eyes that promised laughter, and yet they whispered something tender at the same time; eyes that would caress and tease, and then grow pensive, as though lost in some distant dream as far removed from the present as the Charlottenburger Schloss just across the lake was distant from the bustling city. The old castle sat timelessly, watching her, as though she belonged to its era rather than her own.

Lying on the grass at the edge of the lake, Kassandra looked like a woman in a painting or a dream, her delicate hands sifting gently through the grass, looking for another small pebble to throw. Nearby, the ducks were waddling into the water as two small children clapped their hands with glee. Kassandra watched them, seeming to search their faces for a long moment, as they laughed and ran away.

'What were you thinking just then?' The voice at her side pulled her from her reverie, and she turned towards it with a slow smile.

'Nothing.' Her smile broadened and she held out a hand towards him, her intricate, diamond-encrusted signet ring gleaming in the sun. But he didn't notice it. The jewels she wore mattered nothing to him. It was Kassandra who intrigued him, who seemed to hold the mystery of life and beauty for him. She was a question to which he would never know an answer, a gift he would never quite possess.

They had met the previous winter, at a party to celebrate his second book, *Der Kuss*. In his outspoken fashion, he had shocked all of Germany for a time, but the book had nonetheless won him still more acclaim than his first. The story had been deeply sensitive and erotic and his seat at the pinnacle of Germany's contemporary literary movement seemed assured. He was controversial, he was modern, he was at times outrageous, and he was also very, very talented. At thirty-three, Dolff Sterne had made it to the top. And then he had met his dream.

Her beauty had left him breathless the night they met. He had heard of her; everyone in Berlin knew who she was. She seemed untouchable, unreachable, and she looked frighteningly fragile. Dolff had felt something akin to a shaft of pain when he first saw her, wearing a silky, clinging dress of woven gold, her shimmering hair barely covered by a tiny golden cap, a sable coat draped over one arm. But it wasn't the gold or the sable that had stunned him, it was her presence, her separateness and silence in the clamour of the room, and finally her eyes. When she turned and smiled at him, for an instant he felt as though he might die.

'Congratulations.'

'On what?' He had stared at her for an instant, struck almost dumb, feeling his thirty-three years shrink to ten, until he noticed she was nervous, too. She wasn't at all what he had expected. She was elegant, but not aloof. He suspected that she was frightened of the staring eyes, the milling crowd. She had left early, disappearing like Cinderella as he greeted still more guests. He had wanted to run after her, to find her, to see her again, if only for an instant, to look again into the lavender eyes.

Two weeks later they had met again. In the park, here at Charlottenburg. He had watched her looking up at the

4

castle, and then smiling at the ducks.

'Do you come here often?' They had stood side by side for a quiet moment, his tall, dark good looks in striking contrast to her delicate beauty. His hair was the colour of her sable, his eyes brilliant onyx looking into hers. She nodded and then looked up at him with that mysteriously childlike smile.

'I used to come here when I was a little girl.'

'You're from Berlin?' It had seemed a stupid question, but he hadn't been sure what to say.

She laughed at him, but not unkindly. 'Yes. And you'

'München.' She nodded again, and they stood in silence for a long time. He wondered how old she was. Twenty-two? Twenty-four? It was difficult to tell. And then suddenly he heard a peal of crystal laughter as she watched three children, cavorting with their dog, elude their nurse and wind up knee deep in the water, the recalcitrant bulldog refusing to join them on the shore again.

'I did that once. My nurse wouldn't let me come back here for a month.' He smiled at her. He could have imagined the scene. She seemed young enough still to hike into the water, yet the sable and the diamonds she wore made it seem unlikely that she had ever been unfettered enough to chase into the water after a dog. He could almost see it though, with a governess in starched uniform and cap berating her from the shore. And when would that have been? 1920? 1915? It seemed light-years away from his own pursuits at that time. In those years he had been struggling to manage school and work at the same time, helping his parents at the bakery every morning before school and for long hours every afternoon. How far removed that had seemed from this golden woman.

He had haunted the park at Charlottenburg after that, telling himself that he needed air and exercise after he wrote all day, but secretly he knew better. He was looking for that face, those eyes, the golden hair . . . and at last he found her, again at the lake. She had seemed happy to see him when they met again. And then it became a kind of silent understanding. He would take walks when he finished

5

writing, and if he timed it right, she would be there.

They became spiritual guardians of the castle, surrogate parents of the children playing near the lake. They took a kind of possessive joy in their surroundings, telling each other stories of their childhood, and each listening to the other tell about his dreams. She had wanted to be in the theatre, much to her father's horror, but it had always been her private dream. She understood perfectly that it would never happen, but now and then she dreamed that in her later years she would write a play. She was always fascinated when he spoke of his writing, how he had started, what it felt like when his first book became a success. The fame still didn't seem quite real to him, and perhaps it never would. It had been five years since his first successful novel, seven years since he had left Munich and come to Berlin, three years since he'd brought the Bugatti, two since the beautiful old house in Charlottenburg had become his . . . and still none of it was quite real. Not quite believing it all kept him youthful, and kept the look of delight and astonishment in his eyes. Dolff Stern was not blasé yet, not about life, or writing, and least of all about her.

She was enchanted as she listened. Listening to him talk about his books, she felt the stories come alive, the characters become real; and being with him, she felt herself come alive again, too. And week after week as they met, he saw the fear in her eyes grow dimmer. There was something different about her now when he met her at the lake. Something funny and young and delicious.

'Do you have any idea how much I like you Kassandra?' He had said it to her playfully as the walked slowly around the lake one day, enjoying the balmy spring breeze.

'Are you going to write a book about me, then?'

'Should I?'

But she lowered the lavender eyes for a moment and then, looking back up at him, shook her head. 'Hardly. There wouldn't be anything to say. No victories, no successes, no accomplishments. Nothing at all.'

His eyes held hers for a long moment, the lavender and

6

the black saying words that could not yet be said. 'Is that what you think?'

'It's what is true. I was born into my life and I will die out of my life. And in between I will wear a great many lovely dresses, go to a thousand proper dinners, listen to countless well-sung operas . . . and that, my friend, is all.' At twenty-nine, she already sounded as though she had lost hope . . . hope of life ever being any different.

'And your play?'

She shrugged. They both knew the answer. She was a prisoner in a diamond cage. And then, smiling up at him, she laughed again. 'So, my only hope for fame and glory is for you to make something up for me, put me in a novel, and turn me into some exotic character in your head.' That much he had already done, but he didn't quite dare tell her. Not yet. Instead he played the game with her, tucking her hand into his arm.

'All right. In that case, let's at least do it to your liking. What would you like to be? What seems to you suitably exotic? A spy? A woman surgeon? The mistress of a very famous man?'

She made a face and laughed at him. 'How dreadful. Really, Dolff, how dull. No, let's see . . .' They had stopped to sit on the grass as she flung off her wide-brimmed straw hat and shook loose the golden hair. 'An actress, I think . . . You could make me a star of the London stage . . . and then . . .' She tilted her head to one side, winding her hair around the long, graceful fingers as her rings shone in the sun. 'Then . . . I could go to America and be a star there.'

'America, eh? Where?'

'New York.'

'Have you ever been?'

She nodded. 'With my father when I turned eighteen. It was fabulous. We were – ' And then she stopped. She had been about to tell him that they'd been the guests of the Astors in New York and then of the President in Washington, DC, but somehow it didn't seem quite right. She didn't want to impress him. She wanted to be his friend. She liked him too

7

much to play those games with him. And it didn't matter how successful he had become, the truth was that he would never be part of that world. They both knew it. It was something they never discussed.

'You were what?' He had been watching her, his lean, handsome face close to hers.

'We were in love with New York. At least I was.' She sighed and looked wistfully at their lake.

'Is it anything like Berlin?'

She shook her head, squinting, as though to make the Charlottenburger Schloss disappear. 'No, it's wonderful. It's new and modern, and busy and exciting.'

'And of course Berlin is so dull.' Sometimes he couldn't help laughing at her. To him, Berlin was still all of those things she had said about New York.

'You're teasing me.' There was reproach in her voice, but not in her eyes. She enjoyed being with him. She loved the ritual of their afternoon walks. More and more now, she escaped the fetters and restrictions of her daily obligations and came to meet him in the park.

His eyes were kind when he answered her. 'I am teasing you, Kassandra. Do you mind very much?'

She shook her head slowly. 'No, I don't.' And then, after a pause, 'I feel as though I've come to know you better than anyone else I know.' It was disturbing, but he felt the same way. Yet she was still his dream, his illusion, and she eluded him constantly, except here in the park. 'Do you know what I mean?' He nodded, not sure what to say. He still didn't want to frighten her. He didn't want her to stop meeting him for their walks.

'Yes, I understand.' Far more than she knew. And then, seized by a moment of madness, he took her hand, long and frail, in his own, yet encumbered by the large rings she wore. 'Would you like to come to my place for tea?'

'Now?' Her heart had fluttered strangely at the question. She wanted to, but she wasn't sure . . . she didn't think . . .

'Yes, now. Do you have something else you should do?'

She shook her head slowly. 'No, I don't.' She could have

told him that she was busy, that she had an appointment, that she was expected somewhere for tea. But she didn't. She looked up at him with those huge lavender eyes. 'I'd like that.'

They walked side by side, laughing and talking, secretly nervous, leaving the protection of Eden for the first time. He told her funny stories, and she laughed as she hurried beside him, swinging her hat. There was a sudden urgency to their mission. As though this was what they had been building up to with their months of walks in the park.

The heavily carved door swung open slowly and they stepped into a large marble hall. There was a huge, handsome painting hanging over a Biedermeier desk. Their footsteps echoed emptily as she followed him inside.

'So this is where the famous author lives.'

He smiled at her nervously as he dropped his hat on the desk. 'The house is a good deal more famous than I. It belonged to some seventeenth-century baron and has been in far more illustrious hands than mine ever since.' He looked around him proudly and then beamed at her as she stared up at the carved rococo ceiling and then back at him.

'It's beautiful, Dolff.' She seemed very quiet, and he held out a hand.

'Come, I'll show you the rest.'

The rest of the house fulfilled the promise of the entrance, with tall, beautifully carved ceilings, wonderfully inlaid floors, small crystal chandeliers, and long, elegant windows looking out on a garden filled with bright flowers. On the main floor were a large living room and a smaller one that he used as a den. On the next floor were the kitchen and dining room and a small maid's room where he kept a bicycle and three pairs of skis. And above that were two huge, beautiful bedrooms, with views of the schloss and their park. There were handsome balconies perched outside each bedroom, and in the larger of the bedrooms was a narrow winding staircase tucked into a corner of the room.

'What's up there?' She had been intrigued. The house really was a beauty. Dolff had good reason to be proud.

He smiled at her. He enjoyed the admiration and approval he could see in her eyes. 'My ivory tower. That's where I work.'

'I thought you worked downstairs in the den.'

'No, that's just to entertain friends in. The living room still intimidates me a little bit. But this' – he pointed skyward from the foot of the narrow stairs 'is it.'

'May I see?'

'Of course, if you can wade through the papers around my desk.'

But there were no papers around the well-ordered desk. It was a small, beautifully proportioned room with a three-hundred-sixty-degree view. There was a cosy fireplace, and in every imaginable corner there were books. It was a room one could virtually live in, and Kassandra settled happily into a large red leather chair with a sigh.

'What a wonderful, wonderful place.' She was looking dreamily out at their schloss.

'I think this is why I bought the house. My ivory tower, and the view.'

'I don't blame you, even though the rest is lovely, too.' She had curled one leg under her as she sat down, and she smiled up at him with a look of peace that he had never quite seen on her face before. 'Do you know what, Dolff? This feels like I'm home at last. I feel like I've been waiting all my life just to come here.' Her eyes never wavered from his.

'Perhaps –' his voice was whisper soft in the room – 'the house has been waiting for you all these years . . . just as I have.' He felt a wave of shock ripple through him. He hadn't meant to tell her that. But her eyes showed no anger. 'I'm sorry, I didn't mean to.'

'It's all right, Dolff.' She held out a hand to him, her diamond signet ring catching the sun. He took her hand gently, and without stopping to think, he pulled her ever so slowly into his arms. He held her there for what seemed like an eternity, as they kissed beneath the bright blue spring sky, and they held tightly to each other in his ivory tower. She kissed him with a hunger and passion that only fanned his flame, and it seemed hours before he had the presence of mind to pull away.

'Kassandra . . .' There was both pleasure and torment in his eyes, but she stood up and turned her back to him, looking down at the park.

'Don't.' Her voice was a whisper. 'Don't tell me you're sorry. I don't want to hear it . . . I can't . . .' And then she turned to him, her eyes blazing with a pain akin to his own. 'I've wanted you for so long.'

'But . . .' He hated himself for his hesitations, but he had to say it, if only for her.

She put up a hand to silence him. 'I understand. Kassandra von Gotthard doesn't say things like this, is that is?' Her eyes hardened. 'You're quite right. I don't. But I wanted to. Oh, God, how I wanted to. I didn't even know how much I wanted to until just now. I never have before. I've lived my life until now just as I was meant to. And do you know what I have, Dolff? Nothing. Do you know who I am? No one. I am empty.' And then, with tears misting her eyes, 'And I was looking to you to fill my soul.' She turned away again. 'I'm sorry.'

He came up softly behind her and put his arms around her waist. 'Don't. Don't ever think that you are no one. You are everything to me. All these months, all I wanted was to know you better, to be with you, to give you something of what I am, and to share some part of you. I just don't want to hurt you, Kassandra. I don't want to pull you into my world at the risk of making you unable to live in your own. I have no right to do that. I have no right to take you away to a place where you couldn't be happy.'

'What? Here?' She turned to look at him with disbelief. 'Do you think I could be unhappy here with you? Even for an hour?'

'But that's just it. For how long, Kassandra? For an hour? Two? An afternoon?' He looked anguished as he faced her.

'That's enough. Even a moment of this in my lifetime would be enough.' And then, the delicate lips trembling, she lowered her head. 'I love you, Dolff . . . I love you . . . I . . .'

He silenced her lips with his own, and slowly they walked down the narrow staircase again. But they went no further. Taking her hand gently, he led her to his bed and peeled away the fine grey silk of her dress and creamy beige satin of her slip, until he reached the exquisite lace that lay beneath, and the velvet of her flesh. They lay there together for hours, their lips and their hands and their bodies and their hearts blending into one.

It had been four months since that day, and the love affair had changed them both. Kassandra's eyes sparkled and danced; she teased and she played with him, and sat cross-legged in his big, beautiful carved bed, telling him funny stories of what she had done the day before. As for Dolff, his work had taken on a new texture, a new depth, and there was a new strength about him that seemed to come from his very core. Together they shared something that they felt sure no one had ever shared before. They were a meshing of the best of two worlds: his hard-won, hard-earned, determined struggle to excel, and her fragile fluttering to break free of her golden bonds.

They still walked in the park sometimes, but less often, and when they were together out of his house now, he often found her sad. They were too many other people, too many children and nannies and other couples strolling in the park. She wanted to be alone with him in their own private world. She didn't want to be reminded of a world outside his walls that they did not share.

'Do you want to go back?' He had been watching her quietly for a time. She was stretched gracefully on the grass, a pale mauve voile dress draped over her legs, the sun catching the gold in her hair. A mauve silk hat lay cast aside on the grass, and her stockings were the same ivory colour as her kid pumps. There was a heavy rope of pearls around her neck, and behind her on the grass were her kid gloves and the mauve silk bag with the ivory clasp that had been made to match her dress.

'Yes, I want to go back.' She stood up quickly, with a

happy smile. 'What were you looking at just then?' He had been staring at her so intently.

'You.'

'Why?'

'Because you're so incredibly beautiful. Do you know if I wrote about you I'd be totally at a loss for words.'

'Then just say that I'm ugly and stupid and fat.' She grinned at him and they both laughed.

'Would that please you?'

'Immensely.' She was teasing and mischievous again.

'Well, at least no one would recognise you if I wrote about you like that.'

'Are you really going to write about me?'

He was thoughtful for a long moment as they walked towards the house they both loved. 'One day I will. But not yet.'

'Why?'

'Because I'm still too overwhelmed by you to write anything coherent. In fact –' he smiled down at her from his considerable height – 'I may never be very coherent again.'

Their afternoons together were sacred, and they were often torn about whether to spend them in bed or sit comfortably in his ivory tower talking about his work. Kassandra was the woman he had waited half a lifetime for. And with Dolff, Kassandra had found what she had always so desperately needed, someone who understood the odd meanderings of her soul, the longings, the fragmented pieces, the rebelliousness against the lonely restrictions of her world. They had come to an understanding. And they both knew that, for the moment, they had no choice.

'Do you want some tea, darling?' She tossed her hat and gloves on the desk in the entrance hall and went to her bag for her comb. It was onyx and ivory, inlaid and beautiful, and expensive, like everything else that she owned. She put it back in her bag and turned to Dolff with a smile. 'Stop grinning at me, silly. . . tea?'

'Hmmm . . . what? Yes. I mean, no. Never mind that,

13

Kassandra.' And then he firmly took her hand in his. 'Come upstairs.'

'Planning to show me a new chapter, are you?' She smiled her incomparable smile as her eyes danced.

'Of course. I have a whole new book I want to discuss with you at length.'

An hour later as he slept peacefully next to her, she looked down at him with tears in her eyes. She slipped carefully from the bed. She always hated to leave him. But it was almost six o'clock. After softly closing the door to the large white marble bathroom, she emerged again ten minutes later, fully dressed, with a look of great longing and sadness about her face. She paused for a moment next to the bed, and as though sensing her standing next to him, he opened his eyes.

'You're going?'

She nodded, and for an instant they shared a look of pain. 'I love you.'

He understood. 'So do I.' He sat up in bed and held out his arms to her. 'I'll see you tomorrow, my darling.' She smiled, kissed him again, and then blew him another kiss from the doorway before she hurried down the stairs.

Chapter 2

The drive from Charlottenburg to Grunewald, only slightly further from the centre of the city, took Kassandra less than half an hour. She could make it in exactly fifteen minutes if she kept her foot on the floor in the little navy blue Ford coupe; she had long since established the quickest route home. Her heart pounded slightly as she glanced at her watch.

She was later than usual today, but she still had time to change. It annoyed her that she should be so nervous. It seemed absurd to still feel like a fifteen-year-old girl late for curfew.

The narrow, curved streets of Grunewald came rapidly into view, as the Grunewaldsee lay flat and mirrorlike to her right. There wasn't a ripple on the water, and all she could hear was the birds. The large homes that lined the road sat solidly behind their brick walls and iron gates, concealed by trees and shrouded in their conservative silence, as in bedrooms upstairs maids assisted their ladies to dress. But she still had time, she wasn't too late.

She pulled the car to a quick halt at the entrance to their driveway and hopped rapidly out of the car, fitting her key into the heavy brass lock in the gate. She swung both sides open and drove the car through. She could have someone come back to close the gate later. She didn't have time now. The gravel crunched noisily beneath the wheels of her car as with a practised eye she surveyed the house. It had been built in something of a French manner and stretched out endlessly on either side of the main door. There were three sober-looking storeys of discreet grey stone, topped by yet another floor with lower ceilings nestled beneath the handsomely designed mansard roof. The upper floor housed the servants. Beneath that was a floor that she noticed now was lit by lights in almost every room. Then there were her own rooms, as well as several guest rooms, and two pretty libraries, one looking out over the garden, the other over the lake. On the floor where her own rooms were shone only one light, and beneath that, on the main floor, everything was ablaze. The dining room, the main salon, the large library, the small smoking room panelled in dark wood and lined with rare books. She wondered for a moment why every single light on the lower floor appeared to be on that night, and then she remembered, and her hand flew to her mouth.

'Oh, my God . . . oh, no!' Her heart pounding harder, she abandoned her car outside the house. The huge, perfectly manicured lawn was deserted, and even the abundantly stocked flowerbeds seemed to reproach her as she ran up the short flight of steps. How could she have forgotten? What would he say? Clutching her hat and gloves in one hand, her handbag jammed unceremoniously under her arm, she fought the front door with her key. But as she did so, the door opened and she stood staring into the intransigent face of Berthold, their butler, his bald head gleaming in the bright light of the twin chandeliers in the main hall, his white tie and tails impeccable as always, his eyes too cold even to register disapproval. They simply gazed expressionlessly into her own. Behind him a maid in a black uniform and white lace apron and cap hurried across the main hall.

'Good evening, Berthold.'

'Madam.' The door closed resolutely behind her, almost at the same moment as Berthold clicked his heels.

Nervously Kassandra glanced into the main salon. Thank God everything was ready. The dinner party for sixteen had been the last thing on her mind. Fortunately she had gone over it in detail with her housekeeper the morning before. Frau Klemmer had everything under control, as always. Nodding to the servants as she went, Kassandra rushed upstairs, wishing she could take the stairs two at a time as she did at Dolff's when they were running up to bed . . . to bed . . . . a glimmer of a smile floated to her eyes as she thought of it, but she had to force him from her mind.

She paused on the landing, looking down the long grey-carpeted hall. Everything around her was pearl grey, the silk on the walls, the thick carpets, the velvet drapes. There were two handsome Louis XV chests, magnificently inlaid and topped with marble, and every few feet along the walls were antique sconces with pretty flame-shaped lights. And set between them were small Rembrandt etchings, which had been in the family for years. Doors stretched to her right and left, and a glimmer of light shone beneath only one. She stopped for a moment and then ran on, down the hall towards her own room. She had just reached it when she heard a door behind her open, and the dimly lit hallway was suddenly flooded with light.

'Kassandra?' The voice behind her was forbidding, but when she turned to face him, the eyes were not. Tall, lithe, still handsome at fifty-eight, his eyes were an icier blue than hers, his hair a mixture of sand and snow. It was a beautiful face, the kind of face one saw in early Teutonic portraits, and the shoulders were square and broad.

'I'm so sorry . . . I couldn't help it . . . I got terribly delayed . . .' For an instant they stood there, their eyes holding. There was much left unsaid.

'I understand.' And he did. So much more than she knew. 'You'll be able to manage? It would be awkward if you were late.'

'I won't be. I promise.' She eyed him sorrowfully. But her sadness was not for the dinner party she had forgotten, but for the joy they no longer shared.

He smiled at her from across the vast expanse of distance that seemed to separate their two lives. 'Hurry. And . . . Kassandra . . .' He paused, and she knew what was coming, as waves of guilt surged upward towards her throat. 'Have you been upstairs?'

She shook her head.'No, not yet. I'll do that before I come down.'

Walmar von Gotthard nodded and softly closed his door. Behind that door lay his private apartment, a large, stark bedroom furnished in German and English antiques in dark woods; a Persian carpet in deep wines and sea blues blanketed the rich wood floors. The walls of his bedroom were wood panelled, as were those of the study that was his private sanctum just beyond. There was also a large dressing room and his own bathroom. Kassandra's apartment was larger still. And now, flying through her bedroom door, she tossed her hat on to the pink satin comforter on her bed. Her rooms were as much like her as Walmar's were like him. Everything was soft and smooth, ivory and pink, satin and silk, draped and gentle, and hidden from the world. The curtains were so lavish that they obscured her view of the garden, the room so draped and enclosed that, like her life with Walmar, it hid her from the world beyond. Her dressing room was nearly as large as her bedroom, a solid bank of closets filled with exquisite clothes, an entire wall of

17

custom-made shoes faced by endless rows of pink satin boxes filled with hats. Behind a small French Impressionist painting hid the safe that held her jewels. And beyond the dressing room, a small sitting room with a view of the lake. There was a chaise longue that had been her mother's, and a tiny French lady's desk. There were books she no longer read now, a sketch pad she hadn't touched since March. It was as though she no longer lived here. She only came to life in the arms of Dolff.

Kicking off the ivory kid pumps and hastily unbuttoning the lavender dress, she pulled open the doors of two closets, mentally reviewing what hung inside. But as she stared into the closets' contents, she had to stop, barely able to catch her breath. What was she doing? What had she done? What kind of mad existence had she let herself in for? What hope did she have of ever having a real life with Dolff? She was Walmar's wife forever. She knew it, always had known it, since she had married him at nineteen. He had been forty-eight then, and the marriage had seemed so right. A close associate of her father's, head of her father's sister bank, it had been a merger as much as a marriage. For people like Kassandra and Walmar, that's what made the most sense. They shared a life-style, they knew all the same people. Their families had intermarried once or twice before. Everything about the marriage should have worked. It didn't matter if he was so much older, and it wasn't as if he were elderly or half dead. Walmar had always been a dazzling man, and ten years after their marriage he still was. What's more, he understood her. He understood the frail otherworldliness about her, he knew how carefully she had been cloistered and nurtured during her early life. He would protect her from life's coarser moments.

So Kassandra had her life cut out for her, from a pattern well worn by tradition and cut by hands more skilled than her own. All she had to do was what was expected of her and Walmar would cherish and protect her, guard and guide her, and continue to maintain the cocoon that had been spun for her at birth. Kassandra von Gotthard had nothing to fear from Walmar; in fact, she had nothing to fear at all, except perhaps herself. And she knew that now, better than she had ever known it before.

Having torn one tiny hole in the cocoon that protected her, she had fled now, if not in body, then in soul. Yet she still had to come home at night, to play the role, to be who she was meant to be, to be Walmar von Gotthard's wife.

'Frau von Gotthard?'

Kassandra wheeled nervously as she heard the voice behind her in her dressing room. 'Oh, Anna . . . thank you. I don't need any help.'

'Fräulein Hedwig asked me to tell you –' Oh, God, it was coming; Kassandra turned away from her, feeling guilt pierce her once again to the core – ' the children would like to see you before they go to bed.'

'I'll come upstairs as soon as I'm dressed. Thank you.' The tone of her voice told the young woman in the black lace uniform to go. Kassandra knew all the tones to use to perfection, the right intonations and right words were part of her blood. Never rude, never angry, seldom brusque, she was a lady. This was her world. But as the door closed softly behind the maid, Kassandra sank to a chair in her dressing room with tears brimming in her eyes. She felt helpless, broken, pulled. This was the world of her duties, the existence she had been bred to. And it was precisely what she ran away from each day when she went to meet Dolff.

Walmar was her family now. Walmar and the children. She had no one to turn to. Her father was dead now. And her mother, gone two years after her father, had she been this lonely too? There was no one to ask, and no one she knew who would have told her the truth.

From the start she and Walmar had maintained a respectful distance. Walmar had suggested separate bedrooms. There were little evenings in her boudoir, champagne chilled in silver coolers, which eventually led them to bed, though very seldom since the birth of their last child, when Kassandra had been twenty-four. The child had been born by Cesarean section and she had almost died. Walmar was concerned about what another pregnancy could do to her, as was she. The champagne had cooled less and less often after that. And since March there had been no evenings in her boudoir at all. Walmar asked no questions. It had taken little to make herself understood, the mention of several trips to the doctor, a mention of an ache, a pain, a headache; she retired early to her bedroom every night. It was all right, Walmar understood it. But in truth, when Kassandra came back to this house, to his house, to her bedroom, she knew that it wasn't all right at all. What would she do now? Was this what life had promised? Was she to go on just like this, indefinitely? Probably. Until Dolff tired of the game. Because he would, he'd have to. Kassandra knew it already, even if Dolff did not. And then what? Another? And another? Or no one at all? As she stood staring bleakly into her mirror, she wasn't sure any more. The woman who had been certain in the house in Charlottenburg that afternoon was no longer quite as poised. She knew only that she was a woman who had betrayed her husband and her way of life.

Taking a deep breath, she stood up and went back to her closet. It didn't matter what she felt now, she had to dress. The least she could do for him was look decent at his dinner. The guests were all fellow bankers and their wives. She was always the youngest at any gathering, but she carried herself well.

For an instant Kassandra wanted to slam the door to her closet and run upstairs, to be with the children – the miracles hidden from her on the third floor. The children playing at the lake at Charlottenburg always reminded her of them, and it always pained her to realise that she knew her own children as little as she knew those tiny laughing strangers at the lake. Fräulein Hedwig was their mother now. She always had been and always would be. Kassandra felt like a stranger with the little boy and girl, who both looked so much like Walmar and so little like her . . . 'Don't be absurd, Kassandra. You can't take care of her yourself.'

'But I want to.' She had looked at Walmar sadly the day

after Ariana was born. 'She's mine.'

'She's not yours, she's ours.' He had smiled at her gently as tears filled her eyes. 'What do you want to do, stay up all night and change diapers? You'd be exhausted in two days. It's unheard of, it's . . . nonsense.' For a moment he had looked annoyed. But it wasn't nonsense. It was what she wanted, and she knew also that it was what she would never be allowed to do.

The nurse had arrived on the day they left the hospital and whisked the baby Ariana to the third floor. That night, when Kassandra had walked upstairs to see her, she had been admonished by Fräulein for disturbing the baby. The infant was to be brought to her, Walmar insisted; there was no reason for Kassandra to go upstairs. But her little girl was brought to her only once in the morning, and when Kassandra appeared in the nursery later, she was always told it was too early or too late, the baby was sleeping, fussing, cranky, unhappy. And Kassandra would be sent away to languish in her room. 'Wait until the child is older,' Walmar told her, 'then you can play with her anytime you want.' But by then it was too late. Kassandra and the child were strangers. The nurse had won. And when the second child came three years later, Kassandra was too sick to put up a fight. Four weeks in the hospital, and another four weeks in bed at home. Four more months of an overwhelming sense of depression. And when it was over, she knew it was a battle she would never win. Her assistance wasn't needed, her help, or her love, or her time. She was a pretty lady who would come to visit, wearing pretty clothes and smelling of wonderful French perfume. She would sneak them cakes and candy, spend fortunes on exotic toys, but what they needed from her she was not allowed to give them, and what she wanted from them in return they had long since bestowed upon the nurse.

The tears having subsided, Kassandra pulled herself together, took her dress from her closet, and crossed the room to find a pair of black suede shoes. She had nine pairs of them for evening but she chose the ones she had acquired most recently, with pear-shaped openings over the toes, leaving her brightly polished nails visible. Her silk stockings made a whispering sound as she took them from their satin box and changed from the ivory-coloured stockings she had worn earlier. She was grateful suddenly that she'd taken the time to bathe at Dolff's. Now as she stood there, sliding carefully into the black dress, it seemed incredible that she existed in Dolff's world at all. The house in Charlottenburg seemed like a distant dream. This was her reality. The world of Walmar von Gotthard. She was irretrievably and undeniably his wife.

She zipped herself into the dress, which was a long, narrow sheath of black wool crepe with long arms and high neck, stopping just short of the black suede shoes. It was striking and sombre, and only when she turned around was its full beauty and her own revealed. A large oval opening, like a giant teardrop, revealed her back from neck to waist; her ivory skin glimmering in the opening, like moonlight reflected on a black ocean on a summer night.

Putting a short silk cape over her shoulders to protect the dress, she carefully combed her hair and swept it off her neck, piercing the neat twist she created with long black coral pins. Satisfied with the effect she had created, she wiped the mascara from beneath each eye and redid her face, took one last look in the mirror, and fastened a large pear-shaped diamond to each ear. On her hands were the large emerald she often wore in the evening and the diamond signet ring she always wore on her right hand. The ring had graced the hands of women in her family for four generations. It bore the initials of her great-grandmother in diamonds and glimmered as it caught the light.

With a last glance over her shoulder she knew that she looked as always, striking, lovely, tranquil. No one would have dreamed that underneath there was torment. No one would have guessed that she had spent the afternoon in the arms of Dolff.

In the long, quiet grey hallway, she paused for only an instant at the foot of the stairs leading up to the third floor. A clock in the corner sombrely chimed the hour. She was actually on time. It was seven o'clock, and the guests were expected at seven-thirty. She had half an hour to spend with Ariana and Gerhard before they went to bed. Thirty minutes of motherhood. She wondered, as she climbed the stairs to see them, how much that would add up to in their lifetimes. How many thirty minutes multiplied by how many days? But had she seen her own mother more often? She knew, as she reached the last step on the stairway, that she had not. And that what she had that was most vivid and tangible was the signet ring, which had always been on her mother's hand.

At the door to their large playroom she paused for a moment and knocked. There was no answer, but she could hear squeals and laughter beyond. They would have eaten hours before, and by now they would have had their baths. Fräulein Hedwig would have made them put their toys away, and the nursery maid would have assisted them in this monumental task. But at least they were back now – for most of the summer they had been in the country, and Kassandra hadn't seen them at all. This year, for the first time, Kassandra had not wanted to leave Berlin, because of Dolff. A convenient charity had provided her with the desperately sought excuse.

She knocked again, and this time they heard her, Fräulein Hedwig bid her come in. As she entered, there was sudden silence, the children startled from their playing with a look of awe. Of all of it, it was that that Kassandra most hated. They look they gave her, always as though they had never seen her there before.

'Hello, everybody.' Kassandra smiled and held out her arms. For an instant no one moved, and then, at Fräulein Hedwig's prodding, Gerhard came first. He only needed a moment's urging, and then would fly unharnessed to her arms. But Fräulein Hedwig's voice was quick to stop him.

'Gerhard, don't touch! Your mother is dressed for the party.'

'That's all right.' Her open arms never wavered, but the

23

child backed off to just beyond her grasp.

'Hello, Mummy.' His eyes were wide and blue like hers, but the face was Walmar's. He had lovely perfect features, a happy smile, blond hair, and still the chubby body of a baby, despite his now almost five years. 'I hurt my arm today.' He showed her, still not having arrived in hers. She reached out to him gently.

'Let me see it.' And then, 'Oh, that looks awful. Did it hurt a lot?' It was a small scrape and a smaller bruise, but to him it was important, as he looked from the injured arm to the woman in the black dress.

'Yes.' He nodded. 'But I didn't cry.'

'That was very brave of you.'

'I know.' He looked pleased with himself and then bounded away from her to collect a toy he had forgotten in another room, which left Kassandra alone with Ariana, who was still smiling shyly at her from Fräulein Hedwig's side.

'Don't I get a kiss today, Ariana?' The child nodded and then approached, hesitant, elflike, with delicate looks that promised to outshine even her mother's. 'How are you?'

'Fine, thank you, Mummy.'

'No bruises, no cuts, nothing for me to kiss?' She shook her head and they exchanged a smile. Gerhard made them both laugh sometimes. He was so much a little boy. But Ariana had always been different. Pensive, quiet, much shier than her brother, Kassandra often wondered if it would have been different if there had never been a nurse. 'What did you do today?'

'I read, and I drew a picture.'

'May I see it?'

'It isn't finished yet.' It never was.

'That doesn't matter. I'd like to see it anyway.' But Ariana blushed furiously and shook her head. Kassandra felt more than ever an intruder and wished, as she always did, that Hedwig and the nursery maid would disappear, into another room at least, so that they could be alone. It was only on rare occasions that she was alone with the children. Hedwig stayed near to keep them from getting out of hand.

'Look what I have!' Gerhard had returned to them, bouncing along in his pyjamas, with a large stuffed dog.

'Where did you get that?'

'From Baroness von Vorlach. She brought it to me this afternoon.'

'She did?' Kassandra looked blank.

'She said you were going to have tea with her, but you forgot.' Kassandra closed her eyes and shook her head.

'How awful. I did. I'll have to call her. But that's a very handsome dog. Does he have a name yet?'

'Bruno. And Ariana got a big white cat.'

'Did you?' Ariana had steadfastly kept the news to herself. When would they ever share things? When the girl was grown, perhaps they would be friends. But now it was too late, and yet too soon.

Downstairs the clock chimed again, and Kassandra looked at them, feeling anguish clutch her. And Gerhard looked at her, crestfallen, tiny, chubby, 'Do you have to go?'

Kassandra nodded. 'I'm sorry. Papa is having a dinner.'

'Aren't you having one, too?' Gerhard looked at her curiously and she smiled.

'Yes, me, too. But it's for people from his bank, and some other banks.'

'It sounds very boring.'

'Gerhard!' Hedwig was quick to reprimand him, but Kassandra laughed.

She lowered her voice conspiratorially as she spoke to this delicious child. 'It will be . . . but don't tell anyone . . . that's our secret.'

'You look very pretty anyway.' He looked her over with approval, and she kissed the chubby little hand.

'Thank you.' She pulled him into her arms then and kissed him softly on the top of his blond head. 'Good night, little one. Are you taking your new dog to bed?'

He shook his head firmly. 'Hedwig says I can't do that.'

Kassandra stood and smiled pleasantly at the heavyset older woman.

'I think he can.'

'Very well, madam.'

Gerhard beamed up at his mother and they exchanged another conspiratorial smile, and then her gaze turned to Ariana. 'Will you take your new cat to bed with you, too?'

'I think so.' She glanced first at Hedwig and then her mother, as Kassandra felt something deep inside her die again.

'You'll have to show him to me tomorrow.'

'Yes, ma'am.' The words cut to the quick, but her pain didn't show as Kassandra gently kissed her daughter, waved at both children, and softly closed the door.

As quickly as the narrow black dress would allow, Kassandra made her way downstairs, arriving at the foot of the stairs in time to see Walmar greeting their first guests.

'Ah, there you are, darling.' He turned to smile at her, appreciative, as always, of how she looked. He made the introductions as heels clicked and hands were kissed. It was a couple Kassandra had met often at functions for the bank, but who had not yet visited their home. She greeted them warmly and took Walmar's arm as they entered the main salon.

It was an evening of civilised exchanges, lavish food, and the very best French wines. The guests spoke mostly of banking, travel. Children and talk of politics were strangely absent from the conversation, although it was 1934, although President von Hindenburg's death that year had removed the final threat to Hitler's power. It was a subject not really worth discussing. Since Hitler had become Chancellor the year before, the bankers of the nation had maintained their position. They were important to the Reich, they had their work to do, and Hitler had his. However little some of them might have thought of him, he was not going to stir up problems in their lair. Live and let live. And there were those, of course, who were pleased with Hitler's Reich.

Walmar was not among them, but it was a view he shared with few. He had been astonished at the gathering power of the Nazis, and he had warned his friends several times privately that it would lead to war. But there was no reason to discuss it on that evening. The crêpes flambées, served with champagne, seemed of far more interest than the Third Reich.

The last guest did not leave until one-thirty, when Walmar turned tiredly to Kassandra with a yawn. 'I think it was a very successful dinner, darling. I liked the duckling better than the fish.'

'Did you?' She made a mental note to tell the cook the next morning. They served gargantuan dinners, with an appetiser, soup, fish course, meat course, salad, cheese, dessert, and at last fruit. It was expected, so it was what they did.

'Did you have a pleasant evening?' He looked down at her gently as they walked slowly upstairs.

'Of course I did, Walmar.' She was touched that he would ask. 'Didn't you?'

'Useful. That Belgian deal we've been discussing will probably go through. It was important that Hoffmann come tonight. I'm glad he did.'

'Good. Then so am I.' As she followed him sleepily, she wondered if that was her purpose, then, to encourage him with his Belgian deal, and Dolff with his new book. Was that it, then? She was to help both of them achieve whatever it was that they were going to do? But if them, why not her children? And then it came to her, and why not herself? 'I thought his wife was very pretty.'

Walmar shrugged, and then as they stood on the landing, he smiled at her, but there was a ghost of sorrow in his eyes. 'I didn't. I'm afraid you've spoiled me for everyone else.'

She smiled back into his eyes. 'Thank you.'

There was a moment of awkwardness as they both stood there on the stairs. It was the moment of parting. It seemed easier on the evenings when they had nothing to do. He would retreat to his study, she would go upstairs alone to read a book. But climbing the stairs together left them with a fork in the road that never grew less poignant and left them both feeling so much alone. Before, they had always known they might meet in her bedroom later, but now it was no secret between them that they would not. And there was an aura of adieu each time they reached that landing. It always seemed so much more than just good night.

'You're looking better lately, darling. I don't mean in terms of your looks.' He smiled gently. 'I mean your health.'

She returned his smile. 'I'm feeling better, I suppose.' But there was something gone from her eyes as she said it, and she quickly dropped her eyes away from his. There was an instant of silence as the clock softly chimed the quarter hour.

'It's late, you'd best get to bed.' He kissed the top of her head and walked resolutely to the door of his room. She saw only his back as she whispered softly. 'Good night,' and then walked quickly down the hall to her own.

Chapter 3

The wind whisked briskly around their legs as Dolff and Kassandra walked along the lake at the Charlottenburger Schloss. This afternoon they were alone in the park. The children were back in school, and the lovers and old people who came out to feed the birds were too sensible to go out on such a cold day. But Dolff and Kassandra were happy with their solitude as they walked along.

'Warm enough?' He looked down at her smilingly and she laughed.

'In this? I'd be embarrassed to admit it if I wasn't.'

'You should be.' He glanced admiringly at the new sable coat, which danced only a few inches above the ground. She wore a matching hat tilted to one side of her head, and the sleek golden hair was tied in a knot at the nape of her neck. Her cheeks were pink from the cold, and her eyes looked more startlingly violet than ever. He had an arm around her shoulders and he looked down at her with pride. It was November and she had been his now for more than eight months.

'How do you feel now that you've finished the book?'

'Like I'm out of a job.'

'Do you miss the characters very much?'

'I miss them terribly at first.' And then he kissed the top of her head. 'But less so when I'm with you. Are you ready to go back now?' She nodded and they turned back towards his house, hurrying the few blocks until they reached his door. He pushed it open for Kassandra as they stepped into the front hall. She felt more and more at home here. The week before they had even ventured into some antique stores together and bought two new chairs and another small desk.

'Tea?' She smiled up at him warmly and he nodded comfortably in answer, following her into the kitchen. She put on the kettle and pulled out one of the well-worn kitchen chairs.

'Do you have any idea how lovely it is to have you here, madam?'

'Do you have any idea how lovely it is to be here?' She was coming to terms with the guilt now. This was simply her way of life, and she had been greatly comforted to learn inadvertently several months before that one of her father's sisters had had the same lover for thirty-two years. Perhaps that was her destiny, too. To grow old with both Dolff and Walmar, useful to them both, the fabric of her life irrevocably meshed with that of Dolff's and bordered by Walmar's protecting arms. Was it so terrible after all? Was anyone really suffering? She seldom felt the pangs anymore. Only when she was with the children did she still feel any kind of pain, but she had felt that long before Dolf came along.

'You're looking serious again. What were you just thinking?'

'Oh, about us . . .' She grew pensive again as she poured his tea. How different it was here in the comfortable kitchen,

29

unlike the elaborate ceremony that took place in the house in Grunewald when she invited friends in to tea, with Berthold the butler staring gloomily down at them

'Does thinking about us make you look so serious?'

She turned to face him as she handed him his cup. 'Sometimes I take this very seriously, you know.'

He looked at her gravely. 'I know. So do I.' And then suddenly he wanted to say something to her that he had never said before. 'If things were . . . different . . . I want you to know that . . . I would want you for always.'

Her eyes bore into his. 'And now?'

His voice was a caress in the warm room. 'I still want you for always.' And then with a small sigh, 'But I can't do anything about it.'

'I don't expect you to.' She sat down across from him with a gentle smile. 'I'm happy like this.' And then she told him something she had never said before. 'This is the most important part of my life, Dolff.' It meant everything to him to have her be part of his life. So much had altered in his life over the past year. The rest of the world was changing around them, but he was far more aware of it than she. She touched his hand softly, pulling him back from his own thoughts. 'Now tell me about the book. What does your publisher say?'

But as she said the words, an odd expression came into his eyes. 'Nothing much.'

'He doesn't like it?' She looked shocked. The book was marvellous, She had read it herself, tucked into his bed, on the cold winter afternoons. 'What did he say?'

'Nothing.' She saw his eyes go hard. 'They're not entirely sure they can publish it.' So that was the shadow she had seen in his eyes when she's arrived right after lunch. Why hadn't he told her sooner? But it was like him to hide his problems from her at first. He always wanted to hear about her.

'Are they crazy? What about the success of your last book?'

'That has nothing to do with it.' He turned away from her

and stood up to put his cup in the sink.

'Dolff, I don't understand.'

'Neither do I, but I think we will. Our beloved leader will show us soon enough.'

'What are you talking about?' She stared at his back and then at the anger she saw in his eyes when he turned around.

'Kassandra, do you have any idea what's happening to our country?'

'You mean Hitler?' He nodded. 'It'll pass. People will get bored with him and he'll fall out of favour.'

'Oh, really? Is that what you think?' And then bitterly, 'Is that what your husband thinks?' She was startled at the mention of Walmar.

'I don't know. He doesn't talk about it a great deal. At least not with me. Nobody reasonable likes Hitler, obviously, but I don't think he's as dangerous as some people think.'

'Then you're a fool, Kassandra.' He had never talked to her in that tone of voice before. But suddenly she saw anger and bitterness that he had never unveiled to her before. 'Do you know why my publisher is sitting on the fence? Not because my last book didn't sell, not because he doesn't like the new manuscript. He was stupid enough to let me know how much he liked it before he cooled off. But because of the Party . . .' He looked at her with an anguish that tore at her heart. 'Because I'm Jewish, Kassandra . . . because I'm a Jew.' His voice was a barely audible whisper at the last. 'A Jew isn't supposed to be successful, isn't supposed to win national awards. There will be no room at all for Jews in the New Germany, if Hitler has his way.'

'But that's crazy.' Her face said that she didn't believe him. It was something that they had never discussed. He had told her about his parents, his past, his childhood, the bakery, but he had never talked to her at any length about being Jewish, about what it did and did not mean to him. She had simply assumed that he was and forgotten about it after that. And on the rare occasions when she did think about it, it pleased her, it seemed different and exotic in a

31

very pleasant way. But it was something that simply never entered their discussions, and seldom her mind. But the fact of that difference never left him. And the truth of what it could mean to him was coming slowly clear.

Kassandra thought over the implications of what he had just said. 'You can't mean it. It couldn't be that.'

'Couldn't it? It's starting to happen to some of the others. I'm not the only one. And it's only happening to the Jews. They won't take on our new books, they don't want to publish our articles, they don't answer our calls. Believe me, Kassandra, I know.'

'Then go to another publisher.'

'Where? In England? In France? I'm a German, I want to publish my work here.'

'Then do it. They can't all be fools.'

'They're not fools. They're much wiser than we think they are. They see what's coming, and they're afraid.'

Kassandra stared at him, shocked at what she was hearing. It couldn't be as bad as he thought it was. He was just upset over the rejection. She let out a long sigh and reached for his hand. 'Even if it is true, it won't be forever. They may relax once they see that Hitler isn't going to cause as much trouble as they think.'

'What makes you think he won't?'

'He can't. How can he? The power is still in the right hands. The backbone of this country is the banks, the businesses, the old families – they're not going to fall for all that garbage he spouts. The lower classes might, but who are they, after all?'

Dolff looked grim as he answered. 'The old families,' as you put it, may not fall for it, but if they don't speak out against it, we're doomed. And you're wrong about something else. They aren't the power in this country anymore. The power is the little man, armies and armies and armies of little men, men who are individually powerless, but strong as a group, people who are tired of the "backbone" you're talking about, tired of the upper classes and the "old families" and the banks. Those people believe every word that Hitler is preaching; they think they've found themselves a new god. And if they all get together, that will be the real power in this country. And if that happens, we'll all be in trouble, not just the Jews, but people like you, too.' It terrified her to hear what he was saying. If he was right . . . But he couldn't be . . . he couldn't.'

She smiled at him and stood up to run her hands slowly over his chest. 'Hopefully nothing is as dire as you predict.' He kissed her gently then and led her slowly upstairs with an arm around her waist. She wanted to ask him what he was going to do about the new book, but she hated to press it, she didn't want to revive more of his fears. And for an author of his magnitude, it seemed unlikely that Hitler's prejudice against Jews and Jewish authors could be of any major importance. After all, he was Dolff Sterne.

That evening Kassandra was pensive as she drove back to Grunewald, mulling over again what Dolff had said. The look in Dolff's eyes was plaguing her when she let herself into the house. She had an hour to herself before dinner, and tonight, instead of going to see the children, she sought refuge in her room. What if he were right? What could it mean? What would it mean to them? But as she sank slowly into a tub of warm water, she decided that the whole thing was probably nonsense. The book would be published. He would win another award. Artists were sometimes a little crazy. She smiled as she remembered other moments of the afternoon. She was still smiling to herself when she heard the knock on the door of her bedroom and she called out absently for the maid to come in.

'Kassandra?' But it wasn't Anna. It was the voice of her husband in the other room.

'Walmar? I'm in the bath.' She had left the doors open and wondered if he would come in, but when his voice reached her again, it wasn't approaching, and she continued to talk to him through the open door.

'Will you please come and see me when you're dressed?' He sounded serious, and for an instant she felt fear stir in her

33

heart. Was he going to confront her? She closed her eyes and held her breath.

'Do you want to come in?'

'No, just knock on my door before dinner.'

He sounded more worried than angry.

'I'll be there in a few minutes.'

'Fine.'

She heard the door close again softly and hurried through the rest of her bath. It took her only a few minutes to put on her makeup and run a comb through her hair. She put on a simple dove grey suit for dinner, with a white silk shirt that tied in a loose cravat at the neck. Her shoes were grey suede, her stockings the same subdued hue, and she quickly slipped on the double rope of black pearls that had been her mother's favourite, along with the earrings that matched. She looked subdued and serious as she glanced at herself before walking down the hall. The only touch of colour was her hair, and the deep Wedgwood blue of her eyes. When she reached his door, she knocked softly, and a moment later she heard his voice beyond.

'Come in.' She stepped across the threshold, feeling the silk skirt of the suit rustle against her legs. Walmar was sitting in one of the comfortable brown leather chairs in his study, and he was quick to put down the report he had been reading when she came in. 'You look lovely, Kassandra.'

'Thank you.' She searched his eyes and saw the truth, the pain. She wanted to reach out to him, to ask him, to offer him comfort. But as she watched him, she found that she couldn't approach him. She suddenly found herself staring at him from across an abyss. It was Walmar who had stepped back.

'Please sit down.' She did and he watched her. 'Sherry?' She shook her head. In his eyes she could see that he knew. She turned her face away from him, pretending to enjoy the fire. There was nothing she could say to him. She would just have to live through the accusation and come to some solution in the end. What could she possibly do? Which man

34

would she abandon? She needed and loved them both. 'Kassandra . . .' She kept her eyes on the fire, and then at last turned them to his.

'Yes.' It was a painful rasp.

'There is something I must say to you. It is . . .' He seemed agonised, but they both knew that now there was no turning back. '. . . it is extremely painful for me to discuss this with you, and I'm sure it's quite as distasteful to you.' Her heart pounded so horribly in her ears that she could barely hear him. Her life was over. The end had begun. 'But I must speak to you. For your sake. For your safety. And perhaps ours.'

'My safety?' It was only a whisper, but she stared at him, confused.

'Just listen to me.' And then, as though it were too much for him, he sat back in his chair and sighed. When she looked at him, she also saw the bright light of unshed tears in his eyes. 'I know . . . I've been aware that . . . for the past several months . . . you have been engaged in a somewhat . . . difficult situation.' Kassandra closed her eyes and listened to the sound of his voice drone in her ears. 'I want you to know that I'm . . . I do understand . . . I'm not unsympathetic.' The huge sad eyes opened again.

'Oh, Walmar . . .' Slowly the tears began to roll down her cheeks. 'I don't want to . . . I can't '

'Stop it. Listen to me.' For a moment he sounded like her father, and after another sigh he went on. 'What I'm going to say to you is terribly important. I also want you to know, since this situation is somewhat out in the open now, that I love you. I don't want to lose you, whatever you may think of me now.'

Kassandra shook her head and, taking a lace hand-kerchief from her pocket, blew her nose through her tears. 'I have nothing but respect for you, Walmar. And I love you, too.' It was true. She did love him and she died a little over his pain.

'Then listen to what I have to say. You're going to have to stop seeing . . . your friend.' Kassandra stared at him in silent

35

horror. 'And not for the reasons that you think. I am twenty-nine years older than you are, my darling, and I am not a fool. These things sometimes happen, and they may hurt a great deal for the people involved, but if they're handled properly, one can survive the ordeal. But that's not what I'm telling you now. I'm telling you something very different. I'm saying that for reasons entirely other than me, our marriage, you must stop seeing . . . Dolff.' It seemed to cause him anguish to say the other man's name. 'In fact, even if you were not married just now, if you had never been, it is a relationship in which you could not afford to indulge.'

'What do you mean?' She jumped to her feet angrily, her gratitude for his benevolence instantly gone. 'Why? Because he's a writer? Do you think he's some kind of Bohemian? For God's sake, Walmar, he's a very decent, wonderful man.' The absurdity of her defending her lover to her husband had not yet occurred to Kassandra as she looked into Walmar's eyes.

He sat back in his chair with another sigh. 'I hope you don't think me sufficiently small-minded to eliminate writers and artists and their kind from the roster of those I choose to befriend. I have never been guilty of such narrow opinions, Kassandra. It would do you credit to remember that. What I'm speaking of here is entirely different. I'm telling you' – he leaned forward in his chair and spoke to her with sudden vehemence – 'that you can't afford to know the man, to be with the man, to be seen at his home, not because he's a writer . . . but because he's a Jew. And it makes me sick to tell you that, because I think that what is starting to happen in this country is disgusting, but the fact is that it *is happening* and you are my wife and the mother of my children and I won't have you murdered or put in jail! Do you understand that, dammit? Do you understand how important this is?'

Kassandra stared at him disbelievingly. It was like continuing the nightmare of what Dolff had said to her that afternoon. 'Are you telling me that you think they might kill him?'

36

'I don't know what they'll do, and the truth is that I don't know what I think anymore. But as long as we lead a quiet life and stay out of what's happening, we're safe, you're safe, Ariana and Gerhard are safe. But that man isn't safe. Kassandra, please . . .' He reached out and grabbed her hand. 'If anything happens to him, I don't want you to be a part of it. If things were different, if these were other times, I would be pained at what you are doing, but I would close my eyes, but I can't do that now. I must stop you. You must stop yourself.'

'But what about him?' She was too frightened to cry now. The magnitude of what he had said to her had cleared her head.

Walmar shook his head. 'We can't do anything to help him. If he's smart and if things go on like this, he'd be wise to leave Germany.' Walmar looked at Kassandra. 'Tell him that.' Kassandra sat staring into the fire, not sure what to say. The only thing she was sure of was that she wouldn't give him up. Not now, not later, not ever.

Her eyes found his in a moment, and despite the anger, there was something very tender there for him as well. She went to him and kissed him gently on the cheek. 'Thank you for being so fair.' He hadn't berated her for being unfaithful. He was only worried about her safety, and perhaps even that of her friend. What an extraordinary man he was. For a moment her love for him fanned as it hadn't in years. She looked down at him with her hand on his shoulder. 'Is it as bad as that, then?'

He nodded. 'I think perhaps it's worse. We just don't know it yet.' And then after a moment, 'But we will.'

'I find it difficult to believe that things could ever get so out of hand.'

He looked at her with urgency as she stood up to leave the room. 'Will you do what I asked you, Kassandra?' She wanted to promise him, to assure him that she would, but something had changed subtly between them. He knew the truth, and it was better that way. She didn't have to lie to him any more.

37

'I don't know.'

'You have no choice.' His voice was angry then. 'Kassandra, I forbid you – ' But she had quietly slipped out of the room.

Chapter 4

Six weeks later one of Dolff's writer friend disappeared. He was far less well-known than Dolff, but he, too, had had trouble publishing his most recent work. His girl-friend called Dolff in hysterics at two o'clock in the morning. She had driven home from visiting her mother in Munich that night, and the apartment had been broken into, Helmut was gone, and there was blood on the floor. The manuscript he'd been working on was scattered around the room. The neighbours had heard shouting and then screaming but that was all she knew. Dolff had met her near Helmut's apartment and then driven her back to his place. The next day she sought refuge with her sister.

When Kassandra arrived later that morning, she found him in the depths of depression, and insane with grief over Helmut's disappearance.

'I don't understand it, Kassandra. Little by little, the whole country's going mad. It's like a slow-moving poison travelling in this country's veins. Eventually it will reach our heart and kill us. Not that I'll have to worry about that.' He stared at her gloomily and she frowned.

'What's that supposed to mean?'

'What do you think it means? How long do you think it will be before they come for me? A month? Six months? A year?'

'Don't be crazy. Helmut wasn't a novelist. He was a highly political nonfiction writer who has openly criticised Hitler since he came to power. Don't you see the difference? What do you think they'd be angry about in your case? A novel like *Der Kuss?*'

'You know, I'm not sure I do see the difference, Kassandra.' He glanced around the room with displeasure. He didn't even feel secure in his house anymore, it was as though he expected them to come for him any day.

'Dolff... darling, please ... be reasonable. It was an awful thing to have happened, but it can't happen to you. Everyone knows you. They're not simply going to make you disappear overnight.'

'Why not? Who's going to stop them? Will you? Will anyone? Of course not. What did I do for Helmut last night? Nothing. Absolutely goddamn nothing.'

'All right, then leave for God's sake. Go to Swizerland now. You can publish there. And you'll be safe.'

But he only looked at her bleakly. 'Kassandra, I'm a German. This is my country, too. I have as much right to be here as anyone else does. Why the hell should I go?'

'Then what are you telling me, dammit?' It was the first fight they had had in year.

'I'm telling you that my country is destroying itself and its people and it's make me sick.'

'But you can't stop that. If that's what you believe, then get out before it destroys you.'

'And what about you, Kassandra? You stay here pretending none of it will ever touch you? You think it won't?'

'I don't know ... I don't know ... I don't know anything any more. I don't understand any of it.' The golden woman had been looking tired for weeks. She was getting it from both of them now, and she felt helpless in the face of their fears. She looked to them for reassurance, for the confirmation that everything she believed in would never change, and they were both telling her that everything was changing; yet all Walmar wanted to do about it was for her to stop seeing Dolff, and all Dolff wanted to do was rail, at something that none of them had the power to change. He went on talking in disjointed circles for another half hour, and suddenly she jumped to her feet in a rage. 'What the hell do you want from me? What can I do?'

'Nothing, dammit . . . nothing . . .' And then as tears streamed down his cheeks for his lost friend, he pulled her tightly into his arms as he sobbed. 'Oh, God . . . Kassandra . . . oh, God . . .'

She held him that way for an hour, holding him close, as she would have her son. 'It's all right . . . it's all right, darling . . . I love you . . .' That was really all that was left to say, but the finger of fear that she had been avoiding began to crawl up her spine now, too. What if it were Dolff who were dragged screaming into the night? What if it had been she in the shoes of Helmut's hysterical girl-friend? But that couldn't happen to her . . . or to him . . . those things didn't happen . . . and it wouldn't happen to them.

When she got home late that afternoon, Walmar was waiting for her, not in his study, but in the main salon. He motioned her to join him and quietly closed the double French doors.

'Kassandra, this is becoming impossible.'

'I don't want to discuss it.' She turned her back to him, staring into the roaring fire beneath the portrait of his grandfather, whose eyes always seemed to follow everyone in the room. 'This isn't the right time.'

'There will never be a right time.' And then, 'If you don't do as I ask you, I will send you away.'

'I won't go. I can't leave him now.' It was madness to be discussing this with Walmar, but she had no choice. It had been out in the open for almost two months now, and whatever it cost her, she was going to stand her ground. She had given up too many things in her life already. Her dreams of the theatre, her children – she would not give up Dolff.

She turned to face him. 'Walmar, I don't know what to do. It's very hard to believe what I'm hearing these days. What's happening to us? To Germany? Is it all because of that silly little man?'

'It would seem to be. Or perhaps he has aroused some

incipient insanity we had somewhere in our soul all along. Perhaps all of these people who have welcomed him have simply been waiting for someone to lead them on.'

'Can't somebody stop him before it's too late?'

'It may already be too late. He excites the people. He promises them progress and riches and success. For those who've never tasted that, it's hypnotic. They can't resist.'

'And what about the rest of us?'

'We wait and see. But not your friend, Kassandra. If things go on as they are, he won't have the luxury of waiting. Oh, God, please listen to me, you must. Go and stay with my mother, for a few days. Think it over. It'll give you time away from us both.' But she didn't want time away from them. And she knew didn't want to leave Dolff.

'I'll think about it.' But he knew from the tone of her voice that she would not. There was nothing more he could do. For the first time in the almost sixty years of his lifetime, Walmar von Gotthard felt like a beaten man. She watched him stand up and walk to the doorway, and then quietly stretched out a hand. 'Walmar . . . don't look like that . . . I'm . . . I'm sorry . . .' But he only turned to look at her from the door.

'You're sorry, Kassandra. And so am I. And so will the children be before this is over. What you are doing will destroy you, and perhaps in the long run destroy all of us.'

But Kassandra von Gotthard didn't believe that.

Chapter 5

It was in February that Walmar and Kassandra attended the Spring Ball. The weather was still icy, but it was cheering to celebrate the prospect of spring. She wore her full-length ermine over a starkly simple white velvet gown. The top was cut halter fashion, and the skirt fell in total perfection from her waist to her white satin-clad feet. Her

41

hair was an upswept mass of delicate tendrils, and she looked lovelier than ever and as though she had not a care in the world. The fact that Dolff had been testy all day again over the unpublished manuscript and that Walmar and she were barely speaking as their battle raged on didn't show. Trained from the cradle to show nothing but graciousness beyond the sanctum of her own bedroom, she smiled benevolently at every introduction and danced willingly with all of Walmar's friends. As always their entrance had caused a small sensation, as much for the clothes that she wore as for the face with its striking beauty, which outshone even her clothes.

'You look ravishing, Frau Gotthard. Like a snow princess.' The compliment came from the man she had just met, some banker or other. Walmar had greeted him with a curt, friendly nod and quick assent when he had asked his permission to escort Kassandra to the floor. They were waltzing slowly as Kassandra watched Walmar chat with some friends.

'Thank you. I take it you know my husband?'

'Only slightly. We have had the pleasure of doing business once or twice. But my . . . activities have been a little less commercial in nature during the past year.'

'Ah? Enjoying a sabbatical?' Kassandra smiled pleasantly as they waltzed.

'Not at all. My efforts have been engaged in assisting our leader in establishing the finances of the Third Reich.' He said it with such force that Kassandra was startled and looked into his eyes.

'I see. That must keep you busy.'

'Decidedly so. And you?'

'My children and my husband keep me busy most of the time.'

'And the rest of the time?'

'I beg your pardon?' Kassandra felt herself growing uncomfortable in this bold stranger's arms.

'I understand that you're something of a patron of the arts.'

'Really?' Kassandra found herself praying for the dance to end.

'Indeed.' He smiled pleasantly at her, but there was a glint of something chilling lurking in his eyes. 'I wouldn't waste a great deal of my time on that, though. You see, our concept of the arts is going to change greatly with the assistance of the Third Reich.'

'Is it?' For a moment she felt faint. Was this man warning her about Dolff? Or was she growing as crazy as he was, fearing threats at every turn.

'Yes, it is. You see, we've had such . . . such inadequate artists, such sick minds holding the pen.' Then it was Dolff he meant. 'All of that will have to change.'

But suddenly she was angry. 'Perhaps it already has. They don't seem to be publishing the same people any more, do they?' Oh, God, what was she doing? What would Walmar say if he could hear? But the dance was coming to an end. She was about to be free of this evil stranger. But now she wanted to say more.

'Don't worry about all of this nonsense, Frau Gotthard.'

'I wasn't planning to.'

'That's encouraging to hear.' What was? What did he mean? But he was leading her back to Walmar now. It was all over. And she didn't see the man again that night. On the way home she wanted to tell Walmar, but she was afraid of making him angry – or worse, afraid. And the next day Dolff was back in such good spirits that she didn't tell him what had happened either. And after all, what did it mean? Some moron banker who was in love with Hitler and the Third Reich? So what?

Dolff had come to a decision. He was going to write whether they published him or not. And he was going to go on trying to publish. But if he starved to death, he was going to stay. No one was going to drive him out of his homeland. He had a right to be there, and to prosper, even if he was a Jew.

'Can I interest you in a walk near the castle?' She smiled at him. It would be the first time they had gone out for a walk in two weeks.

'I'd love that.'

They walked for almost two hours, near the schloss and next to the lake, watching the few children who had come to play there, and smiling at other strollers passing by. It felt at long last like their first winter, when they had met by chance there time and time again, anxiously seeking each other, yet afraid of what might lie ahead.

'Do you know what I used to think when I looked for you here?' He was smiling down at her, his hand tightly clasping hers as they walked.

'What?'

'I used to think that you were the most elusive, mysterious woman I had ever known, and if I could only spend one day with you, I'd be happy for the rest of my life.'

'And now? Are you happy?' She drew closer to him, her short fur jacket a ball of fluff over a long tweed skirt and dark brown suede shoes.

'I've never been happier. And you? Has the last year been too hard on you?' He still worried about that much of the time. She was the one with the pressures, with Walmar and the children, especially now that Walmar knew. She had told him of Walmar's warning.

'It hasn't been hard. It's been lovely.' She looked up at him with the fullness of their loving in her eyes. 'It's all I ever wanted – and always thought I couldn't have.' And she still couldn't have it. Not really. Not all the time. But even this was enough. Just these precious afternoons that she shared with Dolff.

'You'll always have me, Kassandra. Always. Even long after I'm dead and gone.'

But she looked up at him unhappily. 'Don't say things like that.'

'I meant when I was eighty, silly lady. I'm not going anywhere without you.' She smiled then, and they found themselves running hand in hand along the lake. Without explaining or asking, they made their way home and wandered happily upstairs after making tea. But they drank

44

it quickly, they had other things on their minds, and their lovemaking was passionate and urgent, as though each of them needed the other desperately and more than anything on earth. At the end of the afternoon they lay sleeping, Kassandra curled tightly in her lover's arms.

It was Dolff who stirred first, aware of someone pounding on his door on the floor below them, and then there was the sudden battering of feet on the steps leading up from the main floor. He lay listening for an instant and then came fully awake and sat straight up in bed. Feeling the motion of his body, Kassandra stirred, and then, as though sensing danger, her eyes went wide. Without saying anything at all to her, he flung the covers over her and sprang from the bed, standing naked in the centre of the large bedroom just as they pressed through the door. At first glance it looked like an army of brown uniforms and red armbands, but there were only four.

Pulling his robe around him. Dolff stood firm. 'What is this?' But they only laughed. One of them grabbed him roughly and spat in his face.

'Listen to the Jew!' He was suddenly pulled taut between two of them, as a third delivered a ferocious punch to his belly, and Dolff grunted with the pain and bent double towards the floor. This time the third man kicked him, and instantly blood gushed from a gash near his mouth while calmly the fourth surveyed the room.

'What have we here under the covers? A Jew bitch keeping our illustrious writer warm? With a sudden motion he pulled back the covers, exposing every inch of Kassandra to their interested gaze. 'And a pretty one. Get up.' Immobile for a moment, she did, sitting upright, and then gracefully slipping her legs on to the floor, her lithe, supple body trembling slightly, her eyes wide in terror as she stared silently at Dolff. The four men watched her, the three around Dolff questioningly gazing at the fourth to see what he would do. He surveyed her carefully, his eyes scouring her flesh, but she could only watch Dolff, still gasping, standing hunched and bleeding between the two uniformed men.

45

And then the fourth turned to them with a sneer. 'Get him out of here.' And then in amusement as he touched his belt, 'Unless he'd like to watch.'

Suddenly Dolff came to his senses, his eyes frantically reaching for Kassandra and then turning furiously to the man in charge. 'No! Don't touch her!'

'Why not, Mister Famous Author? Has she got the clap?' The four men laughed in unison as Kassandra gasped. The full realisation of what was about to happen filled her with a terror she had never known. At a signal from their sergeant, they shoved Dolff from the room, and an instant later a resounding crash told her that Dolff had just been pushed down the stairs. There was an exchange of angry voices and Kassandra heard Dolff's above them all. He was calling her name and attempting to fight his captors, but a series of scuffling noises silenced him quickly, and then there was a dragging sound at the bottom of the stairs, and Dolff's voice did not rise to her ears again as, horrified, she turned her eyes to the man who was about to unzip his pants.

'You'll kill him . . . oh, my God, you'll kill him!' She shrank back from him, her eyes wide, her heard pounding wildly. She could barely think of herself now, only of Dolff, who may even already have been dead.

'And if we do?' Her assailant looked amused. 'It's no great loss to our society. Perhaps even not so great a loss to you. He's only a little Jew boy. And you, my sweet? His pretty Jewish princess?' But now Kassandra's eyes flashed; there was anger mixed with terror in those wild lavender-blue eyes.

'How dare you! *How dare you!*' It was an anguished scream as she ran from the wall towards him, clawing at his face. But with one deft sweep of his arm he slapped her, backhanded, across the face.

When he spoke to her, his voice was quiet, but his face was tense. 'That's enough. You've lost your boy-friend, little Jewess, but now you will find out what it is to be had by a better race. I am going to teach you a little lesson, dear one.' And with that, the belt whipped swiftly from its loops and cracked her mightily across the breasts. Stung by biting wings of pain, she clutched her bosom and bowed her head.

'Oh, God . . .' And then, knowing she must do it, she looked up at him with anger mixed with shame. He would kill her. He would rape her and then kill her. She had to tell him. Had to . . . she had no choice. She was not as brave as Dolff was. She looked in fury at the man who had just whipped her, still holding tightly to her bleeding breasts. 'I am not a Jew.'

'Oh, no?' He approached her now, the belt waiting to bite her yet again. As she stared at him, she saw the undeniable erection clawing at the front of his trousers. The calm he had sported only moments earlier was giving way to a frothing frenzy that Kassandra feared was already beyond control.

'My papers are in my handbag. I am –' she winced at the agony of what she was doing, but she had no choice 'Kassandra von Gotthard. My husband is the president of the Tilden Bank.'

For an instant the man paused, eyeing her with anger and suspicion, not quite sure what to do. And then his eyes narrowed. 'And your husband doesn't know you're here?'

Kassandra trembled. To tell him that Walmar knew was to doom Walmar into the bargain. To tell him that Walmar did not was to doom herself. 'My housekeeper knows precisely where I am.'

'Very clever.' The belt slipped slowly back into the loops on his trousers. 'Your papers?'

She pointed. 'Over there.' In two strides he had reached the brown alligator handbag with the gold clip. He almost tore it open, fumbled for a moment, and found the wallet concealed inside. Roughly, he pulled out her driver's licence and identity cards and threw them to the floor. He almost snarled as he did it, and then menacingly he walked back towards her. It hadn't worked. He didn't give a damn who she was. Kassandra stood bracing herself for what would come next.

He stood looking down at her for an endless moment and then slapped her hard again across the face. 'Whore! Filthy whore! If I were your husband, I would kill you. And one day, for something like this, you will die, like that bastard Jew. You are filth. Filth. You're a disgrace to your race, your country. Filthy bitch!' And then, without another word, he turned and left her, his boots clattering down the stairs as he went, until at last she heard the front door slam. It was over . . . over . . . With every inch of her body trembling, she fell to her knees on the floor, a double trickle of blood still running from her breasts, her face bruised, her eyes filled with tears, as she lay down on the floor and sobbed.

It seemed hours that she lay there sobbing, keening for the last instant when she had seen Dolff, and terrified of what would come next. And then suddenly it occurred to her what might happen. They might come back, to destroy his house. Frantically then, glancing hurriedly around her, she pulled on her clothes. Standing for a last moment in the bedroom where she and Dolff had given birth to their dreams, she gazed, sobbing, at the spot where she had last seen him, and then without thinking she reached out a hand to the clothes he had worn only a few hours before. Discarded on the floor before their hungry lovemaking, still smelling of the special spice and lemon scent he wore, she felt them for a moment and ran them through her fingers, pressing his shirt to her face with a sob. And then she ran from the room and down the stairs. It was at the bottom landing that she saw it, the pool of blood where he had lain, and the trail it made where they must have dragged him, unconscious, from his own house. She fled the building and ran frantically towards her car, parked only slightly further down the street.

She was never quite sure how she had got back to Grunewald, but she had driven home, still sobbing, clutching the wheel. She had crawled out of the car, unlocked the gate, driven on to their doorway, and let herself in with her key. Silently, and with tears still streaming from her eyes, she had run up the stairs to her bedroom, slammed the door, and looked around her. She

48

was back, she was home . . . it was the pink bedroom she had
seen so often . . . the pink . . . the pink . . . it was all she could
see as it spun around her and she sank at last, unconscious, to
the floor.

Chapter 6

When Kassandra came to, she was lying on her bed, a cold
compress pressed across her head. The room was dark and
there was a strange buzzing. She realised in a moment that
the sound she heard was in her own head. Somewhere in the
distance there was Walmar, staring down at her and
applying something damp and heavy to her face. In time she
felt her blouse stripped off, and she was aware of a terrible
stinging, and then of something warm draped across her
naked breasts. It seemed a long time before she could see him
clearly, and then at last the buzzing stopped and he sat
down quietly in a chair beside her bed. He said nothing, he
only sat there as she lay staring at the ceiling, unwilling and
unable to speak. He asked her nothing. He only changed the
compresses from time to time. The room stayed dark for
hours, and when now and then there came a knock at the
door, it was Walmar who sent them away. She looked at him
gratefully and then drifted off to sleep. It was midnight when
she woke again; a dim light burned in the distance in her
boudoir, and keeping his silent vigil, he was still there.

At last he couldn't hold back any longer, and he could see
from her eyes that she was conscious and no longer in shock,
and he had to know what had happened, for her sake and his
own. 'Kassandra, you have to talk now. You have to tell me.
What happened?'

'I disgraced you.' Her voice was the merest whisper, and
he shook his head and took her hand.

'Don't be silly.' And then after another moment, 'Darling
tell me. You must tell me. I have to know.' Anna had come

to him screaming that something terrible had happened to Frau von Gotthard and she was lying near death on her bedroom floor. In terror, he had run to find her, not near death, but beaten and in shock. And then he had known. 'Kassandra?'

'He was . . . going to kill me . . . to rape me . . . I told him . . . who I was.' Walmar felt a chill of fear run through him.

'Who was it?'

'Them . . . they took him . . .' And then she whispered horribly. 'They took Dolff . . . they beat him . . . they . . . he was . . . bleeding . . . and then they . . . dragged him . . . down . . . the stairs . . .' She sat up in bed and retched, emptily, on to the bed, as Walmar sat by helplessly, holding out a monogrammed pink towel. When it was over, she stared blankly at her husband. 'And one of them stayed behind . . . for me . . . I told him . . . I told him . . .' She looked at Walmar pathetically. 'They thought I was a Jew.'

'You were right to tell them who you are. You'd be dead by now if you hadn't. They may not kill him, but they would probably have killed you.' He knew that more likely the reverse was true, but he had to lie, for her sake.

'What will they do to him?'

He took her in his arms then and she sobbed for almost an hour. When it was over, she lay there, spent and broken, and he laid her back quietly on her pillows and turned off the light. 'You must sleep now. I'll be here with you all night.' And he was, but when she woke up in the morning, he had at long last gone to rest. For him it had been a night of anguish, watching the pale face writhe and contort in her nightmares beneath the ugly bruises that had darkened it. Whoever the man was who had slapped her, he had spared not an ounce of his strength when he did. And as he watched her, hour by hour, Walmar came to hate them in a way he never had before. This was the Third Reich. Was this what they had to look forward to in the coming years? Was one meant to count one's blessings that one was not a Jew? Walmar would be damned if he'd see his beloved country turn into a nation of thugs and marauders, beating women, raping the innocent, censuring artists for their heritage. What had happened to their world that this was the price his beloved Kassandra had to pay? He was outraged, and in his own way he also mourned for Dolff.

When he left her to bathe and have a cup of coffee, he glanced at the newspaper with dread. He knew just how they would do it, and he fully expected to find a notice that some 'accident' had befallen Dolff. That's how they had done things like that before. But this time there was no small, 'unimportant' news item. Or rather, it was so small that he didn't notice it on a back page.

When Walmar returned to Kassandra's bedside two hours later, she lay silent and awake, her gaze empty as she stared at the ceiling. She had heard Walmar come into her bedroom, but she didn't turn her eyes to him.

'Are you feeling any better?' But she only stared at the ceiling in answer, and now and then she closed her eyes. 'Can I get you anything?' This time she shook her head. 'It might make you feel a little better to take a nice warm bath.' But for a long time she just lay there, staring at the ceiling and then finally the wall, and then as though the effort was almost too much for her, she dragged her eyes to his.

'What if they come to kill you and the children?' It was all she had thought of since she woke up.

'Don't be ridiculous, they won't.' But now she knew differently. They were capable of anything. They dragged people from their beds and killed them, or at the very least took them away. 'Kassandra . . . darling . . . we are all safe.' But even Walmar knew he was lying. No one was safe anymore. One day it wouldn't be just the Jews.

'It's not true, they'll kill you. Because I told them who I was. They'll come here . . . they'll . . .'

'They won't.' He forced her to look at him again. 'They won't. Be reasonable. I'm a banker. They need me. They're not going to hurt me, or my family. Didn't they let you go yesterday when you told them who you were?' She nodded mutely, but they both knew that she would never feel safe again.

'I disgraced you.' It was her only refrain.

'Stop it! Now it's over. It was a nightmare. An ugly, horrible nightmare, but it's over. Now you must wake up!' But to what?' Dolff gone? The same nightmare all over again? There would only be emptiness, and added to that, pain, and a horror that she knew she would never forget. All she wanted to do was sleep. Forever. A deep black sleep from which she would never have to wake. 'I have to go to the office for two hours, for that Belgian meeting, and then I'll be back and I'll stay with you all day. Will you be all right?' She nodded. He bent low next to her and kissed the long, delicate fingers of her left hand. 'I love you, Kassandra. And everything will be all right again.' He left orders with Anna to bring her a light breakfast, leave it on a tray next to her bed, and then go. And whatever she saw was not to be discussed with the other servants.

Anna nodded sagely and delivered the breakfast half an hour later to Kassandra's side. It was the breakfast tray Kassandra used every morning, of white wicker, covered with a white lace cloth. A single bud vase held a long red rose, and the breakfast service had been her grandmother's favourite Limoges. But Kassandra said nothing when the tray appeared. It was only after Anna left the room that Kassandra took an interest, seeing the morning paper tucked into the side basket of the tray. She had to see it, had to – maybe some small item would appear. Some few words that would tell her something of Dolff's fate. Painfully, she struggled up to one elbow and unfurled the paper on the bed. She read every line, every page, every story, and unlike Walmar, her eyes found the story on the back page. It said only that Dolff Sterne, novelist, had had an accident in his Bugatti and was dead. As she read it, she cried out, and then suddenly the room was filled with silence.

She lay there very still for almost an hour, and then resolutely she sat up on the edge of the bed. She was still shaky and very dizzy, but she made it to the bathroom and ran the tub. She stared into the mirror and saw the eyes that Dolff had loved, the eyes that had watched him dragged

52

from the room, from his home, from his life and hers.

The bathtub filled very quickly, and she quietly closed the door. It was Walmar who found her there an hour later, her wrists slashed, her life gone, the bathtub filled with her blood.

Chapter 7

The dark brown Hispano-Suiza carrying Walmar von Gotthard; his children, Ariana and Gerhard; and Fräulein Hedwig rolled solemnly behind the black hearse. It was a grey February morning, and on and on since daybreak there had been mists and rain. The day was as bleak as Walmar and the children, sitting rigid, holding tightly to the hands of their beloved nurse. They had lost their pretty lady. The woman of golden hair and lavender-blue eyes was gone.

Only Walmar fully understood what had happened. Only he knew how deeply and for how long she had been cleft. Not just between two men, but between two minds, two lives, two life-styles. She had never quite been able to adjust to the rigid rules of the life to which she had been born. Perhaps it had been a mistake to force her into the mould. Maybe he should have been wise enough to leave her to a younger man. But she had been so young, so free, so lovely, and so warm, so entirely what he had always dreamed of having in a wife. And other thoughts nagged at him. Maybe he had been wrong to keep her from the children.

As they rode mercilessly onwards, Walmar cast an eye at the nurse to whom his children now belonged. A rugged, sturdy face, kind eyes, strong hands. She had been the governess to his niece and nephew before this. Fräulein Hedwig was a good woman. But Walmar knew that, in part because of her, his wife was gone. She had been a woman without a cause or a reason to live after the tragedy of the

53

day before. The loss of Dolff had been too shocking, the fear of what she had perhaps brought down on Walmar too great to bear. It was perhaps an act of cowardice, or madness, yet Walmar knew full well that it was more. The note she had left beside the bathtub had been written in a trembling hand. Only 'Goodbye . . . I'm sorry . . . K.' His eyes filled with tears again as he remembered . . . *auf Wiedersehen*. my darling . . . goodbye . . .

The brown Hispano-Suiza halted finally outside the gates of the Grunewald cemetery, its gentle mounds of green bordered by bright flowers, its handsome stones staring solemnly at them beyond the rain that had begun again.

'We're leaving Mama here?' Gerhard looked shocked, and Ariana only stared. Fräulein Hedwig nodded. The gates opened and Walmar signalled the chauffeur to drive on.

The service had been brief and private in the Lutheran church in Grunewald, with only the children and his mother present. That evening mention of Kassandra's passing would be printed in the press, attributed to sudden illness, an inexplicable bout of a lethal flu. She had always looked so fragile that it would not be difficult to believe. And the officials who knew would be too intimidated by Walmar to reveal the truth.

The minister from the Lutheran church had followed them to the cemetery in his own bedraggled car. They had been unable to hold the funeral in the Catholic church they normally attended. Her suicide had ruled out that possibility, but the Lutheran minister had been kind. Now he stepped quietly from his automobile, followed by Walmar's mother, the Baroness von Gotthard, emerging from her chauffeured Rolls. The two liveried Von Gotthard chauffeurs stood discreetly by as the casket was lowered from the hearse to the ground. A man from the cemetery was already waiting, his face sombre, his umbrella unfurled, as the minister reached into his pocket, taking from it a small Bible that he had marked.

Gerhard was crying softly, clutching tightly to Fräulein Hedwig's and his sister's hands, and Ariana looked around her. So many markers, so many names. Such big stones, such large statues, so many hills, and such eerie-looking trees. In spring it would be green and pretty, but now, except for the patches of lawn over the coffins, it all looked so awful and so bleak. She knew as she watched them that she would never forget this day. The night before, she had cried for her mother. She had always been a little frightened by the dazzling beauty, those huge, sad eyes, and the shining hair. Fräulein Hedwig had always said not to touch her or they'd put a spot on her dress. It seemed so odd to leave her here now, in that box, out in the rain. It made Ariana sad to think of her, all alone, under one of the smooth green mounds.

Kassandra was to be buried in the Von Gotthard family plot. It was already populated by Walmar's father, his older brother, his grandparents, and three aunts. And now he would leave her with the others, his sparkling bride, the fragile wife of the elusive laughter and the wondrous eyes. His gaze shifted from the headstones to his children; Ariana looked only faintly like her mother, and Gerhard not at all. Ariana, with her long colt legs stood beside him, wearing a white dress, white stockings, and the dark blue velvet coat with the ermine collar, trimmed with the remains of her mother's spendid coat. Beside her stood tiny Gerhard, a portrait much like his sister, in short white trousers, white stockings, and the same dark blue. They were all Walmar had now, these two small children standing at his side. He vowed silently to protect them from the evil that had so brutally destroyed his wife. No matter what happened to his country, no matter how badly their values were betrayed, he would let nothing happen to the children. He would keep them safe from the venom of the Nazis until Germany was free again from Hitler and his kind. It couldn't take for ever, and when the storm had passed, they would still be safe at home.

'. . . to keep Your child, Father, in the eternal peace she has found now at Your Side. May she rest in peace. Amen.'

The five onlookers silently made the sign of the cross and stood quietly for a moment staring at the dark wood box. Walmar's and the minister's umbrellas stood high above them as the sky opened up its heart and cried, too. But none of them seemed to notice the rain as they stood there, as it fell around them in driving sheets. At last Walmar nodded and touched the children's shoulders gently.

'Come now, children, we must go.' But Gerhard wouldn't leave her; he only shook his head and stared. In the end Fräulein Hedwig simply led him back into the car and lifted him inside. Ariana was quick to follow, with one last glance over her shoulder to where the box lay and where her father stood alone, now that Grandmother had also gone. The minister hurried back to his own car, and only Walmar stood there, looking down at the coffin covered with a single wreath of large white flowers. There were orchids and roses, and lilies of the valley, all the flowers that she loved.

For an instant he wanted to take her with him, never to leave her in this place with the others who had been so unlike her. His aunts and his father and the older brother who had died at war. She had been so childlike, and she was still so young. Kassandra von Gotthard, dead at thirty. Walmar stood there, unable to believe she was no more.

It was Ariana who finally came to find him. He felt the small fingers lace into his own and looked down to see her standing there, her blue coat with the ermine collar drenched with rain.

'We have to go now, Papa. We will take you home.' She looked so old and wise and loving, her huge blue eyes a distant shadow of those others he had known. She cared nothing about the rain as she stood there. She only looked up at him, holding tightly to his hand. And then, silently, he nodded, his face wet with tears and winter rain. His Homburg was dripping water on to his shoulders, and the tiny hand was held fast within his own.

He didn't look back over his shoulder, and neither did the child. Hand in hand, they climbed silently into the Hispano-

56

Suiza, and the chauffeur closed the door. The men of Grunewald cemetery then slowly began to cover Kassandra von Gotthard's coffin until it, too, would become a green mound, to rest with all the others who had come before her and whom she had never known.

Book Two

ARIANA
BERLIN

Chapter 8

'Ariana?' He stood at the bottom of the stairs, waiting. If she didn't hurry, they would be late. 'Ariana!' The nursery floor lay above him, transformed now into the rooms more suitable for teenagers. Now and then he had thought of moving the children downstairs to be near him, but they had grown accustomed to their own floor, and he had never been able to bring himself to reopen his wife's room. The doors to Kassandra's empty apartment had stood closed for seven years.

The clock chimed the half hour, and then, as though on cue, light flooded the upper hall. As he looked up, she stood there, a vision in layers of white, organdy, with a spray of tiny white roses woven into her golden hair. Her long neck was like ivory rising above the snowy dress, her features a perfectly carved cameo, and as she looked at him, her bright blue eyes danced. Slowly, she came down the stairs to him, as Gerhard grinned from above her, peeking from what had once been their playroom door. He broke the spell of the moment, calling down to his father, who waited, stunned, at the bottom of the stairs, 'She looks good, doesn't she? For a girl.' Both Ariana and her father smiled then. Walmar nodded and cast his son a tired smile.

'I'd say she looks extraordinary, for a girl!' Walmar had just turned sixty-five that spring. And times weren't easy, not for a man of his years, for anyone these days. The country had been at war for almost three years now. Not that it changed how they lived. Berlin was still vivid with beauty and excitement, almost to the point of frenzy, with constant parties, theatre, opera, and endless novel forms of entertainment that he found tiring for a man of his age. In addition there was the constant strain of maintaining order for his family, running his bank, keeping clear of trouble, and sequestering his children from the poison that now ran

61

freely in the country's blood. No, it had not been easy. But so far he had managed every turn. The Tilden Bank was still solid, his relations with the Reich were good, his life-style was still secure, and because of his importance as a banker, as long as he continued to be useful to the Party, no one would disturb his children, or him.

When Ariana and Gerhard had reached the age when participation in a youth group was expected, it was quietly explained that Gerhard was having trouble with his studies, had a touch of asthma, and was agonisingly shy around children his own age. Ever since the death of his mother . . . of course you understand . . . and Ariana . . . we're not at all sure she will ever recover from the shock. A noble widower of aristocratic background, his two young children, and a bank. One needed nothing more to survive in Germany, except the patience to endure, the wisdom to be quiet, the willingness to be blind and mute.

He still remembered Ariana's horror when she had gone to see her mother's furrier one day three years after her mother's death. When she was a little girl, Rothmann, the furrier, had always given her hot chocolate and cookies, and now and then some small mink tails. But when she had gone to find him, she had found instead a dozen men with armbands standing guard outside the store. It was dark and empty, the marquee torn, the windows smashed, the huge, luxurious emporium empty, and on the windows one single word – *Juden*.

Ariana had run to her father's bank crying, and he had shut the door and been firm. 'You must tell no one, Ariana! No one! You must not discuss it or ask questions. Tell no one what you saw!'

She had stared at him in confusion. 'But other people saw it, too. The soldiers, they were all standing outside with guns, and the window . . . and, Papa . . . I know it – I saw blood!'

'You saw nothing, Ariana. You were never there.'

'But –'

'Silence! You had lunch today with me, in the Tiergarten,

and then we came back to the bank. We sat in here for a while, you drank a cup of hot chocolate, and then the chauffeur drove you home. Is that quite clear?' She had never seen him like that, and she didn't understand. Was it possible that her father was frightened? They couldn't touch him. He was an important banker. And besides, Papa wasn't Jewish. But where had they taken Rothmann? And what would happen to his store? 'Do you understand me, Ariana?' Her father's voice had been raised harshly, almost angrily, yet she had sensed that he was not angry at her.

'I understand.' And then in a little voice that pierced their silence, 'But why?'

Walmar von Gotthard sighed and sank back into his chair. It was a large, impressive office, an enormous desk, and across from him, despite the fact that she was twelve, Ariana looked so small. What could he tell her? How could he explain?

A year after that incident the worst had happened. In September war had come. Since then he had steered his own course with caution, but he knew that it had paid off. The children were safe and protected. Gerhard was twelve and a half now, and Ariana just sixteen. Very little had changed for them, and although the children always suspected that he hated Hitler, it was a suspicion they never discussed, not even with each other. It was dangerous to admit that one hated Hitler. Everyone knew that.

They still lived in the house in Grunewald, went to the same schools, attended the same church, but they seldom visited other people's homes. Walmar kept a tight rein on them for their own sake, he explained carefully, and it made sense to them. After all, the country was at war. Everywhere were uniforms, laughing soldiers, pretty girls, and at night they sometimes heard music when their neighbours gave large parties for officers and friends. In some ways, all over Berlin it was a time of gaiety beyond measure. In other ways the children knew that it was sad, too. Many of their friends' fathers were off fighting. Some of them had already lost fathers and brothers to the war. But for Ariana and

Gerhard, despite other children's teasing, it was a relief to know that their father was too old. They had already lost their mother, they couldn't have borne to lose him, too.

'But you're not too old for parties,' Ariana had told Walmar with a waiflike smile. This was the spring of her sixteenth birthday, and she desperately wanted to attend her first ball. She was old enough to remember that while her mother was alive her parents had been very social. But in the seven years since her passing, Walmar had spent almost every waking moment either at his bank or at home in his rooms or with them playing cards. The life of balls and parties had ended when Kassandra took her own life. But the children knew very little of their mother. The facts of how and why their mother died were painful truths that Walmar had never shared. 'Well, Papa? Can we? Please?' She had looked at him so pleadingly, and Walmar had smiled.

'A ball? Now? During the war?'

'Oh, Papa, everyone else goes to parties. Even here in Grunewald they stay up all night.' It was true – even in their staid residential district, the carousing went on regularly into the wee hours.

'Aren't you a little young for that?'

'Hardly.' She had stared down her nose at him, looking oddly like his mother rather than her own. 'I'm sixteen.'

At last, with the assistance of her brother, Ariana had prevailed, and now she stood there, like a princess in a fairy tale, wearing the white organdy dress Fräulein Hedwig's expert fingers had made.

'You look so lovely, darling.'

She smiled, childlike, at him, admiring the white tie and tails. 'So do you.'

But Garhard was still watching, and they heard him giggle from the top of the stairs. 'I think you both look silly.' But he looked proud of them, too.

'Go to bed, you monster.' She shouted it gaily over her shoulder as she tripped lightly down the last flight of stairs.

The Hispano-Suiza had been replaced just before the war

had come with a black and grey Rolls, and now it waited for them in the driveway, the elderly chauffeur standing beside the door. Ariana had a light wrap around her shoulders, and the white dress swirled around her as she swept into the car. The party was being held at the Opera House, and all the lights were blazing as the Von Gotthards approached. The broad boulevard looked as beautiful as ever, Unter den Linden had not been changed by the onset of war.

Walmar looked proudly at his daughter, sitting like a fairy princess at his side in the Rolls. 'Excited?'

She nodded happily. 'Very.' She was enchanted by the prospect of her first ball.

And it was even better than she had expected. The stairs leading into the Opera House had been carpeted in red, the main hall with its wondrous ceiling was ablaze with light. And everywhere around them were women in evening gowns and diamonds, while the men all wore uniforms and decorations or white tie and tails. For Walmar the only damper on the evening was the large red flag that hung before them with the black and white emblem of the Reich.

The music whispered at them softly, coming from the main hall, and around them swirled and eddied countless bodies bednecked, bemused, bejewelled. Ariana's eyes looked like two huge aquamarines in the delicate ivory face, her mouth a delicately carved ruby.

She shared the first dance with her father, and afterwards he was quick to move her into the safe confines of a group of his friends. There were several familiar bankers clustered at a table near the floor where couples waltzed.

She had been chatting happily with them for some twenty minutes when Walmar became aware of a tall young man standing near them. He was watching Ariana with a look of interest and conversing quietly with a friend. Walmar turned his gaze away from the soldier and invited his daughter to dance with him again. It wasn't quite fair to do that, but he felt he had to postpone the inevitable for as long as he could. He had known when he had brought her that she would dance with other men. Yet the uniforms . . . the uniforms . . .

it was unavoidable ... he could only pray that they would all think her far too young to have any great appeal.

But as Walmar and Ariana slowly circled the floor together, he knew that she would catch the eye of any man. She looked young and fresh and lovely, but more than that, there was a lure to Ariana, a quiet power that pulled at anyone who looked into those deep blue eyes. It was as though she had the answers to a secret. He had seen the reaction in his own friends. It was a quality that hypnotised most men. It was the quiet face, the gentle eyes, and then the sudden smile, like summer sunshine on a lake. There was a quality to Ariana that drew one, a magic and a spirit of which one wanted to know more, despite her youth. She was far smaller than her brother and still more delicately boned. The top of her head barely reached her father's shoulder, and her feet seemed to fly as they waltzed.

It was when he returned her to their table that the young officer finally approached. Silently, Walmar tightened. Why couldn't it have been one of the others? Someone not in a uniform – a man and not a Reich. That's all they were to him, those uniforms, they weren't people, they were simply one band of gluttonous, self-indulgent evildoers, and in unison, with what they stood for and they threatened, they had killed his wife.

'Herr von Gotthard?' Walmar gave a curt nod and the young man's right arm immediately shot out in the familiar signal. '*Heil Hitler.*' Walmar nodded again, this time with a frozen smile. 'I believe this is your daughter?'

Walmar wanted to slap him but, glancing at Ariana and then back at the intruder, he gave a curt answer instead. 'Yes. She's a bit too young to be here tonight, but I gave my consent as long as she remains with me.' Ariana looked shocked at his pronouncement, but she did not protest. And the young man nodded understandingly and then gazed at the fairy princess with a dazzling smile. He had a long row of perfect snowy white teeth, enhanced still further by the curve of his lips and the beauty of his smile. The blue of his eyes was not unlike the colour of Ariana's, but where her hair was palest blonde, his was raven dark. He was tall and graceful and with broad shoulders, small hips, and long legs accentuated by his uniform and gleaming boots.

This time the young officer bowed to Ariana's father, in the fashion of a time before right arms had shot into the air; he clicked his heels and then stood erect again. 'Werner von Klaub, Herr von Gotthard.' The gleaming smile shot towards Ariana again. 'And I can see that Miss Gotthard is indeed a very young lady, but I would be honoured if you would entrust her to me for just one dance.' Walmar hesitated. He knew the boy's family, he realised now, and to refuse would be a slight, both to his name and to the uniform he wore. And Ariana looked so hopeful and so pretty. How could he refuse? He couldn't fight the uniforms when that was what had taken over their whole world.

'I suppose I can't object to that, can I?' He glanced gently down at his daughter, his voice filled with tenderness and regret.

'May I, Papa?' The eyes so large, so hopeful, and so blue and bright.

'You may.'

Von Klaub bowed again, but this time to Ariana, and then led her away. Slowly they danced, like Prince Charming and Cinderella, as though they had been perfectly made for each other's arms. It was a pleasure to watch them, the man at Walmar's elbow said. Perhaps it was, but not for Walmar. He realised as he did so that a new threat had just come into his life. And more importantly, into Ariana's. As she grew older, she grew more lovely, and he could not keep her eternally a prisoner in his house. Eventually he would lose her, and perhaps to one of 'them'. How strange, he thought to himself as he watched them. In another life, another era, Von Klaub would have been welcome in his home and in his daughter's life, but now . . . that uniform had changed everything for Walmar. The uniform and what it stood for. It was more than he could bear.

When the dance ended, Ariana glanced at her father, an

67

open question in her eyes, and he was about to shake his head, denying his permission, but again he found he could not do that to her. So again he nodded. And after that, once more. And then, wisely, the young German officer led her back to her father, bowed again, and bid Ariana good night. But something in the way he smiled at her told her father that they had not yet seen the last of Werner von Klaub.

'How old is he, Ariana? Did he say?'

'Twenty-four.' She looked directly at her father with a small smile. 'He's very nice, you know. Did you like him?'

'The question is, did you?'

She shrugged noncommittally and for the first time all evening her father laughed. 'So it begins, does it? My darling, you are going to break a thousand hearts.' He only hoped that among them, she would not break his. He had kept her so carefully from that poison that it would kill him now if she countered his beliefs.

But she showed no sign of betraying him, or his principles, as the next few years wore on. Werner von Klaub had indeed come to visit them, but only once or twice. He had found her as ravishing as he had that first evening, yet he also found her very young and more than a little shy. She wasn't nearly as amusing as the women who had fallen prey to his uniform in the past three years. Ariana wasn't ready, and Werner von Klaub wasn't interested enough to wait.

Her father was relieved when the visits ended and she didn't seem particularly saddened by the loss. She was happy with her life at home with her father and her brother, and she had lots of friends her own age at school. Walmar's determined battle to protect her had left her, in some ways, young for her years. Yet countered by that innocence was the wisdom she had gained from loss and pain. The loss of her mother, however remote Kassandra may have been, however well veiled the realities of that loss, had marked Ariana, and the absence of a mother she could turn to had left a sadness lurking somewhere in the tiny beauty's eyes. But it was a private kind of sorrow, a window to something amiss within   it was not due to any exposure to the price of war. Despite the considerable increase in the bombings of Berlin since 1943 and the amount of time she spent in their cellar with Gerhard, her father, and the servants during the air raids, Ariana had no real contact with the pain of war until she was eighteen, in the spring of 1944.

All that spring the Allies had increased their efforts, and Hitler had recently issued new decrees confirming his commitment to total war.

Ariana had come home from school to find her father closeted in the main salon with a friend, according to Berthold, who was now quite elderly and also very deaf.

'Did he say who?' Ariana smiled at him. Berthold was one of her earliest memories. He had always been there.

'Yes, miss.' He smiled benignly, the stonelike face cracking into warm creases just for her. He nodded as though he had understood her, but she knew immediately that he had not.

Familiar with his foibles, she spoke louder, unlike her brother, who often teased him openly about being deaf. But from Master Gerhard, Berthold would take anything. Gerhard was his pet. 'I said, did my father say who was visiting?'

'Ah . . . no, miss. He did not. Frau Klemmer let them in. I was downstairs for a moment asisting Master Gerhard with his chemistry equipment.'

'Oh, God, not that.'

'Yes?'

'Never mind, Berthold, thank you.' Easily, Ariana swung through the hallway. The house and its vast crew of servants had also been a constant in her life. She couldn't imagine living elsewhere.

She passed Frau Klemmer in the upper hallway on the way into her room. She and Frau Klemmer had been discussing a secret that morning, about reopening her mother's room. It had been nine years now, and Ariana was about to turn eighteen. It annoyed her to share the upper floor with Gerhard, who was noisy and constantly blowing up his chemistry concoctions, trying to make small bombs.

And she and her father had already decided that she would put off going to university until after the war. So when she finished school in two months, she would be busier around the house. There was volunteer work that she had planned for herself. She already worked in a hospital two days a week. But somehow it seemed to her more suitable that after she graduated from gymnasium, she should at the same time advance her status in the house. The prospect of occupying her mother's quarters pleased her greatly . . . if only she could get her father to agree.

'Have you asked him yet?' Frau Klemmer asked it in a conspiratorial whisper and Ariana shook her head.

'Not yet. Tonight. If I can get rid of Gerhard after dinner.' She sighed and rolled her eyes. 'He's such a pest.' He had just turned fifteen.

'I think if you give your father time to think it over, he'll probably agree. He'll like having you that much nearer. Climbing all those stairs up to the third floor to see you wears him out.' It was a sensible reason, but Ariana wasn't sure that it was the one that would win him over. At sixty-eight, her father did not enjoy being reminded of his age.

'I'll think of something. I wanted to talk to him now, but there's someone with him. Do you know who it is? Berthold said you let someone in.'

'I did.' She looked briefly puzzled. 'It is Herr Thomas. And he doesn't look well at all.' But who did look well these days? Even Ariana's father looked exhausted now when he came home from the bank. The Reich was putting more and more pressure on all of the country's bankers to come up with funds they didn't have.

As Frau Klemmer left, Ariana mused for a moment about whether or not to go back down and join her father. She had wanted to slip into her mother's rooms again, to admire the handsome bedroom and to see if the boudoir was large enough to accommodate her desk. But she could do that later. She would prefer to visit for a moment with her father's friend.

Herr Thomas was some thirty years younger than her

father, but despite the gap of years between them, her father had a great fondness for the soft-spoken man. He had spent four years working for her father and had then decided to go into law. During law school he had married a fellow student, and they had had three children in four years. The youngest child was three now, but Herr Thomas hadn't seen him since four months after his birth. His wife was Jewish, and she and the children had been taken from him. For the first two years of the war, Max had been able to stave off the Nazis. But in the end there was no putting off the inevitable. Sarah and the children had to go. In 1941, three years before, they were taken away. The shock of losing them had almost destroyed him, and now when he visited Ariana's father, he looked fifteen years older than his thirty-seven years. He had fought desperately to find them, and in the past year Ariana knew he had all but given up hope.

Gently she rapped on the double doors, but all she heard was the soft hum of conversation within. She was about to turn away and leave them when at last she heard her father call out.

She opened the door slowly and peeked inside with her soft smile. 'Papa? May I come in?' But what she saw startled her and she didn't know whether to close the door and go, or stay. Maximilian Thomas was sitting with his back to her, his shoulders shaking gently, his face dropped into his hands. Ariana stared at her father, expecting to be sent away again, but to her surprise, he motioned her to stay. He was at a loss now. There was so little to be said. Perhaps his daughter could offer Max some comfort beyond what he had been able to give. It was Walmar's first act of recognition that Ariana was no longer a child. Had it been Gerhard in the doorway, he would have sent him back upstairs again with an urgent wave of his hand. But Ariana was not just a girl now, she also had the gentleness of a woman. He motioned her towards him, and as she approached, Max dropped his hands.

What she saw when she approached him was a look of total despair. 'Max . . . what happened?' She dropped to her

71

knees beside him and without thinking held out her arms. And just as naturally he went to her and sobbed softly as they embraced. He said nothing for long minutes, and then at last he wiped his eyes and pulled slowly away.

'Thank you. I'm sorry to . . .'

'We understand.' Walmar went to the long antique table where a large silver salver bore several bottles of cognac and the remains of his stock of English Scotch. Without asking Max his preference, he poured him a glass of brandy and silently held out the drink. Max took it from him, sipping slowly and wiping once more his still streaming eyes.

'Is it Sarah?' Ariana had to ask. Had he had news? He had sought information unsuccessfully from the Nazis for so long.

His eyes sought hers in answer, and the pain of what he had learned that day was there, etched in all its horror, his worst fears confirmed. 'They're all . . .' He couldn't bring himself to say the word. '. . . dead.' He took a deep, ragged breath and put down the brandy. 'All four of them . . . Sarah . . . and the boys . . .'

'My God.' Ariana stared at him in anguish and wanted to ask him why. But they all knew why. Because they were Jewish . . . *Juden* . . . Jews. 'Are you sure?'

He nodded. 'They told me that I should be grateful. That now I can start fresh with a woman of my own kind. Oh, God . . . oh, God . . . my babies . . . Ariana . . .' He reached out to her again without thinking, and once again she held him tight, this time with tears running down her cheeks as well.

Walmar knew he must get Max to think about leaving at once. He could no longer stay in Berlin. 'Max, listen. You have to think now. What are you going to do?'

'What do you mean?'

'Can you stay here? Now? Now that you know.'

'I don't know . . . I don't know . . . I wanted to leave years ago. In thirty-eight, I told Sarah then . . . but she didn't want to . . . her sisters, her mother . . .' It was a familiar refrain to them both. 'And after that I stayed because I had to find her. I thought that if I knew where she was, I could

72

bargain with them, I could . . . Oh, God, I should have known . . .'

'That wouldn't have changed anything, would it?' Walmar looked down at his friend, sharing his pain. 'But now you know the truth. And if you stay, they will torment you. They will watch what you do, where you go, who you do what with and where. You have been suspect for years, because of Sarah, and now you really must leave.'

Max Thomas shook his head. Walmar knew only too well what he was saying. Twice Thomas's law offices had been destroyed with 'Jew Lover' carved in every piece of furniture and painted on the walls. But he had stayed. He had to. To find his wife. 'I guess I don't understand yet that it's over, that . . . that she . . . that there's no one to look for any more.' He sat back in his chair, his eyes full of terrible understanding. 'But where would I go?'

'Anywhere. Switzerland, if you can get there. Afterwards maybe to the United States. But get out of Germany, Max, she will destroy you if you stay here.' . . . *just as she destroyed Kassandra . . . and before her, Dolff . . .* The memory of that was fresh again as he looked into the young man's face.

Max shook his head. 'I can't go.'

'Why not?' Walmar was suddenly angry. 'Because you're so patriotic? Because you love the country that has been so kind? Good God, man, what is there to stay for? Get the hell out.'

Ariana watched them, frightened; she had never seen her father look like that before. 'Max . . . maybe Daddy is right. Maybe later you could come back.'

But Walmar stood there glowering. 'If you're smart, you won't want to do that. Start a fresh life somewhere. Anywhere, Max, anywhere, but get out of here before it all comes down around your ears.'

Max Thomas looked at Walmar bleakly. 'It already has.'

Walmar sighed deeply and sat down in his own chair again, never taking his eyes from his friend. 'Yes, I know, I understand that. But, Max, you still have your life. You have already lost Sarah and the children.' His voice was gentle, but Max shed fresh tears. 'You owe it to them and to them and to yourself to survive now. Why add yet another tragedy, one more loss?' If only he could have said that to Kassandra. If only she could have understood that, too.

'How would I go?' Max stared at him, thinking, yet not really understanding what it meant to leave his house, his heritage, the country that had once given birth to his sons and his dreams.

'I don't know. We could think it over. I suppose with all the chaos these days, you could just simply disappear. In fact' – Walmar seemed to be thinking – 'if you did it now, immediately, they might well think that you went mad from the news. You could have run off, killed yourself, done anything. They won't be suspicious right away. Later they might.'

'And what does that mean? That I leave your house tonight and start walking towards the border? With what? My briefcase and my overcoat and my grandfather's gold watch?' The watch he spoke of rested, as it always did, in the pocket of his vest.

But Walmar was still thinking. He nodded quietly. 'Perhaps.'

'Are you serious?'

Ariana watched them, shocked at all she was hearing. Was this what was happening, then? They were killing women and children, leaving others to flee on foot to the border in the middle of the night? It filled her with a kind of fear she had not yet known, and the tiny ivory face seemed paler than it ever had before.

Walmar looked at Max then. He had a plan. 'Yes, I'm very serious. I think you should go now.'

'Tonight?'

'Perhaps you shouldn't leave tonight, but as soon as possible, as soon as papers can be arranged. I think that you should disappear tonight though.' And then after another sip of cognac, 'What do you think?'

Max had been listening carefully to Walmar's words, and he knew that what the older man was saying made a great deal of sense. What reason did he have to cling to a country that had already destroyed everything that he held dear?

Silently he nodded. And then after another moment, 'You're right. I'll go. I don't know where – or how.' His eyes never left Walmar's, but now the elder man looked at his daughter. This was a turning point in all three lives.

'Ariana, would you like to leave now?'

For an instant none of the three stirred in the room, and then she looked questioningly at her father. 'Do you wish me to, Papa?' But she didn't want to. She wanted to stay here with him and Max.

'You may stay if you like. If you understand the importance of keeping all this quiet. You must discuss it with no one. Not Gerhard, not the servants. No one. Not even with me. What will happen, will happen in silence. And when it is over, it never happened at all. Is that clear?' She nodded and for an instant he questioned the insanity of involving his daughter, but they were all involved. Soon it could be happening to them. It was time she knew. He had thought that for some time. She had to understand how desperate the situation was. 'Do you understand me, Ariana?'

'Perfectly, Papa.'

'Very well.'

He closed his eyes for a moment, and then he turned to Max. 'You will leave here this evening, by the front door, looking even more troubled than you did when you came in, and you will very simply disappear. Walk towards the lake. And then later you will come back. I will let you in myself after the house is dark. You will stay here for a day or two. And then you go. Quietly. To the border. Into Switzerland. And then, my friend, you are gone for good. To a new life.'

'And how am I supposed to finance all this? Can you get my money out of the bank?' Max looked worried and Walmar shook his head.

'Never mind that. All you have to worry about is getting back here tonight. And then getting to the border after that. Let me take care of the money and the papers.'

75

Max was impressed, if somewhat surprised, by his respectable old friend. 'Do you know anyone who can do that sort of thing?'

'Yes, I do. I researched it about six months ago, in case . . . the need ever arose.' Ariana was astonished but she kept quiet. She had no idea that her father had ever considered such a thing. 'Are we clear, then?' Max nodded. 'Do you want to stay for dinner? You could leave rather obviously after that.'

'All right. But where will you hide me?'

Walmar sat silent for a moment – he had been wondering the same thing. This time it was Ariana who had the answer. 'Mother's rooms.' Walmar looked at her in quick displeasure, and Max watched the exchange that passed silently between their eyes. 'Papa, it's the only place no one goes near.' Except that she and Frau Klemmer had been there only that day. It was what had brought the rooms in question so quickly to her mind. Ordinarily the family and the household almost pretended that Kassandra's room were no longer a part of the Von Gotthard house. 'Papa. It's true. He would be safe there. And I could tidy up again after he's gone. No one would ever know.'

Walmar paused for what seemed an endless moment. The last time he had been in that apartment, his wife had been lying dead in a bathtub filled with blood. He had never entered her rooms again. He couldn't bear the pain of those last memories, that bruised face and those desperate eyes, the breasts shattered from the belt buckle of the Nazi who had almost raped her. 'I suppose there is no choice.' He said it with an agony that only Max understood. They both knew what the Nazis were capable of.

'I'm sorry to be a problem for you, Walmar.'

'Don't be ridiculous. We want to help you.' And then, with a small wintry smile, 'Perhaps one day you will help us.'

There was a long silence in the room then and at last Max spoke. 'Walmar, do you really think of going?'

The older man looked pensive. 'I'm not sure I could. I'm more visible than you are. They watch me. They know me.

76

They need me more than they need you. I am a source of funds to them. The Tilden Bank is important to the Reich. It is the albatross around my neck, but it is also my salvation. One day it may prove to be the gun held to my head. But if I have to, I would do the same as you are doing.' Ariana was shocked to hear him say it. She had never suspected that her father thought one day to flee. And then, as though by exact prearrangement, Berthold knocked and announced dinner, and the three of them left the room in silence.

Chapter 9

Walmar von Gotthard tiptoed silently through his own house and waited in the front hall. He had warned Max Thomas to come barefoot through the garden. It would make less noise than walking on the gravel in his shoes. And he had given him his own key to the front gate. Max had left them around eleven and now it was a few minutes before three. The moon was round and full and it was easy to see him, running quickly across the expanse of lawn. The two men exchanged no greeting, only curt nods as Max Thomas carefully wiped off his feet with his socks. The dirt from the flower beds would have left tracks on the white marble floor. Walmar was pleased with Max's clear thinking. He was a different man now than the one who had sat sobbing and broken in his study only ten hours before. Now that Max Thomas was fleeing, his very survival would depend on his quick wits and his cool head.

The two men walked rapidly up the main staircase and in a brief moment reached the door at the end of the long hall. For an instant Walmar paused there, waiting, as though not sure whether he should go in. But Ariana had been waiting for them and now, sensing their presence, she opened the door a crack to peek. Seeing Max's intent face in the doorway, she opened the door wider to let them in, but

Walmar only shook his head as he stood there, as though he could not yet force himself to go in. Max quickly entered. Perhaps it was time for Walmar to open the doors again; perhaps, like Max, it was time for him to forge ahead.

He closed the door soundlessly behind him and followed as Ariana beckoned them into the small room that had been her mother's study, now faded into a still softer pink. The chaise longue still stood in the corner, and Ariana had put warm blankets on it so Max could sleep there.

She put a finger to her lips and whispered softly. 'I thought if he slept there he'd be safer. Should anyone look in, they won't see him from the bedroom.' Her father nodded and Max looked at him gratefully, but there were lines of fatigue crowding round his eyes. Walmar looked at him one last time, nodded, and then left the room with Ariana following quickly behind. Walmar had promised that he would get the papers as quickly as possible. He hoped for Max's sake to have them by the next night.

Ariana and her father left each other in the hallway with their own thoughts and no words. She returned to her room then, thinking of Max and the lonely journey he was about to undertake. She still remembered little Sarah, a tiny woman with dark, laughing eyes. She had been so full of funny stories, and she had been kind to Ariana whenever they met. It all seemed so long ago now. Ariana had often thought of her over the past three years, wondering where she was and what they had done to her . . . and the boys . . . Now they knew.

They were the same thoughts Max was thinking as he lay quietly on the pink satin-covered chaise longue in the room of the woman he had seen only once when he first met Walmar. She had been a dazzling woman with golden, almost copper-coloured hair. He had thought her the most striking vision of his lifetime. And shortly after, he had learned that she was dead. Of flu, they had told him. But as he lay there, he sensed that there had been some other reason for her death. Some odd feeling had communicated itself from Walmar, as though he knew, as though he, too, had suffered at the Nazis' hands. It didn't seem possible, but one never knew.

In his own room Walmar stood looking out at the lake in the moonlight, but it was not the lake he saw there, it was his wife. Golden, shining, beautiful Kassandra . . . the woman he had loved so desperately so long ago . . . the dreams they had shared in the room. And now it was empty, solemn, draped, forgotten. It had torn a part of him away that night, crossing that doorway with the man they were hiding, and Ariana with those same bottomless lavender-blue eyes. He turned away from the moonlight in sorrow, and at last he undressed and went to bed.

'Did you ask him?' Frau Klemmer asked her after breakfast when they met in the hall.

'About what?' Ariana had other things on her mind.

'The room. Your mother's apartment.' What a strange girl she was, so distant, so withdrawn at times – had she already forgotten? Frau Klemmer often wondered what mysteries lay behind the deep blue eyes.

'Oh, that . . . yes . . . I mean no. He said no.'

'Was he angry?'

'No. Just very definite. I guess I'll just stay where I am.'

'Why don't you push him a little? Maybe he'll think about it some more and give in.'

But Ariana shook her head with determination. 'He has enough on his mind.'

The housekeeper shrugged and moved on. Sometimes it was hard to understand the girl, but then again, her mother had been strange, too.

When Ariana left for school that morning, Walmar had already left the house in his Rolls. She had wanted to spend the day at home – in case, because of Max – but her father had insisted that she go on with her life as always, and to be sure of Max's protection, Walmar had himself relocked Kassandra's door.

It seemed hours before she could get back there, but at last it was time to go home. She had sat in school all day, distracted, thinking of Max and wondering how he was. Poor man, how strange it must feel to him, to be a captive in someone's house. With a calm step, Ariana walked down the main hallway, greeted Berthold, and went upstairs. She declined Anna's offer of tea and went into her bathroom to comb her hair. It was another fifteen minutes before she dared walk back downstairs to the next floor. She paused for a moment at the door of her father's bedroom and then glided past it with the key she had borrowed from Frau Klemmer only two days before.

The door opened easily as she turned the key and then the handle, and she slipped quietly inside and disappeared. On silent feet she ran through the bedroom, soundless, breathless, and then she stood there, in the doorway, a smiling vision in front of the tired, unshaven Max.

'Hello.' It was barely a whisper.

He smiled and invited her to sit down. 'Have you eaten?' He shook his head. 'I thought so. Here.' She had brought him a sandwich hidden in the deep pocket of her skirt. 'I'll bring you some milk later.' That morning she had left him a pitcher of water. They had told him not to run the taps. The pipes would be too rusty after so many years, and they might squeak horribly, alerting the servants that there was someone in these rooms. 'You're all right though?'

'I'm fine.' He gobbled the sandwich quickly. 'You didn't have to do this.' And then he grinned at her. 'But I'm glad you did.' He looked younger somehow, as though years of care had been dropped from his face. He looked worn, and different now that he was unshaven, but still, he didn't have the gaunt, pained look he had worn yesterday. 'How was school today?'

'Awful. I worried about you.'

'You shouldn't have. I'm fine here.' It was odd, he had only hidden there for a few hours, but already he felt cut off from the world. He missed the buses, the noise, his office, the telephone, even the sound of boots goose-stepping down the street. It all seemed so remote here. As though he had drifted into another world. A faded, forgotten world of pink satin, in the boudoir of a woman long since gone. Together they stared around the small study and their eyes met at the same time. 'What was she like . . . your mother?'

Ariana looked around her strangely. 'I'm not sure. I never really knew her. She died when I was nine.' For an instant she remembered Gerhard at the cemetery and then standing in the rain beside her father, holding tightly to his hand. 'She was very beautiful. I'm not sure I know much more than that.'

'I saw her once. She was incredible. I thought she was the most exquisite woman I'd ever seen.' Ariana nodded.

'She used to come upstairs to see us, in evening clothes and smelling of perfume. Her dresses made wonderful sounds as she crossed the room, the swishing noises of silk and taffeta and satin. She always seemed terribly mysterious to me. I suppose she always will.'

Ariana looked at him with her big sad eyes. 'Have you thought about where you're going?' Speaking to him in the whisper they had to use to converse, she seemed like a child asking him a secret, and he smiled.

'More or less. I think your father's right. Switzerland first. Then maybe when the war is over, I'll see if I can get to the States. My father had a cousin there. I'm not even sure if he's still alive. But it's a start.'

'Won't you come back here?' She looked shocked for a moment as he shook his head. 'Never, Max?'

'Never.' And then he sighed softly. 'I never want to see this place again.' It seemed strange to Ariana that he should cut himself off forever from what had been his whole life. But then, perhaps he was right to shut the door so firmly. She wondered if it was like her father's never re-entering her mother's bedroom until the night before. There were places one simply never returned to. One couldn't bear the pain. When she looked up at him again, he was smiling gently. 'Will you and your father come and see me in America after the war?'

She laughed softly. 'That seems a long way off.'

'I hope not.' And then, without thinking, he reached out

and took her hand. He held it for a long moment, and then she bent slowly towards him and kissed him softly on the top of his head. There were no more words needed between them; he only held her, and she gently stroked his hair. Soon he made her leave, telling her it was dangerous for her to be there. But the truth was, he was thinking the unthinkable while hiding out in his old friend's house.

Later that evening Walmar came to see him, and he looked far more tired and subdued than Max. He already had the travel papers and a German passport in the name of Ernst Josef Frei. They had used the picture from Max's passport, and the official seal they'd stamped on it looked real.

'Quite a job isn't it?' Max stared at it with fascination and then glanced back at Walmar sitting uncomfortably in a pink chair. 'What now?'

'A map, some money. I also got you a travel permit. You can make it close to the border on the train. After that, my friend, you're on your own. But you should be able to make it –' he paused for a moment – 'with this.' He handed him an envelope filled with money, enough to keep him handsomely for several weeks. 'I didn't dare take out more than that, or someone might have wondered why.'

'Is there anything you didn't think of, Walmar?' Max stared at him in admiration. What a remarkable old man Von Gotthard was.

'I hope not. I'm afraid I'm a little new at this. But I think it might be good practice.'

'You really think of leaving?' Walmar looked pensive. 'Why you?'

'A number of reasons. Who knows what will happen, at what point they'll lose control. And I have Gerhard to think of now, too. In the fall he'll be sixteen. If the war doesn't end soon, they may draft him. At that point we go.' Max nodded quietly. He understood. If he still had a son to protect from the Nazis, he would do the same thing.

But it wasn't only Gerhard that worried Walmar, it was Ariana too. The flood of uniforms in the city worried him almost all the time. She was so delicately pretty, so enticing in her quiet, distant way. What if they were to harm her, to grab her, or worse, if some high-ranking officer were to take a fancy to his only female child? It frightened him increasingly now that she was older, and in a few months she would no longer be in school. Knowing that she was doing volunteer work at Martin Luther Hospital terrified him most of all. He sat there thinking while Max looked at his new passport again.

'Walmar, what can I do to thank you?'

'Be safe. Start a new life. That's thanks enough.'

'It seems nothing at all. Can I let you know where I am?'

'Discreetly. Just an address. No name. I'll know.' Max nodded. 'The train leaves from the station at midnight.' Walmar fished in his pocket and handed him the keys to a car. 'In the garage behind the house you'll find a blue Ford coupe, an old one. It was Kassandra's. But I checked it myself this morning. Miraculously, it still works. I think the servants still drive it around from time to time to keep it running. Take it, drive it to the station, and leave it there. I'll report it stolen in the morning. You'll be long gone. We'll go to bed early tonight, so there shouldn't be any problem. Hopefully by the time you leave at eleven thirty-everyone will be asleep. And that, my friend, takes care of everything – except one thing.'

Max couldn't imagine anything more. But Walmar had thought of one thing further. He walked quietly into Kassandra's bedroom and lifted two paintings from the wall. With his pocket knife he prised them from the frames that held them, and then sliced them carefully from the wood stretchers that had held them taut for twenty years. One was a small Renoir that had been his mother's, the other a Corot he had bought his wife in Paris on their honeymoon twenty years before. Without saying anything to the man who watched them, he rolled both canvases tightly and then handed them to his friend. 'Take them. Do whatever you have to. Sell them, eat them, barter them. They're both worth a great deal of money. Enough to start

83

you on your new life.'

'Walmar, no! Even what I'm leaving in the bank here would never cover those.' He had spent much of his money trying to find Sarah and the boys.

'You have to. And they do no one any good hanging here. You need them . . . and I could never bear to look at them again . . . not after they were here. They're yours now, Max. Take them. From a friend.'

Just then Ariana slipped quietly into the room. She was puzzled when she saw the tears in Max's eyes and then, when she saw the empty frames beside her mother's headboard, she quickly understood.

'Are you going now, Max?' Her eyes grew wide.

'In a few hours. Your father has just . . . I don't know what to say, Walmar.'

'*Wiedersehen*, Maximilian. Good luck.' The shook hands firmly as Max fought back tears. A moment later Walmar left them, and Ariana stayed for only a few minutes. But before she left him to go to dinner, Max reached out for her and they kissed.

Dinner passed with the utmost propriety, except for Gerhard, who shot small breadball's at Berthold's retreating back. Reprimanded by his father, he grinned and shot one a moment later at his sister's back.

'We're going to have to send you back to Fräulein Hedwig for your dinners if you continue to do that.'

'Sorry, Father.' But despite his friendly chatter, he was unable to rouse either his father or his sister to a great deal of conversation, and eventually he, too, fell silent as he ate.

After dinner Walmar retired to his study, Ariana to her bedroom, and Gerhard to his pranks. She wanted to return once more to Maximilian, but she was afraid to. Her father had insisted that they must take no more chances of drawing the servants' notice. Max's escape depended on no one's knowing where he was, and their safety on no one's knowing where he had been. So she sat in her room for hours, and dutifully, a ten thirty, as per her father's orders, she turned off her lights. But silently she waited, thinking, praying, until at last she could bear it no longer, and at twenty minutes after eleven, she tiptoed softly down the stairs until she reached her mother's door.

She let herself in without a sound and found him waiting, as though he knew that she would come. He kissed her long and hard this time, holding her tightly until she could barely breathe. They kissed for one last long moment, and then buttoning his coat around him, he pulled away. 'I have to go now, Ariana.' He smiled softly. 'Take good care, my darling. Until we meet again.'

'I love you.' It was the merest whisper, as much spoken with her eyes as with her words. 'God be with you.'

He nodded, the briefcase with the priceless paintings hidden in newspapers at the bottom clutched in his right hand. 'We'll meet again after it's over.' He smiled as though he were going to the office. 'Maybe in New York.'

She giggled softly then. 'You're crazy.'

'Maybe.' And then his eyes grew serious. 'But I love you, too.' And it was true. She had touched him, come to him in a moment when he needed a gentle friend.

And then, saying nothing further, he tiptoed softly past her to the door. She held it open, locked it behind them, and waved one last time as he tiptoed softly down the stairs. She quickly took refuge in her bedroom, and then at last she heard the sound of her mother's car driving swiftly through the gate.

'*Auf Wiedersehen*, my darling.' She watched from her window and stood there for almost half an hour, thinking of the first man she had ever kissed and wondering if they would ever meet again.

Chapter 10

There was nothing evident in her father's manner the next morning that would have led anyone to suspect that something was amiss, nor in Ariana's when they shared breakfast. And that afternoon when the chauffeur reported solemnly that Frau von Gotthard's old Ford had been stolen, Walmar immediately called the police. The car was found later that evening, abandoned near the train station and unharmed. And it was slyly but amusingly suggested that Gerhard had been the culprit and had gone for a little ride. The police attempted to conceal their amusement, and Gerhard behaved with appropriate outrage when he was called. But the matter was left to the family to handle, the police were thanked, and the car was put back in the garage.

'But I didn't take it, Father!' He blushed hotly, standing facing Walmar.

'Didn't you? Well, in that case, then I suppose everything is all right.'

'But you think I did!'

'It doesn't matter. The car is back in the garage. Please see to it, however, that neither you nor your friends attempt to . . . er . . . borrow . . . your mother's car again.' It was an attitude he detested taking, but there was no choice. Ariana understood it clearly, and she attempted to console Gerhard as she ushered him from the room.

'But it's so unfair! I didn't!' And then he stared at her. 'Did you?'

'Of course not. Don't be silly. I don't know how to drive.'

'I'll bet you did!'

'Gerhard, don't be silly!' But suddenly they were both laughing, and they walked arm in arm up the stairs to their rooms, Gerhard convinced she'd done it.

But despite her jovial manner with her brother, Walmar

saw that there was something much amiss. She was more quiet than usual in the mornings, and when she returned from school or her volunteer work in the evenings, she disappeared immediately into her room. She was difficult to draw into conversation, and at last, a week after Max had left them, she sought her father alone in his study, and her eyes were washed with tears.

'Have you heard anything, Father?' He knew instantly. It was just as he had feared.

'No, nothing. But we'll hear. It may be some time before he's settled enough to let us know.'

'You don't know that.' She sank into a chair beside the fire. 'He could be dead.'

'Perhaps.' His voice was sad and soft as he watched her. 'And perhaps not. But, Ariana, he is gone now. Gone from us. To his own life, wherever that will lead him. You can't hang on to him. We are only part of the old life he has left.' But it frightened him to see her, and the next words escaped him before he could make them stop. 'Are you taken with him, Ariana?'

She turned towards him, shocked at the question. She had never known her father to ask something like that. 'I don't know I . . .' She closed her eyes tightly. 'It's just that I was worried. He could have . . .' She blushed faintly and stared into the fire, unwilling to tell him the truth.

'I see. I hope you aren't. It's difficult to dictate these things, but . . .' How could he tell her? What could he say? 'In times like these it is best to save our loving for a brighter day. In wartime, in difficult circumstances, there is a sense of romance that is often unreal and may not endure. You may see him again years from now and find him quite different. Not at all the man you remember from last week.'

'I understand that.' It was why she so carefully avoided any involvement with the wounded men at the hospital where she worked. 'I do know that, Father.'

'I'm glad.' He sighed deeply as he watched her. It was another turning point for him. Yet another fork in their ever more treacherous road. 'It could also be dangerous to love a

87

man in Max's position. Now he is fleeing, someday soon he could be hunted by the Nazis. And if you attach yourself to him, they could hunt you, too. Even if no harm comes to you, the pain of it could destroy you, as in some ways the pain of losing Sarah almost destroyed him.'

'How can they punish people because of whom they love?' She looked angry. 'How can one know beforehand which is the right side and which the wrong?'

Her childish question, so naïve, yet so right, brought the memories of Kassandra flooding back . . . he had warned her . . . she knew . . .

'Father?' Ariana watched him search himself. He seemed a million miles away.

'You have to forget him. It could be dangerous for you.' He looked at her sternly and her eyes never wavered from her father's.

'It was dangerous for you to help him, Father.'

'That's different. Even though, in a sense, you're right. But I'm not tied to him with that same bond, the bond of loving.' And then he looked at her more closely. 'And I hope neither are you.'

She didn't answer, and at last he walked to his window looking out over the lake. He could almost see the Grunewald cemetery from his windows. But in his mind's eye, he saw her face. As she had looked when he had warned her. As she had looked the night before she took her life.

'Ariana, I'm going to tell you something that I never wanted to tell you. About the price of loving. About the Nazis . . . about your mother.'

His voice was a gentle, distant sound. Ariana waited, baffled staring at her father's back. 'It is not a judgement I make of her, or a criticism. I am not angry. I am not telling you any of this to make you feel ashamed. We loved each other deeply. But we married when she was very young. I loved her, but I didn't always understand her. In some ways she was different from the women of her times. She had a kind of quiet fire in her soul.' He turned to face her then. 'Do you know that when you were born she wanted to take care

88

of you herself, not to have a nurse? It was unheard of. And I thought it was silly. So I hired Fräulein Hedwig, and I think something happened to your mother. After that she always seemed a little lost.' He turned away again, silent for a moment, and then he went on. 'When we had been married for ten years, she met someone, a younger man than I. He was a very famous writer, he was handsome and intelligent, and she fell in love. I knew about it almost from the beginning. Perhaps even before it began. People told me they had seen them. And I saw something different in her eyes. Something excited and happy and alive again, something marvellous.' His voice grew softer. 'And I think, in a way, it made me love her more.

'The tragedy of Kassandra was not that she was in love with a man other than her husband, but that her country had fallen into the hands of the Nazis, and the man she loved so desperately was a Jew. I warned her, for her own sake and for his, but she wouldn't leave him. She wouldn't leave either one of us, in fact. In her own way she was loyal to us both. I can't say I ever really suffered from her attachment to this man. She was as devoted as she had been before, perhaps more so. But she was equally devoted to him. Even when they stopped publishing his work, even when they shunned him, and at the last . . .' His voice cracked and he could barely go on. 'Even when they killed him.

'She was with him the day they took him. They dragged him from his house, they beat him, and when they found your mother, they . . . beat her . . . they might even have killed her except that she thought to tell them who she was so they left her alone. She made her way home. And when I got here, all she could talk about was that she had disgraced me and how afraid she was that they would hurt us. She felt she had to offer her life to secure ours . . . and she couldn't live with what they had done to him. I went to a meeting for two hours, and when I came home, she was dead. In the bathroom of her rooms down the hall.' He waved vaguely towards the rooms Max had occupied only a week before.

'That, Ariana, is the story of your mother, who loved a

man the Nazis wanted dead. She couldn't bear the pain of the reality they had shown her . . . she couldn't live with the ugliness and the brutality and the fear . . . So –' he turned to face his daughter – 'in a sense they killed her. Just as, in a sense, they may dare to kill you, if you choose to take the risk of loving Max. Don't do it . . . oh, God, please, Ariana . . . don't . . .' His face sank into his hands and for the first time in her life Ariana heard her father cry. She went to him, trembling and silent, and held him tightly in her arms, her own tears falling on to his jacket as his mingled with the gold dust of her hair.

'I'm so sorry . . . Oh, Papa, I'm so sorry.' She said it to him again and again, horrified at what he had told her, and yet for the first time in her life, her mother had become real. 'Papa, don't . . . please . . . I'm sorry . . . I don't know what happened . . . I'm so confussed. It was so strange, having him here in that bedroom . . . in our house, hidden, frightened. I wanted to help him. I felt so sorry for him.'

'So did I.' Her father raised his head at last. 'But you must let him go. There will be a man for you one day. A good man, and I hope the right man, in better times.' She nodded silently as she dried a fresh cascade of tears.

'Do you suppose we'll ever see him again?'

'Perhaps one day.' His arms went around his daughter. 'I hope we will.' She nodded and they stood there, the man who had lost Kassandra and the little girl she had left him with instead. 'Please, my darling, be careful now, while we're at war.'

'I will. I promise.' Her eyes turned up towards his then as she bestowed on him a tiny smile. 'Besides, I never want to leave you.'

But at that he laughed softly. 'And that, my darling, will change, too.'

Two weeks later Walmar got a letter at the office. It had no return address and contained a single sheet of paper with a hastily scrawled address. Max was in Lucerne. It was the last that Walmar von Gotthard ever heard of him.

Chapter 11

The summer passed uneventfully. Walmar was busy at the bank, and Ariana was busy at the hospital three mornings a week. With school no longer an obstacle, she had more time for her volunteer work and more time to run the house. She and Gerhard and her father went on a week's holiday to the mountains, and when they returned, Gerhard turned sixteen. His father announced with amusement on the morning of his birthday that now his son was a man. That was apparently also the opinion of Hitler's army, because in the desperate last puch of the fall of 1944, they were drafting every man and boy within reason. Gerhard received notice that he was being drafted four days after the birthday that he and his father and sister had celebrated with such glee. He had three days to report.

'I don't believe it.' He stared at the notice over his breakfast. He was already late for school. 'But they can't do that . . . can they, Father?' His father looked at him gloomily.

'I'm not sure. We'll see.'

Later that morning Walmar visited an old friend of his, a colonel, and learned that nothing could be done.

'We need him, Walmar. We need them all.'

'It's that bad, then?'

'It's worse.'

'I see.'

They had discussed the war, the colonel's wife and Walmar's bank for a few moments, and then resolutely Walmar had gone back to his office. As he sat in the back of the Rolls-Royce drive by his chauffeur, he pondered what he had to do. He would not lose his son. He had lost enough.

When Walmar got back to his office, he made two calls. He returned to the house at lunchtime, extracted some papers from the wall safe in his study, and returned to work. He didn't get home that evening until after six, and when he did, he found his children upstairs on the third floor, in Gerhard's bedroom. Ariana had been crying and Gerhard's face was filled with fear and despair.

'They can't take him, can they, Father?' Ariana believed her father was able to move mountains. But her eyes held little hope. And neither did Walmar's when he answered softly.

'Yes, they can.'

Gerhard said nothing; he sat there, stunned at what had befallen him. The notice still lay cast open on his desk. He had read it a hundred times since that morning. Two other boys in his class had also received their notices. But he had said nothing of his own. His father had told him to remain silent, lest there be something that he could do. 'So that means I'm going.' He said it in a dull, flat voice and his sister gave way to fresh tears.

'Yes, it does mean that, Gerhard.' Despite the stern voice he eyed his children gently. 'Be proud to serve your country.'

'Are you crazy?' He and Ariana stared at their father in shocked horror.

'Be still.' On his last words he closed Gerhard's bedroom door. With a finger to his lips, he urged them closer and then whispered softly. 'You don't have to go.'

'I don't?' It was a jubilant stage whisper from Gerhard. 'You fixed it?'

'No.' Walmar shook his head seriously. 'I couldn't. We're leaving.'

'What?' Gerhard looked shocked once more, but his father and sister exchanged a knowing glance. It was like Max's flight only a few months before. 'How will we go?'

'I'll take you into Switzerland tomorrow. We can say that you're sick here at home. You don't have to report until Thursday that's not for another three days. I'll take you over the border and leave you with friends of mine in Lausanne, or in Zurich if I have to. Then I'll come back for your sister.' He glanced gently at his daughter and touched her hand. Perhaps she would see Max again after all.

'Why doesn't she come with us?' Gerhard looked puzzled, but his father shook his head.

'I can't get everything ready that quickly, and if she stays here, they won't suspect that we're pulling out for good. I'll be back here in a day anyway, and then I'll leave with her for good and all. But you're all going to have to be absolutely, totally quiet about this. Our lives depend on it. Do you understand?' They both nodded.

'Gerhard, I've ordered you a different passport. We can use it at the border if you have to. But whatever you do in the meantime, I want you to look resigned to going into the army. I even want you to seem pleased. That also means in this house.'

'Don't you trust the servants?' With all his sixteen years Gerhard was still naive. He overlooked Berthold's preoccupation with the Party, and Fräulein Hedwig's blind faith in Adolf Hitler.

'Not with your lives.'

Gerhard shrugged. 'All right.'

'Don't pack anything. We'll buy everything we need there.'

'Are we taking money?'

'I have money there already.' Walmar had been prepared for years. 'I'm only sorry that we waited this long. We should have never come back from vacation.' He sighed deeply, but Ariana tried to console him.

'You couldn't know. When will you be back from Switzerland, Papa?'

'Today is Monday. We leave in the morning . . . Wednesday night. And you and I will leave on Thursday night after I go to the bank that day. We can say we're going out to dinner, and then we will never come back. It will take a little manoeuvring to get the servants to think Gerhard reported to the army without saying goodbye. As long as you keep Anna and Hedwig out of Gerhard's rooms tomorrow and Wednesday, we can just say he left too early Thursday morning to see anyone at all. If you and I are here, no one will suspect anything. I'm going to try and be back in time for dinner.'

'What have you told them at the bank?'

'Nothing. I won't have to explain my absence. There are enough secret meetings going on these days that I can easily cover myself there. All right, both of you? Is everything clear now?

'The war is almost over, children, and when it ends, the Nazis will pull everything down with them when they go. I don't want either of you here for that. It's time for us to go. We can pick up the pieces later. Gerhard, meet me in the café around the corner from my office at eleven in the morning. We'll go to the train station together from there. Is that clear now?'

'Yes.' The boy looked suddenly grave.

'Ariana? You'll stay up here tomorrow and look after Gerhard, won't you?'

'Absolutely, Father. But how will he leave the house in the morning without being seen?'

'He'll leave at five before anyone gets up. Right, Gerhard?'

'Right, Father.'

'Wear warm clothes for the trip. We'll have to walk the last part.'

'You, too, Father?' Ariana was worried as she searched her father's eyes.

'Me too. And I'm quite capable of doing it, thank you. Probably a great deal more so than this boy.' He stood up then, rumpled his son's hair, and prepared to leave the room. He smiled at them, but there were no answering smiles from his children. 'Don't worry. It will go safely. And one day we'll be back.' But as he closed the door behind him, Ariana wondered if they would.

Chapter 12

'Frau Gebsen.' Walmar von Gotthard looked down imperiously at his secretary, his Homburg in his hand. 'I will be gone for the rest of the day, in meetings. You understand . . . where I'm going.'

'Of course, Herr von Gotthard.'

'Very well.' He marched quickly from the room. She had no idea where he was going. But she thought she did. To the Reichstag of course, to see the Minister of Finance again. And if he didn't appear on the morrow, she would understand that the meetings had resumed again. She understood about those things.

Walmar knew that he had timed his exit perfectly. The Minister of Finance was spending a week in France, consulting over the situation of the Reich's finances in Paris and taking inventory of the vast store of paintings they were sending back to Berlin. Quite a windfall for the Reich.

He had told his driver not to wait for him that morning, and he walked quickly around the corner to the workers' café. Gerhard had left the house on schedule at five that morning, with a kiss from his sister and a last look over his shoulder at the home he had grown up in, before he walked the twelve miles to the centre of Berlin.

As Walmar entered the café, he saw his son there but offered no sign of recognition. He merely walked towards the men's rest room, his face obscured by his Homburg, his briefcase in his hand. Once behind the locked door of the rest room, he quickly stepped out of his suit, putting on a pair of old work pants he had taken from the garage. Over his shirt he pulled a sweater, on his head a nondescript old cap, then an old warm jacket, and back into the briefcase went his suit. The Homburg he shoved brutally to the bottom of the trash. A moment later he joined Gerhard and with a vague nod and a coarse greeting signalled for him to go.

They took a cab to the station and were quickly lost in the milling throng. Twenty minutes later they were on the train bound for the border, their travel papers in order, their identification secure, their faces masks. Walmar was increasingly proud of Gerhard, who had played his part to perfection. He was overnight a fugitive, but learning quickly how to be a successful one.

'Fräulein Ariana? . . . Fräulein Ariana?' There came a sharp knocking at the door. It was Fräulein Hedwig, her face peering into the girl's as Ariana gingerly opened the door. But Ariana was quick to press a finger to her lips to silence Hedwig, and she rapidly joined the older woman in the hall.

'What's going on here?'

'Sshh . . . you'll wake him. Gerhard isn't feeling well at all.'

'Does he have a fever?'

'I don't think so. I think mostly just a dreadful cold.'

'Let me see him.'

'I can't do that. I promised him that we'd let him sleep all day. He's terrified he'll be too sick to go to the army on Thursday. He just wants to sleep it off.'

'Of course. I understand. You don't think we should call the doctor?'

Ariane shook her head. 'Not unless he gets much worse.'

Fräulein Hedwig nodded, pleased that her young charge should be so anxious to serve his country. 'He's a good boy.'

Ariana smiled benevolently in answer and kissed the old woman on the cheek as they stood in the hall. 'Thanks to you.'

Hedwig blushed at Ariana's compliment. 'Should I bring him tea?'

'No, it's all right. I'll make him some later. Right now he's asleep.'

'Well, let me know if he needs me.'

'I will, I promise. Thank you.'

'*Bitte schön.*' And a moment later Fräulein Hedwig went on her way.

Twice that afternoon and once that evening she pressed her services on Ariana again, but each time Ariana insisted that her brother had awakened earlier, eaten something, and then gone back to sleep. It was by then late Tuesday evening, and she only had to play the game until her father returned on Wednesday night. After that they were home free. Her father could claim that he had taken Gerhard to the army himself at the crack of dawn. All they had to do was make it through Wednesday. It was only a matter of another twenty-four hours. She could do that. And on Thursday evening she and her father would be gone, too.

Her body felt tired and achy when she went downstairs late Tuesday night. It had been a strain, listening all day for Hedwig or Anna, keeping up the ruse, and standing guard near Gerhard's room. She needed to escape the third floor, if only for a few minutes. So she let herself into her father's study and sat staring at the ashes in the grate. Had he only been in the room that morning? Had this been where he had said his quick goodbye? It seemed like a different room now without him, the papers carefully ordered on the desk, the books so neatly put away in the bookcase. She stood up, looking out at the lake, remembering his words when he had said goodbye . . . 'Don't worry, I'll be back day after tomorrow. And Gerhard will be fine.'

'It isn't Gerhard I'm worrying about. It's you.'

'Don't be silly. Don't you trust your old father?'

'More than anyone alive.'

'Good. Because that is precisely how much I trust you. And that is why, my darling Ariana, I am going to show you some things now, which one day may come in very handy. I think they're things you need to know.' He had shown her the secret safe in his bedroom, another in the main library, and the last one in her mother's bedroom, where he still kept all her jewels. 'One day these will be yours.'

'Why now?' Tears had sprung to her eyes. She didn't

want him showing her all this now. Not the day he was leaving to spirit Gerhard away.

'Because I love you, and I want you to know how to take care of yourself if you must. If something happens, you must tell them that you knew nothing about it. Tell them you thought Gerhard was sick upstairs and you had no idea he was gone. Tell them anything you have to. Lie. But protect yourself, with your fine mind and with this.' He showed her a small pistol and a dozen stacks of freshly minted bills. 'If Germany falls, these will be worth nothing, but your mother's jewellery will always take care of your needs.' He then showed her the false volume of Shakespeare, in which were the large emerald, which had been her engagement ring, and the diamond signet ring she had worn on her right hand. As Ariana saw it, she unthinkingly reached out to touch it. Its glimmer was familiar. She could remember seeing it on her mother's hand so many years before. 'She always wore that.' Her father's voice had been dreamlike as together they looked at the diamond signet ring.

'I remember.'

'Do you?' He seemed surprised. 'Remember it is here if you need it. Use it well, my darling, and her memory will be well served.'

As she thought back on the morning, she realised that standing in her father's study wouldn't bring him back to her any faster than if she went to bed upstairs. And she had to be up early in the morning to resume her vigil, lest Fräulein Hedwig grow zealous and insist on seeing Gerhard for herself.

Silently, Ariana turned off the lights in her father' study, closed the door, and went back upstairs.

At the Müllheim station Walmar gently nudged Gerhard, sleeping peacefully in his seat. They had been on the train for almost twelve hours, and the boy had been asleep for four. He looked so young and innocent as he lay there, his head tucked away in the corner, pressed against the wall of the coach. Soldiers had come aboard at several stations, and their papers had been checked twice. Walmar had only referred to Gerhard as his young friend; the papers appeared in order, and when he spoke to the officers, his tone had been deferential and his accent coarse. Gerhard had said little, only widening his eyes in awe of the soldiers, and one of them had ruffled his hair and teasingly promised him a commission soon. Gerhard had smiled winningly, and the two men in uniform had moved on.

At Müllheim no one boarded and the stop was brief, but Walmar wanted him awake before they reached Lörrach, their last stop. He would come awake quickly then in any case, in the cool night air. They had a nine-mile walk then, and their greatest challenge – to cross the border and reach Basel as early as they could. From there they would take a train to Zurich. Walmar had decided to leave him there – he would be safe in Switzerland. He would return two days later with Ariana, and they could go on together to Lausanne after that.

He was anxious to return to Ariana as soon as he could. She would not be able to keep up the charade forever, and the main thing was to get Gerhard safely to Zurich. But first, Lörrach, and their long walk. It was eighteen miles from Müllheim to Lörrach, and half an hour after Gerhard had stirred sleepily in his seat and gazed absently around him, the train came to a full halt. It was the end of the line for them.

At one thirty in the morning, with a handful of others, they stepped down, and for an instant Walmar felt his legs tremble beneath him at the unfamiliar sensation of solid ground. But he said nothing to Gerhard, he simply pulled his cap down, pulled up his collar, gestured towards the station, and they moved on. An old man and a boy going home. In their rough clothes they did not look strange in Lörrach: only Walmar's carefully manicured hands and well-barbered hair would have given them away, but he had worn the cap during the entire journey and had seen to it that he got his hands good and dirty in the dusty station before they left Berlin.

99

'Hungry?' He glanced at Gerhard, who yawned and shrugged.

'I'm all right. You?'

His father smiled at him. 'Here.' He handed him an apple he had pocketed from the lunch they'd bought on the train. Gerhard munched it as they walked along the road. There was no one in sight.

It took them five hours to cover the nine miles. Gerhard would have done it faster, but Walmar couldn't walk quite as quickly as he had as a young man. Still, for a man of almost seventy, he had done remarkably well. And then they knew that they had reached the border. Miles of fence and barbed wire. In the distance they could hear border patrols rumbling past them. Two hours earlier they had left the road. But in the dark before the first light of daybreak, they looked like two farmers getting an early start. No bags to attract suspicion, only Walmar's briefcase, which he would have thrown into the bushes had he heard someone approach. From his pocket he quickly pulled wire cutters as Gerhard watched, and as he snipped, the boy held back the wires. In a few minutes there was a hole big enough to crawl through.

Walmar felt his heart pounding . . . If they caught them, they would be shot . . . He didn't care for himself now, but the boy . . . Quickly, quickly, they climbed through and he could hear his jacket tearing, but a moment later they both stood in Switzerland, near a clump of trees in a field. Silently Walmar gestured, and they both began to run, darting through the trees for what seemed like hours until at last they stopped. But no one had followed, no one had heard. Walmar knew that a year or two earlier it would have been much harder to get across, but in the past months, the army had been in such desperate need of soldiers, there were ever fewer on the Swiss border patrols.

They walked for another half hour, reaching Basel by the first bright light of day. There was a splendid sunrise on the mountains, and for an instant Walmar put an arm around Gerhard's shoulders and stopped to watch the mauves and pinks streak across the sunlit sky. He thought in that brief moment that he had never felt so free. It would be a good life for them there until the war was over, and perhaps for even longer than that.

With aching feet they reached the train station and were just in time to catch the first train. Walmar bought two tickets to Zurich and settled back in his seat to rest. He closed his eyes and felt sleep begin to pull him deeper. It seemed only moments later when Gerhard was tugging at his arm. For the four-and-a-half-hour journey, glancing at the pleasant views of the Frick Valley, Gerhard had not wanted to wake him.

'Papa . . . I think we're here.'

Walmar looked sleepily around him, glancing out at the familiar Bahnhof Platz and the Grossmünster cathedral in the distance, and further away he could just glimpse the mountains of the Uetliberg. For that moment it felt like home. 'We are.' As they stepped down safely from the train in Zurich, despite his tired back and aching legs, Walmar wanted to take his son's arm and dance. Instead a long, slow grin lit his face and he put an arm around his son's shoulders. They had done it. They were free. Gerhard's life was assured now. He would never serve in Hitler's army. They would never kill his son.

They walked quickly to a small pension that Walmar remembered vaguely. He had had lunch there once while waiting for a train. And it was still where he remembered, small, unimportant, quiet, friendly. It was a place where he felt comfortable leaving Gerhard while he went back for his last hours in Berlin.

They ate a mammoth breakfast and then Walmar took him up to his room. He looked around, satisfied, and then turned to face the boy who had grown to manhood in so few days. It was a precious moment between father and son. It was Gerhard who spoke first, looking with damp-eyed admiration at the father who had led him to safety, cut the wires, walked across the border, and brought him here. 'Thank you, Papa . . . thank you.' He flung his arms around his father's neck. This was the father his friends had sometimes teasingly called 'old'. But this wasn't an old man who held him, it was a man who would have walked barefoot and bleeding across the mountains to save his son. For a long moment Walmar held him, and then slowly he pulled away.

'It's all right. You're safe now. You'll be all right here.' He walked swiftly to the simple desk then, pulled out a piece of paper and his carefully concealed gold pen. 'I'm going to give you the address and number of Herr Müller . . . in case Ariana and I get delayed.' The boy's face clouded over, but Walmar ignored his fears. 'Just a precaution.' He never thought to give him Max's number. It was too dangerous. The other man was a banker whom Walmar knew well. 'And I'm going to leave you my briefcase, there are papers, some money. I don't think you'll need much of that in the next two days.' All he was taking back with him was a slim purse filled with money, cash, nothing with which he could have been identified should they stop him this time on the road. This time is would be harder. It would be broad daylight, but he didn't want to take a chance delaying his return to Ariana. He wanted to get back to her by that night. He turned then to face Gerhard and saw that the boy was crying. They embraced again and said goodbye. 'Don't look so worried. Get some sleep now. When you wake up, have a good dinner, walk around, and see the sights. This is a free country, Gerhard, no Nazis, no armbands. Enjoy it. And Ariana and I should be back here by tomorrow night.'

'Do you think Ariana can make that walk from Lörrach?' Even for them it had been rough.

'She'll manage. I'll tell her not to wear her fancy high-heeled shoes.'

Gerhard smiled through his tears then and held tightly to his father for one last time. 'Can I see you to the station?'

'No, young man, what you can do now is go to bed.'

'What about you?' He looked exhausted, but Walmar only shook his head.

'I'll sleep on the way back to Basel, and probably all the

way back to Berlin.'

They looked at each other long and hard then. There was nothing left to be said.

'*Wiedersehen*, Papa.' He said it softly as his father waved at him and hurried down the stairs to the pension's main hall. He had ten minutes to catch the train back to Basel, and he ran the few blocks to the station, just in time to buy his ticket and board the train. At the pension, Gerhard was stretched out on the bed and already fast asleep

Chapter 13

'Well, how is he?' Fräulein Hedwig looked worriedly at Ariana as she stepped out into the hall to pick up their trays for breakfast. With an air of reassurance, Ariana smiled at their old nurse.

'He's much better, but he's still coughing a little. I think after another day in bed he'll be just fine.'

'That and a visit from the doctor, Fräulein Ariana. We don't want him reporting to the army with pneumonia. That would be a fine thing for the Reich.'

'Hardly pneumonia, Fräulein Hedwig.' Ariana looked at her kindly but with hauteur. 'And if his bad humour is any sign that he's improving, then he ought to be in fine shape for the Reich.' She made to re-enter their apartment with her brother's tray. She would come back in a moment for her own tray, but Fräulein Hedwig had already picked it up. 'That's all right, fräulein, I'll get it in a minute.'

'Don't be so independent, Ariana. If you've been taking care of that boy since yesterday, trust me, you need help.' She clucked and muttered, and in their little sitting room set down Ariana's tray.

'Thank you, fräulein.' She stood expectantly, clearly waiting for the old nurse to leave.

'*Bitte*.' And then she reached out for the tray Ariana was

still holding. 'I'll take him his.'

'He won't like that. Really, you'd better not.' Her grip was firm. 'You know how he hates being treated like a baby.'

'Not a baby, Fräulein Ariana, a soldier. It's the least I can do.' Sternly, she was reaching for the tray.

'No, thank you, Fräulein Hedwig. I have my orders. He made me promise that I wouldn't let anyone else in.'

'I am hardly "anyone", fräulein.' She drew herself up to her full height. On any other occasion Ariana would have been intimidated. In this case she had no intention of being out-maneouvered by their old nurse.

'Of course you're not "anyone," but you know how he is.'

'Even more difficult than he used to be apparently. I think the army will do him good.'

'I'll be sure to tell him you said so.' She smiled gaily, whisked the tray into Gerhard's room, and closed the door. She set the tray down instantly, leaning her full weight against the door lest Fräulein Hedwig persist, but a moment later Ariana heard the door to the sitting room close firmly and she let out a long sigh of relief. She hoped her father returned on schedule that night. It would be impossible to keep Hedwig at bay for much longer.

She sat nervously in the sitting room that morning and eventually put out both trays, with evidence that there had been damage done to both. She thanked Anna for a stack of fresh towels, and thanked God that Hedwig did not come up again until that afternoon.

'How is he?'

'A lot better. I think he'll be all ready for the army by tomorrow. He may even blow up his room before he goes. He saw saying something about dragging out his chemistry equipment for one last try.'

'That's all we need.' She glared at Ariana disapprovingly. She did not like the high-handed way the girl had been behaving at all. At nineteen, she may have been a grown woman, but not as far as Fräulein Hedwig was concerned. 'Tell him he owes me an explanation for hiding like this, like a spoiled schoolboy, in his room.'

'I'll tell him, Fräulein Hedwig.'

'See that you do.' She stalked off again, this time ascending to her own room on the fourth floor. And twenty minutes later Ariana heard another determined knock on the sitting room door. Expecting to see Hedwig, she opened the door with a strained smile. But this time it was Berthold, still panting from his long climb up two flights of stairs.

'It's a phone call from your father's office. Apparently it's urgent. Will you come down?' For an instant Ariana hesitated – should she leave her guard post? But after all, Hedwig had already been staved off. For a few minutes it would be safe. She hurried after Berthold and took the call in the alcove in the main hall.

'Yes?'

'Fräulein von Gotthard?' It was Frau Gebsen, her father's secretary at the bank.

'Yes. Is something wrong?' Perhaps she had some word of her father? Had there been some change of plans?

'I don't know . . . I'm sorry . . . I don't mean to worry you, but your father . . . I assumed . . . He mentioned something when he left yesterday morning. I rather thought that he was with the Minister of Finance, but I realise now that he was not.'

'Are you quite sure? Perhaps he had some other meeting. Does it matter?'

'I'm not quite sure. We had an urgent call from Munich, and I had to reach him, but he wasn't there. The minister is in Paris, and he has been all week.'

'Then maybe you misunderstood him. Where is he now?' Her heart was pounding.

'That's why I called. He didn't come in this morning, and if he wasn't with the Minister of Finance, then where is he? Do you know?'

'Of course not. He's probably at some other meeting. I'm sure he'll call you later.'

'But he hasn't called all day, fräulein. And –' she sounded vaguely embarrassed, after all Ariana was still young – 'Berthold said he didn't come home last night.'

'Frau Gebsen, may I take leave to remind you that my father's nocturnal whereabouts are none of your concern, or Berthold's, or my own.' Proper outrage shook her voice, or so it seemed; in point of fact it was raw fear.

'Of course, fräulein. I must apologise, but the call from Munich . . . and I was concerned, I thought perhaps he'd met with an accident. It's unusual for your father not to call.'

'Unless he's in a secret meeting, Frau Gebsen. The Minister of Finance can't be the only man of importance with whom my father disappears. I really don't understand why this is so important. Simply tell them in Munich that momentarily he can't be reached, and as soon as he gets home, I'll have him call you. I'm sure it won't be long.'

'I do hope you're right.'

'I'm quite certain of it.'

'Very well, then please ask him to call.'

'I shall.'

Ariana hung up gingerly, hoping that her terror didn't show as she marched with proper outrage back up the stairs. But she paused on the first landing to catch her breath before continuing upstairs. And when she reached the second landing, she saw the door to the sitting room ajar. Hurriedly, she pushed it open, only to find Berthold and Hedwig in grim conference in front of her brother's open door.

'What are you doing here?' She almost shouted it.

'Where is he?' Hedwig's voice was an accusation, her eyes cold as ice.

'How do I know? He's probably hiding somewhere downstairs. But as I recall, I distinctly asked you –'

'And where is your father?' Now it was Berthold's turn.

'I beg your pardon. My father's whereabouts are none of my business, Berthold, nor yours.' But as she faced them, her face went deathly pale. She prayed that her voice wouldn't tremble and give her away to Hedwig, who knew her so well. 'And as for Gerhard, he's probably gone off somewhere. He was here the last time I looked.'

'And when was that?' Hedwig's eyes filled with suspicion. 'That boy has never made his bed in his life.'

'I made it for him. And now, if you would both be good enough to excuse me, I would like to take a nap.'

'Certainly, fräulein.' Berthold bowed with precision and he signalled Hedwig to follow him from the room. When they had left her, Ariana sat pale and trembling in Gerhard's favourite chair. Oh, God, what would happen now? With her hands pressed to her mouth and her eyes closed, a thousand terrifying images ran helter-skelter through her head. But none of them as terrifying as what happened half an hour later when there came a firm knock on her door.

'Not now, I'm resting.'

'Are you really, fräulein? Then you must excuse this intrusion into your private rooms.' The man who spoke to her was not a servant, but a full lieutenant of the Reich.

'I beg your pardon.' She stood up in astonishment as he strolled in. Had they come for Gerhard? What was he doing here? And not just the lieutenant – she saw as he wandered confidently into the room that there were three more soldiers walking up and down her third-floor hall.

'I'm afraid I must beg your pardon, fräulein.'

'Not at all, Lieutenant.' She stood up with a decided presence, smoothing her soft blonde hair into the tidy figure-eight chignon she wore. She dropped a dark blue cashmere sweater around her shoulders and attempted to walk unhurriedly towards the door. 'Would you care to talk downstairs?'

'Certainly.' He nodded pleasantly. 'You can pick your coat up on the way.'

'My coat?' Her heart was pounding.

'Yes. The captain thought we might get down to business more quickly if you came to see him at his office, rather than playing tea party with you here.' His eyes glittered unpleasantly and she found herself hating his steely grey eyes. This man was to his very core a Nazi, from the lapels of his uniform to the depths of his soul

'Is something wrong, Lieutenant?'

'Perhaps. We will let you explain that to us.' Had they caught Gerhard and her father, then? But no, it couldn't be. She wouldn't allow herself to believe that as she followed him, seemingly calm, to the second floor, and then she understood. They had come to question her, but they knew nothing. Not yet. And she mustn't tell them. No matter what.

Chapter 14

'And you thought your father was in a secret meeting, Fräulein von Gotthard? Really? How interesting. With whom?' Captain Dietrich von Rheinhardt looked her over with interest. She was a very pretty piece. Hildebrand had told him as much before he escorted her into the room. And a cool one, for a girl so young. She looked totally unruffled, a lady from the top of her shining blonde head to the tips of her black-alligator-clad feet. 'With whom did you say you thought your father was meeting?' This had gone on for almost two hours, ever since they escorted her from the big black Mercedes on to the Königsplatz, over which rose the forbidding six-columned splendour of the Reichstag, and then hastily into the building and this impressive-looking room. It was the office of the commanding officer, and it had chilled many before her, to the very bone. But she showed no terror, no anger, no exasperation. She merely answered their questions, politely, calmly, and with that unshakably ladylike manner, again, and again, and again.

'I have no idea whom my father was meeting with, Captain. He doesn't share his professional secrets with me.'

'And do you think he has secrets?'

'Only in terms of the work he does for the Reich.'

'How charmingly said.' And then as he sat back and lit a

cigarette, 'Would you care for some tea?' For a moment she wanted to snap at him that they had said they didn't want to play tea party, which was why they had brought her here, but she simply shook her head politely.

'No, thank you, Captain.'

'Some sherry perhaps?'

The amenities were wasted on Ariana. She could not be put at ease here, with a life-size portrait of Hitler staring her in the face.

'No, thank you, Captain.'

'And these secret meetings of your fathers? . . . Tell me about those.'

'I didn't say he had secret meetings. I just know that on some evenings he comes home rather late.' She was growing tired, and in spite of herself, the strain was slowly beginning to show.

'A lady perhaps, fräulein?'

'I'm sorry, Captain, I don't know.'

'Of course not. How rude of me to suggest it.' Something ugly and angry and wicked jumped at her from his eyes. 'And your brother, fräulein? He goes to secret meetings, too?'

'Of course not, he's just barely sixteen.'

'But he doesn't attend youth meetings either, does he? Does he, fräulein? Is it possible, then, that your family is not as sympathetic to the Reich as we had previously thought?'

'That's not true, Captain. My brother had a great deal of trouble with his studies, as well as asthma, and of course . . . since the death of my mother . . .' She trailed off, hoping to discourage further questions, but that was beyond hope.

'And when was it that your mother died?'

'Ten years ago, Captain.' *Thanks to people like you.*

'I see. How touching that the boy even remembers his mother. He must be a very sensitive young man.' She nodded, not sure what to answer, and let her eyes stray from his face. 'Too sensitive for the army, fräulein? Could it be that he and your father have deserted their homeland in its final hour of need?'

'Hardly. If they had done that, why would they leave me here?'

'You tell me, fräulein. And while you're about it, perhaps you could tell me something about a friend named Max. Maximilian Thomas? A young man who used to visit your father on occasion, or was it that he visited you?'

'He was an old friend of my father's.'

'Who only five months ago fled Berlin. Interestingly, he disappeared on precisely the same night that one of your father's cars was stolen, and then found again, of course, safe and sound, outside the train station in Berlin. A happy coincidence, of course.' Oh, God, did they know about Max, then? And had they tied her father to that after all?

'I don't think the car being stolen had anything to do with Max.'

He took a long drag on his cigarette. 'Now let's talk about your brother again for a moment, fräulein. Where do you suppose he could be?' He spoke to her in a singsong voice of someone speaking to the mentally retarded or a very young child. 'I understand that you've been nursing him through a very bad cold for the past two days.' She nodded. 'And then, miraculously, when you went downstairs to answer a phone call, the boy disappeared. Annoying of him, of course. What I'm rather wondering, though, is if he didn't disappear several days earlier. Like yesterday morning perhaps, around the time your father was last seen at his office? What kind of coincidence do you suppose that might be?'

'A very unlikely one, I'd say. He was in the house all day yesterday, last night, and this morning, in his room.'

'And how lucky he is to have a devoted sister like you. I understand that you guarded him with the zeal of a young lioness guarding her cubs.' And he said the words, a chill ran down her spine. There was only one way he could have known that. From Hedwig or Berthold. A wave of nausea seized her as she understood the truth. For the first time Ariana felt the full force of the facts. And then suddenly she felt raw fury run through her for their betrayal. But she couldn't let him see it. She had to play the game, at any price.

The captain pressed relentlessly on. You know, fräulein, what I find intriguing is that they seem to have run off and left you here, your father and your brother together, perhaps to save the boy from joining the army, or perhaps for even more malicious purposes than that. But whatever the reason, they seem to have abandoned you, my dear. And yet you protect them. Is it that you know your father is coming back? I assume that's what it must be. Otherwise I'm afraid I don't understand your unwillingness to talk.'

For the first time she snapped at him in irritation; the strain of the interrogation was finally fraying her nerves. 'We have been talking to each other here for almost two hours, but I simply don't have the answers to the questions you ask. Your accusations are inaccurate, and your presumption that my brother and father have run off and left me is ridiculous. Why would they do that?'

'In truth, my dear lady, I don't think they would. And that is precisely why we're going to wait and see. And when your father returns, he and I will talk over some business.'

'What kind of business?' Ariana eyed Von Rheinhardt with suspicion across his desk.

'A little trade, shall we say? His charming daughter for . . . well, let's not discuss the details. I'll be happy to arrange it with your father when he gets back. And now, fräulein, if you'll excuse me, I will have Lieutenant Hildebrand escort you to your room.'

'My room? I'm not going home, then?' She had to fight to keep the tears from springing to her eyes. But the captain was shaking his head firmly while still wearing his unbearable false smile.

'No, fräulein, I'm afraid we'd prefer to show you our hospitality here, at least until your father returns. We'll make you quite comfortable in your . . . er . . . room here with us.'

'I see.'

'Yes.' He looked at her sombrely for a moment. 'I suppose that by now you do. I must offer your father my compliments when I see him, if I see him, that is. He has a most impressive daughter, charming, intelligent, and extraordinarily well bred. You haven't cried, begged, or pleaded. In fact, I've thoroughly enjoyed our little afternoon.' Their 'little afternoon' had consisted of hours of gruelling interrogation, and she wanted to slap his face when she heard the words.

He rang a buzzer at the side of his desk then and expected Lieutenant Hildebrand to appear. They waited for a long moment and the captain buzzed again. 'The good lieutenant appears to be busy; apparently I'll have to find someone else to escort you to your room.' He spoke of it as of a suite at the Danieli in Venice, but Ariana knew full well that what awaited her was not a hotel room, but a cell. With his boots gleaming in the lamplight, the captain, obviously irritated, strode to the door. He pulled it open by its large brass doorknob and glared angrily outside. It was almost seven o'clock in the evening and Lieutenant Hildebrand had apparently gone in pursuit of his dinner. The only officer visible outside the office was a tall man with a stern face and a long narrow scar that ran down one cheek. 'Von Tripp, where the hell are all the others?'

'I believe they've all gone to eat. It's – ' he glanced at the clock and then at his captain – 'it was getting late.'

'Pigs. All they think of is filling their stomachs. All right, never mind. You'll do just as well. And why aren't you with them, by the way?' He glared in annoyance at the chief lieutenant, who returned his superior's look of annoyance with a small, frigid smile

'I'm on duty this evening, sir.'

He waved back in the direction of his office at the woman who was partially concealed by the door. 'Take her downstairs, then. I'm through with her.'

'Yes, sir.' He stood up, saluted smartly, clicked his heels, and walked rapidly into the room.

'Stand up.' He issued a brisk order and Ariana jumped in her chair.

'I beg your pardon?'

Captain von Rheinhardt's eyes glinted malevolently as he returned to the room. 'The lieutenant has ordered you to stand up, fräulein. Be so kind as to do what he says. Otherwise, I'm afraid . . . well, you know, it would be awkward . . .' He touched the riding crop at his waist.

Ariana instantly rose to her feet, trying to stem the thoughts running through her mind. What were they going to do to her? The tall blond officer who had ordered her to stand up so brusquely looked terrifying, and she was not encouraged by the small, nasty scar on his cheek. He looked cold-blooded and machinelike and he stood by like an automaton as she walked out of the room.

'Have a good evening, fräulein,' Von Rheinhardt smirked at her back.

Ariana did not answer the captain, and in the outer office the lieutenant grabbed her firmly by the arm. 'You will follow me and do exactly as I tell you. I do not enjoy quarrelling with prisoners, and most particularly women. Be good enough to make this easy for yourself, as well as for me.' It was a stern warning, and despite his long strides, she walked along quickly beside him. He had made himself clear. She was a prisoner now. Nothing more than that. And suddenly she couldn't help wondering if even her father would be able to get her out of this.

The tall blond lieutenant led her down two long corridors and then down a long flight of stairs into the bowels of the building, where it was suddenly both damp and cold. They waited for a heavy iron door to be opened after a guard had peeked through a window and nodded his head at the man at her side. The door closed horrifyingly behind them, was bolted, then locked, and she found herself travelling down another flight of stairs. It was like being led to a dungeon, and when she saw the cell where her journey ended, she realised that it was just that.

The lieutenant said absolutely nothing as a woman

sergeant was called and Ariana was frisked and searched. She was then shoved into the cell and the lieutenant stood by as the woman locked the doors. In cells around them women were calling and crying, and once she thought she heard the wails of a child. But she couldn't see any faces, the doors were solid slabs of metal with barred windows only a few inches square. It was the most terrifying place Ariana could imagine, and once inside the dark cell, she had to fight every moment so as not to scream and totally lose control. In the tiny shaft of light that came through the minute window, she could see what she thought was a toilet, and discovered moments later was only a large white metal bowl. She truly was a prisoner – somehow that made it real.

In the stench of the cell she began to cry softly, until at last she sank into a corner, dropped her head on her arms, and was wracked by sobs.

Chapter 15

When Walmar von Gotthard left the station in Basel that morning, he looked around him carefully before beginning his long walk back to Lörrach, to catch the train back to Berlin. Every muscle in his body ached, and he looked finally as dirty and ragged as he had pretended to be the morning before. He looked very little like the banker who ran the Tilden, sat in meetings with Minister of Finance, and was in effect the most eminent banker in Berlin. He looked like a tired old man who had had a long journey, and no one would have suspected him of having the vast amount of cash that he secretly carried.

He reached the border by noon without problem, and now the long haul was about to begin: the nine-mile walk back to Lörrach, which he had finished with such victory at the Swiss border only six hours before. Then came the most difficult part of the journey, the road back to Berlin. And then he had to undertake once again the same terrors with Ariana. And once both his children were safely on the Swiss side of the border, he didn't care if he dropped dead in his tracks. In fact, as he crawled through the wires he had cut that morning, he thought that he would be very lucky if he didn't drop dead long before. For a man of his years it had been quite an adventure, but if he could save both Ariana and Gerhard, nothing mattered. He would have done anything in his power, and beyond that, for them.

Once again he stopped, looked around, and listened. Once again he hurried towards the cover of the trees. But this time he was not as lucky as he had been that morning, and he heard footsteps in the brush only a few feet away. He tried to run deeper into the bushes, but the two soldiers were instantly on his heels.

'Hi there, grandpa, where you going? To join the army in Berlin?'

He tried to grin stupidly at them, but one of the two men on the border patrol nonetheless cocked his gun and took aim at his heart. 'Where you going?'

He decided to tell them, in a thick country accent. 'To Lörrach.'

'How come?'

'My sister lives there.' He felt his heart dancing in his chest.

'Does she? How nice.' He waved his gun again in the direction of Walmar's breastbone and signalled to the other to commence a search. They tore open his jacket, patted his pockets, and then felt his shirt.

'I have my papers in order.

'Oh, yeah? Let's see.'

He began to reach for them, but before his fingers got there the soldier who had been searching felt something long and smooth concealed under Walmar's right arm.

'What's this, grandpa? Hiding something from us?' He laughed coarsely and winked at his friend. The old ones were funny. They all thought they were so smart. The soldiers tore open the shirt that was now wilted and dirty, never noticing the fine fabric they tore. They had no reason to suspect him. He was just an old country man. But what they found in the secret wallet impressed them, for there was a fortune in large bills and small ones, and their eyes grew round with amazement as they counted what they had found. 'You were taking this to the Führer?' They laughed at their own joke and grinned happily at the old man.

He kept his eyes cast down lest they see the anger there and hoped they'd be content just to take his money. But the two soldiers were wise in the ways of war by now. Exchanging a quick glance, they then did what had to be done. The first man stood back while the second one fired. Walmar von Gotthard fell lifelessly into the tall grass around him.

They dragged him firmly by the heels into the deeper brush, stripped him of his papers, pocketed the money, and went back to their hut, where they sat down to count the money in earnest and threw into their open fire the papers of the old man. They never bothered to read them. It didn't matter who he had been. Except to Gerhard, waiting in a hotel room in Zurich. And to Ariana, sitting terrified in her cell in Berlin.

Chapter 16

Lieutenant von Tripp signalled to the soldier with the large key ring to open Ariana's cell. The door creaked slowly open, and both men attempted not to react to the stench that always emanated from inside. All the cells were like that because of the dampness, and of course because no one ever cleaned them out.

Freed from her darkness, Ariana was instantly blinded, unable to see in the bright light. She didn't know for how long she'd been there. She only knew that she had been crying for most of the time. But when she heard them coming, she had quickly dried her eyes and attempted to wash the mascara she knew had run down her face with a corner of her lace slip. She smoothed her hair down quickly, and she waited as she heard them unlock her door. Perhaps there was news of her father and Gerhard? She waited and she prayed, longing to hear familiar voices, but there was only the metallic sound of their keys. At last she could see dimly, and she saw the outline of the tall blond lieutenant who had led her there only the day before.

'Walk out of your cell, please, and come with me.' She stood up shakily, steadying herself against the wall of her cell, and for an instant he wanted to reach out and help her as she stumbled. She looked so incredibly small and so frail. But the eyes that looked into his a moment later were not those of a fragile beauty begging for help; they were the eyes of a determined young woman desperate for survival and trying to maintain an air of dignity against impossible odds. Her hair had come loose from the sleek figure-eight she had worn the previous evening. It hung down her back now, like a loose shaft of wheat. Her skirt was wrinkled, but expensive, and despite the appalling stench in which she had lain for almost twenty-four hours, a faint hint of her perfume still lingered about her hair.

'This way, please, fräulein.' He stepped carefully to one side and walked just behind her, so he could be sure that she didn't escape him, and as he watched her, he felt even sorrier for her than before. She straightened the narrow shoulders and held her head high as they walked, her heels clicked determinedly down the corridors, and again as they walked up the stairs. Only once did she falter, for an instant, bowing her head as though she were too dizzy to go on. He said nothing as he waited, and in a moment she continued up the stairs, grateful that he hadn't pushed her or shouted at her for not moving on.

But Manfred von Tripp was not like the others. Only Ariana did not know that. He was a gentleman, as she was a lady, and not for an instant would he have pushed her, or shouted, or prodded, or whipped. And there were those who didn't like him for that. Von Rheinhardt himself didn't particularly like Von Tripp. But it didn't matter too much because Von Rheinhardt was the captain and he could make Von Tripp dance if he so chose.

As they reached the top of the last flight of stairs, Lieutenant von Tripp once again took a firm grip on her arm and led her back down the familiar hallway, where once again, the captain was waiting, grinning and leisurely smoking a cigarette, as he had been the day before. The lieutenant rapidly saluted, clicked his heels, and disappeared.

'Good afternoon, fräulein. Did you spend a pleasant evening? I hope you were not too . . . er . . . uncomfortable in your . . . ah . . . room.' Ariana didn't amswer. 'Sit down. Sit down. Please.' She took a seat without speaking and stared at him from her seat. 'I do regret to tell you we have not heard from your father. And I rather fear that some of my conjectures may have been all too true. Your brother has also not surfaced, which makes him, as of today, a deserter. All of which leaves you, dear fräulein, for the moment, rather high and dry. And somewhat at our mercy, I might add. Perhaps today you'd like to share with us a little more of what you know?'

'I know nothing more than what I told you yesterday, Captain.'

'How unfortunate for you. In that case, fräulein, I will not waste your time or mine interrogating you further. I will simply leave you to your own devices, sitting in your cell, while we wait for news.' *Oh, God, for how long?* She wanted to scream as he said it, but nothing showed on her face.

He stood up and pressed the buzzer, and a moment later Von Tripp appeared again. 'Where the hell is Hildebrand? Every time I call for him, he's off somewhere.'

'I'm sorry, sir. I believe he's out to lunch.' In fact, Manfred had absolutely no idea where he was, nor did he care. Hildebrand was always wandering, leaving everyone else stuck with his damn errand-boy job.

'Escort the prisoner back to her cell, then. And tell

Hildebrand I want to see him when he comes back.'

'Very well, sir.' The lieutenant shepherded Ariana from the room. She was familiar with the routine now, the long halls, the endless walk. At least she was not confined in her cell and for these moments she could breathe and move and touch and see. She wouldn't have cared if they had walked her down those halls for hours. Anything except the horrors of the tiny, filthy cell.

It was on the second stairway that they ran into Hildebrand, smiling happily and singing a snatch of a tune. He looked up at Von Tripp, startled, and then with interest his eyes combed Ariana, as they had done the morning before when he had walked into her room in her father's house.

'Good afternoon, fräulein. Enjoying your stay?' She didn't answer, but the look she gave him would have burned holes in rocks. He glanced back at her with irritation and then smiled at Manfred. 'Taking her back?' Manfred nodded with disinterest. He had better things to do than talk to Hildebrand. He couldn't bear the man, or most of the officers he worked with, but ever since he'd been wounded at the front, he'd had to put up with jobs like this.

'The captain wants to see you. I told him you were out to lunch.'

'I was, dear Manfred. In fact, I was.' He grinned again then, saluted briefly, and moved on up the stairs as they continued down. He cast a last glance over his shoulder at Ariana as Manfred moved her through the last door, back down the halls, and into the bowels of the building and at last to the door of her cell. Somewhere nearby there was a woman screaming. Ariana shut her ears to the sound and found herself relieved at last to collapse on the floor of her cell.

After three days she walked the corridor again to see the captain; again he told her that her father and brother had not returned. But now she could not understand it, and she knew that either they were lying – that they had found her father and Gerhard – or something had gone desperately wrong. If they were in fact telling her the truth, then there seemed to be no news of either her father or her brother, and after a few brief moments in his office, Von Rheinhardt sent her away.

This time it was Hildebrand who led her down the corridors, his fingers pressing her flesh to the very bone, yet at the same time, his hand was placed high enough on her arm so that with the back of his hand he could touch her breast. He spoke to her in odd familiar bits and pieces, as though she were some animal to be urged on, with kicks and shoves if necessary, and as he never failed to mention, there was always his whip.

This time when they reached the door to her private dungeon he did not wait for the woman to conduct the search. He slipped his hands slowly over her body, down her stomach, up her buttocks, and across her breasts. With every inch of her body, Ariana shrank from him, looking with hatred into his face as he laughed and the woman firmly shut the door between them. 'Good night, fräulein.' And with that she heard him walk away then, but the footsteps stopped only a few feet away. She heard him bark curtly at the matron.

'This one. I haven't tried this one before.' Listening intently with her eyes closed, Ariana heard the keys rattle, the door open, and then his footsteps disappeared. Moments later she could hear screams and pleading, the sound of his crop whizzing through the air and into flesh, and then silence, no more screaming, only a long series of horrific grunts. But she could no longer hear the woman, and in her worst fantasies, she couldn't quite imagine what he'd done. Had he beaten the woman into unconsciousness? Had he whipped her till she died? But at last she heard quiet sobbing, and she knew the woman was alive.

Standing pressed against the wall in her tiny cell, she waited, listening for the footsteps, fearing that they would approach her door again, but instead they turned down the long corridor and rhythmically disappeared. Sighing softly with relief, she sank back to her seat on the floor.

It went on for days and weeks, and regular visits to the captain, who informed her that they had heard nothing of her father and he had not returned. By the end of the third week, she was exhausted, filthy, starving, and she couldn't understand what had happened, why they hadn't come back for her. Or was Von Rheinhardt lying? Perhaps Gerhard and her father had been captured and were prisoners, too. The only answer she couldn't let herself accept was the worst one. They had been killed.

It was after her last visit to the captain, after three weeks of those visits, that Hildebrand escorted her back to her cell. Up until then it had often been the other lieutenant, and now and then it had been someone else.

But today it was he who held her arm as they made their way into the depths of the prison. She was exhausted and three or four times she stumbled. Her hair hung in a tangled mass down her back and around her face. She swept it back often with long, delicate fingers, but the nails were broken now, and there was no longer any trace of perfume in her hair. The cashmere sweater she had first worn so jauntily around her shoulders, she clutched tightly around her for warmth, and her skirt and blouse were torn and dirty – her stockings she had thrown away after the first few days. He took it all in with a look of interest, like a man investing in a herd of cattle or buying sheep, and on the last stairway in the prison they ran into Lieutenant Manfred von Tripp. He greeted Hildebrand curtly, and his eyes avoided Ariana's gaze. He always looked just above her, as though he had no particular interest in her face.

'Good afternoon, Manfred.' Hildebrand was oddly casual as they passed, but Von Tripp saluted and murmured only, 'Afternoon.' And then as though to watch them, he turned briefly and stared. Ariana was too tired to notice, but Hildebrand cast him a knowing look and grinned. Von Tripp turned away then and went upstairs, back to his desk. But as he sat there, his anger burned. Hildebrand was taking much too long to come back to work. He had taken her down there almost twenty minutes earlier; there was no reason for it to take so long. Unless . . . slowly the realisation dawned on him. The fool. He would even pull a stunt like that with her. Did he have any idea who the girl's father was, or from what world she came? Didn't he realise that she was a German, a girl of class and breeding, no matter where her father was or what he'd done? Maybe he could get away with his appalling behaviour with some of the prisoners, but surely not with a girl like this. And whoever the victims were, Hildebrand's outrageous antics made Manfred sick. Without thinking further, he found himself hurrying down the hallways and then clattering down the stairs. Manfred knew it didn't matter in his heart who the hell her father was, not to them. To them she was only a girl. He found himself praying that he was not too late.

He grabbed the key ring from the matron, gesturing to her to stay seated, and barked curtly, 'Never mind. Stay there.' And then with a quick look over his shoulder he asked a question. 'Is Hildebrand down there?' The woman in uniform nodded, and Manfred hurried down the last flight of stairs with the keys, the heels of his boots clicking smartly.

The sounds within told him that Hildebrand was in her cell. Without uttering a single syllable, Manfred turned the key and pulled open the door, and what he saw there was Ariana, almost naked, her clothes in shreds around her, and blood streaming from a cut on the side of her face. Hildebrand stood there also, his face gleaming, his eyes wild with lust, the whip in one hand, the other tearing at Ariana's tangled hair. But from the skirt still barely draped around her middle and from the fight he still saw in her eyes, he knew that the worst had not yet happened. He was grateful that he hadn't been too late.

'Get out.'

'What the hell business is it of yours, damn you? She ours.'

'She's not "ours", she belongs to the Reich, just as you do, just as I do, just as everyone does.'

'The hell she does. You and I aren't sitting in this prison.'

'So you rape her, is that it?' The two men stared at each other in blind fury, and for an instant Ariana, panting and breathless in the corner, wondered if her assailant would also whip the lieutenant who outranked him. But he was not quite that made. Von Tripp spoke first and stood back from the door. 'I told you to get out. I'll see you upstairs.' Hildebrand snarled as he swept past him, and for an instant in the dark cell neither Manfred nor Ariana spoke. And then, bravely sweeping tears from her cheeks and pushing her hair back from her eyes, she attempted to cover herself decently, as Manfred gazed quietly at the floor. When he sensed that she was calmer, he looked up at her again, and this time he did not avoid her face, or the painfully blue eyes. 'Fräulein von Gotthard . . . I'm sorry . . . I should have known. I'll see to it that this doesn't happen again. It shouldn't.' And then, 'We're not all like that. I can't tell you how sorry I am.' And he was. He had had a younger sister who was close to Ariana's age, although he himself was thirty-nine. 'Are you all right?' They stood there talking in the dark, with only a small wedge of light peeking through the door.

Her blonde hair flying, she nodded, and he handed her his handkerchief to dab at the blood still dripping down her face. 'I think I'm all right. Thank you.' She was far more grateful than he knew. She had thought that Hildebrand was going to kill her, and when she understood instead that he was going to rape her, she'd hoped that he would kill her first.

Manfred looked at her again for a long moment, and then sighed deeply. As much as he had once believed in it, he had come to hate this war at last. It had become a corruption of everything he had once trusted and defended. It was like watching a woman you once respected become a whore. 'Is there anything else I can do?'

She smiled at him then, holding her sweater wrapped around her torso, with those big, sad, waiflike eyes. 'You've already done everything you can. The only other thing you can do for me is find my father.' And then, suddenly, daring to ask him the truth, her eyes met his. 'Is he here somewhere? In the Reichstag?'

Slowly Manfred shook his head. 'We've had no news.' And then, 'Perhaps he'll still come. Don't give up hope, fräulein. Never do that.'

'I won't. After today.' She smiled at him again, and looking at her gravely, he nodded, stepped outside, and once more locked the door. Slowly Ariana sank to the floor again, thinking of what had happened, and of the officer who had providentially arrived just in time. As she sat in the darkness of her cell, her hatred for Hildebrand dimmed with her gratitude for what Von Tripp had done. They were an odd lot, all of them. She would never understand their kind.

She did not see either man again until the end of the next week. By then she had been locked in the cell in their dungeon for exactly one month. And what she feared most was that her father and Gerhard had been killed, Still, she couldn't accept it. She only allowed herself to think of the present moment. Of the enemy. And of getting back at them.

An officer she had never seen before came to get her and dragged her roughly from her cell. He pushed her up the stairs when she stumbled and cursed her when she tripped and fell. She was barely able to walk now, from fatigue and hunger and the lack of exercise that left her legs eternally stiff and numb. When she reached Dietrich von Rheinhardt's office, she was a different young woman than the one who had sat there so self-possessed and poised only a month before. Von Rheinhardt stared at her with something akin to revulsion, but beneath the filth and tangles he knew precisely what was there. She was a beautiful young woman, well-bred, intelligent, she would have been an enchanting present to give to any man of the Reich. Not for him though, he had other pleasures, other needs. But she would make a handsome gift to someone. He was not sure yet whom.

He no longer wasted time on the 'fräuleins' or on the fancy speeches. She was of no further use to them. 'And so, I'm afraid you've become useless. A prisoner held for ransom when there is no one to pay that ransom is not a valuable possession, but a burden instead. There is no reason why we should feed and house you any longer. Our hospitality, in fact, is at an end.' Then, they were going to shoot her. That was it, she decided. But she no longer cared. It was a better fate than the other possibilities. She didn't want to become a prostitute for the officers and she was no longer strong enough to scrub floors. She had lost her family, her reason for living. If they shot her, it would be over forever. Listening to him, she was almost relieved.

But Von Rheinhardt had more to say. 'You will be driven home for one hour. You may collect your belongings and then you may leave. You may take nothing of great value from the house, no money, no jewels, only whatever personal possessions you may need in the immediate future. After that, you can take care of yourself.'

Then, they weren't going to shoot her? But why not? She stared at him in disbelief. 'You will live in the women's barracks, and you will work like everyone else.

'I'll have someone drive you to Grunewald in an hour. In the meantime, you may wait in the hall.' How could she wait outside, in view of everyone, in her disgraceful condition? Half-naked, in the clothes that Hildebrand had torn off her body a week before. They were truly animals.

'What will happen to my father's house now?' Her voice was a croak in her throat, so seldom had she spoken in the past month.

Von Rheinhardt busied himself with the papers on his desk and at last looked up. 'It will be occupied by General Ritter. And his staff.' His 'staff' consisted of four willing women he had collected carefully over the past five years. 'I'm sure he'll be very happy there.'

'I'm sure.' So had they been. Her father and her brother, and once upon a time her mother, and she. They had all been happy there. Before these bastards had arrived to smash their lives, and now they were stealing the house in Grunewald. For an instant there were tears swimming in her eyes. Maybe – she thought hopefully of the air raids she'd grown so used to – maybe the bombs would come and kill them all.

'That's all, fräulein. Report to your barracks by five o'clock this afternoon. And I might add that the barracks arrangement is optional. You are free to make other . . . eh . . . living arrangements within the confines of the army . . . of course.' She knew what that meant. She could offer to be the general's mistress and he would let her stay in her own home. She felt a stab of indignation as she sat numbly on a long wooden bench in the hall. Her only consolation was that when she returned to Grunewald, her clothes in tatters, her face scratched and bruised, filthy, hungry, beaten, then Hedwig and Berthold could see what they had done. This was the precious Party that the old fools loved. This was what you got with '*Heil Hitler.*' Ariana was busy with her thoughts and her fury and she didn't see Von Tripp approach.

'Fräulein von Gotthard?' She looked up in surprise to see him. They hadn't met since the day he had saved her from Hildebrand and his whip. 'I understand that I'm to take you home.' He didn't smile at her, but he no longer averted his eyes from hers.

'Do you mean that you're to take me to my barracks?' She looked at him icily. And then, regretting her anger, she sighed. It wasn't his fault. 'I'm sorry.'

He nodded slowly. 'The captain said I was to take you to Grunewald to get your things.' She nodded silent assent, her eyes huge in her hungry face. And then, as though he couldn't help it, he seemed to unbend a little, and his voice was kind. 'Have you had lunch yet?' Lunch? She hadn't even eaten breakfast or dinner the night before. Meals in her stinking dungeon had arrived once a day and were never worthy of a name, breakfast, lunch, dinner. It was pigslop no matter what time they served it. Only the prospect of total starvation had in the end forced her to eat. She didn't answer him, but he knew what she was thinking. 'I understand.' And then he gestured her to leave her bench. 'We should go now.' He said it somewhat sternly, and Ariana followed him slowly from the brightly lit hall. Her knees felt weak for a minute, and the sunlight briefly blinded her eyes, but she stood there, breathing deeply, and when she slid into the car beside him, she turned her head away as though to look out at the rows of houses being used as barracks so he wouldn't see her cry.

They drove on for a few minutes, and then he pulled the car over and sat staring for a moment at the back of her head. Ariana only sat there, staring, totally unaware of the tall blond man with the gentle eyes and the aristocratic duelling scar. 'I'll be back in a moment, fräulein.' Ariana didn't answer, she only lay her head back against the seat and pulled the blanket he had given her more tightly around her. She was thinking again of her father and Gerhard, wondering where they were. She hadn't been this comfortable in over a month, and she didn't care what happened now, she was out of that stinking cell at last.

Von Tripp was back in the car again a moment later with a small steaming bundle he extended towards her without words. Two fat bratwurst wrapped in paper, with mustard, and a large hunk of brown bread. She stared at it as he handed it to her, and then at him. What an odd man he was. Like Ariana, he seldom wasted words, yet he saw everything; and again like her, there was a kind of sorrow in his eyes, as though he felt the world's pain in his own flesh, and now her pain as well.

'I thought you might be hungry.'

She wanted to tell him that it was nice of him. Instead she just nodded and took the bundle in her hands. No matter what he did, she couldn't forget who he was or what he was doing. He was a Nazi officer, and he was taking her home to pick up her things . . . her things . . . which things? Which of them was she to take with her now? And after the war, what then? Would she get the house back? Not that it mattered anymore. With her father and Gerhard gone, she didn't care. The thoughts and questions ran maddeningly through her head as they drove along and she took small bites from the bratwurst Von Tripp had bought for her. She wanted to devour them but she didn't dare. After living for so long on bread and meat scraps, she was afraid that she would be sick if she ate the pungent sausage too quickly.

'Is it near the lake in Grunewald?' She nodded. In truth she was surprised that they were letting her come home for anything at all. It was odd how suddenly she was no longer a prisoner.

And horrifying to realise that the house was theirs now. The art, the silver, whatever jewels they found, even her furs would be given to mistresses of the generals, and of course there were all her father's cars. His money and investments had been appropriated by them weeks before. So on the whole they were not unhappy with their profits in the deal. And Ariana – she was merely an extra, a pair of hands to perform whatever work she could, unless of course she struck someone's fancy. Ariana herself had figured that much out. But she would rather have died than become the mistress of a Nazi. She would spend the rest of her life in their stinking barracks rather than do that.

'It's there, a little further down the road, on the left.'

Ariana's eyes widened and once again she turned her head to hide her tears. She was almost home now . . . the home that she had dreamed of so desperately in those dark hours, lying in her dark cell, the home where she had laughed and played with Gerhard and waited for her father to return at night, where she had sat and listened to stories for hours, as Fräulein Hedwig read to them by the fire, and where she had stolen glimpses of her mother so very long ago . . . the home that now she had lost. To them. The Nazis. In seething hatred she glanced at the man in uniform at her side. To her, he was part of what they represented. Terror, loss, destruction, rape. No matter that he bought her food and had saved her from Hildebrand. In truth he was simply part of a terrifying whole. And given the opportunity, in time he would do the same things to her as the others.

'There it is, there.' She pointed suddenly as they rounded the last bend, and Von Tripp slowed the car as they saw it, as she stared at it with sorrow and regret, and he with respect and awe. He wanted to tell her that it was lovely, and that he, too, had once lived in such a home. That his wife and children had died in the house near Dresden during the bombings, that now he, too, would have nowhere to go. The schloss that had been his parents' had been 'borrowed' by a general at the very beginning of the war, leaving his parents virtually homeless until they had joined his wife and two children at the Dresden home. And all of them were gone now. Dead beneath the Allies' bombs. While the general went on living at their castle, he had been safe there, as would have been Manfred's children, had his parents been allowed to stay.

The Mercedes Manfred was driving crunched along on the gravel, making the sound Ariana had heard ten million times before. If she closed her eyes, it would be Sunday and she and Gerhard and her father would be returning from their drive around the lake after church. She would not be sitting here with this stranger, sitting here in the rags of what had once been her dress. Berthold would be standing at attention. And once inside she would serve tea. '. . . never again . . .' She said the two words softly to herself, stepping down on to the gravel, staring up at the beloved house.

'You have half an hour.' He hated to remind her, but they had to be back, and those had been Von Rheinhardt's orders. They had wasted enough time on the girl already. Von Rheinhardt had been clear about Manfred's spending as little time as possible on the project and then hurrying back. '. . . and watch her!' he had told him, lest she try to spirit something of value out of the house. Also, it was possible that there were hidden safes and secret panels, and whatever Manfred could discover would be of some help. They had already had teams, skilled in just those pursuits, go over the house, but nonetheless it was possible that Ariana would lead them to something more than they had already found.

Uncertainly, Ariana rang the doorbell, wondering if she would see Berthold's familiar face, but what she saw instead was the general's aide. He looked very much like the man who stood just behind her, but somewhat sterner as he stared down in horror at the girl in rags. He glanced from her to

Manfred, the two men saluted, and Lieutenant von Tripp explained.

'Fräulein von Gotthard, sir. She's come to fetch some clothes.'

There was a brief further exchange between the two men.

'There's not much left, you know.' He said it to Manfred, not to Ariana, who was looking up at him in shock. Not much left? Not much, from four closets filled with clothes? How wonderfully greedy they had been, and how quick.

'I don't think I'll be needing much.' There were sparks of anger in her eyes as she stepped inside the front door. Everything looked the same, yet different. The furniture was in the same place, yet, intangibly, some quality of the house had changed. There were no familiar faces, none of the sounds of the people she and the house had always known. Berthold's aging shuffle, Anna's increasing limp, Gerhard's constant slamming and running, her father' dignified progress down the long marble hall. Somehow she expected to see Hedwig – after all her devotion to the Party, surely they would have kept her on – but even Hedwig's familiar face was not among those who stared at Ariana as she made her way upstairs. There were mostly uniforms hurrying in and out of the main study, and several more waiting outside the main salon; there were orderlies carrying trays of schnapps and coffee, and there were several unknown maids. It was like coming back in another lifetime, after everyone you'd known had long since died and another generation had repopulated all the places you had once loved. Her hand touched the familiar banister as she quickened her step and ran upstairs with her eternal shadow still behind her; Lieutenant von Tripp maintained a discreet distance, but he was always there.

She stopped for a moment on the first landing, staring at her father's bedroom door. Oh, God, what could have happened to them?

'In there, fräulein?' Von Tripp's voice was soft behind her.

'I beg your pardon?' She wheeled on him, as though she

130

had just discovered an intruder in her home.

'Is that the room where you are going to fetch your things?'

'I . . . it . . . my room is upstairs. But I'll have to come back here later.' She had just remembered. But perhaps it was too late. The book may already be gone. Or maybe not. But she didn't really care now. With the loss of Gerhard and her father, and then the house, all was already lost.

'Very well. We haven't much time, fräulein . . .' She nodded and ran up the last flight of stairs to the room where Hedwig had betrayed her, the doorway through which the officers had first walked. Hildebrand, with his arrogant gait, strolling into her sitting room as she prayed for her father's return. She pushed open the first door, and then the door to her own room, keeping her eyes averted from Gerhard's doorway across the hall. She didn't have time for nostalgia, and it would have caused her too much pain.

After a moment she hurried out of the room to find a suitcase in a storeroom above them, on the floor where the servants' rooms were, and it was there that she found her, the traitor, hurrying with bent head towards her own room.

Like a dart cast at the woman's retreating back, Ariana hurled the word. 'Hedwig!' The old woman stopped and then hurried on, never turning to face the girl she had raised since birth. But Ariana would not let go of her now. In fact, she never would again. 'Can you not face me? Are you so afraid?' The words a venomous caress, an invitation to drink poison, a machete concealed in a gift of fur. The woman stopped and slowly she turned.

'Yes, Fräulein Ariana?' Calmly, she attempted to face the girl, but her eyes were fearful, and her hands trembled on the stack of linens she had been taking to her room to mend.

'Sewing for them, are you? They must be grateful to you. Just as we were. Tell me, Hedwig.' No more 'Fräulein,' no more respect, only hatred now: Ariana stood with her hands clenched, her fingers tensed like claws. 'Tell me, after you sew their clothes for them, after you take care of their children, if they have any, will you betray them, too?'

'I did not betray you, Fräulein von Gotthard.'

'My, my, how formal. Then it was Berthold and not you who called the police?'

'It was your father who betrayed you, fräulein. He should never have run away as he did. Gerhard should have been allowed to serve his country. It was wrong for him to run away.'

'Who are you to judge that?'

'I am a German. We must all judge each other.' So that was what it had come to. Brother against brother. 'It is our duty, and our privilege, to watch over each other and see that Germany is not destroyed.'

But Ariana spat her answer at her. 'Germany is already dead, thanks to people like you; people like you have destroyed my father and my brother and my country –' she stood there with tears pouring down her face, then, unable to go on as her voice sank to a whisper – 'and I hate you all.'

She turned away from her old nurse, stormed into the storeroom, and took the single valise in which she would pack her remaining belongings from the house. Silently, Von Tripp followed her back to her room and lit a cigarette as he watched her hurriedly stack sweaters and skirts and blouses, underwear and nightgowns, along with several pairs of sturdy shoes. There was no room for frills now. There were no frills in Ariana von Gotthard's life.

But even what she was packing was of a finesse and calibre that was hardly suited to a life in an army barracks – the skirts she had worn to school, the shoes she wore when she went to watch Gerhard play polo or walk slowly with her father around the lake. She cast a glance over her shoulder as she threw a silver and ivory hairbrush into the suitcase. 'Do you suppose they'll mind if I take that? It's the only hairbrush I have.'

Manfred looked momentarily embarrassed and shrugged. For him, it was odd to see her packing. The moment she had walked into the main hallway, it was evident that this was where she belonged. She moved around with an assurance, an authority, that made one want to bow slightly and step aside. But it had been that way for him in Dresden, too. Their house had been only slightly smaller, and in fact even more impressively staffed. The house had been his wife's father's, and when he died two years after they married, it had become theirs. A handsome addition to the schloss he was to inherit when his parents died. So Ariana's life-style was not unknown to him, nor was the pain of her fate as she left home. He could still hear his mother crying, when she got the word that she would have to give up the schloss for the duration of the war. 'And how do we know we'll get it back?' she had sobbed to his father.

'We'll get it back, Ilse, don't be silly.'

But now they were all dead. And the schloss would belong to Manfred, when the Nazis finally left it after the war. Whenever that would be. And now Manfred didn't really care. There was no one to go home to. No home where he would care to be. Not without them . . . his wife, Marianna, and the children . . . he couldn't bear to think of it as he stood there, watching Ariana put another pair of walking shoes into the bag.

'You're planning to take up hiking, Fräulein von Gotthard?' He used a smile to force the pain from his own mind. She had certainly packed a good supply of rugged equipment.

'I beg your pardon? You expected me to wash out bathrooms in a ballgown? Is that what Nazi women do?' Her eyes widened sarcastically as she threw another cashmere sweater on the pile. 'I had no idea they were so formal.'

'Perhaps they're not, but I doubt very seriously that the captain intends to have you scrub floots until the end of the war. Your father had friends, they will invite you. Other officers – '

She cut him off brutally with eyes of stone. 'Like Lieutenant Hildebrand, Lieutenant?' There was a long silence between them and then she turned away. 'I'm sorry.'

'I understand. I just thought . . .' She was so young, so pretty, and there would be plenty of opportunity for her to do more than just scrub floors. But she was right and he knew it. She would be better off hiding in the barracks. There would be others like Hildebrand. Even more of them now that she was free. They would see her now, polishing doorknobs, raking leaves, scrubbing toilets . . . they would see the huge blue eyes, the cameo face, the graceful hands. And they would want her. She would be accessible to them all now. There was nothing to stop them. She was helpless, not as much as she was in the fetid cell, but almost. She belonged to the Third Reich, a possession, an object, like a bed or a chair, and she could be used accordingly, if someone chose to. And Manfred knew that someone would. At the thought of it, Manfred von Tripp felt sick. 'Perhaps you're right.' He said nothing further, she finished her packing and then lowered her suitcase to the floor. She had left on the bed one heavy brown tweed skirt, a dark brown cashmere sweater, and a warm brown coat, along with suitable underwear and a pair of flat brown suede shoes.

'Do I have time to change my clothes?'

He nodded silently and she disappeared. Officially, he was probably supposed to watch her, but he would have put neither of them through that ordeal. She was not a prisoner to that extent, that she had to be watched every moment. That kind of nonsense was what Hildebrand would have done, forcing her to undress in front of him while he drooled and eventually reached out to pull her towards him. Those were not the games that Manfred von Tripp played.

She returned from the bathroom a moment later, a solemn portrait in brown, with only her pale golden hair providing some sunlight on the sombre scene. She pulled the coat on over her sweater and Manfred had to fight the urge to help. It was painful and confusing standing there beside her. He had to let her carry her own suitcase as well. It fought against everything he had been taught, everything he felt for this tiny, fragile stranger who was leaving her house for the last time. But he had already bought her lunch and saved her once from rape. He could not do much more, not now.

Ariana paused at the top of the last flight of stairs, glancing again at her father's door, and then at Von Tripp standing beside her. 'I'd like to . . .'

'What's in there?' His brows knit uncomfortably.

'My father's study.' Oh, Christ, what was she after? Some cash he had hidden somewhere? Some treasure? A tiny pistol she could aim at an assailant's head, or even at his own as they returned to the heart of Berlin? 'Is it purely sentimental? Fräulein, that is the general's study now . . . I really ought to . . .'

'Please.' She looked so bereft and so helpless, he couldn't force himself to refuse. Instead he nodded slowly, sighed, and cautiously opened the door. An orderly was inside laying out a dress uniform for the general, and Manfred looked at him questioningly.

'Anyone else here?'

'No, Lieutenant.'

'Thank you, we'll only be a moment.'

She walked quickly to the desk, but touched nothing, then more slowly she walked to the window and stared out at the lake. She remembered when her father had stood there talking about Max Thomas, and then telling her the truth about her mother, and when he had stood there again the night before he left with Gerhard. If only she had known it would be their last parting . . .

'Fräulein . . .' She pretended not to hear him, her eyes rooted to the still blue Grunewaldsee. 'We have to be going.' And then, as she nodded, once again she remembered. The reason why she had wanted to come to the study. The book.

She glanced casually over the bookcase, knowing long before she reached it where it was, and the lieutenant watched her, hoping that she would do nothing desperate that would force him to report her or return her to her cell. But she was only touching one or two of the old leather-bound books that stood in such abundance in the bookcase of her father's room. 'May I take one?'

'I suppose so.' It was harmless after all, and he really had to get back to his office in Berlin. 'But do hurry. We've been here for almost an hour.'

'Yes, I'm sorry . . . I'll take this one.' After looking at three or four, she settled on one, a volume of Shakespeare, translated into German, leather-bound and well worn. Manfred glanced at the title, nodded, and opened the door. 'Fräulein.'

'Thank you, Lieutenant.' She glided through it with her head held high, praying that her look of victory would not give her away. In the book she had taken from her father's bookcase reposed the only treasure that she still had. The diamond signet ring was there safely couched by Shakespeare, along with the emerald engagement ring. She slipped the book quickly into the deep pocket of her brown tweed coat, where no one could see it and where she couldn't lose the very last of what she had. Her mother's rings. That and her father's book were all that she had left of her lost life. Ariana's head was filled with memories as she walked sedately down the long hall.

As she did so, the suitcase slapping heavily at her legs, rendering her a refugee where she had once been hostess, a door opened suddenly on her right and a uniform dripping medals instantly appeared.

'Fräulein von Gotthard, how nice to see you.'

She looked at him in astonishment, too startled to be repulsed. It was the aging General Ritter, who was now the master of her father's house. But he held out a hand to her, as though he had met her on the way to tea.

'How do you do.' She responded by reflex and he quickly took her hand, looking into the deep blue eyes, and then smiling as though he had found something with which he was very pleased.

'I'm very happy to see you.' She didn't suggest that he had no reason not to be. He was already the proud possessor of their house. 'It has been a very long time.'

'Has it?' She couldn't ever remember meeting him before.

'Yes, I believe the last time we met you were, oh . . . about sixteen . . . at a ball at the Opera House.' His eyes glowed.

'You looked lovely.' For a moment she looked absent. It had been her first ball. And she had met that officer she liked so much . . . and that Father hadn't quite approved of . . . what had been his name? 'I'm sure you don't remember it. It was about three years ago.' She almost expected him to pinch her cheek, and for a moment Ariana felt sick. But she was grateful for the training that made her able to endure as well as pretend. She owed Hedwig a debt after all.

'Yes, I remember.' Her voice was flat, but not quite rude.

'Ah, do you?' He looked immensely pleased. 'Well, you'll have to come back again sometimes. Perhaps for a little party here.' He rolled the words from his tongue in nauseating fashion and for an instant Ariana thought she might throw up. She would die first. In fact, the prospect of death was becoming rapidly more enticing as she began to understand what really was to be her fate. She did not answer him. But the blue eyes shrank from him as he reached out and touched her arm. 'Yes, yes, I do hope we see you here again. We will be having lots of little celebrations, fräulein. You must share them with us. After all, this was your house.' *Is, you bastard, not was!* She wanted to shout the words, but she only dropped her eyes politely, so he could not see the fury that raged in her heart.

'Thank you.'

The general's eyes shot a cryptic message at Von Tripp, and then he waved vaguely at the aide who stood behind him. 'Remember to call Von Rheinhardt and tell him . . . er . . . give him an . . . er . . . invitation for Fräulein von Gotthard. That is if . . . er . . . there are no other invitations for her already.' He was being careful this time. The last concubine he had added to his pack had been a woman he had stolen from right under yet another general's nose. It had caused a lot more trouble than the woman had been worth. And although this one was pretty, he had enough headaches on his hands just then. Two of the trainloads of paintings he had been waiting for from Paris had just been bombed. So this pretty little virgin was not quite the most pressing affair. Yet he would have enjoyed adding her to his other girls. He smiled at her one last time, saluted, and disappeared.

The suitcase was in the backseat, her head was held high, and the tears streamed down her face. She didn't bother to hide them from the lieutenant. Let him see. Let them all see how she felt about what they'd done. But what Ariana didn't see as she watched the house disappear behind them was that there were tears in Manfred von Tripp's eyes, too. He had all too clearly understood the general's cryptic message. Ariana von Gotthard was about to be added to the lecherous old bastard's harem. Unless someone else put in a claim for her first.

Chapter 17

'All finished with the girl?' Captain von Rheinhardt looked at Manfred irritably as he stalked past his desk later that afternoon.

'Yes, sir.'

'Did you take her out to Grunewald to get her things?'

'Yes, sir.'

'It's a nice house, isn't it? Lucky man, the general. I wouldn't mind having a house like that.' But he wasn't doing badly either. A family whose home had a view of the Charlottenburger Lake and Schloss had been fortunate enough to give up its home for him.

The captain went on to speak to Manfred of other matters. Hildebrand kept busy answering the phones. Time and time again Manfred found himself wondering if one of the calls was General Ritter's aide asking about the girl. Then he would stop his thoughts. What difference did it make to him? She was nothing to him, just a young woman who had fallen on hard times, lost her family and her home. So what? Thousands of others were in the same boat. And if she was attractive enough to catch the eye of a general, then it was just something that she would have to learn to handle herself. It was one thing to protect her from the viciousness of a junior officer planning to rape her in her cell, but quite another to steal her from a general. That would mean trouble. For him.

Manfred von Tripp had been careful to avoid problems with his superiors and other officers during the entire course of the war. It wasn't a war that he approved of, but this was the country that he served. He was a German, first and foremost, and more than many others he had paid dearly for the fervour of the Reich. But still he did not argue, he kept his mouth shut and endured. And one day it would be over, he would go back to the land of his parents, and the schloss would be his. He wanted to restore the castle to its medieval splendour, rent out the farms, and bring the surrounding lands around the castle back to life. And there he would remember Marianna, the little boy and girl, and his parents. He wanted nothing more than to survive the war for that. He wanted nothing further, nothing from the Nazis, no stolen priceless paintings, no misbegotten jewels or cars, he wanted no plunder, no rewards, no gold, no money. What he had wanted and held dear was already gone.

But what troubled Manfred as he sat at his desk and listened was that she was so innocent and so young. In a way their lives were much the same now, But Manfred was thirty-nine and she was nineteen. He had lost everything but he hadn't been helpless the way she was now. He had been agonised, broken, anguished, but not frightened and alone . . . Manfred had heard the stories. He knew the kinds of games the old man played, the girls together, he and the girls, a little perversion, a little brutality, a little sadomasochism, a little whip, a little . . . Thinking of it made him sick. What was wrong with all of them? What happened to men when they went to war? God, he was tired of it. He was tired of it all.

He threw his pen down on his desk after Captain von Rheinhardt left the office and sat back in his chair with a sigh. It was then that the call came from the general, or rather from his aide, who spoke to Hildebrand, who only grinned. He put the phone back in its cradle after taking the message that the captain should call him back in the morning. 'Something about a woman. Christ, that old fart is going to end this war with his own army – an army of women.'

'Did his aide say who?'

Hildebrand shook his head. 'Just a little matter he would like to arrange with the captain. Unless, as the aide put it, it's already too late. The aide said this is one cookie the general figures will be off the pastry shelves pretty quick. She may already be gone. Knowing Ritter, she'll be lucky if she is. I wonder who he's got his eye on this time.'

'Who knows.' But after the phone call Manfred stirred restlessly in his seat. Hildebrand left for the day, and Manfred found himself sitting there, at his desk, for another two hours. He couldn't get his mind off her and what Hildebrand had said. The general wanted Ariana . . . unless the cookie was already off the pastry shelf . . . He stood there for a long moment, as though spellbound, and then, hurriedly grabbing his topcoat, he turned off the light in the office and ran down the stairs, out of the building, and across the street.

Chapter 18

Lieutenant Manfred von Tripp found Ariana von Gotthard easily at the barracks. He had been planning to inquire at the desk, but it turned out to be unnecessary. She was outside raking leaves and placing great armloads of them in a barrel, which afterwards she would have to burn. It was easy to see that it was the first time in her life she had done any manual labour.

'Fräulein von Gotthard.' He looked official, his shoulders

squared, his head terribly erect, like a man about to make a major pronouncement, and had Ariana known him better, she would have seen, too, that lurking in his blue-grey eyes was also fear. But she didn't know him that well. In fact, she didn't know Manfred von Tripp at all.

'Yes, Lieutenant?' She said it with exhaustion, pushing a long stray lock of blonde hair from her eyes. She was wearing delicate brown suede gloves to work in, they being the only ones she had. She imagined that he had arrived to give her still more orders. Since that afternoon she had scrubbed down two bathrooms, cleaned trays in the cafeteria, carried boxes from the top floor to the basement, and now this. It hadn't exactly been a leisurely afternoon.

'Please be so kind as to collect your bag.'

'My what?' She looked at him in total confusion.

'Your suitcase.'

'Can't I keep it here?' Or what was it, had someone admired the leather, and now they were taking her suitcase, too? She was still carrying the little leather book with the false compartment in her coat. And when she had had to leave it in her room, she had hidden it in a ball of laundry under the bed. It was the only place she had been able to think of in her rush to get to work. The matron in charge was a large bull-shaped woman with a voice better suited to the drill ground than a women's barracks. She had kept Ariana appropriately terrified all afternoon. But now Ariana looked at Manfred with fresh disgust. 'So someone wants my suitcase. Well, let them have it. I'm not going anywhere for a while.'

'You misunderstand.' His voice was gentle, but hers was not. She had to remind herself always that this was the man who had saved her from Hildebrand that night in her cell. Otherwise it was too easy just to think that this man was like the others. Because, after all, he was. He was inextricably woven into the fabric of her nightmare, and she could no longer separate his needs from theirs. She didn't believe in anything anymore, or anyone. Not even this tall, quiet officer who looked at her gently but firmly now. 'In fact,

Fräulein Gotthard, you're quite wrong. You are going somewhere.'

'I am?' At first she looked at him in sudden terror. Now what? What were they planning for her now? Some terrible internment in a camp somewhere? Then a sharp stab of joy – Could it be? 'Have they found my father?' His quick look of dismay told her all she needed to know.'

'I'm sorry, fräulein.'

His voice was soothing. He had seen the terror in her face. 'You will be safe.' For a while at least. And that was something these days. A while was better than nothing at all. And which of them were safe? In the past years of never-ending air raids, the bombs never ceased to fall.

'What do you mean, I will be safe?' She eyed him with fear and suspicion, clutching tightly to her rake, but he only shook his head now and spoke softly.

'Trust me.' With his eyes he tried to reassure her but she still looked desperately afraid. 'Now please be so kind as to pack your suitcase. I will wait for you in the main hall.' She looked at him with despair blending into desperation. What did it matter now?

'What should I tell the matron? I didn't finish out here.'

'I'll explain.'

She nodded and walked into the building as, silently, Manfred watched her. He found himself wondering what the devil he was doing. Was he as crazy as the general? But it was nothing like that, he told himself. He was only doing it to protect the girl. Yet he, too, had felt the stirrings. He was not unaware of the beauty that lay only faintly obscured by the drab clothes and her distress. It would take very little to polish the diamond to its old lustre, but that was not what he was doing, it was not why he was taking her to Wannsee that night. He was taking her there to save her from the general, to take the cookie off the bakery shelf. Ariana von Gotthard would be safe in Wannsee, no matter what.

Manfred spoke briskly to the matron, explaining that the girl was being removed. He managed to explain with inferences and subtle nuances that it was a matter of someone's pleasure rather than any military decision regarding the girl. The matron understood perfectly. Most of the girls like Ariana were snatched up by officers within a few days. Only the ugly ones stayed to help her, and when she had first seen Ariana, she had known it wouldn't last. It was just as well really. The girl was too small and delicate to do much work. She saluted the lieutenant smartly and assigned another girl to go outside and rake.

Ariana was back in the main hall not quite ten minutes later, with her suitcase clutched tightly in her hand. Manfred said nothing, but turned on his heel and marched swiftly out of the building, expecting Ariana to follow him, which she did. He opened the door of his Mercedes, took her suitcase from her this time, and tossed it in the back, and then he walked around the car, got behind the wheel, and started the motor. For the first time in a very long time, Manfred von Tripp looked pleased.

Ariana still didn't understand what was happening, and she watched the city around them curiously as they drove off. It took her almost twenty minutes to figure out that they were going in the direction of Wannsee. They had almost reach Manfred's house. But by then she had already figured out what was happening. So this was what he had saved her for, that night in her cell. She wondered if he also used a whip. Perhaps that was how he had got the hairline scar that travelled a short distance along his jaw.

A few moments later they pulled up outside a small house. It looked respectable but not sumptuous in any way, and inside it was dark. Manfred signalled for her to get out of the car, and he grabbed the suitcase from the backseat as she walked towards the front door with her spine ramrod straight and her eyes avoiding his. How charmingly he had arranged things. Apparently she was to be his. For good, she found herself wondering, or just the night?

Without further ceremony he unlocked the front door, waved her in, and stepped inside. He shut the door firmly behind them, flipped on some lights, and looked around. His cleaning woman had been there that morning, and everything looked tidy and clean. There was an unceremonious but friendly living room, with lots of books and plants, and a stack of freshly cut wood next to the fireplace where each night he made a fire. There were photographs, mostly of his children, and a journal of some kind lying closed on his desk. There were big, friendly, country windows that opened out on to a garden filled with flowers, a view shared by the kitchen, a small den, and a tiny, cosy dining room, all of which occupied the main floor of the house. There was a narrow wooden stairway, carpeted with a well-worn but once handsome rug, and all Ariana could see from below was a low-ceilinged upstairs hall.

As though he expected her to understand his intentions, Manfred stalked silently from room to room, throwing open doors and then moving on to the next room, until at last he stood at the foot of the stairs. He looked at her hesitantly for a moment and stared into her deep, angry blue eyes. She still wore her coat and the gloves she'd worn to gather leaves outside the barracks; her hair was falling from its tightly woven golden knot. Her suitcase stood behind them, forgotten near Manfred's front door.

'I'll show you around upstairs.' He said it quietly as he waved her up before him. He didn't quite trust her behind him yet. She was too afraid, too angry, and he knew enough to protect himself, even from a child like this.

Upstairs, there wasn't a great deal to show her. A single bathroom and two ominous-looking doors. Ariana stared at the doors with terror, her huge blue eyes wandering slowly to Manfred's hands and then his face. 'Come, I'll show you.' The words were gentle, but it was useless, he could see from her face that she was so frightened, she could barely hear. What could he do to reassure her? How could he explain what he had done? But he knew that in time she would come to understand.

He threw open the door to his bedroom, a stark and simple room done in browns and blues. Nothing in the house was very fancy, but it was all comfortable and it had been precisely what he wanted when he decided to find his own quarters in Berlin. It was a place where he could escape everything, where he could sit peacefully at night, watch the fire, smoke his pipe, and read. His favourite pipe lay on a table in his bedroom, next to the fireplace where he sat in a well-worn, always welcoming chair. But instead of seeing the harmless surroundings, Ariana stood there, eyes wide, arms down, her feet rooted to the ground.

'This is my bedroom.'

The eyes stared at him in helpless horror, and she nodded. 'Yes.'

And then, touching her arm gently, he walked past her and swung open a door she had assumed would be a closet. But he stepped inside and disappeared. 'Come this way, please.' Gingerly and trembling she followed him, only to discover that it was yet another small room. There were a bed, a chair, a table, a desk so small, it was almost better suited to a child, but there were pretty little curtains and a bedspread covered with roses that matched the wallpaper in the small room. There was something reassuring about it as Ariana stepped inside. 'And this is *your* room, fräulein.' He looked at her warmly, but still he saw that she didn't understand. Her eyes went to his again, with the same pain, same sorrow, and he smiled at her, and let out a long sigh.

'Fräulein von Gotthard, why don't you sit down, you look exhausted.' He waved her gently to the bed, which she stared at for a moment, and finally rigidly sat down. 'I'd like to explain something to you. I don't think you understand.' He looked suddenly very different as he spoke to her, not like the stern officer who had trotted her up and down those endless halls and stairs, but like the kind of man who came home at night, who ate dinner, sat by the fire, and fell asleep over his paper because he was so tired. He looked like a real person, but still Ariana shrank from him as she watched him from the bed. 'I brought you here tonight because I believed that you were in danger.' He sat back slowly in his chair and prayed that she'd relax. It was impossible to talk to her when she sat there like that, staring at him. 'You're a very pretty woman, Fräulein von Gotthard, or I should say that you're

145

a very pretty girl. How old are you? Eighteen? Seventeen? Twenty?'

'Nineteen.' It was more of a gasp than a word.

'I wasn't so far off, then, but there are those who wouldn't care.' His face grew serious for a moment. 'Like our friend Hildebrand. He wouldn't give a damn if you were twelve. And there are others . . .' *If you were a little older, if you had been out in the world for a bit before all this misfortune befell you, you would have some idea how to take care of yourself.* He frowned at her and she stared at him. He sounded more like her father than a man who was going to take her to his bed and rape her. And in his chair he was thinking of her raking the dead leaves outside the barracks; she had looked about fourteen years old. 'Do you understand, fräulein?'

'No, sir.' She looked infinitely pale and wide-eyed. Gone was the young woman who had tried to brazen it out with Von Rheinhardt in the beginning. This was no woman, it was a child.

'Well, it came to my attention this evening that there was a possibility you might be urged to . . . er . . . join the general . . .' Fresh terror flew into her eyes but he held up a hand. 'I felt that that would hardly be a fortuitous beginning to your life on your own. So, fräulein – ' he looked around the room that would be hers – 'I brought you here.'

'Will they make me go to him tomorrow?' She stared at him in desperate anxiety as he tried to keep his eyes from noticing the flawless gold of her hair.

'No, that's quite unlikely. The general doesn't ever exert himself over anything. If you had still been there at the barracks, he would have taken you with him to Grunewald, but if you're already gone, then you have nothing to fear.' And then he thought of something. 'Do you mind that? Would it have been worthwhile putting up with him in order to be back in your own house?'

But she shook her head sadly. 'I couldn't have borne to see it like that, with strangers in it, and – ' she choked on the words – 'I would have died rather than be with him.' Manfred nodded, and he saw her looking at him appraisingly, as though to see what she'd got herself instead, and he couldn't repress a burst of laughter. He knew exactly why she was looking him over. And at least she had understood that he wasn't going to tear her clothes off halfway through the bedroom door.

'How does the arrangement suit you, fräulein?' He eyed her and she sighed softly.

'I suppose it will do.' What did he expect? Her thanks for making her his mistress instead of the general's?

'I'm sorry these things have to happen. It has been an ugly war . . . for all of us.' There was a distant, pensive look on his face. 'Come. I'll show you the kitchen.'

In answer to his question about her cooking, she smiled. 'I've never really cooked before. There was no need.' There had always been servants to do the cooking.

'Never mind. I'll teach you. I won't make you rake leaves or scrub toilets – I have a cleaning woman who comes in to do all that – but it would certainly be pleasant if as part of our exchange you did the cooking. Do you suppose you could do that?' He looked so serious and suddenly she felt so tired. She was his concubine now. Like a bought-and-paid-for slave.

She sighed and looked at him. 'I suppose so. And what about the laundry?'

'All you'll have to worry about is your own. That's it really, just the cooking.' It was a small price to pay for her safety. The cooking, and the fact that she was to become his mistress. That much she understood.

She stood quietly by as he taught her how to make eggs, sliced bread, and showed her how to cook carrots and potatoes, and then he left her to wash the dishes in the sink. She heard him put the wood on and start the fire, and then she saw him writing peacefully at his desk. Now and then he would look at photographs of one of the children, and then he'd bow his head again and write some more.

'Would you like some tea, sir?' She felt oddly like one of the maids in her own house, but remembering that she had inhabited the nightmarish cell in the Reichstag only that

147

morning, she was grateful suddenly to be in the lieutenant's house at all. 'Sir?'

'What, Ariana?' And then he blushed faintly. It was the first time, he had called her by her first name. But he had been absentminded. For a moment she hadn't even been sure if he had said Ariana or Marianna. It was hard to tell. 'Sorry.'

'It's all right. I asked you if you would like tea.'

'Thank you.' He would have preferred coffee, but by now it was almost impossible to get. 'Would you like some?' She hadn't dared to pour herself a cup of the precious substance, but at his bidding she ran to the kitchen for a cup and poured herself some tea. For an instant she just sat there enjoying the exotic fragrance. For a month now she had dreamed of just such long-forgotten luxuries as tea.

'Thank you.' For a long moment he wondered about the sound of her laughter. Would he ever hear it? Twice that evening he had won her bedazzling smile. He felt his heart stir as he watched her. She was so desperately serious, so unhappy, her eyes and her face were so marked by her recent trauma. She was looking around the room then, her eyes stopping at the photographs of the children. 'Your children, Lieutenant?' She looked at him curiously, but he didn't smile. It was an odd little tea party they were sharing, the two of them with the broken lives. He only nodded in answer to her question and suggested she pour herself another cup of tea, as he lit his pipe and stretched his long legs towards the fire.

They sat there together quietly, until almost eleven o'clock, saying little, simple being there, Ariana growing slowly accustomed to her surroundings, and the lieutenant enjoying having another living, breathing human being in his home. His eyes would stray towards her now and then, and he would watch her, sitting there, dreamily staring into the fire, as though she had drifted back to a world of long ago. At eleven o'clock Manfred stood up and looked down at her, then he began to turn out the lights.

'I have to get up early tomorrow morning.' As though on

cue, she rose, too. But there was fresh fear in her eyes now. What would happen next? This was the moment she had dreaded all night.

He waited for her to walk sedately from the room, and then followed her. They reached his door first and stood there. He hesitated for a long moment and then with a small smile he held out a hand. She watched him in amazement, and she had to remind herself to put her hand in his. This was so totally not what she had expected that her jaw almost dropped as he shook her hand. 'I hope that one day, fräulein, we shall be friends. You are not a prisoner here, you know. This just seemed the wisest arrangement . . . for your sake. I hope you understand.' Her eyes lit up slowly then and she smiled at him.

'You mean . . .'

'Yes, I mean.' His eyes were gentle and she could see that he was a kind man. 'Did you really think that I would stand in for the general? Don't you think that would have been a little bit unfair? I told you, you are not my prisoner. In fact –' he bowed very properly and clicked his heels – 'I shall regard you as my guest.' But Ariana only stared at him, stunned. 'Good night, fräulein.' The door closed softly behind him, and in utter amazement, she walked soundlessly down the hall.

Chapter 19

'Well, where the hell is she?' Von Rheinhardt stared at Hildebrand in annoyance. 'Von Tripp said he took her over there yesterday. Did you ask the matron?'

'No, she was away from her desk.'

'Then go back. I have better things to worry about than this nonsense, for God's sake.'

Hildebrand went back to see the matron and reported to the captain once again an hour later while Von Tripp kept busy with a number of projects he had not completed the day before.

'What did the matron say?' The captain glowered at Hildebrand from across his desk. Everything had been going wrong for him all day. And he didn't give a damn about the general and that damn Von Gotthard girl. They'd finished with her, and what happened to her now was of no interest whatsoever to him. If General Ritter had the hots for her, that was his own problem. He should have sent his own damn aide running around to look for her.

'She's gone.'

'What the hell do you mean, "she's gone."' And then he looked suddenly furious. 'Has she run away?'

'No, nothing like that, Captain. Someone took her. The matron said it was an officer, but she wasn't sure who.'

'Did you check the logbook?' Von Rheinhardt stared at him.

'No. Should I go back?'

'Never mind. If she's gone, she's gone. He'll find half a dozen others he wants by next week. And that little joyride might not have been worth the price of admission. There is always the chance, though admittedly remote, that her father will turn up one day. And there would be hell to pay if Ritter had made her one of his harem.' Von Rheinhardt rolled his eyes and Hildebrand laughed.

'You really think her old man is still alive?' He looked at his captain with interest.

'No, I don't.' The senior officer shrugged then and admonished Hildebrand to get back to work. And it wasn't until late in the afternoon that the captain himself wandered over to the barracks to have a little chat with the matron. A few moments later she quietly produced the logbook, and Von Rheinhardt got the information that he had come for. He read the name on the logbook with interest and mused to himself all the way back across the street. Perhaps Von Tripp was returning to the land of the living after all. It had been his suspicion that Von Tripp would never recover from the loss of his wife and children, nor from the wound he had suffered just the Christmas before. After he was wounded, Manfred seemed to give up life. He was like a shell of a man – not ever participating in the freer social scene. But perhaps now . . . it was interesting . . . He suspected as much, which was why he had gone across the street to check the log. There was very little that escaped Dietrich von Rheinhardt's attention.

'Von Tripp?'

'Yes, sir?' Manfred looked up with surprise. He hadn't seen the captain come in. What's more, he hadn't seen him go out half an hour before. He had been busy across the hall, looking for some files that someone had mislaid.

'I'd like to see you in my office, please.' Manfred followed him with an uneasy feeling. The senior officer wasted no time. 'Manfred, I happened to take a look at that logbook across the street.' But they both knew that the captain never 'happened' to do anything.

'Oh?'

'Yes, "oh." You have her?' It was impossible to read his face, but slowly Manfred nodded.

'Yes, I do.'

'May I ask why?'

'I wanted her, sir.' It was the kind of blunt answer Von Rheinhardt would easily understand.

'I can of course understand that, but were you aware that General Ritter wanted her, too?'

'No, sir.' Manfred felt his skin crawl. 'No, sir, I didn't know. Although we did meet him for a moment in the hall at the house in Grunewald yesterday. However, he gave no indication . . .'

'All right, all right, never mind.' The two men eyed each other for a long time. 'I could make you give her up to Ritter, you know.'

'I hope you won't do that, sir.' It was the understatement of a lifetime, and for a long moment neither man spoke.

'I won't, Von Tripp.' And then after another moment, 'It's good to see you alive again.' He grinned broadly. 'It's nice to see you give a damn. I've been telling you for three years that was all you needed.'

'Yes, sir.' Manfred grinned convincingly, wanting to slap his commanding officer across the face. 'Thank you, sir.'

'Not at all.' And then he chuckled to himself. 'Serves Ritter right. He's the oldest man here and he always gets the youngest girls. Don't worry, I've got another one I'll send him. She should keep him happy for weeks.' He laughed raucously to himself and waved Manfred from the room.

So . . . he had won her, and by the captain's grace in the end. He felt a long sigh escape him as he looked around the office and realised that it was time to go home.

'Lieutenant?' Her face peered into the hallway, her pretty golden hair looped gracefully on top of her head and her big blue eyes dancing out nervously to see that it was he.

'Good afternoon, Ariana.' He seemed unbearably formal as he gazed into the blue eyes while she stood before him with an anxious look on her face.

'Did . . . was . . .' She stumbled over the words with a look of terror, and instantly Manfred understood.

'It's all right. Everything's settled.'

'Were they very angry?' The huge blue eyes looked larger than ever as gently he shook his head. Every moment of the terror of the past month was etched in her eyes as she stood there. As brave as she had so often seemed to him, now she seemed like a tiny, defenceless child.

'I told you, it's all right. You'll be safe here now.' She want to ask him for how long, but she didn't dare. Instead she only nodded.

'Thank you.' And then, 'Would you like a cup of tea?'

'Yes.' He paused for a moment. 'If you'll have one, too.' She nodded silently and disappeared into the kitchen. She was back a few moments later with a tray and two steaming cups with the precious brew. For her, it was one of the greatest luxuries in his household, after her month in the cell. Being able to be clean again, and to drink tea again. She had actually dared to drink a cup by herself that afternoon as she wandered aimlessly around his living room, glancing at the books and thinking of her father and Gerhard once again. She could barely keep her mind from them. And the ache of worry and sorrow still showed in her eyes. Manfred looked at her gently as she set down his cup. There was so little he could say to her. He knew only to well what it was to cope with the burden of loss. He sighed quietly and picked up one of his pipes as they sat down. 'What did you do today, fräulein?'

She shook her head slowly. 'I . . . nothing . . . I . . . looked at some of your books.' It made him think of the splendid library he had seen in her home the day before, and long before in his own. Thinking back to that made him decide to take the bull by the horns. His eyes carefully sought hers as he lit the pipe.

'It's a beautiful home, fräulein.' She knew instantly which home he meant.

'Thank you.'

'And one day it will be yours again. The war cannot go on forever.' He put the pipe down and his heart reached out to her through his eyes. 'My parents' home was taken over, too.'

'Was it?' There was a flicker of interest in her face. 'Where was it, Lieutenant?'

The sadness came back to his eyes as he answered. 'Outside Dresden.' He instantly read the question in her eyes. 'It wasn't touched by the bombings.' The schloss wasn't . . . but everything else was . . . everyone else . . . everyone . . . the children, Theodor and Tatianna . . . Marianna, his wife . . . his parents, his sister, all of them . . . gone. Just like her father and brother. Just as certainly. Forever.

'How lucky for you.' He looked up, startled by her words, and then remembered that they had been speaking of the schloss.

'Yes.'

'And your family?'

He drew a sharp breath. 'Not as lucky, I'm afraid.' She waited, the silence growing heavy between them. 'My children ... my ... wife ... and my parents ... were all in the city.' He stood up and walked to the fireplace. All she could see now was his back. 'They were all killed.'

Her voice was a gentle whisper. 'I'm so sorry.'

He turned to face her then. 'No more so than I am for you, fräulein.' He stood there for a long moment, and their eyes met and held.

'Has ...' She could hardly bring herself to ask him, but she had to know. 'Has there been some news?'

He shook his head slowly. It was time she faced the truth. He had sensed that somewhere in her heart, in her mind, she had refused to face it all along. 'You father, fräulein, I don't think he just left you ... forgot you. From what I have heard, he was not that kind of man.'

She shook her head slowly. 'No, I know that. Something must have happened to them.' And then she looked up at him defiantly. 'I will find them after . . . after the war.'

He looked at her sorrowfully and there was a dampness in his eyes. 'I don't think so, fräulein. I think you should understand that now. Hope, false hope, can be a very cruel thing.'

'Then you've heard?' Her heart raced as she stood there.

'I've heard nothing. But ... my God, think of it. He left to keep the boy from the army, didn't he?' She said nothing. Maybe this was just a cruel trick, to finally get her to betray her father. And she wouldn't. Not even to this man she had almost come to trust. 'All right, don't tell me. But it's what I assume.' And then he shocked her. 'It's what I would have done. What any sane man would have done to save his son. But he must have been planning to come back for you, Ariana. And the only thing that could have kept him from it was his own death. His and the boy's. There's no way they could have got into Switzerland, no way he could have got back. I'm sure that the border patrol got them. They must have.'

'But wouldn't I have heard?' There were tears on her cheek now, rolling slowly down towards her chin as she

154

listened to his words, and her voice was only a whisper when she spoke.

'Not necessarily. They're not exactly the most refined troops we've got out there. If they killed them, and they must have, they would simply have disposed of them. I . . .' He looked embarrassed for a moment. 'I already tried to find out. But no one told me anything, fräulein. I think, though, that you must face what happened. They're gone. They must be dead.'

She turned slowly away from him, her head bowed, her shoulder shaking, and on quiet feet he left the room. A moment later she heard his bedroom door close. She stood there, sobbing softly, and at last she lay on the couch and let herself cry. It was the first time since the whole nightmare had happened that she had truly let herself go. And when it was over, she felt numb.

She didn't see Manfred again until the next morning, and when she did, she avoided his eyes. She didn't want to see his pity, his compassion, his own sorrow – it was all she could do to cope with her own.

Often in the next few weeks, Ariana would see him looking at the photographs of the children, and she would feel an ache rise in her own heart as she watched him, thinking of Gerhard and her father, knowing that she would never see them again. And now, as she sat in the living room all afternoon alone, the smiling faces of Manfred's children haunted her, as though they reproached her for being there with their father, when they could be with him no more.

Sometimes she resented them for staring at her, the one with pigtails and white satin bows, the other with such straight blond hair and big blue eyes looking out at her above a smattering of boyish freckles . . . Theodor . . . But what she resented most about them was that they made the lieutenant human, they made him seem somehow more real. And she didn't want him to be. She didn't want to know about him, or care about him. Despite what he had said when he brought her to Wannsee, he was in a sense her jailer. She didn't want to see him in any other light. She didn't want to know of his dreams or hopes or sorrows, any more than she wanted to tell him of her own. He had no right to know how deeply she felt her grief. He had already seen too much of her life, of her pain and vulnerability. He had seen her at Hildebrand's mercy in the cell at the Reichstag, he had seen her last anguished moments in her own home. He had seen too much, and he had no right to. No one did. She would share no part of herself with anyone ever again. Manfred von Tripp sensed this in her, as he sat silently staring into the fire night after night, smoking his pipe and saying little to Ariana as she sat politely by, lost in her own thoughts, behind a wall of her own pain.

She had been in his house for three weeks when he turned to her suddenly one evening and took her by surprise as he stood up and put down his pipe. 'Would you like to go for a walk, fräulein?'

'Now?' She looked startled and a little bit afraid. Was it a trap? Where was he taking her, and why? The look in her eyes pained him, as he understood all too quickly how great was her fear and her mistrust, still, after all these uneventful days. But it would take a lifetime to blot out the memory of those days in the bowels of the Reichstag. Just as it would take him a lifetime to forget what he'd seen when he'd gone back to Dresden to comb through the ruins of his house . . . the dolls lying torn under beams and broken plaster, the twisted silver ornaments of which Marianna had been so proud . . . now melted and tarnished . . . like her jewellery . . . like their dreams. Manfred forced his thoughts back into the present as he looked down into the frightened blue eyes.

'Wouldn't you like some exercise?' He knew that she had never ventured beyond his garden in the weeks that she'd been there. She was still afraid.

'What if there's an air raid?'

'We'll run to the nearest shelter. You don't have to worry. You'll be safe with me.' She felt foolish arguing with the deep, calm voice and the gentle eyes, and slowly she nodded. It would be her first turn out in the world in two months. For a month she'd been in jail, and for almost that long now she'd been in Wannsee, too frightened to stir more than a few feet outside the house. She was haunted by all kinds of terrors, and tonight for the first time Manfred understood to what extent she was afraid. He watched her put her coat on and nodded quietly. Ariana didn't know it, but it was the look he had used on Tatianna, his daughter, when he knew that she was afraid. 'It's all right. The air will do us both good.' All evening he had been warring with his own thoughts. It had been happening more and more now. Not just the thoughts of the children or his parents or his wife . . . but there were other thoughts now . . . thoughts of Ariana, which had begun to taunt him weeks before. 'Ready?' She nodded silently, her eyes wide, and as they stepped out into the cool evening, he slipped her small gloved hand into the crook of his arm. He pretended not to notice that she absentmindedly clutched his sleeve tightly as they walked along.

'It's lovely, isn't it?' She glanced up at the sky and smiled again. Her smile was so rare and so beautiful, it made him smile, too.

'Yes, it is. And you see, no air raid.' But half an hour later, as they had begun to head back towards his house, the sirens started and people began to rush from their houses to the shelters nearby. At the first sound of the sirens. Manfred put an arm around her shoulders and ran towards the shelter with the others.

Ariana ran with him but in her heart she didn't really care if she was safe or not. There was nothing for her to live for.

In the shelter there were women crying, babies screaming, and children playing as they always did. It was always the grown-ups who were frightened. The children had grown up with this war. One of them was yawning, and two others were singing a silly song as the shieking above them continued and in the distance they heard bombs. Through it all, Manfred watched Ariana, her face quiet, her eyes sad, and without thinking, he reached out and took her hand. She said nothing, she only sat there, holding the big smooth hand in her own and watching those around her, wondering what they lived for, why they went on.

'I think it's safe now, fräulein.' He still called her that most of the time. He stood up and she followed him, and they walked rapidly home. It was a different kind of walk than it had been earlier that evening. He wanted to get her home again where she was safe. As they walked into the front hallway, they stood there for a moment, silent, staring at each other, something new and different in their eyes. But Manfred only nodded and then turned and walked up the stairs.

Chapter 20

Ariana was standing on a chair in the kitchen when he came home the next evening, trying desperately to reach a canister that had been put away on a high shelf. And as he wandered down the hall and saw her, he went quickly to her side and reached it, handing it to her, and then unthinkingly put his hands around her waist and lifted her down from the chair. She blushed slightly and thanked him, and then went to make him his usual cup of tea. But it was as though she sensed something different now, too. Some current of electricity that had not been there before, or that had been, but that had lain dormant between these two troubled people who had so much on their minds. This time when she handed him his teacup she had forgotten the sugar and she blushed again as she turned away.

They were both quiet and strained at dinner, and afterwards he suggested another walk. This time everything went smoothly, and there were no air raids until later that night. They both awoke quickly, but too late to flee – they had to take refuge in the cellar, bundled into bathrobes and wearing heavy shoes. Manfred kept a suitcase in the cellar with a change of clothes, in case he had to leave in a hurry, but he realised as he sat there that he had never asked Ariana to bring down some of her things. He suggested it to her now, and she shrugged softly in the light of his pipe. There were pieces of black cloth on the windows, so no one could have seen the tiny speck of light as he smoked. He was puzzled by her gesture, and then he understood.

'Don't you care, Ariana, about surviving?'

Slowly she shook her head. 'Why should I?'

'Because you're still so young. You will build your whole life. When all of this is over, you will have everything ahead of you.' She looked unconvinced.

'Do you care so much?' She had seen the look in his eyes when he looked at those pictures of his children and his wife. 'Does surviving mean so much to you?'

'It means more now than it did.' His voice was oddly soft. 'And in time it will mean more to you again, too.'

'Why? What does any of it matter now? This will never end.' Together they listened to the distant bombs. But she didn't seem afraid, only desperately sad. She wanted the bombs to kill all the Nazis, and then she would be free – or dead.

'It will end one day soon, Ariana. I promise you.' His voice was so soft as they sat in the dark, and as he had the night before, he reached silently for her hand. But this time when he took it, she felt a stirring in her body. He held it for a long time and then she felt him slowly pulling her towards him. She felt unable to resist the gentle motion, and unwilling to push him away. As though it had been what she had always wanted, she felt herself enveloped in the powerful arms, and she felt his mouth come down slowly on hers. The sounds of the bombs in the distance faded, and all she could hear was the pounding in her ears as he held her and kissed her and stroked her, and then breathlessly she pulled away. There was a brief awkward silence and then he sighed. 'I'm sorry . . . I'm so sorry, Ariana . . . I shouldn't – ' But this time it was Manfred who was astonished as she silenced him with a kiss and then let herself quietly out of the cellar and went upstairs to her room. The next morning neither of them made any mention of what had happened the night before. But each day now there was a drawing closer, a still greater attraction that each found more and more difficult to resist, until at last one morning she awoke to find him standing in her room.

'Manfred?' She looked at him sleepily, unaware that for the first time she had called him by his first name. 'Is something wrong?' Slowly he shook his head and walked towards the bed. He was wearing blue silk pyjamas beneath a dark blue silk robe. For a long instant she wasn't sure what he wanted, and then slowly she understood. She wasn't sure what to say to him as he stood there, but she knew as she looked at him that she wanted this man desperately. She had fallen in love with her captor, Lieutenant Manfred von Tripp. But as he gazed down at her, hungrily, sadly, he realised that he had made a terrible mistake, and before she could say anything he turned away and hurried towards the door. 'Manfred . . . what are you doing . . . where – '

He turned to look at her. 'I'm sorry . . . I shouldn't have . . . I don't know what . . .' But she held out her arms to him. Not the arms of a child, the arms of a woman. And he turned slowly to face her and walked towards her with a gentle smile and shook his head. 'No, Ariana . . . you're only a child. I . . . I don't know what happened. I was lying in bed thinking of you for hours and . . . I think for a moment I lost my mind.' She slipped quietly from her bed then and stood there, waiting for him to come to her, waiting for him to understand. He looked at her with an air of amazement as she stood there, wearing a white flannel nightgown and a small smile. 'Ariana?' He couldn't believe what he saw in her eyes. 'Darling? . . .' It was the merest whisper as he came to her and swept her into his arms, and her mouth found his and she nestled softly into his arms.

'I love you, Manfred.' She hadn't even known until then that she meant that, but as he held her next to his wildly pounding heart, she knew that she did. And moments later they lay together, and he took her with the tenderness of a man very much in love. He loved her expertly and gently and again and again.

It went on like that until Christmas, as Manfred and Ariana revelled in their private world. Ariana spent all day around the house and in the garden, tidying up and reading, and in the evenings they ate quiet dinners and then stretched out for a little while by the fire, but they went upstairs far more quickly now that there was the lure of the wonders Manfred was teaching Ariana in bed. It was a deep romantic love they shared, and in spite of the loss of her father and Gerhard, Ariana had never been so happy in her life. As for Manfred, he had come back to the land of the living with zest and joy and humour. Those who had known him since the death of his children couldn't quite believe that he was the same man. But for the past two months he and Ariana had been infinitely happy, and now only the threat of Christmas worried both of them a little bit, with ghosts from past lives, past years, no longer around them to share in the young couple's new-found joy.

'Well, what are we going to do about Christmas? I don't want either of us to sit around here and get depressed thinking about what isn't anymore.' Manfred eyed her sagely over their morning tea, which they now shared in bed. It had been his turn to bring the tray up that morning. 'Instead I wanted to celebrate what we've got this Christmas, not cry about what we don't. Speaking of which, what do you want for Christmas?' It was still two weeks away, and the weather had been crisp and icy for the past week.

She smiled at him now from her pillows, the look in her eyes a caress. 'You know what I want for Christmas, Manfred?'

'What, my darling?' He could barely keep his hands off her when she looked like that, the golden hair spread around her like a sheet of spun gold, the delicate breasts bare, the look in her eyes one of invitation and loving.

'I want a baby. Your baby.' For an instant he was quiet.

It was something he had thought of more than once.

'Do you mean that, Ariana?' But she was still so young. So much could change. And after the war . . . He didn't like to think about it anymore, but it could be that when she no longer had to live under his protection, maybe then someone younger would come along and . . . He hated the thought.

But she was looking at him seriously. 'I mean it, my darling. I'd like nothing more than our son.'

He held her tightly for a long moment, unable to speak. It was what he wanted one day. But not yet. Not in these ghastly times. 'Ariana, my darling, I promise you that' – he pulled away to look at her gently – 'when the war is over, we will have a baby. You'll have your gift of a son.'

'Is that a promise?' She smiled happily at him.

'A solemn promise.'

She held tightly to him and laughed the silvery laugh that he loved so much. 'Then I don't want anything else for Christmas. That's all I want in the world.'

'But you can't have that yet.' Her joy was infectious and he was laughing now, too. 'Isn't there something else you'd like as well?'

'No. Except one thing.' She glimmered at him happily.

'What's that?' But she was embarrassed to say it. Talking about having a baby was one thing, but asking a man to get married just wasn't done. So instead she hemmed and hawed and teased and wouldn't answer, and he threatened to get it out of her by that night. But Manfred had his own ideas in that direction. He desperately wanted to marry Ariana, but he wanted to wait until the country was once more at peace. The war couldn't last forever, and it would have meant a lot to him to get married at his family's schloss.

But he had another idea about Christmas, and when Christmas morning came, there were half a dozen boxes under the tree. One was a sweater Ariana had knitted for Manfred, another was a series of poems she had written him and rolled up in a scroll. And third was a box of his favourite cookies, which she had struggled over for several mornings and finally got just the way he loved. Lebkuchen, for

Christmas, in all the traditional shapes, some chocolate covered, some not, with little brightly coloured sugar decorations sprinkled on them. He was touched to the core when he saw how hard she had worked.

Manfred's gifts to Ariana were a little less homegrown, and she rattled all the boxes with anticipation and glee.

'What should I open first?'

'The big one.' In fact, he had two other big ones hidden in the closet down the hall, but he hadn't wanted to overwhelm her all at once. The first package she opened held a beautiful ice-coloured blue dress, which hung from her shoulders and danced softly over her bare skin. It was a halter neck with a low V in the back, and after her winter of rugged skirts, sturdy shoes, and heavy sweaters, Ariana squealed with delight over the beautiful dress.

'Oh, Manfred, I'll wear it tonight to dinner!' Little did she know that that was more or less what he had in mind. The second package yielded a pretty aquamarine necklace to go with it, and the third a pair of absolutely perfect silver evening shoes. Draped in all her finery, Ariana lay across their bed, swilling tea like champagne and singing in a throaty baritone. Manfred laughed happily at her as he went to collect the rest of the boxes, which yielded a white cashmere dress that was a far cry from what she had been wearing, and a simple black wool that was easily worthy of the wardrobe she had had before. He had bought her a pair of plain black pumps, a black alligator bag, and a perfectly simple black wool coat that she slid into with delight, trying on one outfit after the other. 'Oh, I'm going to be so elegant, Manfred!' She hugged him fervently and they both laughed again.

'You already are elegant!' She was wearing the aquamarine necklace, the silver sandals, and the new black coat over white lace underwear. 'In fact, I'd say you look sensational! But there's one thing missing . . .' He began fishing in the pocket of his bathrobe for his last gift to her, this one hidden in a very small box. He tossed it into her open hands and sat back against the headboard with a grin.

'What is it?'

'Open it and see.'

She opened it slowly and carefully, and when the box lay open in her hand, there was the joy of one who is loved in her eyes. It was a very handsome engagement ring from Louis Werner on the Kurfüstendamm. 'Oh, Manfred, you're crazy!'

'Am I? Somehow I thought that if eventually you wanted to have a baby, it might be a nice touch if somewhere along the way we got engaged.'

'Oh, Manfred, it's so lovely!'

'And so are you.' He slipped the round diamond on to her finger and she lay there grinning at it in the wild costume she had put together from the mountain of gifts he had just bestowed on her.

She propped herself up on one elbow as they sat there. 'I wish we could go out so I could show off all pretty things.' But it was said pensively, without any great urgency. For the past three months they had been content just to go for walks or strolls around Wannsee or one of the other small lakes. They went to an occasional restaurant for lunch, but in effect they had lived like hermits, and they were both happier with each other at home. But he had bought her such pretty things to wear that all of a sudden she was tempted to step out into the world again.

'Would you really like that?' He looked cautious.

She nodded excitedly. 'I would.'

'There's a ball tonight, you know, Ariana.'

'Where?' In fact, there were several. Dietrich von Rheinhardt was having a party, as was General Ritter in her father's old house; then there was one at headquarters, and there were two other big parties being given by the brass. They could have gone to any of the parties they wanted to. Only Ritter's was one Manfred was anxious to avoid. But other than that one, Manfred relayed the list to her and they chose three. 'I'll wear my new blue dress and my necklace . . . and my engagement ring.' She grinned at him ecstatically, and then suddenly she remembered something she had never showed him before.

'Manfred?' She looked at him hesitantly.

'What, my love?' Her face had grown serious so rapidly that he wasn't sure what to think. 'Is something wrong?'

'Would you be angry if I showed you something?' He grinned at the question.

'I won't know until you show me.'

'But what if you're angry?'

'I'll control myself.' She went to the room that had been her old room and returned with her father's book. 'You're going to read me Shakespeare now? On Christmas morning?' He sank back into their bed with a groan.

'No, be serious, Manfred. Listen to me . . . I have something to show you. Remember the day you took me to Grunewald, and I got Papa's book. Well, the night my father left with Gerhard and . . .' For a moment her eyes were sad, her thoughts turned inwards. She had long ago told him everything, and holding the book in her hand, she went on. 'My father left me these, in case I should ever need them, if something went wrong. They were my mother's.' Without further ado, she flipped open the secret compartment and revealed the two rings, the diamond signet and the emerald. She hadn't dared to include the tiny gun her father had given her. When she had removed the book, she had quietly pushed the gun to the back of the shelf. To have been caught concealing a weapon would have meant instant death. But the rings were her treasures – all she had left. Not expecting what she was about to show him, Manfred gasped.

'My God, Ariana.' And then, 'Does anyone know you have these?' But of course no one did. She shook her head. 'They must be worth a fortune.'

'I don't know. Papa said they might help if I had to sell them.'

'Ariana, I want you to hide the book again. If something ever goes wrong, if the war ends and we do not win, those rings could buy your life someday, or get you somewhere where you could be free.'

165

'You make it sound like you're going to desert me.' Her eyes looked large and sad.

'Of course not, but anything could happen. We could get separated for a time.' Or he could get killed, but he didn't want to remind her of that on Christmas morning. 'You just hold on to them. And as long as you're so good at keeping secrets, Fräulein von Gotthard – ' he looked at her mock reproachfully – 'I think you should be aware of this.' Without explaining further, he pulled out a drawer and behind it showed Ariana where he had concealed money and a small, efficient-looking gun. 'Should you ever need that, Ariana, you know it's there. Do you want to put the rings there with it?' She nodded and they put her mother's rings away, and she sat gazing happily again at her own. As of Christmas morning, 1944, Ariana Alexandra von Gotthard had become engaged to Lieutenant Manfred Robert von Tripp.

Chapter 21

Their evening began at the Opera House on the broad boulevard Ariana loved so much, Unter den Linden, it's graceful tree-lined expanse interrupted only by the Brandenburg Gate, which lay directly ahead.

Manfred watched with pleasure as she alighted from the car, the pale blue dress hanging from her body like a single sheet of ice, the aquamarines dancing from her neck. It was the first time in months that Ariana had worn clothes that even faintly resembled her old ones, and for just one evening it was lovely to forget the tragedies of the past year.

She clung to him tightly as they made their way through a sea of uniforms, to those of highest rank, to whom Manfred had to pay homage before they joined the others to enjoy the ball. Manfred introduced her sombrely to two generals, several captains, and a handful of colonels whom he knew, each time making a formal introduction as Ariana stood very still, her head held high, her hand outstretched. She would have done any man honour, and Manfred's heart swelled with pride as he watched how poised she was. This was her first time under the scrutiny of half the senior officers of the Reich. Captive princess that she was, they were all a little bit intrigued, and she knew it. Only Manfred knew how frightened she was at the beginning of the evening, as he felt her hand tremble in his, leading her out on to the dance floor to waltz.

'It's all right, darling, you're always safe with me.' He smiled down at her gently and her chin went up just a little higher than before.

'I feel as though they're all staring at me.'

'Only because you look so lovely, Ariana.' But she knew even as she danced with him that she would never feel completely safe again. They could do anything, these people, take her home from her again, kill Manfred, lock her in a cell. But it was absurd to think that way – it was Christmas, and she and Manfred were dancing – and then suddenly, as they whirled around the floor, she remembered and her eyes laughed again as she looked into his.

'Do you know, I came to my first ball here! With my father.' Her eyes glowed, remembering the evening that she had come here, so excited and so filled with awe.

'Aha, should I be jealous, fräulein?'

'Hardly. I was only sixteen.' She looked at him imperiously and he laughed.

'Of course, how foolish of me, Ariana. You're so much older now.' But she was in many ways. She was a lifetime older than the girl who only three years before had danced in this same ballroom, in her layers of white organdy with flowers in her hair. It seemed a thousand years before. And as she thought of it dreamily, someone took their picture. She jumped in surprise and looking, blinking, into his eyes.

'What was that?'

'They took our picture, Ariana. Is that all right?' It was customary to collect dozens of photographs of the officers and their ladies, at each party, every ball. They ran them in the papers, put them up in the officers' clubs, had copies made for relatives. 'Do you mind, Ariana?' For a moment disappointment filled his eyes. Six months before he would have been livid to have his photograph taken with any woman, but now he wanted a photograph of them, as though seeing their faces before him on paper would make it all seem more real. She understood the look in his eyes quickly and inclined her head with a small smile.

'Of course it's all right. I was just surprised. Will I be able to see the pictures?' He nodded and she smiled.

They stayed at the Opera House for over an hour, and then, looking at his watch, he whispered in her ear and went to fetch her wrap. This had been only the first stop of the evening, and the more important stop on their agenda was yet to come. He had wanted to get her accustomed to the sea of uniforms around her, the curious stares, the flashbulbs sending little black dots dancing before her eyes, because at the next stop she would be even more closely watched. As his fiancée she would pass under considerable scrutiny, and he suspected also that the Führer would be there.

When they drove up to the Royal Palace, Manfred immediately spotted Hitler's black 500 K Mercedes. There were dozens of special guards surrounding the palace, and once inside in the splendorous, mirrored gilt and inlay of the old Throne Room, Manfred felt Ariana tighten her grip on his arm. He patted her small hand gently and looked down at her with a warm smile. One by one he made the necessary introductions, wandering slowly through the lines of uniforms, introducing her to the generals and their wives or their mistresses. Watching her incline her head very slightly and hold out the graceful little hand, he felt his heart swell. Until at last they reached a face that was familiar, and General Ritter clutched the delicate young hand.

'Ah, Fräulein von Gotthard . . . what a pleasant surprise.' He cast a look of jubilation at her, and then a glance of brief disapproval at Manfred at her side. 'Lieutenant.' Manfred clicked his heels and bowed. 'Would you care to join us later, fräulein? There will be a small supper at my house.' 'His' house. Manfred saw her eyes begin to dance with anger, and he only tightened his pressure on her left hand and then smoothly tucked it into his arm so that the general could easily set the diamond ring.

'I regret, General – ' Manfred's voice was all sugar and cream – 'my fiancée and I have an earlier commitment for this evening, but perhaps – ' he spoke reverently with a hopeful smile – 'another time?'

'Of course, Lieutenant. And . . . your fiancée, did you say?' He asked the question of Manfred, but his eyes never left Ariana's as he spoke. She could feel the man's eyes almost undressing her, it made her skin crawl as she pretended not to notice.

But this time Ariana spoke before Manfred, her eyes cast deep into the general's, her tone polite but cold. 'Yes, we are engaged now, General.'

'How nice.' His lip curled. 'Your father would be very pleased.' *Not nearly as pleased as he would be to have you in his house, dear General . . . filthy bastard . . .* She wanted to hit him as she stood smiling into the repulsive face. 'May I offer my congratulations?' Manfred bowed again, and Ariana nodded demurely before they wandered off.

'I though we handled that rather nicely.' Ariana looked up at Manfred with a small smile.

'We did, did we?' He was amused and, at the same time, madly in love with her. It was lovely taking her out. 'Are you enjoying yourself at all, Ariana?' He looked down at her with concern, his own pride at being with her showing in his eyes.

She returned the look of pleasure and nodded. 'Yes, I am.'

'Good. Then on Monday we're going shopping.'

'Good God, for what? You gave me three dresses and a coat this morning . . . and a necklace . . . and shoes and an engagement ring.' She ticked it all off on her fingers like a child.

'Never you mind, fräulein. I think it's time that you and I started getting out.' But no sooner had he said it than an odd hush fell over the room, and in the distance they could hear the bombs. Even on Christmas night the war was with them, and he found himself wondering which lovely monument, which home, whose children, had just been destroyed. But they stopped quickly, and no one had to flee to the shelter beneath the building, and the music played on. And they all went on pretending that this was like any other Christmas night. But the Grosses Schauspielhaus had recently been destroyed, and there were other buildings and churches that disappeared now almost every day. For almost a year now many Berliners had gone to bed fully dressed, with suitcases standing next to their beds, ready for a quick trip to the shelters where many of them spent almost every night. The Allies weren't going to let up now, and it frightened Manfred terribly. What if Berlin were another Dresden? What if something should happen to Ariana, too, before the end of the war? But at his side she instantly sensed his feelings, and she reached quickly for his hand, holding it tightly in her own, her deep, lovely blue eyes reaching up towards his to reassure him, her mouth so sensual and gentle. Looking down at her, he could only smile.

'Don't worry, Manfred. Everything will be all right.'

He smiled slowly, looking at her. 'On Monday we go shopping.'

'All right, if that will make you feel better.' And then she stood up on tiptoe and whispered in his ear. 'Now can we go home?'

'Already?' At first he looked surprised and then he grinned, whispered back to his little princess. 'Have you no shame, fräulein?'

'None at all. I'd much rather be home with you than waiting here to see the Führer.' But he put a finger on his lips.

As it turned out, they saw him anyway. He swept into the room surrounded by his henchmen just before they left, a small man with his dark hair and moustache and un-prepossessing looks, yet a current of electricity shot through the entire room. Ariana could feel bodies tighten, voices rise, and suddenly there was a wild chanting of Hail to the Fürher, and she watched in astonishment as the crowd of men in uniform and women in evening clothes went wild. She and Manfred stayed until the frenzy ended and the crowd had settled down to their entertainment once again, and then slowly they wended their way through the crowd. It was near the doorway that someone touched her, just a quick touch on her arm, and as she turned, she saw Manfred suddenly and ferociously at attention, his right arm held aloft. And she saw then it was Hitler who had touched her, and now he smiled benignly and moved on, as though he had bestowed a blessing. Then, quickly, she and Manfred left. For a long moment they said nothing, and then at last in his car again, she spoke. 'Manfred, they almost went crazy.'

He nodded quietly. 'I know. They always do.' And then he turned to her. 'Have you never seen him before in person?'

She shook her head. 'No, Papa didn't want me involved in all that.' And then she regretted saying it – perhaps Manfred would take it as a reproach of him. But he nodded quickly. He understood.

'He was right. And you brother?'

'He kept him out of it as much as he could. But I think he was afraid in a different way for me.'

'And very rightly.' He drove on for a minute and then turned back to Ariana again. 'Do you know what they're doing at that party at General Ritter's tonight? They're having beauty dancers and tranvestites to entertain the guests. Hildebrand tells me that's a regular feature with him.' A look of disgust crossed his face.

'What are beauty dancers and tranvestites?' She sat back with the wide, curious eyes of a child and Manfred grinned.

'Oh, my darling innocent, I love you.' At moments like that he remembered that she was only five years older than his oldest child would have been. 'A beauty dancer is a naked woman who dances in suggestive ways to entertain, and a tranvestite is a man masquerading as a woman, usually in evening clothes. They dance and sing, and can also be quite suggestive.'

But Ariana was laughing as she watched his face. 'Aren't they terribly funny?'

He shrugged. 'Sometimes, but generally not. Ritter doesn't have the "funny" ones, he has the good ones. And when they're all finished performing, everyone . . .' Suddenly he remembered that it was she he was talking to. 'Never mind, Ariana. It's all rather disgusting entertainment. I don't want you involved in that.' And there was more and more of it lately. Not just at Ritter's house in Grunewald; the others were all indulging the same whims. As though with each day, with the war around them worsening, they had to indulge their most outrageous fantasies and go to more and more indecent lengths. This was not what he wanted to introduce her to now. But having taken her out that night, he had been reminded of the pleasure of going out into the world with a pretty woman on one's arm, strolling in the midst of admiring glances, seeing her shine in a special kind of way. It made their seclusion in the house in Wannsee still more precious, yet he suddenly liked the idea of going out with her as well.

'You're not disappointed to miss the other parties tonight, Manfred?' Happily, he shook his head.

'There was one at the Summer Palace in Charlottenburg that might have been nice. But actually, there's a much nicer party I know about in Wannsee.' He looked at her lovingly and they both smiled.

They made their way upstairs quickly and fell happily into each other's arms in the large comfortable bed.

The next morning at breakfast Ariana was pensive and Manfred gazed at her quietly. It was Sunday and he didn't have to go to work. This was Hildebrand's Sunday on.

They went for a long walk in the Tiergarten. He induced her to try ice skates on the Neuer See, and together they glided around the ice like smiling children among the pretty women and the man in uniforms. It was difficult to believe that they were still at war.

Afterwards he drove her to a café on the Kurfürsten-damm, which always looked to Ariana almost exactly like the Champs-Élysées in Paris, where she had gone before the war with Gerhard and her father on a brief trip. On the Kurfürstendamm they sat down amidst the few artists and writers who were still left in Berlin. There were many men in uniform, but the atmosphere was genial and Ariana stifled a happy yawn as they sat in the cosy café.

'Tired, darling?' He smiled at her, when suddenly in the distance they could hear the screech and wail of bombs. They left and walked quickly back to the car.

As they drove back along the Kurfürstendamm on their way to Wannsee, Ariana moved closer to him and tucked a hand into his arm.

'Do you see that church, Manfred?' She pointed and for an instant he took his eyes from the road. It was the familiar Kaiser Wilhelm Memorial Church on the Kurfürsten-damm.

'Yes? Are you feeling religious at this time of night?' He was teasing and they both smiled.

'I just wanted to let you know that is the church where I want to marry you one day.'

'At the Kaiser Wilhelm?'

'Yes.' She glanced again at the pretty little diamond ring.

And he gently put an arm around her shoulders. 'I'll remember that, my love. Happy?' He looked over at her in the dark. The bombs had stopped, at least for a while.

'Never happier in my life.'

And when they got the photographs of the Christmas Eve balls, it was easy to see that she was telling Manfred the truth when she said she was happy. Her face beamed out at the camera, her head held high, her eyes bright with love, as just behind her Manfred, in full dress uniform, gazed into the camera with undisguisable pride.

Chapter 22

At the end of Christmas week, at Manfred's insistence they went shopping in downtown Berlin at Grunefeld's. He had to buy her more clothes. Captain von Rheinhardt was pressing him to come out of hiding to rejoin his comrades of the Reich.

'Was he angry, Manfred?' She looked concerned as they drove downtown, but Manfred only patted her hand and smiled.

'No, but I suppose I've got away with being a hermit for as long as I'm going to. We don't have to go out every night, but we should start accepting a few invitations to dinner. Think you can stand it?'

'Sure. Can we go and see General Ritter's tranvestites?' She looked mischievous and he couldn't suppress a laugh.

'Ariana, really!'

They staggered out of the store three hours later, so burdened by a stack of boxes, they could hardly get to Manfred's car. Another coat, a little jacket, half a dozen lovely wool dresses, three cocktail dresses and a ballgown, and a divine little dinner suit that looked like a man's tuxedo, except that instead of trousers there was a long narrow skirt with a slit up one side. And in honour of her mother's memory there was also a long, slinky dress in gold lamé.

'My God, Manfred, where am I going to wear it all?' He had spoiled her rotten. He felt as though he had a wife again, a woman to spoil and cherish, to dress and protect and amuse. They were in no way strangers to each other, and she was more at ease with Manfred than she had ever been with anyone in her whole life.

She had many places to wear the clothes. They went to several concerts at Philharmonic Hall, an official reception at the Reichstag for the Parliament and favoured officers stationed in Berlin; there was a party at Bellevue Castle and several small dinners near them in Wannsee, where other officers had sought quieter quarters than they would have found in the heart of town. Little by little, Manfred and Ariana became an accepted couple, and it was understood by everyone that they would marry after the war.

'Why wait, for God's sake, Manfred? Why not do it now?' A fellow lieutenant took Manfred aside at a dinner party one night.

But Manfred only sighed and stared down at the simple gold signet ring that he wore on his left hand. 'Because she's so young, Johann; she's really only a child.' He sighed again. 'And these are special times. She should have the opportunity to make that decision in normal times.' And then, shaking his head slowly, 'If we ever see normal times again.'

'You're right, Manfred. Times are not good. For that reason I think you'd be all the wiser to marry Ariana now.' He lowered his voice conspiratorially. 'We can't hold out forever, Manfred.'

'The Americans?'

Johann shook his head. 'I'm a lot more worried about the Russians. If they get here first, we're dead. God knows what they'll do to us, and if we even survive it, they may ship us all off to camps. But you may have some slim chance of staying together if you're married. Also, practically, the Americans may be nicer to her if she's the legitimate wife of a German army lieutenant instead of a concubine.'

'You think it's that close?'

There was a moment's silence as Johann averted his eyes. 'I think it might be, Manfred. I think even those closest to the Führer think so, too.'

'How much longer do you think we can hold out?'

The other man shrugged. 'Two months . . . three . . . if a miracle happens, maybe four. But it's almost over. Germany will never again be what you and I have known her to be.' Manfred nodded slowly – in his eyes she had not been for a long time the country he had once loved. Perhaps now, if the

Allies didn't totally destroy her, she would have the opportunity to be reborn.

Over the next few days Manfred made discreet inquiries. Johann's information was borne out by everyone of influence whom Manfred knew. It was no longer a matter of if Berlin would fall, but when. Manfred realised he had to make plans.

Some questions in the right ears turned up the first item on his shopping list. He brought it home to Ariana two days later, and she squealed with glee.

'Manfred, I love it! But aren't you keeping your Mercedes?' It was an ugly grey Volkswagen, three years old now, but when it had been made in 1942, it had been one of the first. The man from whom he had bought it insisted that it was reliable and useful. It was just that he no longer needed it, having lost both his legs in an air raid the year before. Manfred did not tell Ariana the reason why the car had been up for sale. He simply nodded quietly and opened the door for her to get inside.

'Yes, I'm keeping my Mercedes.' And then after a moment, 'Ariana, this one is for you.'

They drove around the block, and he was satisfied that she could handle the little car fairly well. For a month now, he had been teaching her to drive his Mercedes, but this was a much easier car to drive. He was looking serious as they pulled back in front of their house. Ariana easily sensed his mood. Quietly she touched his hand.

'Manfred, why did you buy it?' She suspected the truth, but she wanted to know from him. Were they leaving? Were they going to run away?

He turned to her slowly with a look of pain and worry in his eyes. 'Ariana, I think the war will end soon, which will be a relief for us all.'

Before he could go on, he pulled her into his arms and held her tight. 'But before it ends, my darling, things may get very rough for us. Berlin may be taken. Hitler's army isn't going to let go easily. It isn't going to be another Anschluss, or like when we took over France. The Germans will fight to

176

the death, and so will the Americans and the Russians . . . This last bit may be one of the bloodiest battles of the war.'

'But we'll be safe here together, Manfred.' She didn't like it when he was afraid, and she could tell now that he was.

'Perhaps, perhaps not. But I don't want to take any chances. If anything happens, if the city falls and is occupied, if something happens to me, I want you to take this car and get out. Go as far as you can.' He said it with an iron determination and there was sudden horror in Ariana's eyes. 'And when you can't drive any more, leave it and start walking.'

'And leave you? Are you crazy? Where would I go?'

'Anywhere you can get to. The closest border. Maybe Alsace, and from there, you could make your way into France. You can tell the Americans you're Alsatian if you have to. They won't know the difference.'

'To hell with the Americans, Manfred. What about you?'

'I'll come and find you. After I've sorted things out here. I can't run, Ariana. I've got a duty to uphold. No matter what – I am an officer.'

But she shook her head emphatically, and then she reached out and clung to him, holding him more tightly than she ever had before. 'I'm not leaving you, Manfred. Never. I don't care if they kill me. I don't care if all of Berlin comes down around my ears, I'll never leave you. I'll stay with you until the end, and they can take us away together.'

'Don't be so dramatic.' He patted her gently and held her close. He knew that what he was saying was frightening her, but it had to be said. It had been three months since Christmas, and the situation had worsened considerably. The British and Canadians had reached the Rhine and the Americans were in Arbrucken. 'But as long as you're so determined not to leave me . . .' He smiled down at her gently. He had decided to take Johann's advice. It was possible that for her safety it might make a difference, and for that reason he had decided not to waste any more time. 'As long as you are so hopelessly stubborn, young lady, and we seem to be in this together and for good – ' he grinned down at her – 'do you suppose that I could induce you to marry me?'

'Now?' She stared at him, shocked. She knew how strongly he felt about waiting, but as he nodded, she smiled, too. She didn't look any further for a reason than the look in his eyes.

'Yes, now. I'm tired of waiting to make you my wife.'

'Hurray!' She held him tight and pounded him happily on the back, then she pulled away again, her head tilted, her eyes bright and childlike, her mouth in a broad smile. 'Could we have a baby right away?'

But this time Manfred only laughed. 'Oh, Ariana, darling . . . do you suppose that could wait just a few months until after the war? Or do you think I'll be too old to be a father by then? Is that why you're in such a hurry, little one?' He smiled down at her gently and she returned a smile in answer and shook her head.

'You'll never be too old, Manfred. Never.' And then, pulling him tightly into her arms again, she closed her eyes. 'I will always love you, my darling, for the rest of my life.'

'I will always love you, too.' He said the words, praying that they would both survive what lay ahead.

Chapter 23

Ten days later, on the first Saturday in April, Ariana walked slowly down the aisle of the little Maria Regina Kirche just off the Kurfürstendamm on the arm of Manfred Robert von Tripp. There was no one to give her away; there were no bridesmaids, no matron of honour. There was only Manfred and Ariana, and Johann, who had come to witness the event.

As she walked down the aisle of the lovely church towards the elderly priest waiting for them at the altar, Manfred could feel the light pressure of her hand on his arm. She had worn a simple white suit with broad shoulders that set off her own tiny frame. Her golden hair was swept up in a soft roll that framed her face, and she had artfully tucked in a soft cloud of veil behind the roll. She looked prettier than Manfred had ever seen her as she walked down the aisle. Miraculously, he had been able to find a number of white gardenias; she was wearing two on her lapel and one in her hair. Also, on this most special day, she was wearing her mother's intricate diamond signet ring on her right hand, as well as the engagement ring he'd given her on her left.

The wedding ring, which Manfred had bought her at Louis Werner's, was a narrow band of gold. At the end of the ceremony he slipped it on her finger and kissed her with an enormous feeling off relief. It was over, they had done it. Ariana was now Frau Manfred Robert von Tripp, and whatever happened to Berlin, that would offer her some protection. It was only now that it was over that he thought of his first wife, Marianna, who seemed so much older and stronger than this delicate girl. It was as though this were part of another lifetime. He felt bonded to Ariana as he had to none other, and as he looked into her eyes, he could see that she felt the same way.

'I love you, darling.' He said it to her softly as they got back into his car. She turned to him with a smile that lit her face from within, and she knew that they had never been happier as they waved to Johann and drove away towards the Kurfürstendamm in the direction of the restaurant where Manfred had promised to take her for their 'honeymoon' before going home. Ariana glanced back over her shoulder once at the church, just as they reached the Kurfürstendamm and turned. There was an enormous thundering and explosion all around them, and Ariana clutched in desperation and terror at Manfred's arm. She turned just in time to see the church explode in a million pieces behind them, and Manfred stomped hard on the gas, telling her to crouch on the floorboards lest debris from other buildings shatter the windshield and cut her face.

'Stay down, Ariana!' He was driving quickly and

lurching terribly to avoid pedestrians and fire trucks streaking by. At first Ariana was too stunned even to react, but then, as she realised that they had escaped death by only moments, she softly began to cry. But they were almost in Charlottenburg before Manfred would pull over. And when he did, he reached down to her gently and pulled her into his arms. 'Oh, darling, I'm so sorry . . .'

'Manfred . . . we could have . . . the church.' She sobbed hysterically.

'It's all right, my darling, it's over . . . It's over . . . Ariana . . .'

'But what about Johann? Do you suppose . . .'

'I'm sure he'd got as far from it as we had by then.' But inwardly Manfred wasn't quite as sure as he led her to believe. And as they drove on a few moments later, he felt a wave of exhaustion come over him. He was so desperately tired of the war. All the people one cared about, all the places one had loved, all the homes and the monuments and the cities, wasted.

Silently they drove home, Ariana quiet and trembling next to him in her veil and her pretty white suit, the gardenias wafting their exotic fragrance towards him. He realised then that the smell of gardenias would always remind him of that night, the night of their wedding, and of their escape from death. Suddenly he wanted to cry then, from relief, from exhaustion, from terror, from concern for this tiny, beautiful woman he had just made his own. Instead, he simply held her very tightly, swept her into his arms, and carried her into their house, up the stairs to their bedroom, where this time, thinking only of each other, they abandoned all care, all thought, all reserve, all precaution, and became one.

Chapter 24

'Did you find Johann?' Ariana looked at Manfred worriedly as he came home from the office the next day.

'Yes, he's fine.' He said it curtly, afraid that she would discover that he was lying. In truth, Johann had died outside the church the night before. Manfred had sat trembling in his office for an hour, unable to accept that yet another person he cared about was gone. With a sigh he sat down heavily in his favourite chair.

'Ariana, I want to talk to you about something very serious.' She wanted to tease him, to take some of that terrible earnestness from his eyes, but as she looked at him she knew there was no point. Life in Berlin was very serious these days.

She sat down very quietly and looked into his eyes. 'What is it, Manfred?'

'I want to establish a plan for you, so that you know what to do if something goes wrong. I want you to be prepared at all times now. And, Ariana . . . I'm very serious . . . you must listen.'

She nodded quietly. 'All right, I will.'

'You know where I keep the money and the gun in the bedroom. If something terrible happens, I want you to take that and your mother's rings and go.'

'Go where?' She looked momentarily overwhelmed.

'Towards the border – there's a map in your Volkswagen. And I always want you to keep the tank filled with gas. I have a spare can in the garage for you. Fill the tank before you go.' She nodded, hating his instructions and explanations. She would never go anywhere. She would never leave him.

'But just how do you think all this would happen? I would just drive off and leave you here, Manfred?' It was a ridiculous suggestion, she never would.

'Ariana, you may have to. If your life is at stake, I want you to go. You have no idea what this city will be like if it is overrun by Allied troops. There will be pillaging, plundering, murders, rapes.'

'You make it sound like the Dark Ages.'

'Ariana, it will be the darkest moment this country has ever known, and you will be totally helpless here if for some reason I cannot reach you. I may get caught at the Reichstag for example, for weeks – or days at the very least.'

'And you really think they'll just let me drive out of here, in that ridiculous little car, with my mother's rings and your gun? Manfred, don't be crazy!'

'Don't you be crazy, dammit. Listen to me! I want you to get as far as you can in the car and then get rid of it. Run, walk, crawl, steal a bicycle, hide in the bushes, but get the hell out of Germany. The Allies are already west of here, all the way to the French border, and I think you'd be safest in France. You can make your way through the Allied lines. I don't think you'll be able to get into Switzerland any more, Ariana. I want you to try to get to Paris.'

'Paris?' She looked stunned. 'That's six hundred miles from here, Manfred.'

'I know. And it doesn't matter how long it takes you to make it, but you have to. I have a friend in Paris, a man I went to school with.' He took out a notebook and carefully inscribed a name.

'What makes you think he's still there?'

'From the reports I've heard for the last six years, I'd say he is. He had polio as a child, so he has been safe from our army and his own. He is the Assistant Minister of Culture in Paris, and he has driven our officers insane.'

'Do you think he's with the Resistance?' She was intrigued.

'Knowing Jean-Pierre, I'd say there was a possibility of that. But if he is, he's smart enough to be discreet. Ariana, if anyone can help you, he will. And I know he'll keep you safe for me until I can get back to you. Stay in Paris if he tells you to, go wherever he thinks you should go. I trust him with my entire being.' He looked at her soberly. 'Which means I trust him with you.' He wrote the name down and handed it to her. Jean-Pierre de Saint Marne.

'And then what?' She looked unhappy as she fingered the note, but she was slowly beginning to wonder if maybe Manfred was right.

'You wait. It won't be long.' He smiled gently. 'I promise.' And then his face hardened again. 'But from now on I want you ready at all times. The gun, the rings, the money, Saint Marne's address, some warm clothes, enough food to carry with you, and a full tank of gas in the car.'

'Yes, Lieutenant.' She smiled softly and saluted, but he didn't smile.

'I hope we never need it, Ariana.'

She nodded, the smile fading, her eyes quiet. 'So do I.' And then after a time, 'I want to try to find my brother after the war.' She still believed Gerhard had got out safely. Time and distance had made her come to realise how much riskier it had been for Walmar, but there was a chance Gerhard had escaped.

Manfred nodded in understanding. 'We'll do your best.'

They spent the rest of the evening quietly, and the next day they went for a long walk on the deserted beach nearby. In summer, the beach at Strandbad on Grosser Wannsee was one of the most popular beaches near Berlin. But now it looked lonely and empty as Manfred and Ariana walked along in the sand.

'Maybe by next summer it will all be over and we can come here and relax.' She smiled at him hopefully and he stooped to pick up a shell. He handed it to her a moment later and she fingered it slowly. It was smooth and pretty and exactly the same blue-grey colour as his eyes.

'I hope that's exactly what we'll do, Ariana.' He smiled as he looked out over the water.

'Can we go to your schloss?'

He looked amused at the matter-of-fact look in her eyes.

'If I have it back by then. Would you like that?'

She nodded at him. 'Very much.'

'Good. Then we'll go there as well.' It was becoming something of a game, as though they could hasten the end of the war and the beginning of their own life by, just wishing the nightmare away and talking of what they would do 'after.'

But the next morning, as she had promised before he went to work, she gathered the things he wanted her to keep in order – the gun, her mother's rings hidden in their hiding place, some food, some money, the address of his French friend – and she went outside to check that the Volkswagen had a full tank of gas. When she went outside, in the distance – but not very distant – she could hear the roar of guns. That afternoon bombs were dropped further into the city. Manfred came home early. As usual during air raids, she was waiting in the cellar with a radio and a book.

'What happened? It said on the radio – '

'Never mind what it said on the radio. You're ready, Ariana?'

She nodded, terrified. 'Yes.'

'I have to go to the Reichstag tonight. They want every available man to defend the building. I don't know how soon I'll be back. You have to be a big girl now. Wait here, but if they take the city, remember all I've told you.'

'How will I get out if they take the city?'

'You will. They'll let refugees out, especially women and children. They always do.'

'And you?'

'I'll find you when it's over.' But then, glancing at his watch, he went upstairs to look for some of his own things, and then he came downstairs again slowly. 'I have to go.' They clung to each other silently for an endless moment, and Ariana wanted to beg him not to leave. To hell with Hitler, with the army, with the Reichstag, with all of it. She only wanted him there with her, where they would both be safe.

'Manfred . . .' From the panic in her voice he knew what was coming. He silenced her with a long tender kiss and shook his head.

'Don't say it, my darling. I have to go now, but I'll be back soon.'

There were tears streaming from her eyes as she walked upstairs with him and stood beside the Mercedes. He turned and wiped her cheeks gently with his hand. 'Don't cry, my darling, I'll be fine. I promise.'

She threw her arms around his neck then. 'If something happened to you, Manfred, I would die.'

'Nothing will happen, I promise.' And then, smiling at her through his own pain, he slipped his signet ring from his finger and put it in the palm of her hand, closing his fingers around hers. 'Take care of that for me until I get back.' She smiled softly at him, and they kissed for a long time before he backed out of the driveway, waved, and drove back to the Reichstag in Berlin.

Day after day she heard the reports on the radio, of battles being waged in every corner of Berlin. By the night of 26 April, she knew that every sector had been affected, Grunewald as well as Wannsee. She herself had not left her cellar in days. She had heard the shots and explosions around her and hadn't dared emerge to the main floor. She knew that the Russians were advancing along the Schonhouserallee up to the Stargarderstrasse, but what she did not know was that everywhere in Berlin people like her were blocked in their cellars, most of them without food, water, or air. There had been no plans made for an evacuation. Even the children were condemned to the same fate as their parents, trapped like rats, waiting for it all to end. And what none of them knew was that the High Command had already fled Berlin.

On the night of 1 May Hitler's death was announced on the radio, which the populace listened to in sombre stupefaction as they waited in their black holes, in basements, trapped beneath buildings, as the battle raged and the city burned. The Allies stepped up their fire to a terrific degree. After Hitler's death was announced the sound of Wagner and Bruckner's Seventh Symphony wafted on the radio into the cellar where Ariana hid. It seemed an odd note as she listened to the gunfire and explosions in the distance, remembering the last time she had heard that symphony, with Gerhard and her father, at the Opera House years before. And now she sat, waiting for it all to end, wondering where Manfred was in the holocaust that was Berlin. Later that night she learned that the entire Goebbels family had committed suicide as well, poisoning all six children.

On 2 May she heard the news of the cease-fire given in three languages on the radio. She did not understand it in Russian, and it seemed unreal to her in German, but when an American voice came over the radio, telling her in halting German that it was all over, at last she understood. But still it made no sense to her – she could still hear guns exploding in the distance, and around her in Wannsee she could hear the battle raging on. The skies were still now; the battle was being waged on foot, as looters attacked the houses around her, although in the heart of the city, the Berliners had left their homes. But in Wannsee, for three more days it continued, and then there was an eerie silence as everything seemed to stop. For the first time in weeks there was no sound at all, except an occasional shout, and then again silence. Ariana sat, waiting, listening, alone in the house, as the sun dawned in the eerie stillness of 5 May.

As soon as it was daylight, she decided to search for Manfred. If the Allies had taken the city, she had to know where he was. He no longer had to defend the Reichstag – there was no longer a Reich to defend.

For the first time in days she climbed the stairs to her bedroom and put on one of the warm, ugly skirts, wool stockings, and her old solid shoes. She pulled on a sweater and grabbed a jacket, shoving Manfred's gun deep into her pocket and concealing it with a glove. She would make no other preparations. She was only going to find Manfred, and if she could not find him, she would come back to the house and wait. A few moments later, outside for the first time in what seemed years, she took a deep gulp of air and was suddenly aware of the acrid smell of smoke. She slipped into her little Volkswagen unseen, turned the ignition, floored the gas.

It took her only twenty minutes to reach the heart of the city, and when she did, she gasped at what she saw. The streets were strewn with debris and rubble, there was no way to get through. At first glance it looked as though there was nothing left. Closer inspection showed that there were still some buildings standing, but none had gone unmarked by the battle that had raged for days. Ariana sat staring with disbelief at what lay around her, and finally she realised how hopeless it would be to try to drive through the mess. Backing her car away slowly, she pulled it into a back alley and as best she could, pulled it out of sight. She pocketed the keys, felt the gun still in its hiding place, pulled her scarf tighter, and got out of the car. All she knew was that she had to find Manfred.

But all she saw as she wandered in the direction of the Reichstag were droves of British and American soldiers hurrying past, and here and there an island of curious Berliners, staring at them from doorways or hurrying away to leave the city as they wondered what would come now. And it was only much later, as she came closer to the Reichstag, that she saw men in German uniforms, huddled together, filthy, exhausted, waiting for buses to come to take them away as Americans stood guarding them, machine-guns pointed, but looking equally filthy and tired. As Ariana watched them and stumbled over the torn sidewalks, she realised to her very soul just how tough a fight it had been. So this was what had happened to her country, this is what the Nazis had brought them in the end. Over 5000 soldiers had attempted to defend the Reichstag and half of them had died. As she stood, not knowing where to turn, a second group of men in German uniforms passed by. Ariana gasped when she recognised Hildebrand, one eye bruised and swollen, his head bleeding through a bandage, his uniform torn, and a vacant look in his eyes. She waved frantically to catch his attention and ran towards him. Surely he would know where Manfred was. She was instantly stopped by two

Americans with guns crossed to block her. She pleaded with them in German. But it was obvious that they would not be moved. She shouted at Hildebrand, urgently calling his name until he turned.

'Where is Manfred? . . . Hildebrand . . . Hildebrand . . . Hildebrand! . . . Where is – ' His eyes darted to the left and when she followed his gaze, she was overcome by the sight. A stack of broken bodies waiting for trucks to haul them away. The uniforms were besmirched beyond recognition, the faces clenched in the rictus of death. She walked slowly towards them, and then, as though she were meant to find him, she saw the familiar face almost at once.

Her heart knew before her mind, and then she stood, rooted, disbelieving, her mouth open, giving birth to a scream that would not come. Even the American soldier couldn't make her leave him. She knelt beside him and wiped the dirt from his face.

She lay there beside him for almost an hour, until suddenly, terrified, she understood what it meant now, and with a last kiss on the sleeping eyes, she touched his face and ran away. She ran as hard and as fast as she could towards the alley where she had left the funny little car. And when she reached it, she found that two men were already working it over, trying to start it without the key. With eyes narrowed and voice trembling, she pulled out the small gun, pointing it at her fellow Berliners until they stood back with hands raised. Quietly she slid into her car then, locked the door, still holding the gun pointed at them with one hand, and with the other she started the car. And then, pushing the car as hard as it was willing, she shot into reverse out of the alley and drove away.

She had nothing to lose now . . . nothing for which to live . . . and as she drove along, she could see the looters, other Germans, some soldiers – some even were Russians. Her city was about to be dragged over the coals again. And if they killed her, so be it, she didn't really care now. It didn't matter if they killed her or not. But she had promised Manfred she would try to get to safety. And because of that, she would try to get out.

She drove as quickly as she could back to Wannsee, put the few things she had ready into the car. Some cooked potatoes, some bread, a little bit of stew meat. And then she took the package with the money, the address of the Frenchman, and the book concealing the two rings. Her engagement ring from Manfred she left on her finger – let someone dare to try and take it from her – along with her gold band and his signet. She would have killed them before they'd got the rings off her. Her eyes hard, her mouth set, she set the gun in her lap and once more started the car; and then, with a last look over her shoulder, she glanced at the house where Manfred had first brought her, and great anguished sobs tore at her heart. He was gone now, the man who had saved her . . . gone forever. At the pain of that realisation, Ariana thought she would die. She had slipped among her papers the only letter he'd ever written her, a love letter filled with tenderness and promise that he had written after the first time they'd made love. And she had also brought with her some pictures – of them at their first party together at the Opera House, some more from the ball at the Royal Palace, a few others from the Tiergarten, and even those of his children and his dead wife. Ariana would not leave those pictures for anyone else's eyes. They were hers, as would be Manfred, for the rest of her life.

Chapter 25

Along with thousands of others fleeing – on foot, riding bicycles, and now and then in cars – Ariana left the city and headed west. The Allies didn't try to stop the women and children and old people who were leaving the city like frightened rats. Ariana couldn't bear the agony of what she was seeing, and again and again she stopped to give someone a hand, until she knew that she could stop no more. Each time she did, there were attempts to take the car from her, and only at the last did she agree to give two old women a ride. They were silent and grateful, they lived in Dahlem, and all they wanted was to get out of town. Their store on the Kurfürstendamm had been destroyed earlier that morning, their husbands were dead, and now they were afraid for their lives.

'The Americans will kill us all, fräulein,' the older of the two women told her, crying. Ariana didn't think so, but she was too tired to argue with either of them. She was too anguished even to talk. But she knew that if the Americans truly wanted to kill them, they had plenty of opportunity, as the refugees thronged the roads. Driving along beside them was also slow going for Ariana, but at last she was able to reach some familiar back roads. And in the end she managed to get as far as Kassel, some 200 miles from Berlin, where she finally ran out of gas.

She had long since dropped off her passengers in Kalbe, where they had cousins and had been received with open arms and tears. As Ariana watched them, she felt a pang of envy. Unlike these old women, she had no one now. And after she had left them, she had driven on mindlessly until the car came to a slow, grinding halt. The jerry can in the back seat was empty. She had come halfway from Berlin to Saarbrücken, the town north of Strasbourg where Manfred had wanted her to try to cross into France. But she had another 200 miles until she reached it. She sat there for a moment thinking of the sea of refugees swarming out of Berlin. She was just another face among them now, shuffling towards nowhere, with no friends and no possessions, and nowhere to go. Fighting back tears as she looked over her shoulder at the lost safety of the little grey car, she tightened her grip on her bundles and began the long walk towards France.

It took her two days to walk the forty miles to Marburg, and from there an old country doctor let her drive with him to Mainz. They made little conversation as they rode along for three hours. The trip covered some eighty miles, and when they reached Mainz, he looked at her sympathetically and offered to take her to Neunkirchen – it was on his way after all. Gratefully she accepted, her mind still whirling from the night before.

In Neunkirchen, Ariana thanked him, staring at him blindly and somehow wanting to say more, but in the endless hours that she had driven and then walked and then finally ridden beside him, something deep inside her had frozen into place, a sense of loss, of broken hope, of deep despair. She was no longer even sure of why she was running, except that Manfred had told her to and she was his wife. He had told her to go to Paris, so she would. Maybe the friend in Paris would have the answers; perhaps he'd tell her that what she had seen in the dawn three days before had been a lie. Perhaps Manfred would be there in Paris, waiting for her to arrive.

'Fräulein?'

The old man had seen the ring but he found it difficult to believe that she was really married. She looked so young. Perhaps she had worn it for protection. Not that it would protect her from the soldiers or that she needed that kind of protection from him. He smiled gently at her as she pulled her little bundle off the seat.

'Thank you, sir.' She looked at him for a long, empty moment.

'You'll be all right?' She nodded in answer. 'Would you like a ride back from Neunkirchen in a few days? I'll be going back to Marburg.' But she would not be going back again. For her it was strictly a one-way journey and her eyes were filled with the tragedy of last goodbyes.

Quietly she shook her head. 'I'm going to stay with my mother. Thank you.' She didn't want to admit to him that she was trying to flee the country. She trusted no one now. Not even this old man.

'*Bitte.*' She shook his hand politely, stood back, and he drove off. Now all she had to do was to get the twenty miles to Saarbrücken, and then another ten miles to the French border and she'd be all right. But this time there was no old man driving, and it took her three long days to make the trek. Her legs were aching, she was tired and cold and hungry. She had run out of food on the first day. Twice she had seen frightened farmers; one had given her two apples, the other had only shaken his head. But at last she reached the border, six days after her journey had begun. She had done it . . . done it . . . done it . . . All she had to do was crawl through the wire and into France. She did it slowly, with her heart pounding, wondering if someone would see her and shoot her on the spot. But it seemed as though the war was truly over – no one cared if one filthy, exhausted young girl in a torn skirt and sweater crawled through the wire, scratching her face and arms and body. Ariana looked around in exhaustion and murmured, 'Welcome to France,' before she lay down to rest.

She awoke some six hours later, to the sound of church bells pealing, her body aching and agonisingly stiff. For the girl who had lived under her father's kind wing in Grunewald and then under Manfred's protection for the past eight months, this was not what she had been prepared for. She began walking again and it was half an hour later that she fainted on the road. An old woman found her two hours later and thought that she was dead. Only a slight stirring beneath the sweater, as her heart beat softly still, led the old woman to wonder, and she hurried home to find her daughter-in-law, and together they dragged her inside. They touched and they prodded and they held her and when she awoke at last she vomited horribly, and she ran a fever for the next two days. At times they thought that she would die there with them. All the old woman knew about the girl was that she was German, for she had found the German gun and the Reichsmarks among the currency she carried. But the old woman did not hold it against her; her own son had gone to work for the Nazis in Vichy four years before. One did what one had to in wartime, and if this girl was running now, the old woman was willing to help her. The war was over, after all. They nursed her for two more days while she lay and vomited, and then at last Ariana insisted that she was well enough to go. She spoke to them in their own language, and with her cultured accent and fluent knowledge of French, she could just as well have been from Strasbourg as Berlin.

The old woman looked at her wisely. 'Do you have far to go?'

'Paris.'

'That's more than two hundred miles. You can't walk the whole way, you know. Not in the condition you're in.' Already Ariana was showing signs of malnutrition and she figured she must have got a concussion when she'd fallen, else she wouldn't have vomited so violently or had so much pain afterwards in her eyes. And she looked some ten years older than she had when the journey had begun.

'I can try. Someone may give me a ride.'

'In what? The Germans took all our cars and trucks, and what they didn't take, the Americans did. They're all stationed in Nancy, and they've already been up this way to get more cars.' But her daughter-in-law remembered that the old priest was going up to Metz at nightfall. He had a horse he used for his travels. And if Ariana was lucky, he'd give her a ride. As it turned out, Ariana was lucky, and the priest took her along.

They reached Metz by morning, and after the long hours of jolting over the countryside, Ariana was desperately sick again. Too sick to eat, too sick to move, she had to nonetheless. From Metz she had to get another forty miles to Bar-le-Duc. She set out once again, walking, this time praying that someone in a truck would come along, and after the first four miles her prayers were answered – a man with a horse cart happened by. He was neither old nor young. Neither hostile nor friendly. She flagged him down, offered some French money, and climbed into his cart. Four hours she sat beside him, with the spring sun beating down on her head, as the man sat beside her in silence and the horse ploughed on. It was sunset when the man finally halted.

'Are we at Bar-le-Duc?' Ariana looked at him in surprise, but he shook his head firmly.

'No, but I'm tired. And so is my horse.' As it so happened, she was also exhausted, but she was anxious to continue on. 'I'll stop for a while and rest, and then we continue. It's all right with you?' She didn't have much choice in the matter. He had already spread his jacket out on the ground and was preparing to devour some bread and cheese. He ate it hungry and roughly, offering none to Ariana, who felt too tired and sick to eat, let alone watch him eat. She lay down quietly on the grass some distance from him, her head on her precious bundle, and she closed her eyes. The grass was soft and warm beside her from the bright May sun that had pounded down on it all day, and she felt herself doze off in exhaustion. It was then she felt the man put his hand up her skirt. He grabbed her roughly, letting himself down hard on top of her, at the same time pushing up her skirt and pulling at her pants, while in astonishment she pushed at him, fighting wildly and flailing at his face with both her hands. But he was indifferent to her lack of interest in his seduction; he pushed hard at her with his hands and body, and then with something hard and warm she felt pulsing between her legs, and then just before he could enter her there was a stirring, a shout, and a shot fired in the air. The man jumped back, startled and, much to his chagrin, fully exposed. Ariana quickly leaped to her feet and then stumbled suddenly as a wave of dizziness overtook her and she almost fell. Two strongs hands took hold of her shoulders and she was gently set back on the ground.

'Are you all right?' She hung her head and nodded, not wanting to see his face, and also not wanting him to see hers. The voice that had saved her spoke to her in English, and she knew that now she had reached the Americans' hands. Thinking that she didn't understand him, he spoke to her then in awkward French. She forced herself not to smile at him when finally she looked up. It seemed funny that he so easily believed her French.

'Thank you.' He had a friendly face and lots of soft brown hair, curled beneath a helmet, and in the distance she could see three more men and a jeep.

'Did he hurt you?' he asked her firmly, and she shook her head. Without discussing matters further, the young American in the helmet took a long swing and hit the Frenchman squarely in the face. 'That ought to take care of him.' What pissed him off was that they were always being accused of raping the locals, when in point of fact the sons of bitches were raping their own. And then he looked down at the tiny blonde girl again as she stood up and shook the grass and dust from her fine gold hair. 'Do you need a ride somewhere?'

'Yes.' She smiled weakly. 'To Paris.' It was crazy even to be standing here talking to him.

'Would you settle for Châlons-sur-Marne? It's about a hundred miles outside Paris, and from there I ought to be able to find someone to drive you the rest of the way.'

Was it possible he would help her get to Paris? She stared at him as tears rolled down her cheeks.

'Okay? Would that help?' His eyes were gentle and his smile widened as she nodded her head. 'Come on, over here.'

The Frenchman was still dusting himself off as Ariana followed the American to the jeep. They were young and raucous and happy as they drove along, the four young men staring curiously at silent Ariana, crushed between them; their eyes would touch on the gold hair, the delicate face, the sad eyes, and then they would shrug and go on talking, or now and then break into an off-colour song. The young man who had saved her from the Frenchman wore the name Henderson on the pocket of his fatigues, and it was he who arranged for two other soldiers to drive her into Paris, an hour after they arrived at Châlons. 'You'll be okay with them, miss,' he reassured her in his clumsy French and she put out a hand.

'Thank you, sir.'

'You're welcome, ma'am.' She turned to follow the two soldiers, who were driving to Paris on some mission that involved two colonels who apparently sent each other messages at least three times a day. But it wasn't of the colonels that Henderson was thinking. He was thinking of the look of despair and desperation that he had seen in that tiny pale face. He had seen that look before in wartime. And he knew something else from looking at that face with the sunken blue eyes, the taut skin, the dark circles. That girl was sick as hell.

Chapter 26

The two young American soldiers explained to Ariana that they were going to an address on the rue de la Pompe. Did she know where she was going? She pulled out the paper Manfred had given her. The address was on the rue de Varenne.

'I think that's on the Left Bank, but I'm not sure.' As it turned out, it was. Paris was also showing signs of the war, but it was in no way as shocking as Berlin had been. More than damage by bombs, Paris had suffered at the hands of the Germans, who had attempted to remove everything available and ship it back to the Pinakothek in Berlin.

An old man with a bicycle explained to the two young soldiers where it was Ariana wanted to go and then volunteered gamely to lead the way. It was then that Ariana got her first view of Paris since she'd been there as a child with her father and brother. But she was too tired to appreciate the sights, or even the beauty of the city. The Arc de Triomphe, the Place de la Concorde, the Pont Alexandre III whizzed by her. She simply closed her eyes and rumbled along in the jeep, hearing the old man shout instructions now and then and the young American at the wheel shout his thanks. At last they reached the address and Ariana opened her eyes. She had no choice but to step down then, though she would have preferred infinitely to sleep in the back of their car. In the end her flight from Berlin had taken her a full nine days, and now here she was in Paris, with no idea why she had come or what this man she was looking for would be like. Perhaps he was even dead by now. It seemed to her that everyone was. And as she stood outside his huge ornate doorway, she longed more than ever for the cosy little house in Wannsee she and Manfred had shared. But there was nothing there any longer, she had to remind herself. Nothing at all. Manfred was gone.

'*Oui, mademoiselle.*' A fat, white-haired old woman swung open the main door, revealing a handsome courtyard on the other side. Across it was a lovely eighteenth-century *hôtel particulier* and a short flight of marble stairs. '*Vous désirez?*' The house lights glowed invitingly in the dark.

'Monsieur Jean-Pierre de Saint Marne.' Ariana answered her in French, and for a long moment the woman stared her down, as though she didn't want to understand. But Ariana persisted. 'Is he away from home?'

'No.' The woman shook her head slowly. 'But the war is over, mademoiselle. There is no need to trouble Monsieur de Saint Marne any more.' She was tired of these people who had come calling and begging and entreating for so long. Let them go to the Americans now. They would kill Monsieur with their exhausting tales, their terrors, their emotions. For how long would this imposition continue to go on? Preying on the poor man like that. Watching her face, Ariana did not understand.

'I . . . I'm sorry . . . my husband and Monsieur de Saint Marne were old friends. He suggested that I look Monsieur de Saint Marne up when I got here . . .' She faltered and the old woman shook her head.

'That's what they all say.' And this one didn't look any better than the others. Sickly, skinny, deathly pale, in torn clothes and worn-out shoes, with only that tiny bundle in her hands. Lord, she looked as though she hadn't bathed in at least a week. And just because Monsieur had money, there was no reason for all this refugee riffraff to prey on him. 'I'll see if Monsieur is at home.' But the handsome Rolls in the courtyard suggested that her master was indeed in. 'Wait here.' Ariana sank down gratefully on a narrow bench in the courtyard, shivering slightly in the chill night air. But she was used to being cold and tired and hungry. Had she ever been otherwise? It was difficult to remember as she closed her eyes. It seemed hours later that someone was shaking her and she looked up to see the old woman, her lips pursed in disapproval, but nodding her head. 'He'll see you now.' Ariana felt a wave of relief overcome her, not at the prospect so much of seeing him, but only because she would have to go no further that night. At least she hoped not. She didn't care if he made her sleep in the attic, but she didn't think she had the strength to go another step before morning. She hoped desperately that he'd let her stay.

Following the old woman, she climbed the short flight of marble stairs to the main doorway, and a sombre-looking butler opened the door and stepped aside. For an instant he reminded Ariana of Berthold, but this man had kinder eyes. He looked down at her for a brief moment and then, without speaking a single word, turned on his heel and disappeared. With that the old woman shook her head again in patent disapproval and muttered to Ariana in the front hall. 'He's gone to get the Master. They'll send for you in a minute. I'll go now.'

'Thank you.' But the old woman cared not two pins for Ariana's thank you.

The butler returned. She was led down a handsomely appointed hallway, draped in velvets and punctuated at regular intervals with portraits of the Saint Marne ancestors. Ariana stared at them blindly as she walked along, until at last they reached a large doorway and the butler flung open a single mirrored door. What she saw inside the room he had thus opened reminded her very much of Berlin's Royal Palace, with cherubs and gilt panels, inlays and marquetries and endless mirrors over white marble mantelpieces, and in the midst of all the splendour was a single serious-looking man, of Manfred's age but slighter build, with deep, worried furrows running between his eyes. He sat watching her from a wheelchair in the centre of the room.

'Monsieur de Saint Marne?' She felt almost too tired for the etiquette that seemed required by the circumstances and the room.

'Yes.' He made no move in the wheelchair, but his face bid her approach. He turned welcomingly towards her, his eyes still serious, yet somehow warm. 'That's who I am. Now, who are you?'

'Ariana . . .' She hesitated for a moment. 'Mrs Manfred von Tripp.' She said it quietly, looking into the gentle eyes that watched her. 'Manfred told me that if Berlin fell, I was to come here. I'm sorry, I hope that . . .' The wheels approached her swiftly as she struggled on. He stopped very near to her and held out a hand.

'Welcome, Ariana. Please sit down.' His face had not yet broken into a joyful welcome. He felt certain that this girl had more to tell him, and he wasn't sure at all that it would be good news.

She sat down quietly, looking into the Frenchman's face. In an odd way he was good-looking, though so totally unlike Manfred that it was almost difficult to imagine that they had been friends. As she sat looking at her husband's schoolmate, Ariana found herself lonelier than ever for the man she would never see again.

'How long did it take you to get here?' His eyes searched her face as he asked her. He had seen so many like her before. Sick, tired, broken, afraid.

She sighed. 'Nine days.'

'You came how?'

'By car, by horse, by foot, by jeep . . .' *By barbed wire, by prayer, by almost being raped by a disgusting man* . . . Her eyes stared emptily at Saint Marne. And then he asked the question he had wanted to ask her from the first.

'And Manfred?' He said it very softly, and she dropped her eyes.

Her voice was nothing more than a whisper in the grandiose room. 'He's dead. He died . . . in the . . . fall of Berlin.' She looked up at him then squarely. 'But he had told me to come to you here. I don't know why I left Germany, except that now I have nothing left there anyway. I had to go.'

'Your family?' His eyes seemed inured to the bad news he had just had about his friend.

In answer to his question, she sighed jaggedly into the silent room. 'I believe that my father is dead. My mother died before the war. But my brother . . . he may be alive still. In Switzerland. My father took him there last August to avoid the draft. My father never returned from Switzerland, and I never heard from Gerhard. I don't know if he's alive or not.'

'Gerhard was to stay?' She nodded. 'And was your father meant to come back?'

'Yes, to get me. But . . . our nurse – that is, they called the Nazis. They took me and held me for ransom. They thought my father would be back, too.' She looked up at him quietly. 'After a month, they let me go. Manfred and I . . .' She stopped before the tears came.

Jean-Pierre sighed and pulled a piece of paper towards him on the desk. 'I assume this is why Manfred sent you to me.'

Ariana looked confused then. 'I think he only sent me to you because you were his friend and he thought that I'd be safe here.'

Jean-Pierre de Saint Marne smiled tiredly. 'Manfred was indeed a very good friend. But a wise one as well. He knows what I've been up to all during the war. I kept in touch. Discreetly, of course.' He waved vaguely to the wheelchair. 'As you can see, I am somewhat . . . hampered . . . but I have managed very nicely in spite of it. I have become something of a philanthropist, shall we say, bringing families back together, sometimes in other countries, and arranging for "vacations" in warmer climates.'

She nodded at the euphemisms. 'In other words, you've been helping refugees to escape.'

'Mostly. And now I'm going to spend the next few years attempting to reunite families. That ought to keep me busy for a while.'

'Then can you help me find my brother?'

'I'll try. Give me whatever information you have, and I'll see what I can discover. But I'm afraid you have to think of more than that, Ariana. What about you? Where will you go now? Home to Germany?'

She shook her head slowly and then looked up at him blankly. 'I have no one there.'

'You can stay here for a while.' But she knew also that that would not be a permanent arrangement, and then where would she go? She hadn't thought of it at all, hadn't thought of anything.

Saint Marne nodded quietly with sympathetic understanding and made several notes. 'All right, in the morning I will see what I can do for you. You must tell me everything that you know to help me find Gerhard. If that's what you want me to do.' She nodded slowly, scarcely able to absorb it all. His presence, the room, this offer to help her find Gerhard. 'And in the meantime – ' he smiled gently – 'you must do something else.'

'What's that?' She tried to return the smile but it was an enormous effort just to look him in the eye and not fall asleep in his intolerably comfortable chair.

'What you must do now, dear Ariana, is get some rest. You look very, very tired.'

'I am.'

They all looked like that when they got to him, exhausted, wounded, frightened. She would look better in a day or two, he thought. What a pretty little thing she was, and how unlike Manfred to marry someone so frail, so ethereal, so young. Marianna had been a good deal more solid. First Jean-Pierre was shocked to realise that Ariana was Manfred's new wife. Somehow, he hadn't expected Manfred to marry. He had been so distraught when his wife and children had died. But here was this girl. And he could easily understand Manfred's passion. She was so elfenlike, so pretty, even in her torn, filthy clothes. He would have liked to have seen her with Manfred in better times. And after he was once again alone in the drawing room, he mused to himself about his old friend. Why had he really sent her to him? To wait for him as she had told him, if he had managed to survive the fighting in Berlin? Or did he want something more? Some protection for her? Help in her search for her brother? What? Somehow he felt as though sending her had been a kind of message, and he desperately wanted to decipher what it was. Perhaps, he thought to himself as he sat looking out the window, in time it would become clear.

And in her room, with the view of the pretty cobbled courtyard, Ariana was already fast asleep. She had been put to bed by a kindly middle-aged woman in full skirts and an apron, who had turned back the covers, exposing thick blankets, a comforter, and clean sheets. It seemed a hundred years since Ariana had seen anything so lovely, and without another thought of Jean-Pierre or her brother or even Manfred, she climbed into the bed and slid into a deep sleep.

Chapter 27

The next morning Ariana joined Jean-Pierre after breakfast. It was clear in the light of day that she was ill. She sat in his study, her face tinged a sickly green.

'Were you sick before you left Berlin?'

'No, I wasn't.'

'You may just be worn out from the trip – and your loss.' He had seen the reaction to grief too many times before. Sweating, vomiting, dizziness. He had seen grown men faint from the sheer relief of at last reaching the safety of his home. But he was less concerned with her physical state than her emotional state right now. 'Later I'll have a doctor come to see you. But first, I want to find out everything I can about your brother. His description, height, size, weight. Then where was he going, what was he wearing, what were his exact plans. Who did he know?' He faced her squarely and one by one she answered all his questions, explaining in detail the plan that her father intended to follow, walking from the train station at Lörrach across the Swiss border to Basel, where they would take another train to Zurich, and then her father would come back for her. 'And in Zurich, what?'

'Nothing. He was simply to wait.'

'And after that what were the three of you going to do?'

'Go on to Lausanne, to friends of my father.'

'Did the friends know you were coming?'

'I'm not sure. Papa may not have wanted to call them from his house or the office. He may have just planned to call them when he got to Zurich.'

'Would he have left your brother with their number?'

'I'm sure he would.'

'And you never heard from any of them, not the friends, your brother, your father?'

She shook her head slowly. 'No one. And then Manfred said that he was certain that my father was dead.'

He could hear in her voice that she had already made peace with that. Now it was the losing of Manfred that she couldn't bear.

'But my brother . . .' Her eyes looked up pleadingly and he shook his head.

'We'll see. I'll make some calls. Why don't you go back to bed. I'll let you know as soon as I hear anything at all.'

'You'll come and wake me?'

'It's a promise.' But in the end he didn't bother. He found everything there was to learn within the hour, and it wasn't enough to bother waking Ariana up for. As it turned out, she slept through till nightfall, and when Lisette told him she was finally sitting up in bed and looking better, he wheeled himself into her room. 'Hello, Ariana, how do you feel?'

'Better.' But she didn't look it. She looked worse. Paler, green, and it was obvious that she had to fight each moment not to be ill. 'No news?'

He paused only for an instant, but right away she knew. She looked at him more intently and he held up a hand. 'Ariana, don't. There is really no news at all. I will tell you what I found out, but it is less than nothing. The boy is gone.'

'Dead?' Her voice trembled. She had always hoped that he might still be alive. Despite what Manfred thought.

'Maybe. I don't know. This is what I learned. I called the man whose name you gave me. He and his wife were killed in an automobile accident exactly two days before your father and the boy left Berlin. The couple had no children, the house was sold, and neither the new owners of the house nor the man's associates in the bank ever heard from your brother. I talked to an officer of the bank who knew your father of course, but he never heard from him. It's possible that he left the boy and came for you, and that your father got killed somewhere on the way back. In which case, eventually the boy would have called the name your father gave him and discovered that they were both dead, husband and wife. Then I assume he would have either contacted the bank where the man worked or figured he was on his own, rolled up his sleeves, and got to work somewhere, simply to survive. But there is no trace of him, Ariana, not in Zurich, not with the central police, not with the bankers in Lausanne. There is not even a trace of Max Thomas.' She had given him that name, too. He looked at her unhappily. He had tried desperately all day. But there was nothing. No trace at all. 'I tried all the usual routes as well as some of my better contacts. No one ever came across the boy. That may be a good sign or a very bad one.'

'What do you think, Jean-Pierre?'

'That he and your father died together, between Lörrach and Basel.' He knew by her silence that she was paralysed with grief. He kept talking to keep contact with her. To pull her through. 'Ariana, we must go on.'

'But to where? . . . To what? . . . And why?' She sobbed angrily at him. 'I don't want to go on. Not now. There's no one left. No one but me.'

'That's enough. That's all I have now.'

'You, too?' She stared at him and blew her nose as he nodded quietly.

'My wife was Jewish. When the Germans occupied Paris, they took her and – ' his voice caught strangely and he turned the wheelchair away from Ariana – 'our little girl.' Ariana closed her eyes tightly for a moment. She suddenly felt desperately ill. She couldn't bear it anymore. The endless losses, the immeasurable pain. This man, and Manfred, and Max, and she herself, all of them losing people they loved, children and wives and brothers and fathers. She felt the room spinning, herself spinning; she lay down in a feeble attempt to anchor herself. He wheeled to her side quietly and gently stroked her hair. 'I know, *ma petite*, I know.' He didn't even tell her about the one lead he had had. It would only have made the bitter truth harder to bear. There had been a clerk in a hotel in Zurich who thought he remembered a boy like the one Jean-Pierre described. He had struck up a conversation with the boy and remembered he had said he was waiting for his relatives. He had been at the hotel alone for two weeks, waiting. But then the clerk remembered that he had met up with the relatives and left. It couldn't have been Gerhard. He had no relatives left. Ariana's father would have told her if this had been part of his plan. It was clear he was a very thorough man. The clerk remembered the boy going off with a couple and their daughter. So it wasn't Gerhard after all. And that had been all. There were no other leads, no other hopeful signs. The boy was gone, and like thousands of others in Europe, Ariana had no one left.

After a long time Jean-Pierre spoke to her again. 'I have an idea for you. If you're brave enough. It's up to you. But if I were young enough, I'd do it. To get away from all of these countries that have been destroyed, twisted, broken, bombed. I'd go away and start all over again, and that's what I think you should do.'

She lifted her head and wiped her eyes. 'But where?' It sounded terrifying. She didn't want to go anywhere. She wanted to stay anchored, hiding in the past forever.

'To the States.' He said it very quietly. 'There is a refugee ship leaving tomorrow. It's been arranged by an organisation out of New York. Their people will meet the ship when it docks and help you to relocate.'

'What about my father's house in Grunewald? Don't you think I could get that back?'

'Do you really want it? Could you live there? If you could ever get it back, which I doubt.' The truth of his words struck her with force. And then suddenly as he spoke to her, he understood what had been Manfred's message. This was why Ariana had been sent to her husband's boyhood friend. He had known that Jean-Pierre would come up with a solution. And now he knew that this was the right one.

The one question he had was if she was well enough to travel. But he knew from long experience with the people he had helped in the last six years, it would be months before she was herself again. She had simply lost too much, and the nine days of mad running across Germany, after the shock of seeing Manfred dead, had been the final straw. That was all that ailed her really, fatigue, exhaustion, hunger, too much walking, too much sorrow, too much loss. There was also a problem in that there might not be another ship for a long time. 'Will you do it?' Jean-Pierre's eyes never left hers. 'It could be a whole new life.'

'But what about Gerhard? You don't think that maybe he went to Lausanne after all? Or stayed somewhere in Zurich, that if I got there, maybe I'd find him?' But the hope was gone now from her eyes, too.

'I'm as good as certain, Ariana. There is absolutely no trace of him, and if he were alive, there would be. I think it happened as I told you. He and your father must both have been killed.' She shook her head slowly, letting the finality of it sink in. She had lost them all. She could let herself lie down and die, too – or keep going.

Fighting back the waves of dizziness and nausea, she looked at Jean-Pierre sitting in his wheelchair beside her bed and nodded. Some instinct deep inside her made her say it, and to her ears the voice didn't sound like her own. 'All right. I'll go.'

Chapter 28

Jean-Pierre's large black Rolls pulled sedately into Le Harve harbour. Ariana sat wanly in the back of the car. They barely spoke all the way from Paris. The roads were cluttered with trucks and jeeps and small convoys conveying equipment between Paris and the port. But the situation around Paris had settled down nicely, and apart from the drab colour of the army vehicles, the roads looked almost normal as they drove along.

Jean-Pierre had watched her quietly during most of the journey, and for the first time in his years of assisting the homeless refugees, broken and frightened, he felt at a loss for words that would offer comfort. The look in her eyes said so clearly that nothing anyone could say would ease her terrible burden.

As they drove along, the reality of her situation was hitting her. There was no one left in the world she cherished, no one to turn to; no one could ever share a memory of what had been her past, no one would ever understand without translation, have memories of her brother, her father, the house in Grunewald . . . her mother . . . Fräulein Hedwig . . . the summers at the lake . . . or the laughter behind Berthold's back at the table . . . No one who would have smelled Gerhard's chemistry set as it burst into flame. Nor would there be anyone who had known Manfred – not in this new world she was going to. There would be no one who understood what it would be like to be caged in that cell. Attacked by Hildebrand . . . and then saved by Manfred, spirited away to Wannsee. With whom could she possibly share the memory of the 'stew' she had made from liver sausage, the colour of the bedspread in that first room – or the look in his eyes when he had first made love to her – or the touch of his face when she had found him at last outside the Reichstag in Berlin. They would never know anything of the past year of her life, or the past twenty, and as she rolled along beside Saint Marne on the way to the ship that would take her away forever, she couldn't believe she would ever share herself with anyone again.

'Ariana?' He called her with his deep voice and French accent. He had barely dared speak to her that morning until they left for Le Harve. She'd been too ill to get up. On the day before, she had fainted twice. Jean-Pierre noticed that now she seemed a little stronger, and he prayed silently that she was well enough to survive the trip to New York. As long as she made it, they'd let her into the States. The United States had opened her arms to the refugees of war. 'Ariana?' He spoke to her again gently, and slowly she returned from her distant thoughts.

'Yes?'

'Were you and Manfred together for very long?'

'Almost a year.'

He nodded slowly. 'I suppose right now that a year must seem to you like a lifetime. But – ' a small smile attempted to offer her hope – 'at twenty, a year seems enormous. Twenty years from now, it won't seem very long.'

Her voice was frigid when she answered. 'Are you suggesting I'll forget him?' She was outraged that Saint Marne would say it, but sadly he shook his head.

'No, my dear, you won't forget him.' For an instant he thought of his wife and daughter, lost only three years before, and the pain of it seared his heart. 'No, you won't forget. But I think in time the pain will be duller. It won't be as unbearable as it is for you now.' He put an arm around her shoulder. 'Be grateful, Ariana, you're still young. For you, nothing is over.' He tried to warm her, but there was nothing hopeful he could read in her great big blue eyes.

When at last they reached Le Harve, he didn't leave the car to accompany her to the boat. It was too complicated to get his wheelchair out of the trunk and have the chauffeur help him get into it. There was nothing more he could do for her now. He had arranged passage to New York, where he knew she would be cared for by the New York Women's Relief Organisation.

He reached out a hand to her through the open window, as she stood there with the small cardboard suitcase his housekeeper had brought up from the basement and packed with some of his wife's clothes, probably none of which fit. She was so tiny and childlike as she stood there, her eyes so huge in the unbelievably finely carved face, that suddenly he wondered if he had done the wrong thing in arranging her passage. Perhaps she was really too frail to make the trip. But she had managed the 600 miles from Berlin, on foot and by car and by horse and cart and jeep, over nine treacherous days – surely she could manage yet another week to cross the ocean. It would be worth it, just to put that much distance between herself and the nightmare, just to find a new life in a new land. 'You'll let me know how you are, won't you?' He felt like a father banishing a treasured child to a school in a foreign land.

Slowly a wintry smile came to her mouth and then to the blue eyes. 'Yes, I'll let you know. And Jean-Pierre . . . thank you . . . for all that you've done.'

He nodded. 'I only wish . . . that things could have been different.' He wished that Manfred had been standing there at the side of his bride.

But she had understood his meaning, and she nodded. 'So do I.'

And then in a gentle voice he whispered, '*Au revoir*, Ariana. Travel safely.'

Her eyes thanked him one last time, and she turned towards the gangway to the ship she'd be taking. She turned back one last time, waved solemnly, and whispered, '*Adieu*' with tears streaming from her eyes.

Book Three

ARIANA

NEW YORK

On the last voyage there had been three sisters who had lived half in steerage half in an extra cramped below the quarters, giving up to the nurse. But only five of the women survived the journey and the last four crews were limp— nine at Nancy Townsend's with the women passengers aboard. She knew that not all of them would reach New York. Often

Chapter 29

The SS *Pilgrim's Pride* was appropriately named. She looked as though she had been used by them long before they had switched their business to the *Mayflower*. She was small, narrow, dark, and smelled of mould. But she was seaworthy. And she was filled to the gills. The *Pilgrim's Pride* had been bought jointly by several American rescue organisations and was run primarily by the New York Woman's Relief Organisation, which thus far had overseen four trips of this nature, bringing more than a thousand refugees from war-torn Europe to New York. They had provided sponsors for everyone through their assorted sister organisations across the United States, and they had hired a decent crew to make the journey, bringing men, women, children, and the aged from the wasteland of Europe to their new lives in the States.

The people travelling on the ship were all in fairly poor condition and had reached Paris from other countries as well as other regions of France itself. Some had travelled on foot for weeks and months; others, like some of the children, had been roaming, homeless, for years. None of them had seen real food in longer than they could remember, and many of them had never even seen the sea before, let alone sailed it in a ship.

The Relief Organisation had not been able to find a doctor to sign on with their ship to make these crossings, but they had hired a remarkably competent young nurse. On each crossing so far, her services had been vital. She had already delivered nine babies, assisted at several grim miscarriages, four heart attacks, and six deaths. So Nancy Townsend, as ship's nurse, had to contend with homesickness, fatigue, hunger, deprivation, and the desperate needs of people who had suffered the price of war for much too long.

On the last voyage there had been four women who had been held in jail outside Paris for almost two years before the Americans arrived to set them free. But only two of the women had lived through the sea voyage to New York. Each time, as Nancy Townsend watched the passengers boarding, she knew that not all of them would reach New York. Often it was easy to spot which were the strongest and which were those who never should have undertaken the trip. But often, too, there were those who seemed sturdy and then suddenly gave way on this last leg of their escape. It would seem that the tiny blonde woman on the lower deck, in a room with nine other women, was one of those.

A young girl from the Pyrenees had come running to find Nancy, screaming that someone was dying right below her bunk. When Nancy saw the girl, she knew she was dying of seasickness, hunger, dehydration, pain, delirium – it was impossible to tell what had pushed her over the edge, but her eyes were rolled back in her head, and when Townsend touched her, the girl's forehead was hot and parched with a raging fever.

Taking her pulse, the nurse knelt quietly beside her and motioned to the others to stand back. They had been staring at Ariana in discomfort, wondering if she was going to die in their room that night. It had already happened to them two days earlier, on their fourth day out from Le Havre. A small rail-thin Jewish girl who had travelled from Bergen-Belsen to Paris had not survived the last leg of her trip.

Twenty minutes after she had first seen her in the overcrowded cabin, Nurse Townsend had Ariana moved to one of the two isolation rooms. It was there that the fever raged higher and that she developed fierce cramps in her arms and legs. Nancy thought she might go into convulsions, but she never did, and on the last day of their voyage, the fever finally broke. Ariana was vomiting constantly, and each time she had attempted to sit up in bed, her blood pressure dropped so low that she fainted. She was able to remember almost none of her English, and she spoke to the nurse constantly in desperate, frightened German, none of which Nancy understood except the names that had recurred over and over ... Manfred ... Papa ... Gerhard ... Hedwig . . . again and again she had shrieked, '*Nein*, Hedwig!' when she had unseeingly looked into the eyes of the American nurse. And when she sobbed late into the night, it was impossible to console her. At times Nancy Townsend wondered if this girl was so sick because she no longer wanted to be alive. She wouldn't have been the first.

Ariana looked at her blankly on the last morning; her eyes were less feverish but filled with pain.

'I hope you're feeling better.' Nancy Townsend smiled gently.

Ariana nodded vaguely and went back to sleep. She never even saw the ship pull into New York harbour or the Statue of Liberty with the sun glinting gold on its arm holding the torch. Those who could stood on the decks and cheered wildly, tears streaming down their faces, their arms locked around each other – they had made it at last! But of all this Ariana knew nothing. She knew nothing at all until the special immigration officer came downstairs after they docked. He greeted the nurse quietly and read her reports. Generally they were able to send most of the passengers on to their sponsors, but this was one of those who would have to wait. Given the delirium and the fever, they wanted to be sure that she carried no disease. The immigration official praised the nurse for putting the girl in isolation and then, looking down at the sleeping girl and then at the uniformed woman, he raised an eyebrow in open question.

'What do you think it is?'

The nurse gestured silently towards the corridor and they left her sleeping. 'I can't tell you for certain, but it could be that in some way she's been tortured, or maybe been in one of the camps. I just don't know. You'll have to watch her.' He nodded in answer, sympathetically glancing through the open door.

'No open wounds, infections, obvious lesions?'

'Nothing I could see. But she vomited all the way across the Atlantic. I think you ought to keep an eye on that. There could be some internal damage. I'm sorry – ' she looked at him apologetically – 'I'm just not sure about this one at all.'

'Don't worry, Miss Townsend. That's why you're turning her over to us. She must have kept you pretty busy.' He glanced down at the charts again.

But the nurse smiled a slow smile into the harbour. 'Yes, but she made it.' Her eyes went quietly back to his. 'I think now she'll live. But for a while there . . .'

'I can imagine.' He lit a cigarette and glanced below them to watch the others disembarking. He waited while two orderlies came and gently moved the girl on to a stretcher. Ariana stirred slightly, and then with a last look at the nurse who had kept her alive, Ariana left the ship. She didn't have any idea where they were taking her, and she didn't really care.

Chapter 30

'Ariana? . . . Ariana . . . Ariana . . .' The voice seemed to call at her from a great distance, and as she listened, she wasn't sure if it was her mother or Fräulein Hedwig, but whoever it was, she couldn't make herself answer. She felt terribly tired and heavy, she was on a long journey, and it was too much trouble to come back. 'Ariana . . .' But the voice was so insistent. Frowning gently in her sleep, Ariana was aware of a sensation of coming back from a long distance. She would have to answer them after all . . . but she didn't want to . . . what did they want? 'Ariana . . .' The voice kept on calling, and after what seemed like a very long time Ariana opened her eyes.

There was a tall grey-haired woman dressed in black. She wore a black shirt and a black sweater, and her hair was pulled back into a heavy knot. And she was smoothing Ariana's hair back from the pillow with strong, cool hands. When at last she took her hand away, Ariana could see a large diamond ring on her left hand.

'Ariana?' The girl found that her voice seemed to have left her and she could only nod in response. But she couldn't remember what had happened. Where was she? Where had she been last? Who was this woman? Everything in her mind was jumbled and out of context. Was she on a ship? Was she in Paris? . . . Berlin? 'Do you know where you are?' The smile was as gentle as her hands had been on Ariana's tangled hair, and she spoke English. Now Ariana remembered, or at least she thought so, as she looked questioningly at the woman. 'You're in New York. In a hospital. We brought you here to make sure that you were all right.' And the odd thing was that as far as they could tell, she was.

Ruth Liebman knew full well by now that there was much about these people one never knew and never would know, much that one had no right to ask. 'Are you feeling any better?' The doctor had told Ruth that they could find no reason for the exhaustion, the deep sleep, the weakness, except of course for the vomiting and the fever when she had been on the ship. But now they felt that it was urgent that someone make the effort to pull the girl back from the edge of the abyss where she lingered still. It was their official opinion that the girl was simply quietly giving up the fight to go on living, and it was crucial now that someone step in and pull her back before it was too late. As the head of volunteers of the New York Women's Relief Organisation, Ruth Liebman had come to see the girl herself. This was the second time she had been back to visit. The first time despite the soft stroking of her hair and the persistent calling, Ariana hadn't stirred. Quietly Ruth had looked her over, and stealthily she had looked for the numbers tattooed inside the girl's right arm. But there had been nothing. She had been one of the very lucky ones if she had escaped that fate. Perhaps she had been hidden somewhere by a family, or perhaps she had been one of their special victims, those they left unmarked by numbers but used in other ways. The peaceful, sleeping face of the tiny blonde beauty told her nothing, and all they knew of her was her name and that her sponsorship had been arranged through Saint Marne's refugee organisation in France. Ruth knew of the man slightly, a cripple who had lost his wife and daughter to the war.

She had endured her own tragedies since Pearl Harbor had dragged America into the war. When the war broke out, she had had four healthy, happy children; now she had two daughters and only one son. Simon had been shot down over Okinawa, and they had almost lost Paul in Guam. When the telegram had come, Ruth had almost fainted, but with stern face and trembling hands she had closeted herself in her husband's den. Sam was at the office. The girls had been upstairs somewhere, and in her hands she held the paper that looked so much like the first one . . . the paper that would reveal to her her last son's fate. Ruth had decided to face the news alone. But when she read the telegram, the shock was that of relief. Paul had only been injured and he would return stateside in the next few weeks. When she called Sam, there had been the hysterics of rejoicing. She no longer had to maintain her iron calm. For them, the war was over. Her joy had given fresh vigour to her every move, her every thought. She had been distraught over reports of German horrors and stricken with a special kind of guilt, which came of not having suffered as the Jews in Europe had. She threw herself into her volunteer work. She saw these people now with even greater love and compassion, and the gratitude she felt over Paul's survival spilled over into her hours with them – helping them to locate the unknown sponsors, putting them on trains to distant cities in the South and Midwest, and now, visiting this small, frightened girl. Ariana stared at her intently and then closed her eyes.

'Why am I here?'

'Because you were very sick on the ship, Ariana. We wanted to be sure that there wasn't something wrong.' But at this Ariana smiled at her in tired irony. How could they be sure of that? Everything was wrong.

With the older woman's help she sat up slowly and sipped a little of the warm broth the nurse had left, and then Ariana fell back exhausted. Even that small effort had been too much. Gently, Ruth Liebman smoothed the girl's pillows and looked into the troubled blue eyes. And then she understood what the doctors had been saying. There was something terrifying in those eyes that said the girl who lay there had already given up hope.

'You're German, Ariana?' She nodded in answer and closed her eyes. What did being German mean now? She was only a refugee like those others, running away from Berlin three weeks before. Ruth saw the eyelids flutter as the girl remembered, and she gently touched her hand as Ariana once more opened her eyes. Perhaps she needed to talk it out with someone, perhaps she needed to say it, so that the ghosts would not haunt her any more. 'Did you leave Germany alone, Ariana?' Again Ariana only nodded. 'That was very brave of you to do that.' She spoke carefully and precisely. The nurse had told her that Ariana spoke English, but she was not yet sure how well. 'How far did you travel?'

Ariana looked into the kindly face with suspicion, and then she decided to answer. If this woman was with the army or the police or immigration, that didn't matter either any more. For an instant she thought of her endless interrogation at the hands of Captain von Rheinhardt, but that only brought back thoughts of Manfred once again. She pressed her eyes shut for an instant, and then opened them again as two huge tears slid slowly down her cheeks. 'I travelled six hundred miles . . . into France.' Six hundred miles? . . . And from where? Ruth didn't dare to ask her. It was obvious that just barely touching on the memories, the girl was gripped with fresh anguish.

Ruth Liebman was a woman who never gave up hope. It was an attitude she communicated to others, which was why she was so extraordinary at this kind of work. She had always wanted to be a social worker when she was younger, but as the wife of Samuel Liebman, she had her work cut out for her in other ways.

She sat very still now, watching Ariana, wanting to understand the young girl's sorrow, wanting to know how she could help. 'Your family, Ariana?' The words were spoken very gently, yet it was clear that to Ariana they were words she was not yet ready to hear. Crying more freely, she sat up now and shook her head.

'They're all gone now . . . all of them . . . my father . . . my brother . . . my – ' She started to say 'my husband,' but she was unable to go on, and without thinking further Ruth took Ariana in her arms. 'All of them . . . all of them. I have no one . . . nowhere . . . nothing . . .' Fresh waves of grief and terror overtook her. She felt tormented by all of it as she lay there and prayed for her life to end.

'You can't look back now, Ariana.' Ruth Liebman spoke to her softly as she held her, and for an instant Ariana felt as though she had found a mother as she lay in the woman's arms and sobbed. 'You must look ahead. This is a new life for you, a new country . . . and people whom you loved in that other life will never leave you. They are here with you. In spirit, Ariana, you will always take them along.' Just as she did Simon . . . just as she would never lose her firstborn son. She believed that, and Ariana caught a glimpse of hope as she clung to the tall, spare woman whose optimism and strength seemed almost tangible as their eyes met and held.

'But what will I do now?'

'What did you do before?' But even Ruth understood quickly that it was a foolish question. Despite the look of added years and fatigue around her eyes now, it was obvious that the girl was probably no more than eighteen. 'Did you work at all?'

Ariana shook her head slowly. 'My father was a banker.' And then she sighed. It was all a joke now. All those shattered unimportant dreams. 'I was to go on to the university after the war.' But even she knew that she would never have used the education. She would have married and had children, given luncheons and played cards, like the other women. Even with Manfred, she would have done nothing more, except travel between their town house and the schloss on weekends and vacations, where she would have had to see that all was in order for her husband . . . and then of course there would have been children . . . She had to squeeze her eyes shut again. 'But all of that was so long ago. It doesn't matter any more.' Nothing did. And it showed.

'How old are you, Ariana?'

'Twenty.' Paul was only two years older, and Simon would have been twenty-four. Could she really only have been twenty and come so far? And how had she got separated from her family? Why had they killed the parents and brother and spared her? But as Ruth watched her, she understood the answer to the question, and a fresh ache was born in her heart for the girl. Ariana was so devastatingly pretty, even in her present wan condition, with those huge, sad blue eyes. Ruth suddenly felt certain that the Nazis had used her. It was clear to her in an instant what had befallen Ariana during the war. And that was why they hadn't killed her, why they hadn't marked her body, tattooed her arms. As the full realisation came to her, her heart went out to the girl, and she had to fight the tears that pushed from behind her eyes. It was as though they had taken one of Ruth's own beloved girls and used her as they had Ariana, the thought of it almost made Ruth Liebman ill.

For a long moment there was silence between the two women, and then Ruth gently took Ariana's hand. 'You must forget all that's behind you. All of it. You must allow yourself to have a new life.' Otherwise it would taint her forever. She was obviously a girl of good breeding, but if she let it, her nightmare with the Nazis would destroy her life. She could wind up a drunk, a whore, disturbed, in some institution, or she could lie in her bed in Beth David Hospital and choose to die. But as she held Ariana's hand, Ruth made a silent promise – to give this tiny, broken child a fresh chance in life. 'From today, Ariana, everything is new. A new home, new country, new friends, new world.'

'What about my sponsors?' Ariana stared bleakly at Ruth, whose answer to her was vague.

'We still have to call them. First we wanted to make sure you were all right. We didn't want to frighten them by calling before we knew.' But the truth was that they had called them, a Jewish family in New Jersey who had done what they considered their duty, but they were less than thrilled. A young girl was going to be a problem; they ran a business and she would be of little help; besides, they hated Germans. They had told the Women's Relief Organisation that they wanted someone French. And what the hell were they going to do with her if she was lying in a hospital bed in New York? . . . Just a precaution, Ruth had assured them, nothing major, we're almost sure. But the people had been curt and unpleasant. And Ruth wasn't sure they'd take her. Unless . . . A thought suddenly came to her as she sat there – unless she could convince Sam to let Ariana come to them. 'As a matter of fact – ' Ruth Liebman looked pensively down at Ariana and stood to her considerable height. A smile dawned slowly on the large, kindly features and she patted Ariana's hand again. 'As a matter of fact, I have to see them later this morning. I'm sure everything will work out just fine.'

'How long do I have to say here?' Ariana looked around the small bleak room. They had continued to keep her in isolation, mostly because of the endless shrieking night-mares, but they wouldn't keep her there much longer. Ruth had heard them talking that morning of putting her out in the ward.

'You'll probably only be in the hospital for a few more days. Until we know that you're stronger.' She smiled gently at Ariana. 'You don't want to leave too quickly, Ariana, you'd just go out and really get sick. Enjoy the rest here.' But as she prepared to leave, she saw a fresh wave of panic wash over Ariana, who looked in terror around the empty room.

'My God, my things – where are they?' Her eyes flew to Ruth Liebman's, who reassured her quickly with a warm smile.

'They're safe, Ariana. The nurse on the ship gave your suitcase to the ambulance driver, and I understand that they have it locked up here. I'm sure you'll find everything in it that you had there, Ariana. There's no need to worry.' But she was worried – her mother's rings! And with that, she looked down at her own hands. Her wedding band and her engagement ring from Manfred were both gone as well as his signet ring. She looked wildly at the older woman, who immediately understood. 'The nurse put all your valuables in the safe, Ariana.

'Trust us a little.' And then more softly, 'The war is over, child. You're safe now.'

But was she? Ariana wondered. Was she safe and did it matter?

A few minutes later she rang for the nurse, who came running. She was curious to see the girl they had all been talking about. The one who had escaped the camps in Germany and who had slept for four days straight.

Ariana waited nervously until the woman brought the suitcase.

'Where are my rings? From my hands?' Her English was slightly rusty. She hadn't had her English tutor to give her lessons since before the war. 'I'm sorry . . . I was wearing rings.'

'You were?' The nurse looked vague and hurried off to check. She was back a moment later with a small envelope, which Ariana took from her and held tightly in her hand, and then she opened it slowly after the nurse had left the room. They were all there, the narrow gold band that had joined her to Manfred, the engagement ring he'd given her at Christmas, and his own signet ring, which she had been wearing behind the rest so it wouldn't fall off. Her eyes filled with tears again as she slipped them on her hands. And when she did, she realised that she had in fact been sicker than she'd realised in the twenty-two days since she had left Berlin. When she pointed her fingers downward, the rings fell swiftly into her lap. Nine days getting to Paris, two days sick with exhaustion and grief and terror there, seven days desperately ill on the ocean, and now four days in this hospital . . . twenty-two days . . . that seemed more like twenty-two years . . . Four weeks earlier she had been in the arms of her husband, and now she would never see him again. She held the rings tightly in the palm of her left hand as, sobbing with determination, she pulled herself together. She opened the suitcase.

The clothes Jean-Pierre de Saint Marne's housekeeper had provided were still packed neatly. After the first two days on the ship, she had been too sick to move or change. Beneath them was an extra pair of shoes, and beneath that the bundle she was desperately seeking, the envelope with the photographs, and the small leather book with the secret compartment in which still rested her mother's jewels. Slowly she brought them out into the open, the large, handsome emerald, and the smaller diamond signet her father had given to her that night before he left. But she didn't put either ring on, she only stared at them as she held them. They were her only possessions, her only security, her only tangible memories of the past. They were all she had of the past. They were all she had of that lost world now. The two rings of her mother's, her rings from Manfred, his simply carved gold signet ring, and a packet of photographs that showed a man in full dress uniform and a happy, smiling nineteen-year-old girl.

Chapter 31

The secretary outside Sam Liebman's private office on Wall Street guarded his presence there like an avenging angel with a sword. No one, not even his wife or children, was allowed to enter unless he had sent for them. When he was at home, he was all theirs, but when he was at work, he considered it a sacred world. Everyone in the family knew that, especially Ruth, who seldom came to his office except on matters of ultimate importance, which was why she sat there now.

'But he may be tied up for hours.' Rebecca Greenspan looked across at her employer's wife with faint exasperation. Ruth Liebman had already been sitting there for almost two hours. And Mr Liebman had left strict orders that he was not to be disturbed.

'If he didn't go to lunch today, Rebecca, he'll have to come out sooner or later to eat. And while he's eating, I can catch a word with him.'

'Couldn't it wait until tonight?'

'If it could, I wouldn't be here. Would I?' She smiled pleasantly but firmly at the girl who was close to half her age – and also close to half her height. Ruth Liebman was an imposing-looking woman, tall, broad-shouldered, but not manly. She had a warm smile and kind eyes. She herself was dwarfed by her husband's overwhelming height. Samuel Julius Liebman stood six feet five in his stocking feet; he was broad-shouldered, had bushy eyebrows and a leonine mane about which his children teased him – his hair was almost the colour of flame. It had dulled now that he was older and had settled down to a kind of coppery bronze, fading ever more as the red hair was dimmed by an increase of grey. Like him, his oldest son, Simon, had been a redhead, but the rest of his children were dark haired like his wife.

He was a man of wisdom, charity, and kindness, and in the world of merchant banking, he was a man of great importance. The house of Langendorf & Liebman had withstood even the crash of twenty-nine, and over the twenty years that he'd built it, it had become an investment house respected by all. And one day Paul would replace his father. That was Sam's dream. He had, of course, always assumed it would be Simon and Paul. Now the entire mantle would fall on his youngest son's shoulders as soon as he was back on his feet.

At last, at three o'clock the door to the inner sanctum opened and the giant with the lion's mane emerged in a dark pin-striped suit and Homburg, his brows knit and his briefcase in his hand.

'Rebecca, I'm going to a meeting.' And then, in

astonishment, he saw Ruth waiting patiently in a chair across the room. For an instant terror seized him.

What now?

She smiled mischievously at her husband and his worry faded. He returned the smile and kissed her gently as she stood beside him in the anteroom and the secretary discreetly disappeared.

'This isn't the way respectable old people should be behaving, Ruth. And certainly not at three o'clock in the afternoon.'

She kissed him softly and slipped her arms around his neck. 'What if we pretend it's later?'

'Then I miss the meeting I was already late for.' He laughed softly. 'All right, Mrs Liebman, what did you have on your mind?' He sat down and lit a cigar expectantly. 'I'll give you exactly ten minutes, so let's try to get whatever it is settled quickly. Think we can do that?' His eyes danced over the cigar and she smiled. They were notorious for their long-drawn-out battles of will. She had her own ideas on some subjects, and Sam had his, and when the two were not in perfect harmony, the battles could rage on for weeks. 'How about making this a quick one?' The smile broadened to a grin. During the twenty-nine years they had been married, they had learned that in the end it was a compromise that drew on the best from each.

'I'd like to. It's up to you, Sam.'

'Oh, God, Ruth . . . not another one of those. The last time you told me something was "up to me," you almost drove me crazy about that car for Paul before he went into the army. "Up to me," my eye, you had already promised him that before you ever asked me. "Up to me."' He chuckled. 'All right, what is it?'

Her face sobered and she decided to come right to the point. 'I want to sponsor a girl we brought into this country a few days ago, Sam. The Women's Relief brought her over on the ship. She's been at Beth David since she got here and the family that sponsored her doesn't want her.' Her eyes showed bitterness and anger. 'They wanted someone

French. What, a French maid from a Hollywood movie maybe, or a French whore?'

'Ruth!' He glared at her disapprovingly. It was rare that she ever spoke so sharply. 'What is she, then?'

'German.' Ruth said it quietly and Sam nodded silently.

'Why is she in the hospital? Is she very sick?'

'Not really.' Ruth sighed and walked slowly around the room. 'I don't know, Sam, I think she's broken. The doctors can't find any trace of a specific disease, and certainly nothing communicable.' Ruth hesitated for a long moment. 'Oh, Sam, she's so . . . so hopeless. She's twenty years old and she's lost her whole family. It's heartbreaking.' She looked at him, pleading.

'But they're all like that, Ruth.' He sighed softly. For a month now they had been learning daily more of the horrors of the camps. 'You can't bring them all home.' The truth was that with all her work for the Women's Relief Organisation, she had never wanted to bring any of them home before.

'Sam, please . . .'

'What about Julia and Debbie?'

'What about them?'

'How will they feel to have a total stranger brought into the house?'

'How would they feel if they lost their whole family, Sam? If they can't at least feel for other people's problems, then I think we've failed as parents. There's been a war, Sam. They have to understand that. We all must share the consequences.'

'They've suffered the consequences.'

Sam Liebman's thoughts turned instantly to his eldest son. 'We all have. You're asking a lot of the family, Ruth. What about Paul when he comes home? It may be hard for him to have a total stranger there while he's coping with whatever problems he may have with his leg, and . . .' Sam paused, unable to go on, but Ruth instantly understood. 'He's going to have a number of shocks when he gets home, Ruth, you know. It won't make it any easier for him to have a strange girl in the house.'

The tall, dark-haired woman smiled at her husband. 'It may have just the opposite effect. In fact, I think it may do him a lot of good.' They both understood only too well what Paul had to face when he got home. 'But that isn't the point. The point is this girl. We have the room in our home for her. What I want to know from you is if you'll let me bring her home to live with us, for a while.'

'How long a while?'

'I don't know, Sam. Realistically, six months, a year. She has no family, no assets, nothing, but she seems to be well-educated, she speaks English quite well. In time, when she's recovered from the shock of all that's happened, I assume she'll be able to get a job and take care of herself.'

'And if she isn't able to, what do we do with her? Keep her forever?'

'Of course not. Maybe we could discuss that with her. We could offer to take her for six months, and perhaps to extend it for another six months after that; but we could make it clear to her from the beginning that after a year she'd have to go out on her own.'

Sam knew she had won. In her own way, she always won. Even when he thought he'd been winning, somehow she always got her point across. 'Mrs Liebman, I find you disturbingly persuasive. I'm glad you don't work for any rival firms down here.'

'Does that mean yes?'

'It means I'll think it over.' And then after a moment, 'Where is she?'

'Beth David Hospital. When will you see her?' Ruth Liebman grinned and her husband sighed and put down his cigar.

'I'll try to see her on my way home tonight. Will she recognise the name if I tell her who I am?'

'She should. I was with her all morning. Just tell her you're the husband of the volunteer named Ruth.' And then she saw he was worrying over something. 'What's the matter?'

'Is she disfigured?'

Ruth went to him and touched his cheek gently. 'Of course not.' She loved the weakness and fears that she sometimes saw in him; it made her even more aware of his strengths and reduced him to a scale that seemed more human to her. Catching those glimpses always made her love him more. She looked at him with a small smile and a twinkle. 'In fact, she's very pretty. But she's so . . . so desperately alone now . . . you'll understand when you see her. It's as though she's lost all hope.'

'She probably has after what she's been through. Why should she believe in anyone now? After what they did to those people . . .' There was suddenly fire again in Sam Liebman's eyes. It made him crazy to think of what those sons of bitches had done. When he had read the first reports of Auschwitz, he had sat alone in his study, reading and thinking and praying, and finally crying all night. And then he looked at Ruth again as he reached for his Homburg. 'Does she trust you?'

Ruth thought for a minute. 'I think so. As much as she trusts anyone now.'

'All right, then.' He picked up his briefcase. 'I'll go meet her.'

He looked at her for a long moment, then they walked to the elevator. 'I love you, Ruth Liebman. You're a wonderful woman, and I love you.'

She kissed him gently in answer, and then just before the doors opened for them, 'I love you, too, Sam. So when will you tell me?'

He rolled his eyes as the doors opened and they stepped into the elevator. 'I'll tell you tonight when I get home. Will that do?' But he was smiling at her, and she nodded happily, and then she kissed him quickly on the cheek as he went off to his meeting and she climbed into her new Chevrolet and drove home.

Chapter 32

In her hospital room, Ariana sat quietly on the bed all morning, looking out the window into the bright sunlight and, when that became tiresome, staring at the floor of her room. After a while, a nurse came by to urge her to go walking, and after a few feeble attempts to crawl down the corridor, holding on to railings and doorways, she finally went back to bed. But after lunch they told her she was moving, and by dinnertime she found herself in a bed in the bustling ward. The nurse had told her that it would do her good to see other people, but soon Ariana asked them to put a screen around her; and listening to the laughter and the noises, and smelling the trays of dinner all around her, Ariana lay miserably in her bed overcome by waves of nausea. She was still holding the towel to her mouth, her eyes watering pathetically after another bout of dry heaves, when there was a knock on the screen that shielded her from the others and with a look of panic she put down the towel and looked up.

'Who is it?' Not that it mattered – she didn't know anyone here. Her words were spoken softly and her eyes seemed to grow larger as a huge man loomed at her from around the screen. She had never felt smaller or more frightened than she did at that moment, and as Samuel Liebman looked down at her, she began to tremble visibly and had to fight not to cry out. Who was he? What did he want from her? In his Homburg and dark suit, he looked so official, she was sure he was with the police or immigration. Were they sending her back to France?

But the man looked at her gently, the eyes soft and warm despite his towering height. 'Miss Tripp . . . ?' That was the name on her papers. Saint Marne had conveniently dropped the 'von.'

'Yes?' It was barely more than a whisper.

'How are you?' She didn't dare answer. She was shaking so badly that he wasn't even sure if he should stay. She was sick and frightened and alone and he could understand why Ruth's heart had gone out to this girl. She was a lovely child. And it was clear to him as he watched her that she was barely more than a child. 'Miss Tripp, I'm Ruth Liebman's husband.' He wanted to hold out a hand to her, but he was afraid that if he moved towards her, she would leap, trembling, off the bed, so precarious did she seem there, so terrified and poised for flight. 'You know, Ruth Liebman, the lady who was here this morning? The volunteer.' Sam fought to jar her memory. Slowly the light dawned in her eyes. Even in her total state of panic, the name Ruth rang a bell.

'Yes . . . yes . . . I know . . . she was here . . . today.' Ariana's English sounded more than adequate, even cultured, but she spoke so softly that Sam could barely hear.

'She asked me to come to see you. So I thought I'd stop in on my way home.'

Did she? Why? As a social visit? Did people still do things like that? Ariana stared at him in amazement, her eyes a blank stare, and then, remembering her manners, she nodded slowly. 'Thank you.' And then, as though with great effort, she held out a small, wraithlike hand.

'It's a pleasure,' Sam reassured her, though they both knew that that was not quite the word. The ward was perfectly dreadful, and screeches and cries seemed to increase rather than lessen as they attempted to talk. She had waved him to a seat at the foot of her bed, and now he sat there, looking uncomfortable and trying not to stare. 'Is there anything I can get you? Anything you need?' The huge eyes bored into his but all she did was shake her head, while he reproached himself for the stupid question. Her needs could not be easily met.

'My wife and I want you to know that in any way we can, we'd like to help you.' He sighed jaggedly and went on. 'It's difficult for people in this country to really understand what

231

has happened over there... but we care... we care deeply... and that you have survived it is a miracle we must rejoice in. You and the other survivors will remain something of a monument to these times, and to the others, and you must live well now – for yourself, and for them.' He stood up and walked towards her.

It was a difficult speech for him, and Ariana watched him with round eyes. What exactly was he thinking? Did he know she had escaped from Berlin? Of what 'others' was he speaking? Or did he just mean the Germans who had survived? But whatever he meant, and whomever he was referring to, it was clear that this was a man who cared a great deal. With his great height and wild hair, he looked so different from her father, yet she felt her heart go out to him as though to an old friend. This was a man of dignity and compassion, a man she respected, and whom her father would have honoured, too. She leaned forward then and put her arms gently on his broad shoulders, and kissed him carefully on the cheek.

'Thank you, Mr Liebman. You make me glad that I'm here.'

'You should be.' He smiled tenderly at her, touched by the kiss. 'This is a great country, Ariana.' It was the first time he had called her that, but now he felt he could. 'You'll find out what it's like here. It's a new world, a new life for you, you'll meet new people, new friends.' But her eyes only looked sadder as she listened. She didn't want new people, she wanted the old ones, and they were gone for good. But as though seeing the pain that had returned to her eyes then, Sam Liebman touched her hand. 'Ruth and I are your friends now, Ariana. That's why I came here to see you.' And then, as she understood what he was saying, that he had come to see her, there in the hospital, in that hideous ward, that he had come there because he cared about her, her eyes filled slowly with tears. But behind the tears there was a smile.

'Thank you, Mr Liebman.'

As he watched her, he had to fight back tears, too. He

stood up slowly, still holding the small hand, and then he squeezed it for a moment. 'I have to go now, Ariana. But Ruth will be back to see you tomorrow. And I will see you soon, too.' Like a child being deserted she nodded, trying to smile, and desperately fighting the tears that threatened to get out of control. And then, unable to hold himself back any further, Samuel Liebman took her into his arms. He held her that way, bearlike, for almost half an hour, as Ariana gave way to uncontrollable sobs. At last, when she stopped, he handed her his handkerchief and she blew her nose long and hard.

'I'm so sorry . . . I didn't mean to . . . it was just that . . .'

'Sshh . . . stop it.' He stroked her head gently. 'You needn't explain Ariana. I understand.' As he looked down at the elflike golden girl, bowing her head into his handkerchief on the big bed, he asked himself how she had survived it. She looked too frail to have survived even one rugged moment, yet he sensed also that beyond the delicately carved features, the thin frame, the little, graceful figure, there was a woman who could have survived almost anything, and still would. Something tough and invincible had allowed her to survive it, and as Sam Liebman looked at the girl who had just become his third daughter, he thanked God that she had.

Chapter 33

The preparations for Ariana's arrival were undertaken with a mixture of rejoicing and awe. Sam had returned to the house after he had met her and all but ordered Ruth to get the child out of that ward by the next day. As long as the doctors felt that she was not ill in any way that endangered his children, he wanted Ariana brought to the house on Fifth Avenue, as quickly as could be arranged. The girls were called to his den after dinner and it was explained to them that Ariana was about to join them, that she was German, had lost her entire family, and that they would have to be gentle with her for a while.

Like their parents, Julia and Debbie were compassionate. They, too, were overcome with the shock of what the news brought daily about Germany. They, too, wanted to lend their support. The next morning they pleaded with Ruth to let them come along on her visit to the hospital. But in this the elder Liebmans held their position firmly. It would be time enough for the girls to meet Ariana at home. And as worn-out as Ariana had been since the disastrous sea voyage, Ruth was afraid that their visits would be too much. In fact, at the doctor's suggestion, she was planning to keep Ariana in bed at home for the first week. After that, if she felt stronger, they could take her out with them for lunch, or dinner, or even a movie or two. But first, it was obvious that she was going to have to build up her strength.

Ruth appeared at the hospital and announced to Ariana that she and her husband wanted her to move into their home, not for the six months she had first told Sam, but for as long as Ariana needed a family. Ariana stared at her in total amazement, sure that her English had momentarily led her astray and she hadn't properly understood.

'I'm sorry?' She had looked at Ruth inquiringly. It was impossible that she had heard what she thought she'd heard. But Ruth had taken both of Ariana's small hands into her larger ones and sat down on the bed in the ward with a smile.

'Mr Liebman and I would like you to come and live with us, Ariana. For as long as you'd like.' After he had seen her, it was Sam who had dropped the stipulation of six months to a year.

'At your home?' But why would this woman do that? Ariana already had a sponsor, and this woman had already taken so much time just to be with Ariana. She looked at her benefactress now with nothing less than awe.

'Yes, at our home, with our daughters, Deborah and Julia, and in a few weeks our son will be coming home, too. Paul has been in the Pacific, but he recently took some shell fragments around his kneecap, and soon he will be well enough to travel.' She didn't tell her about Simon. There was really no point. She simply rambled on happily, telling Ariana about the children, giving the girl time to sort out her own thoughts.

'Mrs Liebman . . .' Ariana stared at her. 'I don't know what to say.' For a moment she lapsed into German, but Ruth Liebman's knowledge of Yiddish somewhat helped her out.

'You don't have to say anything, Ariana.' And then suddenly the older woman smiled. 'But if you do, you should try to say it in English, otherwise the girls won't understand.'

'Did I speak German again? I'm sorry.' Ariana blushed and then for the first time in weeks she looked at Ruth Liebman and laughed. 'Are you really taking me home with you?' She looked at her friend in total astonishment, and the two women exchanged a long smile as Ruth nodded and held tightly to the young girl's hands. 'But why will you do this? For what reason? It's so much trouble for you and your husband.' And then suddenly she remembered Max Thomas during the two days he'd stayed with them. He had felt just as she did now . . . but that had been different. Max had been an old friend. And her father hadn't offered to house him forever. But as she thought of it, she knew that her father would have. Perhaps this was the same kind of thing.

Ruth was looking at her seriously now. 'Ariana, we want to do this. Because we're sorry about all that has happened.'

Ariana looked at her sadly. 'But it's not your fault, Mrs Liebman. It was just . . . the war . . .' Ariana seemed so helpless for a moment, and Ruth Liebman put an arm around her shoulders, running a hand over the soft golden hair that hung down her back.

'We've felt the teeth of the war, the unfairness, the horror, the anguish, even here.' As she said it, she thought of Simon, who had died for his country, but truly for what? 'But we have never known what you experienced in Europe. Maybe in some way, if we can, we could make up one tiny bit of what happened to you, just so that you can forget for a moment, just so that you get a fresh start.' And then she gazed at the girl gently. 'Ariana, you're still so very young.'

But Ariana shook her head slowly in answer. 'Not any more.'

Several hours later Sam Liebman's chauffeur-driven Daimler drove Ariana sedately to the Fifth Avenue house. Across the street Central Park beckoned with lush trees and bright flowers, and clipping slowly along the park's paths, Ariana could see hansom cabs and young couples in each other's arms. It was a beautiful spring morning at the end of May. And this was Ariana's first glimpse of New York. She looked like a small child as she sat there, tucked in between Samuel and Ruth.

Sam had left his office to go to the hospital, and he himself had carried Ariana's one pathetic little cardboard suitcase to the car. In it she had once more packed her few treasures, and from it she had planned to pull out whatever she had to wear home when the Liebmans picked her up. But Ruth had stopped briefly at Best & Co. that morning, and the box she proudly handed to Ariana yielded a pretty pale blue summer dress, almost the colour of Ariana's eyes, with a tiny gathered waist and a huge softly flowing full skirt. Dressed in it, Ariana looked more than ever like a fairy princess, and Ruth stood back to look at her with a warm smile. She had also brought her white gloves, a sweater, and a pretty little natural straw cloth hat that tilted to one side and showed off Ariana's face. And miraculously, the pumps she had bought fitted Ariana's tiny feet. When they emerged from the hospital, she looked like a different girl, and sitting in Sam Liebman's handsome maroon car, looking at her first glimpse of the city, she looked more like a tourist than a refugee.

For an instant Ariana found herself wondering if it could be a game of let's pretend . . . if she closed her eyes just for a minute, would it feel as though she were back in Berlin, on her way to the house in Grunewald . . . but as in testing a too fresh wound, she found that touching it still brought back waves of unwanted pain. It was easier to keep her eyes open, look around her, and drink it all in. Now and then Sam and Ruth smiled at each other over her head. They were happy with the decision they had made. Fifteen minutes after they had left the hospital, the Daimler drew to halt and the chauffeur got out and held the door. He was a distinguished-looking, careworn black man in a black uniform, a black cap, white shirt, and bow tie.

He touched his cap as Sam alighted and then offered Ruth his arm. She declined it with a warm glance, looking back over her shoulder at Ariana, and then she gently helped her out herself. Ariana had not yet retrieved all her forces, and despite the pretty hat and dress, she was still looking very pale.

'Are you all right, Ariana?'

'Yes, thank you, I'm fine.' But Ruth and Sam watched her with caution. While she had been dressing, she had felt so faint that she had had to sit down, and it was lucky Ruth had been there to help. But it was something else about her that Sam was watching, her finesse, her poise, the calm with which she had moved the moment she got into the car. It was as though she had finally entered a world in which she was entirely at home, and he found himself wanting to ask questions. This was not just a well-brought-up, nicely educated girl; this was a young woman of the uppermost echelons, a diamond of the first water, which made it an even greater tragedy that now she had nothing at all. But she had them now, he consoled himself, as she stood next to Ruth for a moment, looking out at the park with wonder and a long, slow smile. She had been thinking of the Grunewaldsee and the trees and boats. But that might as well have been on another planet as she stood there, feeling far, far from home.

'Ready to go home now?' Ariana nodded and Ruth led her slowly inside, to the main hall, which rose for two floors above them, draped in rich, gem-coloured velvets and filled with antiques they had acquired on trips to Europe before the war. There were medieval paintings, statues of horses, long Persian runners, a small marble fountain, and a grand piano visible in the conservatory at the end of the hall. And in the centre of the entrance a stairway that spiralled skyward, on which stood two wide-eyed, gangling, dark-haired girls.

In silence they stared at Ariana, then their mother, then back at Ariana again, waiting for some silent signal, and then suddenly, not seeming to care about what was expected, they tore down the staircase and threw their arms around Ariana, shouting, giggling, jumping up and down, and dancing with glee.

'Welcome, Ariana! Welcome home!' It was a harmony of shrieking that brought fresh tears to Ruth Liebman's eyes. Gone the solemn moment among the elders – the girls had even obscured Ariana's bittersweet moment and turned it into the celebration that it was. They had a cake waiting, and balloons and streamers, and Debbie had cut a huge bouquet of fresh roses from the bushes in the garden. Julia had baked the cake, and together they had gone out that morning and bought Ariana all the things that they felt a young lady of Ariana's advanced years ought to require; three deep pink lipsticks, several powders and two huge pink puffs, a jar of rouge, several hair ornaments and tortoiseshell hairpins, and even a funny blue hairnet that Debbie insisted was going to be the rage by the fall. They had gift-wrapped each and every item and piled them high on the dressing table of the guest room Ruth had set aside for Ariana the night before.

When Ariana saw the room, she was moved to fresh tears. In some ways it reminded her of her mother's long-closed rooms in Grunewald. This, too, was a paradise of silks and satins done in a spun-candy pink, but this room was even prettier, the bed was larger, and everything was fresh and perfect and cheerful, just as one would have expected a room in America to be. The bed was covered by a huge white organdy canopy, the bedspread a lovely pink and white satin quilt. There were a desk all intricately covered with trompe l'oeil designs and flowers, a huge antique armoire for her clothes, a white marble fireplace topped by a handsome gilt mirror, and an abundance of small, elegantly upholstered chairs covered in pink satin, where the girls could come and sit with Ariana, chatting until the wee hours. Beyond the bedroom was a small dressing room, and beyond that a pink marble bath. And everywhere Ariana looked there were pink roses, and on a table set for five was Julia's cake.

Unable to find the words to thank them, Ariana simply hugged them and continued alternately to laugh and cry. Then she hugged Sam and Ruth again. What miracle was this that now she should wind up in such a home? It was as though she had come full circle, from the house in Grunewald, to the tiny cell where Von Rheinhardt had left her, to the women's barracks, and then to the safety of Manfred's house, and after that out into the world to nothing, and now back into the luxurious comfort of a world she knew, a world she had grown up in, a world of servants and large cars and pink marble bathrooms, like the one she stared at now in disbelief. But the face she glimpsed briefly in the mirror was no longer the face of the young girl she had known. This was a gaunt and tired stranger, someone who did not really belong in this house. Now she belonged nowhere, to no one, and if they wanted to be kind to her for a while, she would let them and be grateful, but she would never count on a world of pink marble bathrooms again.

In solemn celebration, they sat down to eat Julia's elaborately decorated cake. She had written 'Ariana' in pink rose petals in the frosting, and Ariana smiled as she tried to fight the desperate nausea she never seemed able to escape now as they cut her a slice of the cake. She found that she was barely able to eat it, and although the girls were lovely, she was grateful when at last Ruth shooed them out. Sam had to get back to the office, the girls had to visit their grandmother for lunch, and Ruth wanted Ariana to go to bed now. It was time they left her alone to rest. She laid out the robe and one of the four nightgowns she had bought for her that morning at Best's, and once again, Ariana stared at the gifts in amazement. White lace and satin . . . pink lace . . . blue satin . . . it was all so wonderfully familiar, and yet now it all seemed so remarkable and so new.

'Are you all right, Ariana?' Ruth cast her a searching glance as Ariana sank on to the bed.

'I'm fine, Mrs Liebman . . . and you've all been so good to me . . . I still don't know what to say.'

'Don't say anything. Just enjoy it.' And then, after a moment of pensive silence, she looked at Ariana. 'In some ways I think it is our way of living with the guilt.'

'What guilt?' Ariana looked at her in confusion.

'The guilt that we were all safe here while all of you in Europe . . .' She paused for a moment. 'You were no different than we were, yet you all paid the price for being Jews.'

In a moment of stunned silence Ariana understood. They thought that she was a Jew. So that was why they had taken her in like one of their own children . . . that was why they were so good to her – they thought she was a Jew. Bereft and anguished, she stared at Ruth Liebman. She had to tell her. She couldn't let her think . . . but what could she tell her? That she was a *German* . . . a real one . . . that she was one of the race that had killed those Jews? What would they think then? That she was a Nazi. But she wasn't. Nor had been her father . . . nor Gerhard. Her eyes filled with tears as she though of it . . . they would never understand it . . . never . . . they would cast her away from them . . . put her on the boat again. A sob broke from her and Ruth Liebman ran to her and held her tightly as they sat side by side on the bed. 'Oh, my God . . . I'm sorry, Ariana . . . I'm so sorry. There is no need for us to speak to that now.'

But she had to tell her . . . had to tell her . . . but a little voice inside Ariana silenced her. *Not just yet. Once they know you better, then maybe they will understand.* And she was too exhausted to argue with the voice any further. She just let Ruth Liebman tuck her into the canopied bed beneath the bedspread of pink satin, and with a long, jagged sigh, after a few moments, Ariana slept.

And when she awoke, she once again sat thinking over her problem. Should she tell them now or wait? But by then Debbie had already written her a poem, and Julia knocked softly on the door to bring her a cup of tea and another slice of the cake. It was impossible to tell them. Already she had been woven in among them. Already it was too late.

Chapter 34

'Now what are you three up to?' Ruth looked in on the three girls, giggling together in Ariana's bedroom. Ariana had been showing them how to put on rouge. 'Aha! Painted women!' Ruth looked at the three faces and grinned. Ariana looked even sillier than the two others, with her fair cameo beauty and her long blonde hair falling over her shoulders childlike; the rouge looked ridiculously out of place on her cheeks.

'Can't we take Ariana out tomorrow?' Julia looked at her mother pleadingly, a long-legged, sensual colt with huge brown eyes that somehow made her look more than just sixteen. She was fully as tall as her mother, but there was something more delicate about the cast of her face. Ariana thought her very lovely, and somewhat exotic. And she was so wonderfully honest and open, so bright, and she had such a quick wit.

Debbie on the other hand was more gentle, quieter, but very lovely, too. She was still something of a dreamer, and unlike Julia she was not interested in boys at all. She was only interested in her beloved brother, and in another week he was due home. By then, Ruth had promised, Ariana could be out with the girls, every day if she chose. But in the meantime she still wanted her stay quiet, and she could see, too, that despite Ariana's protests, the girl was often grateful to be left alone to lie down.

'Ariana, is it that you feel ill, dear, or only very tired?' It still troubled Ruth greatly, and she was growing more afraid daily that Ariana had in some way been marked for life. At times she was very lively and rapidly becoming a part of the family's roughhousing and cavorting on weekends and after meals, but still Ruth could see that the girl was not at all recovered from her ordeal. She had made Ariana promise that they would return to the doctor again if she didn't feel a great deal better by the following week.

'I promise you, it's nothing. I'm only tired. . . . I think it was just from being so seasick on the boat.' But Ruth knew full well that it wasn't the ocean crossing. It was a sickness of the heart. But Ariana never faltered, never complained. She helped the girls each day with their summer studies, tidied her room, sewed for Ruth, and twice now Ruth had found her downstairs helping their housekeeper to rearrange the linen cupboards, sifting through mountains of sheets and tablecloths and napkins, in an effort to put order in areas where Ruth seldom had the time or interest to interfere. The last time she caught her, Ruth had sent her quickly packing to her room, with orders to go back to rest. But instead she had found her in Paul's room, sewing the new curtains Ruth had started but never had time to finish. It was obvious that Ariana wanted to be part of this homecoming. Everyone else in the house was and she wanted to be, too.

And as Ariana sat quietly in Paul's room, sewing, she wondered what kind of young man he was. She knew how infinitely dear he was to his parents, but she didn't know much more than that, except that he was close to her own age and that the high school pictures that lined the room showed a tall, smiling, athletic-looking boy with broad shoulders and a mischievous light in his eye. She liked the look of him, even before they met, and it wouldn't be long now before she met him. He would be home Saturday and Ariana knew now how desperately they had longed for his return, particularly after the death of their eldest son. Ruth had told her gently about Simon, and of course, Ariana knew the loss of Simon had been a severe blow, which made Paul more precious to them now. But Ariana also knew now that Paul's homecoming was not going to be easy for another reason.

Ruth had told her that when he had left two years before, Paul had wanted to be just like his older brother. Everything he did had to be a mirror image of what his older brother did. And when Simon left, he was engaged. So just before Paul shipped out, he got engaged, too. To a girl he'd known all his life. 'She's a very sweet girl,' Ruth had sighed. 'But they were both twenty, and in some ways Joan was a lot more mature than Paul.' As Ariana watched Ruth's eyes, she suddenly understood. 'Six months ago Joan married another man. It's not the end of the world, of course, or it shouldn't be, but . . .' She had looked up in agony at Ariana. 'She never told Paul. We thought she'd written to him, but finally she told us that she never told him a thing.'

'He still doesn't know?' Ariana's voice was filled with compassion. Miserably, Ruth shook her head. 'Oh, my God. And you're going to have to tell him when he comes home?'

'We are. And I can't think of anything I less want to do.'

'What about the girl? Do you suppose she'd be willing to come and tell him? She doesn't have to tell him she's married after all. She could just break off the engagement, and then if he found out about it later . . .'

But Ruth smiled ruefully. 'I'd love it, but she's eight months pregnant.' Ariana smiled. 'I'm afraid it falls back on me and his father.'

So that was what they had to look forward to. Ariana couldn't help wondering how he'd take the news. She had already heard from his sisters that he had a ferocious temper and that he was a very intense young man. She worried, too, how he would feel about having a stranger there, in his house, when he returned. To him, after all, she would be a stranger, even though before he even came home, Paul was no stranger to her. She had heard dozens of stories about him, his childhood, his jokes, his mischief. She felt that he was already her friend. But what would he feel about this mysterious German girl who had suddenly appeared in their midst? She couldn't help wondering if he wouldn't be put off by her after viewing Germans as the enemy for so long, or if, like the rest of his family, he would trust and accept her as one of their own.

It was precisely this trust and acceptance that made her not tell them she was not Jewish. After days of silent torment she had made up her mind. She couldn't tell them, it would destroy everything. They would never understand that a non-Jewish German could be a decent human being. They were too blinded by their own pain and revulsion at what the Germans had done. It was simpler to keep quiet and suffer her twinges of guilt. It didn't matter now. The past was dead and gone. And they would never find out the truth. If they knew, it would only hurt them. They would feel they had been betrayed. And they hadn't. Ariana had lost as much as anyone. She needed the Liebmans just as much as they had known she needed them from the first. There was no reason to tell them. And she couldn't now. She couldn't bear to lose this family, too. She only hoped that Paul would accept her, too. Now and then she worried that he might ask too many questions, but she'd just have to wait and see.

But Ruth's mind was turned in an entirely different direction. It occurred to her that having a young girl as pretty as Ariana afoot would distract him, too. Despite the fatigue that continued to pull her, the girl had blossomed in the brief two weeks. She had the most perfect complexion Ruth had ever seen on another living human being – it was like a perfect peach velvet, her eyes like heather kissed with dew. Her laughter was bright and sunny, her body lithe and graceful, her mind sharp. She would have been a gift to any mother, and the thought of that did not escape Ruth Liebman whenever she worried about Paul. But she couldn't only think of Paul now; she had to consider Ariana, too, which reminded her that there had been something she wanted to ask her. She narrowed her eyes now as she looked at Ariana, who felt suddenly like a very small child beneath that gaze. 'Tell me something, young lady, why didn't you tell me that you fainted yesterday morning? I saw you at lunchtime, and you told me you were fine.' The servants had told her that afternoon.

'I was fine by then.' She smiled at Ruth, but Ruth did not look pleased.

'I want you to tell me when those things happen. Do you understand that, Ariana?'

'Yes, Aunt Ruth.' It was the name they had decided was most comfortable.

'How often has that happened?'

'Only once or twice. I think it just happens when I'm very tired or when I don't eat.'

'Which, from what I can see, is all the time. You're not eating enough, young lady.'

'Yes, ma'am.'

'Never mind that. If you faint again, I want to be told immediately, and by you, not by the servants. Is that clear?'

'Yes, I'm sorry. I just didn't want to worry you.'

'So worry me a little. It worries me more if I feel I'm not being told.' And then her face softened again and Ariana smiled. 'Please, darling, I really worry about you. And it's important that in these first few months we take especially good care of your health. If you're careful to recover properly now, you won't have ugly reminders of the past forever. But if you don't take care of yourself, you may pay for it for the rest of your life.'

'I'm sorry, Aunt Ruth.'

'Don't be sorry. Just take care of yourself. And if you continue fainting, I want to take you back to our doctor. All right?' He had already seen her at the hospital before she checked out.

'I promise I'll let you know next time. But don't worry about me, you're going to be busy enough next week with Paul. Will he have to be confined to his bed?'

'No. I think he ought to be able to manage, as long as he's careful. I'll have to follow around after both of you to make sure you take care of yourselves.'

But Ruth didn't have far to follow after her son when he got home. When they told him the news of Joanie's

245

marriage, he was so overwhelmed that he spent two days locked in his room. He let no one in, not even his sisters, and it was his father who at last prevailed and convinced him to emerge. When he did, he looked ghastly, exhausted, unshaven. But the rest of the family looked almost as bad. After the long years of terror and worry, to have him home at last, and so distraught over the broken engagement, made them ache with frustration at his pain. But in a roar of anger his father had finally accused him of self-indulgence and childish pouting, and his own anger at his father's words had at last brought him out of his shell. He appeared at breakfast the next morning, clean-shaven, pale, and red-eyed, and although he spoke tersely to all present, he was at least there. It wasn't until the end of the meal that he addressed anyone. He had been staring angrily at everyone, except Ariana, whom he didn't seem to see at all. And then suddenly, as though someone had hit him on the shoulder, he looked across the table at her with a look of surprise.

For a moment she wasn't sure whether to smile at him or just to sit there. She was almost terrified to acknowledge the look in his eyes. It was a piercing stare that went to the very core of her being, questioning her presence in his home, at his table, silently asking her why she was there. Following her instincts, she nodded and then averted her eyes, but she could feel his gaze on her for endless moments, and when she looked up at him again, there seemed to be a thousand questions in his eyes.

'What part of Germany did you come from?' He didn't say her name, and the question fell strangely into his parents' conversation as he speared her with his eyes.

She looked him straight in the eyes. 'Berlin.'

He nodded, his brows suddenly knit together. 'Did you see it after the fall?'

'Only briefly.' Ruth and Samuel exchanged uncomfortable glances but Ariana didn't waver. Only her hands trembled slightly as she buttered a small piece of toast.

'How was it?' He eyes her with increasing interest. In the Pacific, they had only heard distant rumours of what the fall of Berlin had been like.

But for Ariana the question conjured up a sudden vision of Manfred in the stack of bodies outside the Reichstag, and involuntarily she closed her eyes, as though that gesture could banish the memory, as though anything ever could. For a moment there was a terrible silence at the table, and then Ruth stepped rapidly into the gap.

'I don't think any of us needs to discuss things like that. At least not now, and not at breakfast.' She looked worriedly at Ariana, who had once again opened her eyes, but they were heavily veiled with tears.

Ariana shook her head gently and without thinking stretched a hand across the table to Paul. 'I'm sorry . . . it's just . . . it's so . . .' There was a little catch in her throat '. . . it is very . . . difficult . . . for me to remember . . .' The tears were rolling openly down her face now. 'I lost . . . so much . . .' And then suddenly there were tears in Paul's eyes and his hands reached across the table and took hers tightly in their grasp.

'I'm the one who's sorry. I was very stupid. I won't ever ask you anything like that again.' She nodded with a small grateful smile, and then carefully he stood up, walked to her side, and with his linen napkin he wiped the tears from her face. There was total silence in the dining room as he did it, and then quietly the rest of the family collected themselves and went on as before. But a bond seemed to form rapidly between them and she sensed him a friend.

He was as tall as his father but he still had the narrow frame of a very young man. He had the rich dark brown eyes of his mother, and almost raven black hair like the girls', but she knew from photographs that his smile was different from all the others'. It broke across his face with a great splash of excitement, cutting an ivory path of radiance across his otherwise serious face. It was the most serious side Ariana had seen that morning, when he seemed almost sultry, with the black brows knit, the dark eyes angry, like a hurricane gathering and waiting to empty the ire of the heavens on cue. One almost expected thunder and lightning when he looked

247

like that. Thinking of it made her smile as she slipped into a white cotton dress and the cork-soled Wedgie sandals that she and Julia had both bought a few days before. Ruth had insisted that she go shopping and buy a few more things. But Ariana still didn't know what to do about this constant generosity they showered on her. The only solution she could come up with was to keep an elaborate record, and later when she felt well enough to get a job, she would repay them for the hats, the coats, the dresses, the underwear, the shoes. The armoire in her bedroom was rapidly filling with lovely clothes.

As for the rings she still kept hidden, she couldn't think of selling them. Not now. They were the only security she had left. She fingered her mother's rings now and then, and once she had been tempted to show Ruth, but she was afraid that it would seem as though she were showing off. And the rings from Manfred were still much too big for her with all the weight she'd lost. She would like to wear Manfred's rings. In a different way than her mother's, she felt that Manfred's rings were part of her soul, just as Manfred was, and always would be. She would have liked to tell the Liebmans about him, but it was too late. And anyway, to explain to them that she had been married and that her husband had died, too, was more than she could bear to tell them, more than she could stand to think of, and perhaps also more than they cared to hear.

'What are you looking so serious about, Ariana?' Julia had slipped into her room with a small smile. She was wearing the twin pair of sandals, and Ariana looked at the young girl's feet and smiled.

'Nothing special. I like our new shoes.'

'So do I. Do you want to come out with my brother?'

'Wouldn't the three of you rather be alone?'

'No, he's not like Simon was. Paul and I always get into fights, and then he picks on Debbie, and then we all start yelling . . .' She grinned at Ariana invitingly, half woman, half girl. 'Doesn't that sound appealing? Come on, you'll have a ball.'

'You know, maybe you're just assuming that's how he'll behave. He's been at war for two years since you last saw him, Julia. He may have changed a lot.' She had already glimpsed that herself at the table that morning.

But Julia only raised her eyebrows. 'Not judging from the performance over Joanie. Gee, Ariana, she wasn't even all that nice. He was just mad that she went off with someone else. And –' Julia giggled unkindly – 'you should see her –' she stuck her arms way out front – 'she looks like an elephant since she got pregnant. Mother and I saw her last week.'

'Did you?' The voice in the doorway was frigid. 'Well, I'll thank you not to discuss it. With me or anyone else in this house.' Paul strolled into the room, looking livid. Julia turned scarlet in embarrassment as being caught gossiping about his affairs.

'I'm sorry. I didn't know you were standing right there.'

'Apparently.' But as he gazed at her haughtily, Ariana suddenly realised the part he was playing. He was only a boy after all, pretending to be a man. And he had been hurt. Perhaps that was why he had attempted to comfort her pain. He looked in an odd way much like Gerhard. And as she watched him then, she couldn't help smiling softly, and when Paul saw her, he looked at her for a long moment, and then he smiled, too. 'I'm sorry if I was rude, Ariana.' And then after a moment, 'I'm afraid I've been rude to everyone since I came home.' He was indeed much like Gerhard, and she felt more kindly to him now because of it. Their eyes met warmly and held.

'You had good reason to. I'm sure it must be very difficult to come home after so long. A lot of things have changed.'

But he only smiled at her in answer, and then he spoke softly. 'Some things even change for the good.'

They drove to Sheepshead Bay out in Brooklyn to eat oysters, down to the tip of Manhattan to glimpse the Statue of Liberty Ariana had been too sick to see a few weeks before; they drove slowly up Fifth Avenue, and then Paul took them over to Third Avenue so he could race along beneath the elevated train. But as they raced across the cobblestones of

Third Avenue, Ariana became noticeably green.

'Sorry, old girl.'

'It's nothing.' She looked embarrassed.

Paul was grinning at her good-naturedly. 'It would have been something if you'd got sick in my mother's new car.' Even Ariana had to laugh at that, and the group continued on to Central Park, there they picnicked happily by the boat pond and eventually wandered down to laugh at the animals at the zoo. The monkeys were all cavorting in their cages, the sun was high and warm, it was a perfect June afternoon, and they were all young together. And for the first time since she had lost Manfred, Ariana thought that she felt truly happy again.

'Hey, what are we doing this summer?' Paul broached the subject at dinner that night. 'Are we staying in town?'

The parents glanced at each other quickly. Paul always was the one to get things moving. It took some adjusting to get used to his being at home. 'Well, we weren't sure what your plans would be, darling.' Ruth smiled at him as she served herself some roast beef from the large silver tray being held by one of the maids. 'I had thought about renting something in Connecticut or out on Long Island, but your father and I hadn't made any decisions yet.' After Simon's death they had sold their country house in upstate New York. The memories there had been far too painful.

'Which brings to mind,' his father tossed at him casually, 'that you have a few other decisions to make first. But there's no hurry, Paul. You just got home.' He was referring to the office in his own firm, which was being redecorated for his son.

'I think we have a lot to talk about, Father.' He looked directly at the elder Liebman and the old man smiled.

'Do you? Then why don't you come downtown and have lunch with me tomorrow?' He would have his secretary have special trays sent in from their kitchens just below the boardrooms.

'I'd like that.'

What Sam Liebman wasn't prepared for was that his son wanted to negotiate a Cadillac roadster, and he wanted to have one last idle summer before he went to work for his father in the fall. But even Sam had to admit that it made sense for the boy to do that. He was only twenty-two, and if he had been finishing college, the same rules would have applied. He had a right to one last fling, one summer, and the car wasn't so much to ask. They were grateful to have him home now . . . grateful that he had come home at all . . .

At four o'clock that afternoon Paul stood in Ariana's open bedroom doorway; he was surprised to find her alone. 'Well, I did it.' He looked quiet but victorious, and for an instant he looked more man than boy.

'What did you do, Paul?' She smiled at him and waved a hand towards a chair. 'Come in and sit down and tell me what you did.'

'I got my father to give me a summer holiday before I go to work for him in the fall. And –' he beamed at her, once more a boy – 'he's giving me a Cadillac roadster. How does that sound?'

'Amazing.' She had only seen one Cadillac in Germany before the war, and she could barely remember it. She was sure it hadn't been a roadster. This was a whole new world. 'What does it look like, this Cadillac roadster?'

'A perfect beauty of a car. Can you drive, Ariana?' He looked at her with a curious smile, and her brow clouded.

'Yes, I can.'

He didn't know what had happened, but he knew that he had revived some old pain. Gently he reached out and took her hand then, and he reminded her more than ever of Gerhard as she fought back tears. 'I'm sorry, I shouldn't have asked you. It's just that sometimes I forget I shouldn't ask you questions about your past.'

'Don't be silly.' She held on to his hand more tightly. She wanted him to know that he had done no harm. 'You can't always treat me like a fragile package. You can't be afraid to ask me things. And in time I will stop hurting . . . It's just that now . . . some things still hurt very much, Paul . . . it's all .

251

very fresh.' He nodded, thinking of both Joanie and his brother – they were the only losses he had known. One so real and so forever, the other different but painful nonetheless. As Ariana watched him with his head bowed, she smiled again. 'Sometimes you remind me of my brother.' His eyes reached up to hers then – it was the first time that she had willingly told him of her past.

'What was he like?'

'Outrageous sometimes. He once blew up his room with his chemistry set.' For a moment she smiled, but it was easy to see that her eyes were rapidly filling with tears. 'And once he took my father's new Rolls when the chauffeur wasn't looking and drove it into a tree.' By then he could hear the tears in her voice. 'I used to . . .' She closed her eyes for a moment, as though she couldn't bear the pain of what she was about to say. 'I used to tell myself that a boy like him . . . like Gerhard . . . couldn't be dead. That he would find a way to stay alive . . . to . . . survive . . .' She opened her eyes and the tears poured down her face silently, sorrowfully, and when she turned her eyes to Paul, there was more anguish there than he had ever seen in two years of war. 'But now, for months I have told myself that I have to believe what they told me, that I must give up hope.' Her voice was a fragile whisper. 'I have to believe now that he is dead . . . no matter how much he laughed . . . or how beautiful and young and strong he was . . . no matter how much – ' the sobs were jagged in her throat as she whispered the words – 'I loved him. In spite of all that . . . he is dead.' There was an endless silence between them, and then quietly he took her in his arms and held her as she cried.

It was a long time before he spoke again, and when he did, he dabbed gently at her eyes with his white linen handkerchief. But though his words were lighthearted and teasing, his eyes told her that he cared a great deal about her pain. There was nothing flip in what he felt for this girl.

'Were you as rich as that, then? Rich enough to have a Rolls?'

'I don't know how rich we were, Paul.' She smiled softly.

'My father was a banker. Europeans don't talk much of things like that.' And then, with a deep sigh, she attempted to speak of the past without crying. 'My mother had an American car when I was very young. I think it was a Ford.'

'A coupe?'

'I don't know.' She shrugged her ignorance. 'I suppose so. You would have liked it. It sat in the garage afterwards for years.' But thinking of that made her think of Max then, and then somehow Manfred and the Volkswagen she had used in the first lap of her escape . . . every memory led to another for Ariana. It was still a dangerous game. She felt the weight of loss settle down on her again as she sat there. It was as though she had lived in a universe that was no more.

'Ariana, what were you just thinking?'

She eyed him honestly. He was her friend now. As best she could, she would be honest with him. 'I was thinking how strange it is that it's all gone now, that none of it exists anymore . . . none of the people . . . none of the places . . . everyone is dead, everything has been bombed . . .'

'But you aren't.' He eyed her gently. 'Now you're here.' He held tightly to her hand and their eyes held for a long moment. 'And I want you to know how glad I am that you are.'

'Thank you.' There was a long silence between them and then Julia bounded into the room.

Chapter 35

Paul brought home his dark green Cadillac roadster a week later and gave Ariana the first ride. After that he had to give Julia and Debbie each a turn in it, then his mother, and then at last Ariana again. They took a ride around Central Park. The leather upholstery was soft and creamy and the whole car had a brand-new smell to it that Ariana liked.

'Oh, Paul, it's lovely.'

'Isn't it?' He chortled happily. 'And it's all mine. My father says it's a loan until I start working for him, but I know him better than that. The car's a gift.' He smiled proudly down at the new roadster and Ariana was amused. In the past week he had also convinced his mother to rent a house on Long Island, and plans were already under way to find an establishment suitable for all of them for at least a month, if not two. 'And then, the salt mines.' He smiled at Ariana as they drove slowly through the park.

'And then what? Will you get your own apartment?'

'Probably. I'm a little too old to live at home.'

Ariana nodded slowly. He was also a great deal too mature. The apron strings had long since been cut. She had already learned that about him. 'They'll be disappointed if you move out though. Especially your mother and the girls.'

He looked at her strangely then, and Ariana felt something inside her tremble. Then he stopped the car and pulled over. 'And you, Ariana? Will you miss me, too?'

'Of course I will, Paul.' Her voice was very quiet. But she suddenly thought back to their exchange about her past. He had already touched her deeply. And it would hurt to lose him now.

'Ariana . . . if I left the house, would you spend some time with me?'

'Of course I would.'

'No.' He looked at her pointedly. 'I don't mean just as a friend.'

'Paul, what are you saying?'

'That I care for you, Ariana.' Paul's eyes never wavered from hers. 'I'm saying that I care for you very, very much. I've been drawn to you, I think, since that first day.' Her mind went back instantly to the breakfast when he had made her cry by asking about Berlin and then wiped the tears from her cheeks. She had felt a strange pull towards him then, and she had felt it since. But she had resisted it from the first. It was wrong for her to feel that way about him, and it was much too soon.

'I know what you're thinking.' He sat back in his seat, but

his eyes remained on Ariana, ethereally beautiful as always in a clinging white silk blouse. 'You're thinking that I hardly know you, that until a couple of weeks ago I thought I was engaged to some other girl. You're thinking that it's hasty, that I'm on the rebound . . .' He went on matter-of-factly, and Ariana smiled softly.

'Not quite all that.'

'But some of it?'

She nodded. 'You don't really know me, Paul.'

'Yes, I do. You're funny and you're loving and you're kind, you're not bitter in spite of all you've been through. And I don't give a damn if you're German and I'm American. We come from the same kinds of worlds, similar backgrounds, and we're both Jews.' For an instant she looked desperately pained. Every time one of them said something like that, it reminded her again of her lie. But it was so important to them that she be Jewish. It was as though she had to be Jewish to be worthy of their love. She had thought about it often. Everyone they knew, all of the girls' friends, everyone Sam did business with, was Jewish. It was essential. It was a given. An invariable. And the thought that Ariana could be anything but Jewish would have been unthinkable to them. Worse than that, she knew that it would have been seen as a betrayal, perhaps even the ultimate betrayal. Because she had won their love.

Sam and Ruth hated the Germans, the non-Jewish ones. To them, every German who was not a Jew was a Nazi. Ariana would have been a Nazi to them, if they had known the truth. The realisation of that had come to her quickly, and it still hurt. It was the pain of again realising that that Paul saw once more in her eyes. She turned away from him, with a look of distress on her face. 'Don't, Paul . . . don't . . . please.'

'Why?' His hand touched her shoulder. 'Is it really too soon? Don't you feel what I do?' The words were hopeful and for a long moment she didn't answer. For her it was and always would be much, much too soon. In her heart she was still married. Had Manfred been alive, they would have been trying to have their first child. She didn't want to think of any other man. Not yet, not now, and not for a very long time.

She turned slowly to Paul, then with a look of sorrow in her eyes. 'Paul, there are parts of my past . . . I may never be ready . . . it's not fair to let you think . . .'

'Do you like me, even as a friend?'

'Very much so.'

'All right, then, let's just give it some time.' Their eyes met and held and she felt a sudden longing for him that frightened her. 'Just trust me. That's all I ask.' And then ever so gently he kissed her on the mouth. She wanted to resist him, she owed that much to Manfred, but she found that she didn't want to make Paul stop, and she was flushed and breathless when he took his mouth from hers.

'Ariana, I'll wait if I have to. And in the meantime –' he kissed her cheek gently and started the car again – 'I'll be content to be your friend.' But as he said the words, she knew she had to say something more. She couldn't just let it go at that.

'Paul –' she put a gentle hand on his shoulder – 'what can I say to you to tell you how much I appreciate your feelings? What can I say to let you know that I feel for you like a brother, but –'

He cut her off. 'You didn't kiss me like a sister.'

She blushed. 'You don't understand . . . I can't . . . I'm not . . . I'm not prepared to be a woman to any man.'

And then he couldn't bear it any longer, and before they reached the house where the others waited, he turned to her, with a pain in his eyes she had never seen before. 'Ariana, did they hurt you? . . . I mean, the Nazis . . . did they?' At the caring in his eyes, her eyes filled with tears and, hugging him tight for how much he truly cared for her, she shook her head.

'No, Paul, the Nazis didn't do what you think to me.' But that night he knew he did not believe her, when he heard her terrible scream. Many nights he had heard her torment, but this time instead of turning over, knowing that the war she still fought was now hers alone to fight, he walked softly on bare feet into her bedroom and found her sitting there at the edge of her bed, a small light burning, her face in her hands, sobbing softly, a small leather book held in her hands.

'Ariana?' He advanced towards her and she turned. He saw then what he had never seen in her before, the raw anguish of torment. He said nothing more. He only sat beside her and held her until at last the sobs subsided and she was calm.

In her dreams she had seen Manfred again . . . dead outside the Reichstag. But there was no way she could explain that to this young man. After a long time with her head on his shoulder, he took the small leather book from her and glanced at the spine. 'Shakespeare? My dear, how intellectual for this hour. No wonder you were crying. Shakespeare would do that to me, too.' She smiled through the last of her tears, then shook her head.

'It's not real.' And then, taking the book from him, 'I saved this from the Nazis . . . it's all I have left.' She flipped open the secret compartment and for an instant Paul looked stunned. 'They were my mother's.' The tears began to flow again. 'And now they're all I have.'

Paul could see an emerald and a large diamond signet ring among the others, but he dared not ask her anything at all. It was obvious how distraught she was.

Ariana had had the presence of mind to tuck Manfred's photographs into the lining of her purse, but thinking of them now made the tears flow again – thinking that she had to hide him like that.

'Shh . . . Ariana, stop. He held her close and felt her tremble, gazing still at the two rings. 'My God; those are two fairly incredible rocks. You got those out without the Nazis seeing?' She nodded victoriously and he picked up the large emerald ring. 'That's an extraordinary piece of jewellery, Ariana.'

'Isn't it?' She smiled. 'I think it was my grandmother's before her, but I'm not really sure. They say my mother wore it all the time.' She picked up the diamond signet. 'And

this one, too. Those are my great-grandmother's initials.'
But the design was so intricate one had to know that they
were there.

Paul looked at her with awe then. 'It's a wonder no one
stole them from you coming over on the boat.' Or anywhere
else she'd been. He didn't dare say what he was thinking,
but it had taken ingenuity for her to bring that little book so
far. Ingenuity and guts, but he already knew that she had
lots of both.

'I wouldn't have let anyone take them. They were all I
had left. They would have had to kill me first.' And as he
looked into her eyes, he knew that she meant what she said.

'Nothing is worth dying for, Ariana.' Now his own
experiences showed in his eyes. 'I've learned that much
myself.' And she nodded her head slowly. Manfred had
discovered the same thing. What had there been worth
dying over? Nothing. There was winter in her eyes when she
looked back at Paul, and this time when he kissed her, she
didn't pull away. 'Get some sleep now.' He smiled at her
gently and motioned her back under the covers so he could
tuck her in. But she was already reproaching herself silently
for letting him kiss her. It wasn't right. But once he had left
the room, she found her mind drifting back to things he had
said, about the war . . . about himself . . . they were things
Manfred might have said. Paul was young, but he was daily
becoming more a man in Ariana's eyes.

Chapter 36

'Ariana, are you all right this morning?' Ruth Liebman
looked at her over breakfast the next morning and found her
looking strangely pale. It had taken hours for her to get back
to sleep the night before after Paul and left. She felt guilty
about encouraging him. She knew that eventually, after
he'd been home for a while and had played for a bit and had

run into old friends and made some new ones, she would hold less pull for him. But in the meantime he was like a big, devoted puppy, and she didn't want to hurt his feelings. She was annoyed at herself, but he had been so kind to her when she had had the nightmare, and she was only human after all. She looked up at Ruth Liebman with big sad eyes that morning, and the older woman frowned with concern. 'My dear, is something wrong?'

Ariana shook her head softly. 'No, I think I'm just tired, Aunt Ruth. It's nothing. I'll get some more rest and I'll be fine.' But Ruth Liebman was sufficiently concerned that half an hour later she picked up the phone, and later that morning she appeared in Ariana's room.

Ariana picked her head up off the pillow with a wan smile. The sleepless night had had a dire effect on her. After she had eaten breakfast that morning, she had returned to her bedroom and vomited for half an hour. Now it showed in her pallid face as Ruth pulled up a chair and sat down. 'I think that it might be a good idea for you to see Doctor Kaplan today.' Ruth tried to hide her worry in ordinary words.

'But I'm all right . . . really . . .'

'Now, Ariana.' She looked reproachfully at the young girl all but hidden by her covers and reluctantly Ariana nodded.

'All right, but I don't want to go to the doctor, Aunt Ruth. There's nothing wrong with me.'

'You sound like Debbie or Julie. Come to think of it,' she grinned, 'you might even sound like Paul.' And then, having thrown one shoe, she decided to throw the other. 'He hasn't been pressuring you, Ariana, has he?' She watched the girl's face intently as Ariana shook her head.

'No, of course he hasn't.'

'I just wondered. He has an awesome crush on you, you know.' Ariana had not heard the word 'crush' before, but she got the message easily.

'I had that feeling, Aunt Ruth.' Ariana perched on the edge of her bed. 'But I've had no intention of encouraging him. He seems like a brother and I miss my brother so much . . .' Her voice drifted and Ariana looked once more into the older woman's eyes. 'And I would never do something that would so greatly displease you.'

'That's what I thought I'd tell you, Ariana. It wouldn't displease me at all.'

'It wouldn't?' Ariana looked stunned.

'No, it wouldn't.' Ruth Liebman smiled. 'Sam and I talked about it the other day. And we know the boy is still kind of on the rebound from Joanie, but, Ariana, he's a good boy.

'I'm not pushing you in any direction. I just wanted to let you know that if the subject should ever come up . . .' She gazed softly at the young German girl sitting in their guest room bed. 'We love you very much.'

'Oh, Aunt Ruth.' Her arms went instantly around the woman who had been so good to her since they first met. 'I love you so much.'

'We want you to feel free to do what *you* want to do. You're a member of the family now. You must do what's right for you. And if he does get that bee in his bonnet, don't let him pressure you if that's not what you want. I know how stubborn he is!' Ariana laughed in answer.

'I don't think it'll ever come to that, Aunt Ruth.' She wouldn't let it. It still didn't seem right to her.

'I couldn't help wondering if that was what was happening, that Paul was pursuing you and you were consumed with guilt because of us.'

'No –' Ariana shook her head tentatively – 'though Paul did say something the other day, but – ' Ariana shrugged and smiled – 'I just think it's his "crush."' She tried out the new word.

'You just follow your heart wherever it takes you.' Ruth smiled at her hopefully and Ariana laughed as she got out of bed.

'Are mothers supposed to play Cupid?'

'I don't know. I've never done it before.' For a moment their eyes met and held. 'But I can't think of anyone we'd rather have as a daughter-in-law, Ariana. You are a very special, lovely girl.'

260

'Thank you, Aunt Ruth.' With a look of gratitude she turned to the armoire and took out a pink striped sundress and white sandals. The June sun was already warm. And she was about to turn to Ruth again to tell her how foolish it was for them to go to the doctor, when, without any warning, she felt dizzy and slumped slowly towards the floor.

'Ariana!' Ruth was out of her chair instantly and at the girl's side.

Chapter 37

Dr Stanley Kaplan's office was at Fifty-third Street and Park Avenue, and Ruth dropped Ariana off in the doorway of the building and went to park.

'Well, young lady, how are you feeling? I guess that's a stupid question. Not very well obviously, or you wouldn't be here.' The elderly man smiled at her from across his desk as Ariana sat facing him in his office chair. The last time he'd seen her she had been wan, pale, frightened, scraggly. Now she looked like the beautiful girl she was. Almost. There was still that haunted look around her eyes, the look of pain and loss and sorrow that would not be quick to fade. But otherwise her complexion looked good, her eyes bright; her long blonde hair had been shaped into a handsome pageboy. And in the fresh, candy-striped dress she wore that morning, she looked like the daughter of any of his patients, not like a young woman who had fled war-torn Europe some few weeks before. 'So tell me, what's the problem? Still the nightmares, nausea, dizziness, fainting? Tell me.' He smiled warmly and picked up his pen.

'Yes, I still have the nightmares, but not quite as often. Now at least sometimes I can sleep.'

'Yes,' he nodded, 'you look more rested.'

She nodded and then she admitted to him that after almost every meal she was still sick. He looked shocked.

'Does Ruth know?' This time Ariana shook her head. 'You have to tell her. You should be on a special diet. Every meal, Ariana?'

'Almost.'

'No wonder you look so thin. Did you have this before, this stomach problem?'

'Only since I walked most of the way to Paris. Once I didn't eat for two days, and a couple of times I tried to eat some dirt in a field . . .' He nodded quietly.

'And the fainting?'

'It still happens a lot.'

And then he did something she wasn't expecting. He put down his pen and looked at her long and hard, but the look was one of kindness and utter compassion, and when he spoke to her, she knew that this man was her friend. 'Ariana, I want you to feel that there is nothing you can't tell me. I want you to tell me anything I need to know about your past life. It is almost impossible for me to help you if I have no idea what you've been through. But I want you to know that what you tell me is sacred. I'm a doctor, and I've taken a sacred oath. Anything you tell me I cannot repeat to anyone else, and I never would. Not Ruth, not Sam, not their children. No one, Ariana. I'm *your* doctor, and *your* friend, too. And I'm an old man who's seen a lot in his lifetime, maybe not as much as you've just seen in yours, but I've seen enough. Nothing will shock me. So now, if there's something you need to tell me, for your own sake, about things they did to you that could have led to these problems, I want you to go ahead.' His face was so kind that she wanted to kiss him, but instead she only sighed softly.

'I don't think so, Dr Kaplan. I was in a cell once for over a month, and all they fed me was some potato broth and stale bread and water and once a week they gave us meat scraps. But that was a long time ago, almost a year now.'

'Did the nightmares start then?'

'Some of them. I . . . I was terribly worried about my father and my brother.' Her voice dropped painfully. 'I never saw them again after that.'

The doctor nodded slowly. 'And the stomach trouble, that started then, too?'

'Not really.' A smile flashed across her face then, remembering her own first attempts at cooking for Manfred and the liver sausage 'stew'. Perhaps it was that that had destroyed her stomach. But she did not explain the smile.

'Ariana, I feel we know each other a little better now.' He entered the subject slowly. The first time he had seen her, he had not dared to ask.

'Yes?' She looked at him expectantly.

'Were you –' he thought over how most delicately to put it – '. . . used?' Judging from her delicate beauty, he had felt sure from the beginning that she had been, but she shook her head now, and he wondered if she was simply afraid to tell the truth. 'Never?'

'Once. Almost. In that same cell.' But she offered no further explanation and he nodded his head.

'Then perhaps we'd just better look at you.' He buzzed for the nurse, who helped her undress.

The doctor had an odd feeling as he went over her body. His brows knit and he examined her more closely, asked for some more information, and then finally, regretfully, suggested a pelvic. He felt sure that she would regard it as an ordeal. But she seemed steeled for the inevitable, and she was oddly quiet as he prodded her and felt at last what he had suspected, the uterus swollen to twice its normal size. 'Ariana, you can sit up now.' She did, and he looked at her sadly. She had indeed been lying. Not only had they assaulted her, they had impregnated her.

'Ariana.' She sat there after the nurse had left the room, so pale, so young, the sheet draped over her. 'I'm afraid I have something to tell you, and then maybe we ought to talk some more.'

'Is something wrong, Doctor?' She looked frightened. She had only assumed that she was exhausted. She had never really believed that she was seriously ill. Even the lack of menses she had attributed to the shock, the trip, and the readjustment.

'I'm afraid so, little one. You're pregnant.' He waited to see the look of grief and horror. What he saw instead was a look of total amazement, and then a small smile.

'You didn't suspect it?' She shook her head, the smile broadening slightly. 'And you're pleased?' Now it was his turn to stare.

Ariana looked as though she had received a priceless gift beyond hope or expectation, and she stared at Dr Kaplan with wide blue eyes filled with love and awe. It had to have happened right after they got married . . . some time near the end of April, perhaps on that last time before he'd gone to defend the Reichstag . . . which made her about seven weeks pregnant. She stared at the doctor in disbelief. 'Are you quite sure?'

'I'll run a test if you like, but frankly I'm certain. Ariana, do you know . . .'

She looked up at him, smiling gently. 'Yes, I know.' She knew she could trust this man. She had to. 'The baby is my husband's. He is the only man I have ever . . . known.'

'And where is he now, your husband?'

Ariana's eyes dropped slowly, and two long tears drifted from her lashes to her cheeks. 'He is dead . . . like all the others.' She lifted her head again slowly. 'He is dead.'

'But you will have his baby.' Kaplan spoke softly and silently rejoiced with her. 'Now you will always have that. Won't you?' She smiled softly, finally allowing herself to think of Manfred, to see his face in her mind's eyes, to remember his touch. It was as though now she could allow his memory to come back to her, to share in the joy of their child. Until then she had desperately wrestled with the memories, afraid to let them flood her mind. But now, when the doctor left the room, she sat there for a full ten minutes, bathed in the tender memories and the dreams, and now, when the tears came, she was smiling. This was the happiest moment of her life.

When she rejoined the doctor in his office, he looked at her seriously for a time. 'Ariana, what will you do now? You'll have to tell Ruth.' For a long moment there was silence.

Ariana had not yet thought of that. For a moment all the Liebmans had been blotted from her mind. But now she realised she had to tell them, and she knew what they would say. How could they welcome this baby – whose baby? The child of a Nazi officer? She had to defend this unborn child. What would she do now? Silently she thought of her mother's rings. If she had to, she would use them to support herself until the baby was born. She would do anything she had to, but she could not impose on them any longer. In a few months she would leave.

'I don't want to tell Mrs Liebman, Doctor.'

'But why not?' He looked distressed. 'She's a good woman, Ariana, a kind woman, she'll understand.'

But Ariana looked adamant. 'I can't ask her to do more than she's already done. She's done so much for me. And this would be too much.'

'You have to think of the baby, Ariana. You owe that baby a decent life, a decent chance, as good a chance as you've been given, as the Liebmans have given you.'

It was a heavy speech that weighed on her all that evening after she had made the doctor promise that he would not tell Ruth. He simply told her that Ariana was still obviously a bit tired, but that it was nothing to be concerned about. She should not overdo it, she should eat well, she should get lots of sleep, but other than that, she was fine.

'Oh, I feel so much better hearing that,' Ruth had told her on the way home. She seemed even kinder that day than usual, and it tore at Ariana's heart to be deceiving her about the child. But it seemed wrong to ask for still more from them. She had to do this herself, had to take care of this child on her own. It was hers . . . her own . . . and Manfred's. It was the baby they had both wanted so badly . . . conceived amid the ashes of their dreams. He would now return to bloom on greener hillsides, a memory of how bright their love had been. She sat alone in her room that night, wondering, dreaming, would it be a girl or a boy? Would he look like Manfred . . . or perhaps like her father? . . . It was like expecting a visitor from an old familiar world, as she found herself wondering which of the faces she would never see again would be reborn in this small child. The doctor said that the baby would be born at the end of January, or perhaps even early February. Often, he insisted, first babies come late. And he thought that it would start to show some time in September, perhaps even October, if she was careful of what she wore. So by then she would have to leave the Liebmans. And once she was settled, once she had a job, then she would tell them. When the baby came, Julia and Debbie could come to visit. She smiled to herself as she thought of the tiny bundle in knitted clothes that the girls would come to see . . .

'What are you looking so happy about, Ariana?' It was Paul, standing right beside her. She hadn't even seen him come in.

'I don't know. I was just thinking.'

'What about?' He sat down on the floor next to her and looked up into the perfect little face.

'Nothing special.' She smiled slowly at him. Her happiness was almost impossible to hide, and now it touched Paul as well.

'Do you know what I was thinking about today? Our summer. It's going to be wonderful for us out there in the country. We can play tennis and go swimming. We can lie around in the sun and go to parties. Doesn't that sound like fun?' It did but now she had someone else to consider.

She nodded. And then, sobering, she looked at her young friend. 'Paul, I've just made a big decision.'

'What's that?' He smiled in anticipation.

'In September I'm going to get a job and move out.'

'That makes two of us. Want to become room-mates?'

'Very funny. I'm serious.'

'So am I. And what kind of job are you going to get, by the way?'

'I don't know yet, but I'll think of something. Maybe your father can give me some ideas.'

'I've got a better one.' He leaned over and kissed the soft blonde hair. 'Ariana, why won't you listen?'

266

'Because you're not old enough to make sense.' She was happier than she had been in months, and he laughed in answer. He could sense her good mood.

'You know, if you're serious about getting a job in September, then this will be your "last summer", too. Our last fling before we all settle down.'

'As a matter of fact,' she grinned broadly at him, 'that's exactly what it will be.'

He smiled at her and stood up. 'Then let's make it good, Ariana, the best summer we ever had.' She smiled at him, feeling her heart soar.

Chapter 38

A week later they all moved to the huge house in East Hampton. It had a main building with six bedrooms, three maids' rooms, a dining room large enough to feed an army, a large formal living room, a smaller den, and a family room downstairs. The kitchen was gigantic and friendly, and in the back there was a guest-house, and a beach-house where one could change one's clothes. In the guest-house there were five guest bedrooms, which the Liebmans planned to keep filled all summer with relatives and friends. The vacation was off to a great beginning until Ruth heard from Paul the day after they got there that Ariana planned to move out and get a job in the fall.

'But why, Ariana? Don't be silly. We don't want you to leave.' Ruth Liebman looked at her, crushed.

'But I can't impose on you for ever.'

'You're not imposing. You're one of our children. Ariana, this is absurd. And if you absolutely must have a job, why can't you live at the house?' She looked distraught at the prospect of losing the girl already. 'Go to University if you want to – you said once that you'd wanted to do that. You can do all kinds of things, but there is absolutely no reason for you to move out.'

'Oh, Paul, she looked so hurt.' Ariana looked at him in despair as he drove her into the city in his roadster to pick up some special odds and ends they had promised his mother they would get in New York. There were two more bathing suits for Debbie, some medication for Julia, a bunch of papers relating to the Women's Relief Organisation that Ruth had forgotten on her desk. They gathered it all up quickly, and then Ariana looked at the little gold watch Ruth had given her to wear. 'Do you suppose I have time to do one more errand?'

'Sure, what's up?'

'I promised Dr Kaplan I'd stop by for some vitamins if I had time.'

'Absolutely.' He looked at her sternly. 'We should have done that first.'

'Yes, sir.' She laughed at him and they gathered up all the things they'd promised to return with and headed downtown. It felt good to be young and enjoying the summer. The sunshine smiled down at them, and Ariana stretched out happily in the car.

'Want to try driving on the way back?'

'Your precious roadster? Paul, what have you been drinking?'

He laughed, glad she was feeling light-hearted. 'I trust you. You said that you knew how to drive.'

'I'm very flattered that you'd let me drive your new car.' She was touched by his offer, knowing how much the car meant to him.

'I would trust you with anything I own, Ariana. Even my new car.'

'Thank you.' There was little more she could say until they arrived at Dr Kaplan's office and she prepared to go inside. But he jumped out quickly to help her. He was wearing white linen slacks and a blazer, and with his long, easy stride and his warm smile, he looked youthful and elegant as they went inside.

'I'll come in with you for a minute. I haven't seen him in a while.' There was no longer much reason for him to see Kaplan – the knee that had taken him out of action was almost healed. In fact, one couldn't even see much of a limp, and with the exercise he'd get that summer, by fall the knee would be as good as new.

But Dr Kaplan was delighted to see him, and the threesome chatted for a moment until Dr Kaplan asked if he could see Ariana alone. Paul complied easily and sat down in the waiting room, putting his boater on the chair beside him.

In his office Ariana looked at the doctor with wide eyes.

'How are you feeling, Ariana?'

'Fine, thank you. As long as I watch what I eat, I'm fine.' She smiled at him and he thought that he had never seen her more at peace. She was wearing a summer dress with a big skirt and small waist, and a huge straw hat tied beneath her chin with blue ribbons the same colour as her eyes.

'You're looking wonderful.' And then after an awkward pause, he looked at her more intently. 'You haven't told any of them, have you?'

'No.' She shook her head slowly. 'I made up my mind. You said it would show in September, so when we get back from Lond Island this summer, I'm going to move out and find a job. And *then* I'll tell them everything. And I'm sure they'll understand. But I refuse to impose on them any further, or to expect them to support my child.'

'That's noble of you, Ariana. But do you have any idea how you and the baby will eat? Have you thought of the baby at all, or just yourself?' It was an unusually stern speech for him, and Ariana was briefly angry, and then hurt.

'Of course I've thought of the baby. That's all I think of. What do you mean?'

'That you're twenty years old, you have no trade, no profession, that you're going to be alone with a baby in a country you don't know, where people may not hire you simply because you're German. We've just ended a war with Germany and sometimes people hold that kind of grudge for a long time. I'm telling you that you're not giving that baby a decent shake, and you could do it, if you don't wait too long. If you do something about it now.' He looked at her intently and she stared.

'What do you mean?'

'I mean, Ariana – ' his voice gentled – 'get married. Give yourself and the baby a decent chance. I know, it's a hell of a thing to do, but, Ariana, since I saw you last, I've been tormenting myself. I think it's the only answer. I've thought and I've thought and I've thought. I know Paul since he's a baby. I can see what he feels for you. It's hell on my conscience to suggest this – but who will be hurt? If you marry that boy in the waiting room, you'll guarantee your baby's future, and your own.'

'I don't care about me.' She was shocked at what he was suggesting.

'But you do care about the baby. What about that?'

'But I can't do that . . . it's dishonest.'

'Don't you think a lot of other girls do the same thing? Girls who have far less reason to do it than you do . . . Ariana, the baby won't be born for another seven months. I could say that it came early. No one would have to know. No one. Not even Paul.'

She looked at the doctor, shocked by what he was suggesting. 'Don't you think that I could provide for the baby myself?'

'Of course not. When was the last time you saw a pregnant woman work? Who would hire you? And to do what?'

She sat for a long moment and then nodded pensively. Maybe he was right. She had just assumed she'd be able to get a job in a shop. But what a thing to do . . . what a deception . . . what a thing to do to Paul . . . how could she lie to him like that? He was her friend and in a way she loved him. In fact, she cared for him a great deal.

'How could I do such a thing, Doctor? It's wrong.' She felt guilt and shame rise within her just at the thought.

'You could do it for the sake of your unborn child. What

did you do getting to Paris, getting here? Were you always so honest? Wouldn't you have lied or shot or killed to save your life? You must do the same for the baby, Ariana. To provide him with a family, a father, a decent life-style, meals in his belly, an education . . .' Ariana realised she was naïve to think a few rings tucked away in a box could get her through this. Slowly she nodded her head.

'I'll have to think it over.'

'Do that, but don't think for too long. If you wait much longer, it will be too late. This way, if the baby comes at seven months, I can easily explain it by your frail health, the trip from Europe, all of that.'

'You think of everything, don't you?' She looked at him and realised he was giving her the push she needed to survive. He was teaching her the rules to a game she was getting very good at playing, and in her heart she knew he was right. But where would it end?

He was talking. 'If you do this, Ariana, your secret will always be safe with me.'

'Thank you, Doctor – for my life – and my baby's life.'

He handed her the vitamins and touched her shoulder gently as she left. 'Make your decision quickly, Ariana.'

She nodded quietly. 'Yes, I will.'

Chapter 39

'Ariana, do you want to come swimming?' Julia was pounding on her door at nine o'clock in the morning, and Ariana sleepily opened an eye.

'So early? I'm not up yet.'

'Neither was Paul. And he's coming, too.'

'That's right,' he verified as he sauntered through her doorway, 'and if I have to get up to go swimming with these little monsters, so do you.'

'Oh, I do, do I?' She stretched lazily and smiled as he sat

down next to her and kissed the loose blonde hair falling over her face.

'Yes, you do, otherwise, I shall drag you from your bed and pull you screaming down the beach.'

'How charming of you, Paul.'

'Yes, isn't it?' They smiled at each other for a moment. 'By the way, would you like to go to a party in Southampton tonight? My parents are taking the girls somewhere overnight.'

'How come?'

'It's the Fourth of July weekend, my dear. American Independence Day. Wait until you see – it should be quite an event.'

And as it turned out, it was. They went swimming with the girls that morning and on a picnic with the whole family that afternoon. After which Sam and Ruth took the girls off on their excursion and Ariana disappeared upstairs to take her nap. But at seven o'clock she was dressed to go out for the evening, and when she came down the stairs of the big summer home, Paul whistled and grinned.

'Say, lady, nobody ever warned me you'd look like that with a suntan.' She was wearing a turquoise silk dress that highlighted her fresh brown skin. He looked equally dashing in a white linen suit, white shirt, and a wide navy blue tie with tiny white dots, and together they set out for the evening in his new car.

In gala spirit he let Ariana drive it to the party, and once there he immediately brought her a gin fizz. Hesitant about her reactions to the liquor, she only took very small sips. But the party around her was already swinging. There were two bands playing, one in the house and one out on the lawn. Several yachts had pulled up for the occasion and were moored at the long dock where they were tended by a dozen boatsmen, and there was a ripe summer moon hanging overhead.

'Would you like to dance, Ariana?' He was smiling down at her gently, and smoothly she drifted into his arms. It was the first time they had danced together, and in the moonlight it was easy to pretend that it was Manfred, or her father, or anyone at all. 'Has anyone ever told you that you dance like an angel?'

'Not lately, I'm afraid.' She laughed softly at the compliment and they danced on until the end of the set. They walked slowly to a railing where they could look down at the boats bobbing beneath them, and Paul looked at her with a seriousness Ariana had not yet seen.

'I'm so happy when I'm with you, Ariana. I've never known anyone like you before.' She wanted to tease him and ask about Joanie, but she knew that this wasn't the time.

'Ariana –' he looked at her quietly – 'I have something to tell you.' He reached over slowly, took both her heands in his, and then kissed them gently, one at a time. 'I love you. I don't know how else to tell you. I love you. I can't bear being without you. Being with you, I feel . . . well . . . so happy and strong . . . like I can do anything, like everything I touch is some kind of a gift . . . like it's all worth it . . . and I never want to let that feeling go. If you go off on your own after the summer and I do the same thing, we'll lose that.' His eyes misted over as he said it. 'And, Ariana, I can't bear to let you go.'

'You won't have to.' Her voice was a whisper. 'Paul . . . I –'

And then, as though he had timed it, the first fireworks exploded overhead. He reached into his pocket and took out a large emerald-cut diamond ring. Before she had realised what had happened, he had slipped it on her finger, and his mouth was pressing hard on hers as his urgency and his passion reached towards her. She felt a longing and a stirring in her that she had thought never to feel again. She clung to him almost desperately for a moment, returning his kiss and fighting the longing in her own soul.

At last, after their lips parted, she told him that she was tired, and they drove back to his parents' house in East Hampton in a far more subdued state of mind. She was still trying to wrestle with her conscience. How could she go on

273

with this charade? And it wasn't that she didn't love him. She did love him, in a warm, friendly kind of way, but it was wrong to take advantage of his affection, wrong to press on him a child that was not his. When at last they got out of the car in the driveway, Paul put a gentle arm around her and led her inside. And in the front hall he looked down at her sadly.

'I know what you're thinking. You don't want it, not the ring, not what it stands for, not me . . . not any of it. It's all right, Ariana. I understand.' But there were tears in his voice as he pressed her to him. 'But, oh, God, I love you so much, please, please, just let me be alone with you here, just this one night. Let me dream, let me imagine what it would have been like if this were our house, if we were married, if all the dreams had come true.'

'Paul.' She pulled away from him gently, but when she did, she saw the handsome young face washed with tears. And then she couldn't bear it any longer; she pulled him close to her and reached her face up to his, offering him a warmth and a loving that she had never thought she would have to give anyone again. Moments later they reached her bedroom, and with a gentleness far beyond his years, Paul carefully peeled away the silk dress. They lay there for a long time in the moonlight, holding, caressing, dreaming, kissing, and saying nothing at all. And at last by the first light of morning, with the last passion spent, they fell asleep in each other's arms.

Chapter 40

'Good morning, my darling.' Ariana squinted in the bright sunlight as she saw him. He had set a breakfast tray down on the bed and was opening several drawers and putting the contents into a small suitcase he had laid out on the bed.

'What are you doing?' She sat up in bed and had to fight a

274

wave of nausea. The coffee was pungent and it had been a long night.

'I'm packing your suitcase.' He smiled at her over his shoulder.

'But where are we going? Your parents will be back tonight. They'll worry if they don't find us – '

'We'll be back by then.'

'Then why the suitcase, Paul? I don't understand.' She felt totally disoriented as she sat there, still naked, as this man with the long legs in a navy blue silk bathrobe packed her bag. 'Paul, will you please stop and talk to me?' There was a faint note of panic in her voice.

'I will in a minute.' And then, when he had finished, he turned, sat down quietly on the bed, and took her hand in his own, the one that still wore the enormous emerald-cut diamond ring. 'All right, now I'll tell you. We're going to Maryland this morning, Ariana.'

'Maryland? Why?'

But this time he faced her squarely. It was as though overnight he had become a man. 'We're going to Maryland to get married, because I'm tired of playing games and acting like we're both fourteen years old. We're not, Ariana. I'm a man and you're a woman, and if something like last night can happen between us once, then it can happen again and again. I won't play games with you, I won't beg you. I love you, and I think you love me, too.' And then his voice softened again slightly. 'Will you marry me, Ariana? Darling, I love you with all my heart.'

'Oh, Paul.' Tears flooded her eyes as she held out her arms to him. Was it possible that she could make him happy? If she did marry him, out of gratitude for what he would be giving her child, she would always be good to him. But all she could do was cry as he held her. It was such a huge decision, and she still wasn't sure what to do.

'Will you stop crying and give me an answer?' He kissed her neck gently, then her face, then her hair. 'Oh, Ariana, I love you . . . how I love you . . .' He kissed her again, and slowly this time she nodded, and then she faced him, as other faces came to mind ... Manfred ... her father ... briefly she even remembered Max Thomas, kissing her in her mother's room the night he escaped Berlin. What would they all think of her if she married this man? And then she realised that it didn't matter, that it was her decision, her life now. Not theirs. They were all gone. All of them. She was the only one left ... she ... and her baby ... and Paul. He was more real than the others ever could be now. She stretched a hand out to him now with a long, slow smile. She was reaching across a lifetime, reaching out to him with all her heart and soul, and as she did so, she vowed silently never to betray their love.

'Well?' He looked at her, trembling, afraid to take her hand, afraid to move. But she took both of his and brought them slowly to her mouth. And then one by one she kissed his fingers and closed her eyes. When she opened them again, there was a look of tenderness that reached to his very soul.

'Yes.' She smiled at him and pulled him closer. 'Yes, my darling. Yes! The answer is yes.' And then, burying her head in his shoulder, she rejoiced. 'How I will love you, Paul Liebman.' And then she took a step back to look at him. 'What a wonderful man you are.'

'My God.' He grinned at her. 'I think you've gone crazy. But I'm not about to look a gift horse in the mouth. You just stay crazy and let me take care of the rest.'

And so he did. An hour later they were on the road to Maryland, with their suitcases in the back seat and Ariana's temporary identity cards in his pocket. Hours later the wife of a justice of the peace just outside Baltimore snapped their picture as her husband solemnly stared at Paul and nodded, murmuring firmly, 'You may kiss the bride.'

'Mother ... Dad ...' Paul's voice almost trembled as he faced them, but gently he reached out for Ariana's hand. He took it, and he held it proudly, and then he smiled at his parents with a look that said he was a man. 'Ariana and I eloped.' He smiled down at tiny, nervous Ariana. 'I almost had to force her to do it, which is why I didn't want to waste my time waiting around to discuss it with you. So – ' he looked at both his parents warmly, and although they were clearly stunned, they did not look displeased – 'may I present to you Mrs Paul Liebman?' He bowed gracefully towards her, and she dropped a curtsy at his feet. And then with one swift, graceful movement, she reached up and kissed him and then reached out quick arms to Ruth. The older woman took her and held her, holding her close for a long moment, remembering the terrifyingly sick girl she had rescued from the ship. Sam watched them for a moment, he then held his arms out to his son.

Chapter 41

As planned, Ariana and Paul stayed in East Hampton until September, and then after Labour Day they went back to the city to begin their search for their own place. Paul began to work with his father at the office, and Ruth joined Ariana in the hunt for the right home. Just after they all celebrated Rosh Hashanah together, a pretty little town house became available in the upper Sixties, and after very little debate Paul decided that it had to be theirs. For the moment they were only renting, but the owner was interesting in selling the place to them at the end of their lease. The young couple decided that the arrangement was perfect. It would give them a chance to decide if they really liked the house.

Now all they needed was more furniture, and with the girls back in school, Ruth had more time to help. She was a little less busy with her refugee organisation, and she had been spending almost every day with Ariana, enough so to see that once again the girl wasn't feeling well.

'Ariana, have you been back to see Kaplan?' Ruth looked at her worriedly, and Ariana nodded, trying to decide about a swatch of fabric she'd ordered to match their new rug.

'Well, have you?'

'Yes. I went last Thursday.' She avoided Ruth's eyes for a moment and then looked up at her mother-in-law with a small smile.

'What did he say?'

'That the fainting and the problems with my stomach are going to go on for quite a while.'

'Does he think it's permanent?' Ruth looked at her with greater concern now, but Ariana shook her head.

'Not at all. In fact, he isn't even worried about it any more. He said that before it was from the rigours of my trip to get here. But now it's the price I'm paying for what I did after I arrived.'

'What does he mean by that?' And then suddenly she understood the cryptic message. Her eyes widened and she looked at Ariana with a long, slow smile. 'You mean you're pregnant?'

'Yes, I am.'

'Oh, Ariana!' She looked at her happily and quickly crossed the room to give her a hug. But then she looked at the small young woman with fresh worry. 'Does he think it will be all right for you? It's not too soon after you were so sick . . . you're so tiny – you're not a big horse of a woman like me.' But she clung to Ariana's hand tightly, so thrilled with the news. For an instant it reminded her of the joy she had felt when she learned that she was expecting their first child.

'The only thing he wants me to do is start seeing a specialist a little later, when we get closer to the birth.'

'That sounds reasonable, and when will that be, by the way?'

'Early April.' Inwardly, Ariana cringed at the lie, praying that Ruth would never know the truth about the baby, and silently promised herself and Ruth that one day there would truly be a Liebman child. She owed it to Paul to have his baby, and as soon as she was able, she was going to have another, and still more if that was what he wanted. She owed him everything for protecting Manfred's child.

*

As the months wore on, Paul matured, growing more and more paternal, helping Ariana prepare the nursery and smiling at her as she spent night after night knitting clothes. Ruth had also brought over boxes and boxes of things from her own babies, and there seemed to be little tiny hats and socks and dresses and sweaters everywhere Paul looked.

'Well, from the look of this place, Mrs Liebman, I'd say we were having a baby.' It was two weeks before Christmas. Paul thought she was only five and a half months pregnant, but in truth the baby's birth was only six weeks away. But no one seemed to find her enlarged proportions outrageous. They assumed her impressive bulge was simply due to the fact that it all showed more on a woman of Ariana's size. And by now Paul had grown to like the belly – he called it funny names and said that he had to rub it twice for good luck before he left for work every day.

'Don't do that!' She squealed when he tickled her. 'You'll make it kick me again.'

'It must be a boy.' He said it was great seriousness one night while listening to her stomach. 'I think it's trying to play football.'

Ariana groaned and rolled her eyes as she laughed at her husband. 'It certainly is playing football in there . . . with my kidneys, I think.'

The next morning, after Paul had left for the office, something strange happened, and for hours on end Ariana felt overwhelmed by nostalgia for her old life. She sat for hours in a chair thinking of Manfred, got out her jewel box, and tried on his rings. She sat there thinking of their plans and their promises and then found herself wondering what he would have thought of this child. Paul had his heart set on Simon, after the brother who had died. And it was something she felt she should do for him.

As she went through her mementos that morning, she came to the envelope with the photographs of her and Manfred, hidden in a book in a locked drawer at the bottom of her desk. She pulled them out and spread them out in her lap then, staring at the face she had loved, remembering every inch of the uniform, hearing his words at their first Christmas. It was difficult to believe that the photographs of the Christmas Eve balls had been taken only a year before. With two little rivers of tears dripping from her cheeks on to the huge belly, she held the photographs in her hands and never heard her husband come in. A moment later he stood behind her, staring down at the photographs, first in confusion, and then in horror, as the insignia on the uniform finally became clear.

'My God, who is that?' He stared down in fury and amazement, seeing Ariana's smiling face at the man's side. Ariana jumped in terror as she heard him. She had no idea that he was standing there at all.

'What are you doing here?' The tears had stopped and she still held the photographs in her hand as she stood up.

'I came home to check on my wife and see if she wanted to join me for lunch somewhere, but I see that I seem to have interrupted a rather intriguing private time. Tell me, Ariana, do you do this every day, or only on major holidays?' And then after a frozen moment, 'Would you mind telling me who that was?'

'It was . . . he was a German officer.' She looked at Paul almost in desperation. This was not the way that she had wanted him to find out.

'I could tell that much from the Nazi armband. Anything else you'd like to tell me? Like how many Jews he killed? Or which camp he ran?'

'He didn't kill any Jews, and he didn't run any camps. In fact, he saved my life. And he kept me from being raped by a lieutenant and made a whore by a general. If it hadn't been for him – ' she began to sob uncontrollably as she held the picture of the man who'd been dead for seven months now – 'if it hadn't been for him . . . I would very probably be dead now.'

For an instant Paul regretted what he had said to her, but then as he looked at the photograph fluttering in her hand, he felt anger overcome him again. 'Then, what the hell are you doing laughing and smiling in these pictures if your life was so much at stake?' He reached for the pictures and then realised with utter fury that she was dancing with the Nazi officer at a ball. 'Ariana, who is this man?' And then suddenly he understood how she had survived the camps after all. His mother had been right. And he had no right to berate her for what she'd done. The girl had no choice. Tenderly, feeling shaken, he reached out to Ariana, and pulled her as close as he could with her huge belly into his arms. 'I'm sorry . . . oh, darling, I'm sorry. I think for a moment I forgot what happened. I just saw that face and that uniform and it all looked so German, I think for a minute I lost my mind.'

'But I'm German, too, Paul.' She was still crying, sobbing softly in his arms.

'Yes, but you're not like them, and if what you had to do was to be this man's mistress to survive the camps, Ariana, then I don't give a damn what happened.' But as he said it, he felt her freeze in his arms. And quietly she backed away from him and sat down.

'That's what you think, isn't it, Paul?' She eyed him for an endless moment and he said nothing, and then softly she went on. 'You think I was this man's whore to save my own skin. Well, that's not true and I want you to know the truth. After the death of my father and Gerhard, he – Manfred – took me to his house and he expected nothing from me, nothing. He didn't rape me, he didn't touch me, he didn't hurt me. He only gave me his protection and became my only friend.'

'It's a touching story, but that's a Nazi uniform, isn't it, Ariana?' His voice was like ice as it touched her, but she sat there feeling unafraid – knowing she was doing the right thing.

'Yes, Paul, it is. But there were some decent men wearing Nazi uniforms, and he was one. It's not all just good guys and bad guys. Life isn't always as simple as that.'

'My, my, darling. Thank you for the lesson. But frankly I find it a little hard to stomach when I come home and find my wife crying over pictures of some goddamn Nazi, and then I discover that he was her "friend". The Nazis weren't anyone's friends, Ariana. Don't you understand that? How can you say what you're saying? You're a Jew!' He was raging at her as she sat there, but now she stood to face him and shook her head.

'No, Paul, I am not a Jew. I am a German.' He was shocked into silence, and she went on, afraid that if she stopped now, words would fail her.

'My father was a good German, and a banker; he was the head of the most important bank in Berlin. But when they drafted my brother after his sixteenth birthday, my father didn't want Gerhard to go.' She tried smiling at him now. What a relief it was to tell him the story, to tell him the truth, no matter what it cost in the end.

'My father's sympathies were never with the Nazis, and when they tried to draft Gerhard, he knew that we had to escape. He devised a plan to get my brother into Switzerland, and then he would come back for me the day after that. Only something must have happened, and he never did return. Our servants turned me in – people I had trusted all my life – ' her voice rose – 'and the Nazis came and took me away. They kept me in a cell for a month, Paul, holding me for "ransom", in case my father came back, but he didn't. For a month I lived in a filthy, stinking little cell, half starving and half crazy, in a room half the size of one of the closets of your mother's maids. And then they let me go because I was useless. They took over my father's house, kept all our things, and threw me out in the street. But the general who took over my father's home in Grunewald apparently also wanted me, too. Manfred, this man – ' she pointed at the pictures with trembling hands as tears rolled down her face – 'saved me from him, and from everyone. He kept me safe until the war ended.' Her voice broke then. 'Until the fall of Berlin, when he was killed.' She looked up at Paul then but his face looked as hard as rock.

'And were you lovers, you and this stinking Nazi?'

'Don't you understand? He *saved* me! Don't you care

282

about that?' She eyed him for a long moment, her own anger building.

'I care that you were the mistress of a Nazi.'

'Then you're a fool. I survived, dammit. I survived!'

'And you cared about him?' His voice was frigid and suddenly, as much as she had come to love Paul, she hated him now. She wanted to hurt him as he was hurting her.

'I cared very much. He was my husband, and he would be now if he weren't dead.'

For an instant they stood there eyeing each other, suddenly aware of all that had been said, and when Paul spoke again, his voice was shaking. He looked and pointed at her stomach and then raised his eyes to her face.

'Whose baby is that?'

She wanted to lie to him, for the child's sake, but she could no longer do it. 'My husband's,' she answered. Her voice was strong and proud, as though she were bringing Manfred back to life.

'I am your husband, Ariana.'

'Manfred's.' She answered softly, suddenly aware of what she had done to Paul. As the full impact hit her, she almost reeled.

'Thank you,' he whispered, and then, turning on his heel, he slammed the door.

Chapter 42

The next morning Ariana received a packet of papers from Paul's attorney. She was being notified that Mr Paul Liebman had the intention of suing her for divorce. She was being formally notified that four weeks after the birth of the baby, she would have to vacate the premises, but that in the meantime she could stay there. She would also continue to be supported for that brief period, and after she left, once the baby was born, the sum of 5000 dollars would be given to her by cheque. No support was going to be forthcoming for the baby, since it apparently was not Mr Liebman's child, nor for her, given the circumstances of their brief and apparently fraudulent marriage. A letter in the same packet from her father-in-law confirmed the financial arrangements, and a note from her mother-in-law berated her for having betrayed them all. How dared she have pretended to be a Jew. It was, as Ariana had always suspected it would be, the ultimate betrayal, not to mention the fact that she was pregnant with 'some Nazi's' child. The war had hit hard. 'Some Nazi' – Ariana flinched at the word when she read it. Further, she forbade Ariana to set foot near the house on Fifth Avenue, and forbade her also ever to come near any of them again. Should she discover that Ariana had attempted to see Deborah or Julia, Ruth would feel no qualms about calling the police.

As Ariana sat in the apartment, reading what they had sent her, she desperately wanted to reach Paul. But he had sought refuge with his parents, and under no circumstances would he take her calls. Instead, he spoke to her through his attorney, the arrangements were begun, the divorce suit was filed, the Liebmans shut her out, and on 24 December, shortly after midnight, one month early, Ariana went into labour all alone.

Her bravado faded then, as, momentarily, did her courage. She was paralysed with fear – of the unknown, and of her aloneness – but she was able to reach the doctor and got to the hospital in a cab.

Twelve hours later Ariana was still in the throes of her labour, and she was almost incoherent with the pain. Frightened, frantic, still shocked by what had happened with Paul and the Liebmans, she was in no condition to deal with what was happening, and time and again she screamed for Manfred, until at last they gave her something for the pain. At ten o'clock on Christmas night the baby was finally delivered, by Cesarean section, but despite the difficulties of the labour neither mother nor baby had come to any harm. They showed him to Ariana briefly, a tiny bundle of wrinkled flesh with the smallest hands and feet that she had ever seen.

He didn't look like her or like Manfred, or like Gerhard or her father. He didn't look like anyone at all.

'What will you call him?' The nurse asked her softly as she held Ariana's hand.

'I don't know.' She was so tired, and he was so little – she wondered if it was all right that he was so small. But through the pain and the anesthetic, she still felt a warm glow of joy.

'It's Christmas, you could call him Noel.'

'Noel?' Ariana thought for a minute, smiling in her drug-filled half-sleep. 'Noel? That's pretty.' And then, turning her face towards where she imagined the baby, she smiled a peaceful smile. 'Noel von Tripp,' she said to herself and fell asleep.

Chapter 43

Exactly four weeks after the birth of the baby, Ariana stood in the front hall with the last of their bags. As per the arrangement, she was vacating the apartment, and she already had the baby all bundled up in the cab. They were going to a hotel a nurse at the hospital had recommended. It was cozy and inexpensive, and the proprietress would serve meals. So soon after the Cesarean, Ariana wasn't really supposed to be up. One more time she had attempted to reach Paul at his office, and then once more she had allowed herself to try him at home. But it was useless. He wouldn't speak to her. It was over. He had sent her the 5000 dollars. All he wanted now was her keys.

She closed the door softly behind them, and with her clothes and her baby, her photographs of Manfred, and her volume of Shakespeare with a compartment for rings, she began her new life. She had already sent back the large diamond Paul had given her, and she was once again wearing Manfred's rings. Somehow they felt more right on her fingers, and she knew now that she would never take them off again. She would be Ariana von Tripp for ever. If it seemed wiser in the States, she would drop the 'von', but she would never betray her old life, she would never lie or pretend any more about who and what she was. She had suffered at the hands of the Nazis, yet she knew better than anyone that the Nazis were only a horde of men, and in the horde somewhere there had been some good ones. She would never betray Manfred again.

He was the husband she would cherish for a lifetime. He was the man she would talk of to her son. The man who had bravely served his country and the woman who had loved him until the very end. She would tell him about his grandfather and sweet Gerhard. Perhaps she would even tell him that she had married Paul, but she wasn't sure. She knew she had been wrong to try to deceive him, but she had paid for that dearly, too, in the end. But, she smiled down at the sleeping baby, she would always have her son.

Chapter 44

When Noel was two months old, Ariana had answered an ad in the paper and gotten a job in a bookshop that specialised in foreign books. They allowed her to bring the baby and paid her a tiny wage on which, at least, she and the baby could survive.

'Ariana . . . you really ought to do it.' The young woman was looking at her intensely as Ariana tried to keep an eye on her roving child. She had worked at the bookstore for over a year now and Noel had learned to walk early, and he was already fascinated by the bright books stacked on shelves near the floor.

'I don't think I want anything from them, Mary.'

'Yes, but don't you want something for the baby? Do you

286

want to be doing this kind of work for the rest of your life?' Ariana looked at her hesitantly. 'It won't hurt to ask. And you're not asking them for charity, you're asking them for what's yours.'

'What was mine. That's different. When I left, it was all in the Nazis' hands.'

'At least go to the consulate and ask them.' Mary was insistent, and Ariana decided that maybe she would ask on her next day off. The German government had instated a system whereby the people who had lost goods and property at the hands of the Nazis could now ask the government for some compensation for their loss. She had no proof of what had belonged to her, either the house in Grunewald or Manfred's family schloss, which also, by right, would be hers.

Two weeks later on a Thursday, her day off, she rolled Noel's pram to the consulate. It was a cold, blustery day in March, and she almost hadn't gone out for fear that it might snow. But she bundled the baby into his heavy blanket and walked inside the impressive bronze door.

'*Bitte?* May I help you?' For an instant Ariana only stared. It had been so long since Ariana had heard her own language, seen a European, or seen things done in the official way she was used to that for a moment all she could do was look around her in astonishment. It was as though in a single instant she had been transported home. Slowly, she began to answer and to explain why she had come. And to her surprise she was treated with the utmost respect and courtesy, given the information she desired and a raft of forms to fill out, and told to come back next week.

When she returned, there was a fairly large crowd in the lobby. She had the forms all filled out in her pocket, and all she had to do now was wait for an interview with some minor consulate official who would process them through. And then who knew how long it would all take? Maybe years if she got anything from them at all. But it was worth a try.

As she stood at the consulate, Noel sleeping in his pram, she couldn't resist the urge to close her eyes and imagine herself at home again. Around her everywhere were Germans, the sounds of Bavaria, of Munich, of Liepzig, of Frankfurt, and then the patter of Berlin. It sounded so sweet and familiar, and yet at the same time it was painful, too. Among all those familiar words and accents and sayings, not a familiar voice could she hear. And then suddenly, as though she were dreaming, she felt someone grab her arm, there was a quick exclamation, an intake of breath, and when she looked up, she was staring into a pair of familiar brown eyes. They were eyes that she had seen before somewhere . . . eyes she had known . . . and seen for the last time only three years before.

'Oh, my God! Oh, my God!' And then suddenly she was crying. It was Max . . . Max Thomas . . . and without thinking, she hurled herself into his arms. For what seemed like hours he held her tightly while they both laughed and cried. He hugged her, he kissed her, he held the baby – for both it was a dream they had never thought would come true. And then, huddled in the hallway as they waited, she told him of her father and of Gerhard and of how they had lost their home. And then she told him quietly of Manfred; no longer afraid or ashamed, she told Max that she had loved him, that they had been married, and that Noel was his son. But she discovered quickly that, with the exception of Noel, he knew about all that. He had scoured Berlin for her and her father after the war.

'Did you look for them after the war, Ariana?'

She hesitated for a moment and then shook her head. 'I didn't really know how. My husband said that he was certain my father was dead. And then I contacted a friend of his in Paris, a man who ran a refugee assistance organisation of sorts, before I left Europe. He checked out every possible lead, looking for any trace of them, especially of Gerhard.' She sighed softly. 'He even tried to trace you, but there was no sign of you . . . or of Gerhard.' And then suddenly the full impact of what she had just said struck her. There had been no trace of Max and he was alive   couldn't Gerhard be, too? She looked thunderstruck for a moment and Max gently took her face in his hands as he shook his head from side to side.

'Don't. They're gone, Ariana. I know it. I looked, too. After the war, I went back to Berlin, to try to reach your father, and . . .' He had been about to say 'to see you'. 'I heard from the men at the bank in Berlin what happened.'

'What did they tell you?'

'That he disappeared. And that with hindsight, pretty much everyone knew that he had gone to save Gerhard from the draft. There is absolutely no trace of your father, nor of Gerhard. Once in Switzerland a maid in a hotel recognised a photograph I had of him, thought that he looked like a boy who'd been there a year or so before, but she wasn't sure, and after she looked at the photograph for a while, she was certain it wasn't the same boy. I went back to Switzerland and searched for them for three months.' He sighed deeply and leaned heavily against the wall. 'I think the border patrol got them, Ariana. It's the only answer that makes any sense. If they were alive, they'd have eventually gone back to Berlin. And they never did. I've stayed in touch.' Hearing it from him now made it real once again, and he was right. If they'd been alive, they would have turned up, and if Max had stayed in touch with people at the bank in Berlin, then it was certain. Hearing it made the news seem fresh again and she felt grief tear once more at her heart. He put an arm around her shoulders and with one hand smoothed down her golden hair. 'You know, it's amazing. I knew you had come to the States, Ariana, but I didn't think I'd ever see you again.'

She turned to him in amazement. 'You knew? How?'

'I told you, I looked for all three of you. I had to. I owed your father my life and . . .' He looked boyish for a moment. 'I never . . . forgot that evening . . . the night that . . .' He lowered his voice. '. . . I kissed you. Do you remember?'

She looked at him sadly. 'Do you really think that I'd forget?'

'You could have. It's been a long time.'

'It's been a long road for all of us. But you remembered.

So did I.' And then she remembered something else. She still wanted to know all the details of the story. 'How did you know I'd come to the States?'

'I don't know. It was just a hunch. I thought that it was safe to assume that if you'd survived the fall of Berlin, you hadn't stayed. As the wife of a German officer . . . You see, I knew.' He hesitated for only an instant, his eyes looking deep into hers. 'Were you forced to do that?'

She shook her head. Was her lifetime to be filled with denying that? 'No, Max, I wasn't. He was a wonderful man.' She remembered suddenly Hildebrand and General Ritter . . . and Von Rheinhardt and the endless interrogations . . . Coming back here, listening to the countless conversations around her in German brought it all back. But now she pulled her attention back to Max. 'He saved my life, Max.' There was a long pause between them, and then he pulled her slowly into his arms. 'I heard from someone that he'd been killed.' She nodded sombrely in confirmation. 'So I tried various possibilities, and France was one. The immigration people in Paris had a record of issuing you temporary travel papers. I knew the date you left France. I traced you to Saint Marne.' She was touched beyond words.

'What made you search so hard?'

'I felt that I owed your father something, Ariana. I hired a detective to look for you all when I got back to Berlin. And of your father and Gerhard – ' he hesitated painfully – 'there was no trace.' And then he smiled softly. 'But you, *Liebchen*, I knew you were alive, and I didn't want to give up.'

'Then why did you? Why didn't you look here? Surely Jean-Pierre must have told you I came to New York.'

'He did. Did you know he died?'

'Jean-Pierre? Dead?' She was rocked by the news.

'He died in a car accident outside Paris.' There was a moment of silence between them and then he went on.

'He gave me the name of some people in New Jersey. I wrote to them and they claimed that they never even met you. They admitted that they were supposed to be your sponsors, but they had changed their minds.' Slowly Ariana recalled the sponsors in New Jersey. They had faded from her life as she had lain half-dead in the hospital.

'They wrote that they didn't know who had become your sponsors, and no one else seemed to know either. The people who took over Saint Marne's files in Paris had no idea. It was only months after I came here myself that someone at the Woman's Relief Organisation told me about the Liebmans. But when I went there to talk to them myself, things became confused.'

Ariana felt her heart race nervously at the sound of the name.

'What did they say?' She looked strangely anxious.

'They said that they'd never seen you either and that they had no idea where you were. Mrs Liebman said she recalled the name but had no further information to give me.' Ariana nodded slowly. She could imagine Ruth doing that. She was so angry at Ariana that she would deny everything now, especially her marriage to their son. Slowly Ariana's eyes rose until she was looking at Max with an expression that told him there was much more.

'I never found any trace of you after that.'

'It doesn't matter, Max.' She touched his arm gently. 'You found me after all.' She hesitated for a moment and then decided to tell him. Why not? 'Ruth Liebman lied to you. I was married to her son.' Max looked astonished as she told him all of it, keeping nothing back, and there were tears in his eyes as he listened. Without realising it, he took her hand and she held it tightly as she told him the story from beginning to end.

'And now?'

'I'm waiting for the divorce. It will be final in July.'

'I'm sorry, Ariana. What more can I say?'

'It was my own fault. I shouldn't have done it the way I did, but I was stupid and foolish. I'm only sorry because now I've lost them all, and they were very special people. Ruth saved my life – and Noel's.'

'Perhaps one day they'll change their minds.'

'I doubt it.'

'And the little one?' Max smiled pensively, remembering his own children at the same age. 'What is his name?'

'Noel.' Ariana returned Max's smile. 'He was born on Christmas.'

'What a nice gift for you.' And then with a tender look at Ariana, 'Was anyone with you?' She shook her head slowly. 'I'm sorry, Ariana.' But she was sorry for them all. How far they had come, and how much they had lost over the past few years. Only she seemed to be lucky as she looked around at the people waiting to make their claims – she had much-treasured Noel, and he had been worth it all.

'And what about you?' Still waiting in the consular hallways, he told her that her father's paintings had kept him alive through the war and not only allowed him to eat, but to go to law school to become an attorney again once he got to the States.

He had remained in Switzerland until the end of the war, working at odd jobs, living hand to mouth, waiting, until V-E Day, when he had finally sold the last of the paintings and shortly thereafter gone to the States, and that had been two years before.

And now he was finally officially once more a lawyer, which was what brought him here. He wanted to establish his own claim and then make an arrangement with the consulate to handle many of the claims that were going to come in droves. He was hoping the consulate would recommend him since he was certified in Germany and the States.

'It won't make me rich, but it's a living. And you? Did you get anything out, Ariana?'

'My skin, a few pieces of jewellery – and Manfred's photographs.' He nodded slowly, remembering all they had once had, the splendour of her father's house. It seemed incredible that they had all come so far and that there was nothing left of that world. Only memories and trinkets, souvenirs and dreams.

For Max they were memories to which he couldn't have borne to return.

'Do you ever think about going back, Ariana?'

'Not really. I have no more there than I do here. I have no one except Noel now. And here it will be a good life for him.'

'I hope so.' Max smiled at him gently, reminded of his own sons. And then he took Noel carefully from his mother and tousled his hair. Standing there together, they looked like a family, laughing, happy, united; and no one, except others who had been there, would have believe the long road they had come.

Book Four

NOEL

Chapter 45

The ceremony took place on a brilliantly sunny morning in Harvard Yard between the Widener Library and the Appleton Chapel. There seemed to be a sea of sparkling young faces and tall, lean bodies draped in cap and gown, waiting to receive the diplomas they had struggled towards for so long. Ariana watched them, smiling mistily, as Max sat beside her on the narrow folding chairs, holding her hand and noticing how the large emerald she now wore constantly sparkled in the sun.

'Doesn't he look handsome, Max?' She leaned gently towards the distinguished white-haired gentleman he had become, and he patted her arm and smiled.

'How can you tell, Ariana? I'm not even sure which one is he.'

'Some people just have no respect at all.' They whispered at each other like two children, the laughter still fresh in their eyes. He had been her constant companion now for almost twenty-five years, and they still enjoyed each other's company after all this time.

She smiled up at him, her golden beauty not yet faded and only slightly quieter with time. The features were still perfect, her hair a softer gold, the eyes still enormous and the same deep blue. It was Max who had changed greatly, still tall, spare, almost lanky, but with a full mane of white hair now. Nineteen years older than Ariana, he had just turned sixty-four.

'Oh, Max, I'm so proud of him.'

This time his arm went gently around her and he nodded. 'You should be. He's a good man.' And then he smiled again. 'And a good lawyer. It's a damn shame he wants to work for that high-falutin fancy firm. I would be proud to have an associate like him.' But although Max's law practice

297

in New York had grown to considerable proportions, it was still a relatively small show compared to the firm that had already made Noel an offer the summer before. He had clerked for them for one summer, and they were quick to offer him a job the moment he would graduate from Harvard Law. And now that moment had come.

By noon it was all over, and he returned to hug his mother warmly and shake hands with Uncle Max.

'Well, you two, surviving? I was afraid that by now you'd both be cooked by the sun.' The huge blue eyes danced as he looked down at his mother, and she smiled up into the face that was so exactly Manfred's that it still startled her at times. He had the tall, lean frame of his father, the broad shoulders, the graceful hands, yet oddly, now and then there was a look . . . an expression . . . some vague hint of Gerhard, and she would smile as she looked at Noel . . . yes, they did live on in her son.

'Darling, it was a lovely ceremony. And we're both so proud.'

'So am I, you know.' He bent the broad shoulders lower to speak to her softly, and she touched his face with the hand that wore her mother's signet ring on her little finger and the ring Manfred had given her, which had never left her hand since her son had been born. In all those early years after Paul had left her, she had never given up the treasured rings. They were not only her last security, but they remained the only reminder of the past. In time Max had won her the restitution, both for the house in Grunewald and some of its contents and Manfred's schloss. The amount was not an overwhelming fortune, but it was nonetheless very handsome and had been enough to invest well and provide herself and the child with a healthy income, at least for the rest of Ariana's life. She needed no more than that. For her the days of glory now were gone. She was able to quit the bookshop. She bought a small town house on the East Side, in the upper Seventies, invested all her money, and spent every living, waking moment caring for her only child.

For the first years Max had tried to talk her into getting

married, but after that he stopped. Neither of them wanted any more children, and in their own way they were both still too tied to those they had loved in the past. Instead, for a while Max rented a small apartment, and eventually at Ariana's urging he bought a small but handsome co-op across the street from her house. They went to the opera, theatre, dinner, disappeared occasionally together on weekends, but in the end, they went home to their separate retreats. For a long time Ariana did so because of Noel, but eventually it just became a habit. And now, even in the seven years he had been at Harvard, Ariana still spent much of her time in her own place.

'You have every right to be proud, darling.' She gazed at him from under her straw hat and he wondered for an instant, as Max did so often, if she would ever show the signs of age. She was still as spectacularly pretty as she had been when she was a girl.

But Noel was shaking his head and smiling. 'I didn't mean that I was proud of me,' he whispered. 'I meant that I was proud of you.' She laughed at him softly in amusement, touched his face, and tucked her arm into Max's.

'I don't think you're supposed to say things like that to your mother, Noel.'

'That's right. Besides – ' Max smiled at them both – 'I might get jealous.' They both laughed and Ariana took hold of Max's hand. 'So when do you start work, Noel?'

'The hell I'm going to work now, Uncle Max. Are you kidding? I'm taking a vacation!'

Ariana turned to look at him with surprise and pleasure. 'Are you? Where are you going?' He hadn't said anything to her yet. But he was a man how. She didn't expect him to share all his plans. Wisely, with Max's help, she had learned to let go slowly when he had first left for Harvard in the fall of 1963.

'I thought I'd go to Europe.'

'Really?' She looked at him in amazement. On their trips together they had gone to California, Arizona, the Grand Canyon, New Orleans, New England . . . everywhere except

Europe, because neither Max nor she had ever been able to go back. What was the point of returning to old places, seeing the homes and haunts and hideouts of the people they had loved, people who were gone but not yet forgotten? Max and she had both agreed long before never to go back. 'Where in Europe, Noel?' For an instant she paled.

'I haven't decided.' And then he looked at her gently. 'But I'll probably stop in Germany, Mother, I have to . . . I want to . . .' She nodded slowly. 'Can you understand that?'

She smiled gently up at the son who was so suddenly a man. 'Yes, darling, I do.' Yet she was surprised to realise that it hurt her. She had wanted so to give him everything American, to create a world where there would be no room for Germany in his life, where the boy would be content with what he had here, and never want to go back to her old world.

'Don't look so unhappy, Ariana.' Max looked at her gently while Noel went off to get their lunch. 'For him it isn't going "back". It's simply going, to see something he's heard about, read about. It doesn't have all the deeper meaning you want to give it. Trust me.' She looked up at him and smiled slowly.

'Maybe you're right.'

'It's just a healthy curiosity, believe me. Besides, it's not just your country, Ariana, it was his father's.' And they both knew that to Noel that was sacred. To Noel, Manfred had always been something of a god. Ariana had told him all about his father, how he had saved her from the Nazis, how good he'd been, how much they'd cared for each other. He'd seen the photographs of his father in uniform. Nothing had been hidden from him, nothing spared.

Max looked at her again as they sat there, and patted her hand in the warm Cambridge sun. 'You did a good job with him, Ariana.'

'You think so?' She peered at him mischievously from beneath her hat.

'Yes, I do.'

'And you had no hand in it at all, did you?'

'Well, just a little . . .'

'Max Thomas, you're such a fibber. He's as much your son as mine.' For a long moment Max didn't answer, and then he kissed her softly on the neck.

'Thank you, my darling.'

They both jumped, startled as Noel towered above them, carrying two trays and wearing a broad smile. 'I mean really, everyone will know you're not married if you sit around here necking.' The three of them laughed and Ariana blushed.

'Really, Noel!'

'Don't look at me like that, Mother. I wasn't sitting here behaving like a teenager . . . and in *broad daylight*!' He emphasised it again and all three of them laughed together, and then he smiled at them very gently. 'It's nice to see you two so happy.'

'Weren't we always?' Ariana looked at Max in surprise, and then at her son, who nodded slowly.

'Yes, amazingly, you always were. I think that's fairly rare though.' He smiled again. And this time Ariana quietly kissed Max.

'Perhaps it is.'

The three of them settled down to lunch then, and it was almost time for the guest speaker when suddenly Noel stood up and waved to a friend. For a minute the gown billowed as he signalled and tried to urge whoever it was to approach, and then he sat down smiling broadly, with a look of victory he shared with his mother and Max.

'She's coming over.'

'Is *she*?' Max teased, and this time it was Noel who blushed. And a moment later they were joined by a young lady. Noel instantly stood up. She had huge green eyes, and olive complexion, and a long, straight sheaf of shining black hair. She had long, thin legs and Ariana noticed that she wore sandals.

'Max, Mother, this is Tamara.' It was a congenial introduction. The girl smiled, showing perfect teeth. 'Tammy, my mother and Uncle Max.'

301

'How do you do.' She shook hands politely, casting a great shaft of the raven hair over her shoulder, and then she looked into Noel's eyes. For an instant there seemed to be a kind of secret, a message of some kind, an exchange. And Max found himself smiling at them. That kind of look between two people only meant one thing.

'Are you also at the law school, Tamara?' Ariana looked at her politely, trying not to feel awed by the presence of this girl in her son's life. But there was very little awesome about her; she seemed like a very open, friendly girl.

'Yes, I am, Mrs Tripp.'

'Yes, but she's still a baby lawyer,' Noel teased as he touched a lock of the shining hair. 'Just a fledgling greenie,' he teased, and her eyes shot friendly daggers.

'I still have two more years to finish,' she explained to Max and Ariana. 'Noel is all pleased with himself today.' As she said it, it was as though there was an understanding between them. As though Noel was more hers than theirs. Ariana understood the message and smiled.

'Maybe we're all a little impressed with him, Tamara. But your turn will come. Will you be staying on at Harvard?'

'I think so.' But again there was a quick look between the two.

Noel treated the matter casually and glanced quietly at Tamara. 'You'll be seeing her in New York sometime. If she ever does her homework. Right, little one?'

'Oh! Look who's talking!' Suddenly as Ariana and Max watched in amusement, they were both forgotten by the youngsters. 'Who finished your last paper for you? Who did all your typing for the last six months?' But they were both laughing and he quickly put a finger to his lips.

'Sshh, that's a secret, for chrissake, Tammy! You want them to take back my diploma?'

'No.' She grinned at him. 'I just want them to give it to me, so I can get out of here, too.' But at that moment the guest speaker was ready to address them; Noel shushed Tamara, who shook hands again with Max and his mother and then disappeared to rejoin her friends.

'She's a very pretty young lady,' Max whispered to Noel with a smile. 'Quite a striking beauty in fact.'

Noel nodded. 'And one day she'll be a hell of a good lawyer.' He glanced into the distance admiringly, and looking at her son, so young, so tall, so golden, Ariana just sat back and smiled.

Chapter 46

That night they had dinner at Locke Ober's, but all three of them were exhausted, and the subject of Tamara did not come up again. Max and Noel talked law while Arian half listened, watched the people, and thought once or twice of the girl. For some reason she had an impression that she'd already seen her, but she wondered if that was because Noel had had a snapshot of her somewhere in the apartment in New York. Anyway, it didn't seem too important. However taken with each other they seemed to be, their paths were now going to take very different turns.

'Don't you think so, Ariana?' Max looked over at her with a raised eyebrow and then grinned. 'Flirting with the younger men, darling?'

'Oh, my, he caught me. I'm sorry, darling. What did you say?'

'I asked you if you didn't think he'd prefer Bavaria to the Black Forest.'

Her face clouded at the question. 'Maybe. But frankly, Noel, I think you ought to go to Italy instead.'

'Why?' He faced her squarely. 'Why not Germany? What are you afraid of, Mother?' Privately, Max was glad that the boy had the courage to to bring it out.

'I'm not afraid of anything. Don't be silly.'

'Yes, you are.'

She hesitated for a long moment, looked at Max, and then dropped her eyes. The three of them had always been so honest, but now suddenly it hurt her to say what she was thinking. 'I'm afraid that if you go back, you'll find some piece of you that belongs there. You'll feel at home.'

'And then what? You think I'll stay there?' He was smiling gently at his mother and quietly reached out and took her hand.

'Maybe.' She sighed softly. 'I don't really know what I'm afraid of, except that . . . I left there so long ago, and it was such an ugly time. For me, all I can think of is what I lost . . . the people I loved.'

'But don't you think I have a right to know something more about them, too? To see the country where they lived? Where you lived as a child? To see the house where you lived with your father, where my father lived with his parents? Why can't I see it, just so I know it's there, somewhere, a part of me the way it has stayed a part of you?'

There was a long silence at the table and Max spoke first. 'The boy is right, Ariana. He has a right to that.' And then he looked at Noel. 'It's a beautiful country, son. It always was and I'm sure it always will be. And maybe one of the reasons we don't go back is because we still love it so much and it hurt us so deeply to know what happened.'

'I understand that, Max.' And then he looked at his mother again gently, with compassion. 'It can't hurt me, Mother. I never knew it as it was. I'm just going there to see it, that's all, and then I'll come back to you and my own country, a little richer for what I understand about you and myself.'

She sighed softly and looked at them both. 'You're both so eloquent, you should be lawyers.' And then the three laughed softly, finished their coffee, and Max signalled for the cheque.

Noel's plane was to leave Kennedy Airport two weeks later, and he planned to stay in Europe for about six weeks. He wanted to be back in New York by mid-August, so he would have time to find his own apartment and start work on 1 September.

The weeks before he left for Europe were hectic. He had friends he wanted to see, parties to go to, and almost every day now he sat down and went over his travel plans with Max. The trip still bothered Ariana, but she made her peace with it. And she was amused by Noel's constant running. She thought, as she saw him drive off with friends one night, that in twenty years young men had not changed very much after all.

'What were you thinking just then?' Max had seen the glimmer of nostalgia in her eyes.

'That nothing changes.' She smiled tenderly at her beloved.

'Doesn't it? I was just thinking that it does. But maybe that's because I'm almost twenty years older than you are.'

They both thought back to her mother's deserted apartment in the house in Grunewald, when he had first kissed her, while he was hiding from the Nazis. His eyes asked her if she remembered.

Slowly, Ariana nodded. 'Yes, I do.'

He smiled back. 'I told you then that I loved you. And I did, you know.'

She kissed his cheek softly. 'I loved you then, too, as best I knew how in those days.' And then she smiled into the rich brown eyes. 'You were the first man I had ever kissed.'

'And now I hope to be the last. In which case I shall have to live to be at least a hundred.'

'I'm counting on it, Max.' They smiled at each other for a long moment and then purposely he took her hand, the heavy emerald as always on her finger.

'I have something to say to you, Ariana . . . or rather, something I would like to ask.'

Suddenly she knew. Was it possible? Did it still matter, after all these years?'

'Yes, it's very important. To me. Ariana, will you marry me?' He said it so gently, with such a look of love and pleading in his eyes.

For a moment she didn't answer, and then she looked at him with her head tilted to one side. 'Max, why now, my love? Does it really make so much difference now?'

'Yes. To me. Noel is gone now. He's a man, Ariana. When he gets back from Europe, he's moving into his own apartment. And what about us? We maintain appearances, as we always have? For what? My doorman and your maid? Why don't you sell your house, or I'll sell the apartment, and let's get married. It's our turn now. You've devoted twenty-five years to Noel. Now let's devote the next twenty-five to us.' She couldn't help but smile at his argument. In a way she knew that he was right, and she liked what he had in mind.

'But for that we have to be married?'

He grinned at her. 'Don't you want to be respectable at your age?'

'But, Max, I'm only forty-six.' She had smiled at him then, and he had known that finally, he had won her. And he kissed her once more, twenty-eight years after the first time.

They told Noel the next morning, and he was delighted. He kissed his mother, and this time he kissed Max as well.

'Now, I'll feel better going. And especially moving out in September. Are you keeping the house, Mom?'

'We haven't worked that out yet.' She was still a little flustered by their decision. And then Noel suddenly grinned as he kissed her on the cheek again.

'Just think, not every couple gets married to celebrate their silver anniversary . . .'

'Noel!' She still felt a little odd getting married at her age. Getting married, as far as Ariana was concerned, was something one did at twenty-two or twenty-five, not two decades later, with a son who was already a man.

'So when's the wedding?'

Max answered for her. 'We haven't decided. But we'll wait till you get back.'

'I should hope so. Well, do we get to celebrate?' It seemed that that was all they had done for weeks since he'd left Harvard, and he was leaving for Europe the next day.

But Max took them both to dinner at Côte Basque that

evening. It was a sumptuous meal, and a wonderful occasion. They celebrated Noel's flight into the past and their venture into the future, and as always, Ariana shed a few tears.

Paris was everything he'd hoped. He visited the Eiffel Tower, the Louvre. He stopped in cafés, read the paper, and wrote a postcard home addressing it. 'Dear Engaged Couple,' and signing it, 'Your Son.' That night before dinner, he called a friend of Tammy's whom he had promised to call, Brigitte Goddard, daughter of the noted art dealer and proprietor of the Galerie Gérard Goddard. Noel had known Brigitte only slightly during her brief stint at Harvard, but she and Tammy had become good friends. She was an intriguing girl with an odd family, a mother she hated, a father she claimed was obsessed with his past, and a brother whom she laughingly insisted was crazy. She was always teasing and cavorting. She was beautiful and funny.

But there had been something tragic about her as well, as though there was something missing. And when Noel had questioned her seriously about it once, she had said, 'You're right. My family is missing, Noel. My father lives in his own world. None of us matter to him . . . only . . . the past . . . the others . . . the people he lost in another lifetime . . . We, the living . . . we don't count. Not to him.' And then she had said something cynical and funny, but he had never forgotten the look in her eyes – it was an expression of sorrow and loss and desolation well beyond her years. And now Noel wanted to see her, and he was bitterly disappointed when he learned that she was out of town.

As a consolation he took himself out for a big dinner, with drinks at La Tour d'Argent, and dinner at Maxim's. He had promised himself he'd do that before he left Paris, and now he wasn't going to be able to do it with Brigitte. But now he had the extra leisure time for the fancy dinner, and he enjoyed it thoroughly as he watched the elegant French women and their rather dapper-looking men. He noticed how different the styles were here, how much more cosmopolitan people seemed. He liked the looks of the women, the way they moved, the way they dressed, the way they did their hair. In a way, they reminded him of his mother. There was a finished quality about the way they put themselves together that pleased the eye, and extra touch, a something subtle but sexy, like a flower hidden in a garden; it didn't assault the senses, but one sensed instantly that it was there. Noel liked the subtlety of these women; it evoked something in him that he had never known was really there.

The next morning he left for Orly very early, caught his flight to Berlin, and landed at Tempelhof airport, his heart beating with excitement and anticipation. It wasn't a sensation of homecoming, but of discovery, of finding the answers to secrets long unspoken, of tracing people who had long since vanished, where they had been, where they had lived, what they had been and meant to each other. Somehow, Noel knew that the answers would all be there.

He left his things at the Hotel Kempinski, where he had made a reservation, and as he walked out of the lobby, he looked up and down the Kurfürstendamn for a long time. This was the street Max had told him about where writers and artists and intellectuals had congregated for decades. Around him he could see cafés and shops, and swirls of people walking along arm in arm. There was a festive feeling around him, as though they had all been waiting, as though it had been time for him to come.

With a map and a rented car he set out slowly. He had already seen the remains of the Maria Regina Kirche where he knew his parents had been married. What was left of it still stood there, pointing emptily at the sky. He remembered his mother's description of when they had bombed it, and now it remained, a shattered memory of another time. Most of Berlin showed none of the scars, the damage had all been repaired, but here and there were shells of buildings, monuments to that troubled time. He drove slowly past the Anhalter Station, which also stood in ruins, too, then on to the Philharmonic Hall, and then he walked through the Tiergarten to the Victory Column, which stood as it always had, and Bellevue Palace just beyond it, which was as beautiful as Max said it was. And then beyond that Noel came to a sudden halt. There it stood, gleaming in the sunlight, the Reichstag, which had been Nazi headquarters, located on what they now called the Strasse des 17 Tury, the building his father had died defending. Around him, other tourists also gazed at it in silent awe.

To Noel this was no monument to the Nazis; this had nothing to do with history, or politics, or a little man with a moustache who had had an insatiable desire to control the world. This had to do with a man whom Noel had always suspected had been very much like him, the man who had loved his mother, and whom Noel had never known. He remembered his mother's description of that morning . . . the explosions, the soldiers, the refugees, and the destruction of the bombs . . . and then she had seen his father dead. As Noel stood there, a quiet path of tears coursed down his face. He cried for himself and for Ariana, feeling her pain as she had stood there, looking into his father's lifeless face lying in a stack of bodies on the gutted street. How in God's name had she survived it?

Noel quietly walked away from the Reichstag, and it was then that he caught his first glimpse of the Wall; solid, intransigent, determined, it wended its way across Berlin, to one side of the Reichstag and cutting right through the Brandenburg Gate, turning the once flourishing Unter den Linden into a dead end. He looked at it in interest silence, curious about what lay beyond. This was something that neither Max nor his mother had ever experienced, the wall that had left a divided Berlin. Later in his stay he would go there, to see the Marienkirche, the City Hall, and the Dom. He understood that there were many untouched ruins there, too. But first there were other places he wanted to visit, places he had come to see.

With his map on the seat of the Volkswagen he'd rented, he drove from the heart of the city around the Olympic stadium, out to Charlottenburg, where he stopped for a moment by the lake and looked at the schloss. And though he could not know it, this was exactly the place where thirty-five years before his grandmother Kassandra von Gotthard had stood with the man she loved, Dolff Sterne.

From Charlottenburg he drove to Spandau, staring at the great citadel in fascination and getting out to inspect the famous doors. There, the helmets of countless wars were carved in great detail, from the Middle Ages until the last panel, which bore the legend '1939'. The prison held only one prisoner, Rudolf Hess, who was costing the city government more than 400,000 dollars a year to keep. And from Spandau he drove to Grunewald, driving along the lake, looking carefully at all the houses, and searching for the address he had gotten from Max. He had wanted to ask his mother, but when the time had come, he hadn't dared. Max had given him the directions and told him briefly how lovely the house had been, and once again he had told him the story of how Noel's grandfather had saved Max's life when he was fleeing the country, how he had cut the two priceless paintings from the walls where they hung, rolled them up, and handed them to his friend.

At first Noel thought he had missed it, but then suddenly he saw the gates. They had changed not at all from Max's description, and as Noel got out of the car and peered in, a gardener waved.

'*Bitte?*' Noel's German was very rusty. He knew only what he had learned at Harvard in three semesters several years before. But somehow he managed to explain to the old man tending the gardens that long ago this had been his grandfather's house.

'*Ja?*' The man eyed him with interest.

'*Ja.* Walmar von Gotthard.' Noel said it proudly and the man smiled, shrugging. He had never heard the name. An old woman appeared, admonishing the gardener to hurry, the madam would be back from her trip the next evening.

Smiling, the old man explained to his wife why Noel had come there, and looking at him with suspicion, she then stared back at the old man. At first the woman hesitated, but after a moment she grudgingly nodded her head and gestured towards Noel. He looked at the old man question-ingly, not sure he had understood them.

But the old man was smiling as he took Noel's arm. 'She will let you look around.'

'Inside the house?'

'Yes.' The old man smiled gently. He understood. It was nice that this young American cared enough about his grandfather's country to come back. So many of them had forgotten where they came from. So many of them knew nothing of what had happened before the war. But this one seemed different, and it pleased the old man.

In some ways the house looked very different than he had expected, and in others it looked precisely like Ariana's memories of when she was a child, memories she had shared with him constantly through the years. The third floor, where she had lived with her nurse and her brother, still looked as she had described it. The large room that had been their playroom, the two bedrooms, the large bathroom the children had shared. Now it stood made into guest rooms, but Noel could still see exactly where his mother had lived. On the floor beneath that, much seemed to have changed. There seemed to be lots of smaller bedrooms, sitting rooms, libraries, a sewing room, and a small room filled with toys. Obviously the house had been remodelled, and there was little trace of the past. The downstairs still remained impressive and somewhat stuffy. But Noel could more easily imagine his grandfather presiding over the large dining room table in the huge hall. He thought fleetingly of a Nazi general cavorting there with his girls, but quickly dismissed the image from his mind.

He thanked the old couple profusely before he left them, and took a photograph of the house from the spot where he had left his car. Maybe he could get Tammy to do a sketch from the photograph, and he could give it to his mother sometime. The thought pleased him as he drove along to the Grunewald cemetery, where it took him a long time to find the family plot. But there they were, the aunts and the uncles, the great-grandparents; all with names and histories he did not know. The only one that was familiar was that of his grandmother Kassandra von Gotthard. It touched him that she had been only thirty and he wondered briefly how she had died.

There were things that his mother still had not told him – things that he did not need to know. Like the truth about her mother's suicide, which was something that had always disturbed Ariana a great deal. And the fact that she herself had briefly been married to Paul Liebman. She didn't feel Noel needed to know that either. By the time he was old enough to understand things, she and Max had decided that it was a closed chapter in Ariana's life, and one of which her son did not need to be apprised.

Noel wandered slowly through the cemetery, looking at the peaceful green mounds, and then at last he got back into his car and drove out towards Wannsee, but this time he struck out. The house whose address he still vaguely remembered from his mother's stories was no longer there. Instead, there were neat rows of modern buildings. The house where she had lived with Manfred was gone.

He stayed on in Berlin for another three days then, journeying back to Grunewald once, and to Wannsee, but spending most of his time on the other side of the Wall. The eastern side of Berlin fascinated Noel – how different the people were, how barren their faces, how bleak their stories. It was his first and only view of communism, and this was far more real to him than the faded ghosts of the Nazis, which some had attempted to keep alive.

After Berlin he went to Dresden, and went to the few places he knew of there. Mostly he was interested in the schloss for which his mother had been given restitution. He knew only that it was used now as a small country museum where they gave occasional tours. On the day that he reached it, it was all but deserted, blessed with only one sleeping guard. It was dark and somewhat dreary, the furnishings sparse, most having been removed, a plaque said, during the war. But here again, as he had in Grunewald, he could reach out and touch the same walls that his father had touched as a boy. It was a strange, thrilling feeling to look out the same windows, stand in the same doorways, touch the same doorknobs, breathe the same air. This might have been the house of his boyhood, if he had not lived instead on East Seventy-seventh Street in New York. And as he left the house, the guard smiled at Noel from the chair where he sat watching.

'Auf Wiedersehen.'

Without thinking, Noel smiled at him and murmured, 'Goodbye.'

But instead of being depressed by his visits, in an odd, wonderful way, he felt finally free. Free of the questions, of the empty places that they had seen and he hadn't. Now he had seen them all, too. He had seen them as they were now, as part of the present, as part of his times, not of theirs, not as they had been. Now they were a part of his life, and he felt he understood them, and now he felt freer than ever to be himself.

He had the time he needed to put the past into perspective, to understand his mother even more, how much she had endured, how strong she was. He vowed he'd do all he could to make her proud of him for the rest of his life.

He got off the plane at Kennedy Airport, looking relaxed and happy, and for a long moment held his mother tightly in his arms. No matter what he had seen, or how much some of it had meant to him, there was no doubt in his mind whatever, this was home.

Chapter 47

'Well, guys, when's the wedding?' On his return Noel had found his own apartment, in the east Fifties, overlooking the East River, and cozily located near an assortment of friendly neighbourhood bars. He still liked to go drinking with his law school buddies, and his playtime hadn't entirely come to

313

an end, even with his first job. But he was not quite twenty-six yet, and Max and Ariana knew he had time to settle down. 'Have you set a date yet?' It was the first dinner they had shared since he had moved out, and Max's bathrobe had been appearing more regularly on the back of Ariana's bedroom door.

'Well.' She smiled at Max and then at Noel. 'We were thinking about Christmas. How does that sound to you?'

'Wonderful. We can do it before my birthday.' And then he smiled shyly. 'Will it be a big wedding?'

'No, of course not.' Ariana shook her head, laughing. 'Not at our age. Just a few friends.' But as she said it, there was a faraway look in her eyes. For the third time in her life, she was getting married and the memories of her lost family flashed across her heart and her mind. Noel looked at her and seemed to sense her thoughts. Since his trip to Europe they had been even closer than before. It was as though now he *knew*. They seldom spoke of it, but the new bond was there.

'I was wondering if I could bring a friend to the wedding, Mother. Would that be all right?'

'Of course, darling.' Ariana was instantly smiling. 'Anyone we know?'

'Yes. You met her this summer, at my graduation. Remember Tammy?' He tried so desperately to look nonchalant, but instead looked so nervous as he said it that Max couldn't suppress a laugh.

'The ravishing Rapunzel with the long black hair, if I'm not mistaken. Tamara, yes?'

'Yes.' He looked gratefully at Max and his mother smiled.

'I remember her, too. The young law student – she was just finishing her first year.'

'Right. Well, she'll be down to see her parents over Christmas, and I just thought . . . I mean . . . she'd enjoy the wedding.'

'Of course, Noel. Of course.' Max got him off the hook quickly by changing the subject, but the look on Noel's face had not escaped Ariana. That night she turned to Max before they went to bed.

'You don't suppose he's serious, do you?' She looked worried, and Max smiled gently and sat down on the edge of the bed.

'He might be, but I doubt it. I don't really think he's ready to settle down.'

'I hope not. He isn't even twenty-six.' Max Thomas grinned at the woman he was soon to marry.

'And how old were you when you had him?'

'That was different, Max. I may only have been twenty, but that was wartime, and –'

'Do you really think you would have stayed single until you were twenty-six if there hadn't been a war? On the contrary, I think you'd have married in no time at all.'

'Oh, Max, that was another world. Another life!' For a long moment they said nothing and then quietly she joined him in the bed and took him in her arms. She needed him now, to ward off the memories and the pain. And he knew it too. 'Tell me, Ariana, after all these years, will you take my name?'

She looked at him in astonishment. 'Of course I will. Why wouldn't I?'

'I don't know.' He shrugged. 'These days women are so independent. I thought maybe you'd prefer to stay Ariana Tripp.'

'I'd prefer to be your wife, Max, and to be Mrs Thomas.' And then she smiled slowly. 'It really is time.'

'What I like about you, Ariana,' he said gently as his hands caressed her body beneath the sheets, 'is that you make such quick decisions. It's only taken you twenty-five years.' But then she laughed softly at him. The tinkling laugh of crystal had not changed since she was a girl, nor had the passion with which she received him, startled as always by the thrust of his desire as he took her and held her and filled her with his love.

Chapter 48

'And do you, Maximilian, take this woman to be . . .' The ceremony was brief and lovely, and Noel watched them with tears in his eyes, grateful that, as tall as he was, few people could notice if his lashes were damp. 'You may kiss the bride.' They kissed for a long moment, obviously enjoying it more than they should. The friends they had invited giggled, and Noel tapped Max on the shoulder and smiled.

'Okay, you two, break it up. The honeymoon is in Italy. This is only the reception.' Max turned to him with a long smile of amusement and Ariana grinned and smoothed a hand over her hair.

They had decided to hold the wedding and the reception at the Carlyle. It was close to the house and there was a lovely room available that was just the right size. They had, in the end, invited almost forty people for the ceremony and a formal luncheon, and a small quartet was already playing for those who wanted to dance.

'May I, Mother? I think the first dance is supposed to be between the bride and her father, but maybe you'll accept this modern variation on the theme.'

'I'd be delighted.' He bowed and she took his arm and slowly they moved on to the floor for a graceful Waltz. He danced as impeccably as had his father, and Ariana wondered if it was simply in his genes. The boy had a fluid grace of movement that was irresistible to almost any female watching him make his way smoothly around the floor. As she looked happily past him at her new husband, Ariana saw Tammy, standing quietly in a corner, her black hair wound neatly in a knot, wearing small diamond earrings and a pretty black wool dress.

'Will you look at those two?' Noel was smiling at his mother as Tammy stood by. She felt faintly uncomfortable in the crowd of strangers, but she was always happy at Noel's side. It was odd to see him here though. She was so used to seeing him in blue jeans and turtleneck sweaters, playing touch football with his friends in Harvard Yard. He had already been up to see her twice this winter, and she had just told him what she had in mind.

'What do you think, Noel?'

'About what?' He was smiling distractedly at his mother from where he stood.

'You know about what.'

'About your transferring to Columbia? I think you're out of your mind. You have a chance at a Harvard Law degree, kiddo. That's quite a piece of paper to throw away for a piece of ass.'

'Is that all it is to you?' Her eyes narrowed and she looked both angry and hurt. But he was quick to take her hand and kiss it softly.

'No, and you know it. But what I'm trying to point out to you is that because you're so goddamn horny –' he grinned at her gently – 'you're not willing to sit it out at Harvard for the next two years while I commute.'

'But that's silly. It's hard on you and on me. You're going to be having more briefs to write, more research to do, now that you're working. How much time do you think you'll be able to spend coming up to Cambridge? And with law school getting as tough as it has this year, I can hardly get away. If I'm here, then we can just both do what we're doing and be together.' The huge eyes looked at him, pleading, and he had to fight himself not to beg her to do what she said.

'Tammy. I just don't want to influence your decision. It's too important. You're talking about a major change that could affect your whole career.'

'Oh, don't be such a snob, for chrissake, I'm talking about Columbia, not Backwater U.'

'How do you know they'll accept you as a transfer?' He was desperately trying to do his duty, but he equally desperately wanted her to make the switch.

'I already asked, and they said I could start next term.' He looked at her pointedly without commenting. 'Well?' She looked at him expectantly.

He drew a long, slow breath. 'I think this is where I'm supposed to discourage you and be noble.'

'Is that what you want to do?' She searched his face and his eyes met hers squarely.

'No. I want to live with you. Right here. Right now. But that's awfully selfish. You should be aware of that.' He moved closer to her and their bodies touched lightly as they stood side by side. 'I love you and I want you with me.'

'Then let me do what I want to do.' She smiled up at him and he smiled in return just as Max and Ariana approached them, watching them with appreciative smiles.

They were so young and so good-looking, so happy and so free, one wanted just to stand near them, to be a part of what they had before them. It was like looking down a long, long stretch of open road.

'You remember Tammy, Mother?'

'I do.' Ariana gazed warmly at the girl. She liked her. She liked her looks and her spirit. She just wasn't so sure about that tender, earnest look in her son's eyes.

'Maybe I should renew the introductions. After all, my mother has a new name.' This time it was Ariana who blushed gently, as Max stood proudly by and grinned. 'My mother, Mrs Maximilian Thomas, my stepfather, Max Thomas, and my friend, Tamara Liebman.'

'Liebman – ' Ariana was taken by surprise but managed to rein in her emotions quickly. 'Are you related to Ruth and Samuel Liebman?' She hadn't dared mention Paul's name. Tammy nodded quietly, her eyes puzzled by what she saw and did not understand in the other woman's face.

'They were my grandparents, but they died a long time ago. I never knew them.'

'Oh.' Ariana was struck mute for a while. 'Then you're . . .'

'Paul and Marjorie Liebman's daughter. And my Aunt

Julia lives in London. Maybe you knew her, too.'

'Yes . . .' Ariana was almost choking and she was suddenly very pale.

Tammy couldn't know what was behind Ariana's shock. She only knew the anguish of rejection as a few minutes later they spun slowly on the dance floor and tears rolled slowly down her face.

'Tammy? Are you crying?' Noel looked down at her tenderly and she shook her head. But her denials were useless. 'Come on, let's get out of here for a minute.' He took her downstairs to the lobby and slowly they walked the halls. 'What's the matter, baby?'

'Your mother hates me.' A little sob escaped her as she said it. And she had so wanted everything to be all right. She knew how close Noel was to his mother, and it was essential that she fit in from the start. She had known that. But now it was already over.

'Did you see her face when she heard my name? She almost fainted in her tracks because I was Jewish. Didn't you tell her before now?'

'I didn't think I had to, for chrissake. Tammy, this is the Seventies. Being Jewish is no big thing.'

'Maybe not to you, but it is to her. Just like your being German was a shock to my parents. But at least I warned them! How can you not understand that about your mother? She's anti-Semitic, for chrissake, and you don't even know!'

'No, she isn't! Next you'll be calling my mother a Nazi.' That wasn't likely, but it was exactly what her father had called him.

'Noel, you don't understand anything.' She stood shivering in the lobby, watching people hurry down the street.

'I do. I understand perfectly that you're buying into their bullshit and all their old games. It's not our fight, Tammy. It wasn't our war. We're people, black, white, brown, yellow, Jewish, Irish, Arab. We're Americans – that's the whole

319

beauty of this country. That other stuff doesn't matter any more.'

'It does to them.' She looked heartbroken as once more she thought of his mother, but firmly he pulled her into his arms.

'But it doesn't matter to me, do you believe that?' She nodded. 'And I'm going to talk to my mother tonight before she leaves for the airport to see if you're right.'

'I know I'm right, Noel.'

'Don't be so sure.' But she refused to go back to the party. They went upstairs briefly so she could retrieve her coat, and after politely saying goodbye to his mother, Tammy went back downstairs and he put her into a cab.

'Your friend looked very pretty, Noel.' Ariana said it stiffly as they sat down in her living room after they got back from the reception at the hotel. They had three hours until she and Max had to leave for the airport. They were going back to Europe for their honeymoon, but only to Geneva and Rome. 'She seems like a lovely girl.' But there was an odd silence in the room after she said it. She had already discussed it with Max when they had a few moments alone.

Noel stood facing her from where he stood near the fireplace with a look in his eyes that said he didn't understand her tone. 'She thinks you don't like her, Mother.' There was no answer. 'Because she's Jewish. Is that true?' It was a quiet accusation as he stood there, and slowly Ariana lowered her eyes.

'I'm sorry she thinks that, Noel.' And then she looked up at her son again. 'But no, that isn't why.'

'Then she's half right – you don't like her?' He looked angry and hurt by what he was hearing and it killed Ariana to go on.

'I didn't say that. She seems like a very nice person. But, Noel . . .' She looked at him bluntly. 'You have to stop seeing that girl.'

'What? Are you kidding?' He left the fireplace and stalked the room.

'No, I'm not.'

'Well, just exactly what is going on here? I'm twenty-six years old and you're telling me whom I can and can't see?'

'I'm telling you for your own good.' The excitement of the past few hours seemed to have faded, and suddenly Ariana looked tired and old. Max reached out and touched her hand gently, but even Max couldn't comfort her for having to hurt her own son now.

'It's none of your damn business.'

She winced slightly. 'I'm sorry to hear you say that. But the fact is that when her father learns all about you, you're going to be hurt, Noel. You might as well know that now.'

'Why?' It was an agonised wail. 'And what the hell do you know about her father anyway?'

There was a long silence in the room, which Max was going to interrupt to save Ariana, but she quietly held up a hand. 'I was married to him, Noel, when I first came to the States.' This time it was her son who looked shocked. He sat down heavily on a chair.

'I don't understand.'

'I know.' Her voice was gentle. 'And I'm sorry. I just didn't think you'd ever need to know.'

'But weren't you really married to my father?'

'Yes, but when I got here, widowed and frightened, I was terribly sick. I had come over on a boat sponsored by the Women's Relief Organisation here. I don't think they even exist now, but they were very important then. And I was befriended by a lovely woman –' she thought quietly of her for a moment, sorry that she had heard from Tammy that Ruth was dead – 'Ruth Liebman. She was Tammy's grandmother. And they decided to take me into their home. They were wonderful to me. They nursed me back to health, they gave me everything, and they loved me. But they also believed I was Jewish. And I was foolish enough not to correct that belief.' She stopped for what seemed like a long time. And then she looked straight at her son.

'They had a son. He had come back from the Pacific because he was wounded, and he had a crush on me. I was twenty then and he was only twenty-two. And after your father, he seemed . . . well, like a little boy. But he was sweet, and he had just been jilted by the girl he'd been engaged to during the war. And – ' she swallowed hard – 'I discovered that I was pregnant with you, Noel. I was just going to leave them and have you, but . . . something . . . I don't know what happened . . . Paul kept asking me to marry him, and it seemed so simple. I had nothing at all to give you, and if I married Paul Liebman, I could do everything for you.' She wiped a tear from her cheek sadly. 'I thought that . . . he'd give you everything I couldn't, and I would always be grateful to him.' She wiped the tears away with one hand. 'But two weeks before you were born, he came home one afternoon and found me looking at the photographs of your father and it all came out. I couldn't lie to him any more. I told him the truth. And then he knew that the baby was Manfred's and not his.' Her voice seemed very distant as she stared into space. 'He left the house that day, and I never saw him again. He only communicated with me through his lawyers.' Her voice grew softer still. 'I never saw any of them again. To them, I was a Nazi.'

Noel left his chair then and went to his mother, and he knelt beside her, softly stroking her hair. 'They can't do anything, Mama, not to me and not to Tammy. Times are different now.'

'It doesn't matter.'

He pulled her chin up gently with one hand. 'Yes, it does. To me.'

'I agree with you entirely, Noel.' Max stood up and spoke for the first time in half an hour. 'And now, if you will forgive me for being selfish, I would like to have your mother to myself until we leave.' He knew that Ariana had had enough.

'Of course, Max.' Noel kissed them both and stood in the doorway for a long moment.

'You're not angry that I didn't tell you, Noel?' She eyed him with regret as they stood in the door, but he shook his head slowly.

'Not angry, Mother, just surprised.'

'He'll be all right,' Max reassured her as he walked her back inside. 'You don't owe anyone any explanations, darling. Not even him.' And with that he kissed her gently and she followed him inside.

Noel had already gotten into a cab, and he was at his own apartment minutes later, the phone in his hand. She was on the line a moment later, sounding unusually subdued.

'Tammy? I have to see you.'

'When?'

'Now.'

Twenty minutes later she was there.

'I've got a few surprises for you, kiddo.'

'Like what?'

He didn't know where to begin. So he decided to take a dive. 'Like your father was almost my father.'

'What?' She stared at him in confusion and slowly he began to explain. It took almost half an hour to sort it all out, after which they sat and stared at each other. 'I don't think anyone in the family knows he was married before.'

'Well, his parents obviously did, and his sisters. I wonder if your mother does.'

'Probably.' She thought about it for a moment. 'He's so scrupulous about honesty and revealing everything, he probably told her when they met.'

'It's no reflection on him really. It was my mother who tried to pull the wool over his eyes.' But Noel said it kindly, he had nothing but tenderness and compassion for what she had tried to do. He imagined the twenty-year-old pregnant refugee, and his heart reached out to her.

The tragedy that had belonged to another generation had once more become just another piece of history with the passage of time. It made no real difference to them now, it only mattered to those who had participated in the drama long before. 'Are you going to tell him about us, Tammy?'

'I don't know. Maybe.'

'I think you should tell him now. Let's not wait to unveil any secrets till later. I'd like to get all our cards out on the

323

table now. Our parents have had enough surprises in their lives.'

'Does that mean you want to live with me, Noel?' Her deep green eyes were filled with hope, and he nodded solemnly.

'Yes. It does.'

Chapter 49

When the winter term ended, Tammy had already made her decision. She had long since organised the paperwork for her transfer to Columbia Law School, and all that remained was for her to pack her bags and vacate the tiny apartment she had rented in Cambridge with four other girls. Noel appeared bright and early on a Saturday morning, and together they made the brief trip to New York.

At his apartment he had made space for her in every cupboard, and there were flowers and balloons and a cooler of champagne waiting in the fridge. That had been three months earlier, and there had been no problems between them, except one. Neither her parents nor Ariana knew about the arrangement. Contrary to his usual principles of total honesty with his mother, Noel hadn't told his mother that he was living with Tammy. And Tammy had simply installed her own phone on the desk, and when it rang, Noel knew not to touch her line. It would be her father calling·to see if she was in.

But in late May the game halted abruptly one day when Ariana came by to drop off some mail that had come to her house by mistake. She had been about to leave it with the doorman when Tammy came flying out of the building, carrying their laundry and her law books, on her way to school.

'Oh . . . oh . . . hello, Mrs Tripp – I mean Mrs Max . . . Mrs . . .' Her face had been one bright red flame as Ariana greeted her coolly.

'Visiting Noel?'

'I . . . yes . . . I had to check some things in his old law books . . . research . . . a paper . . .' She wanted to lie down on the spot and die. Noel had been right. They should have told them months before. Now Ariana looked disappointed and betrayed.

'I'm sure he's very helpful.'

'Yes, yes . . . very . . . and how've you been?'

'Very well, thank you.' And then with a polite greeting she was off to the nearest phone booth to call her son. In the end he was just as glad it had happened. It was high time they knew. And if Tamara didn't plan to tell her father, Noel had made up his mind that he would. With a steady hand he dialled Information and then called Paul Liebman's office and made an appointment for two forty-five.

The building where the cab stopped was the same building where Sam Liebman had established his offices almost fifty years before, and the office where Paul Liebman ran the firm's investments was the same office in which Sam had sat for so long. It was the office where Ruth had visited her husband and begged him to take the tiny blonde German girl into his home. It was the office that German girl's son walked into with his long, confident stride; he shook hands with Tamara's father and quietly sat down.

'Do we know each other, Mr Tripp?' He had looked Noel over carefully and there was something familiar about the young man. His business card showed him to be associated with a very reputable law firm, and Paul Liebman was wondering if the young man was there on the firm's business or his own.

'We've met once, Mr Liebman. Last year.'

'Oh, I'm sorry.' The older man smiled pleasantly. 'I'm afraid my memory is not quite at its peak these days.'

Noel smiled gently. 'With Tamara. I graduated from Harvard Law last year.'

'Oh, I see.' And then suddenly he remembered, and the smile began slowly to fade. 'I assume, however, Mr Tripp, that you are not here to discuss my daughter. In what way may I assist you today?' They had only given the boy the appointment on the strength of his law firm's name.

'I'm afraid that your assumption, sir, is not quite correct. I am indeed here to talk to you about Tamara. And myself. I'm afraid I have some difficult things to tell you, but I want to be forthright with you from the first.'

'Is Tamara in some kind of trouble?' The man blanched. He remembered who the boy was now. He remembered perfectly. And he already hated his guts.

But Noel was quick to reassure him. 'No, sir. She is not in any kind of trouble. In fact, she's in something very nice.' He smiled and tried to look less nervous than he was. 'We've been in love with each other, Mr Liebman, for quite some time.'

'I find that difficult to believe, Mr Tripp. She hasn't mentioned you in months.'

'I think she hasn't because she's been afraid of your reaction. But before I go any further, there's something I must tell you, because if I don't, sooner or later it will come out. And we might as well get it out right now.' He looked away from the older man for a moment and wondered if he'd been mad to come at all. This was crazy. And it was also the hardest thing he'd ever done. 'Twenty-seven years ago I believe your mother was involved in a refugee organisation here in New York.' Paul Liebman's face tightened and Noel pushed ahead. 'She befriended a young woman, a German girl, a refugee from Berlin. Whom, for whatever reasons, you married shortly thereafter, only to discover that she was pregnant by her husband who had died in the fall of Berlin. You left her, and divorced her, and –' he paused for only an instant – 'I am her son.' There was an electrifying moment of silence and then Paul Liebman stood up.

'Get out of my office!' He pointed savagely towards the door, but Noel didn't move.

'Not until I tell you that I love your daughter, sir, and that she loves me. And that – ' he rose to his full height, towering over even Paul Liebman – 'my intentions towards her are entirely honourable.'

'Do you dare to tell me that you wish to marry my daughter?'

'Yes, sir, I do.'

'Never! Do you understand me? Never! Is your mother promoting this arrangement?'

'Absolutely not, sir.' For an instant Noel's eyes flashed, too, but then the fire left Paul's gaze. Whatever had passed between them, Liebman would not malign Ariana now. He let the matter of Ariana drop.

'I forbid you to see Tamara again.' There was rage in his face, based on an old, old pain he had never quite been able to forget.

But Noel spoke calmly. 'I'm telling you now, to your face, that neither she nor I will obey you. Your only choice is to make peace with what is.' And then, without waiting to hear the remainder of Liebman's anger, Noel walked directly to the door and left. He heard a huge pounding on the desk behind him, but by then the door to the office was already closed.

As Tamara came to know Noel's mother, she came to love her almost as her own, and it was at Christmas, when Noel decided to announce their engagement, that Ariana gave Tammy the gift that so deeply touched her heart. Noel already knew what was coming and for an instant the mother and son exchanged a secret smile as slowly Tammy unwrapped the bright paper, and then suddenly the brilliant ring fell into her hand. It was the signet ring set in diamonds, which had been Kassandra's so many years before.

'Oh, my God . . . oh . . . oh, no!' She looked around her in amazement, first at Noel, then at Ariana standing by, and then at Max smiling broadly, and then, reaching blindly for Noel, she began to cry.

'It's your engagement ring, my darling. Mother had it sized for you. Come on, let's try it on.' But as she slipped it on her finger, all she did was cry more. She knew the history of that diamond ring so well now . . . and now the ring that had been worn by four generations before her was hers. It fit perfectly on the third finger on her left hand, and it sat there, beautifully wrought and skilfully woven, the diamonds sparkling brilliantly as she stared.

'Oh, Ariana, thank you.' But holding Noel's mother tightly only brought fresh tears.

'It's all right, darling. It's all right. It's yours now. May it bring you much joy.' Ariana looked at the girl gently; she had been completely won over. And now she had decided to take matters into her own hands.

Three days after Christmas, with trembling hands, she looked up the number and dialled the phone. She identified herself only as Mrs Thomas, got an appointment, and the next day quietly took a cab downtown. She said nothing to Max or Noel; she didn't feel they had to know, but it was time that, lo these many years later, she faced him, and also time that he faced her.

The secretary announced her, and Ariana, wearing a black dress and a dark mink coat, walked sedately into the room. On her hand she wore only her large emerald now. The diamond signet was Tamara's.

'Mrs Thomas?' But as Paul Liebman stood to greet her, he opened his eyes wide with shock. Even in his surprise it flashed through his mind how little she had changed, even in almost thirty years.

'Hello, Paul.' She stood there bravely and waited for him to ask her to sit down. 'I thought that I should come to see you. About our children. May I sit down?' He waved her into a chair and then, still staring, sat down himself. 'I believe my son had already been to see you once.'

'It served no purpose.' His face hardened still more. 'And your visit will be useless, too.'

'Perhaps. But the point, I think, is not how we feel, but how our children feel. At first I felt the same way you did. I was violently opposed to their getting together. But the fact is that whether or not we like it that's what they want.'

'And may I ask why you'd have any objection?'

'Because I assume you're bitter about me and equally so about Noel.' And then she paused and her voice was softer when she went on. 'What I did was terribly, terribly wrong. Afterwards I understood that, but in the desperation of the moment, wanting the right things for the baby . . . the things you could have given him, and I couldn't . . . what can I say to you, Paul? I was wrong.'

He sat looking at her for a long, long time. 'Did you have other children, Ariana?'

She shook her head with a small smile. 'No. And I never remarried until last year.'

'Not because you pined for me, I might assume.' But there was less anger in his voice now and the hint of an old warmth in his eyes.

She sighed briefly. 'No, because I knew that I had been married, that I had cast my lot for good or bad with what happened. I had my son, and I never wanted to marry again.'

'Who changed your mind?'

'An old friend. I gather though that you remarried very quickly.'

He nodded. 'As soon as the divorce became final. She was a girl I had gone to school with.' And then he sighed across his desk, across his lifetime, at Ariana. 'In the end, those are the best kind. And that is why I've been so opposed to Tamara and your boy. Not so much because he's your son.' He sighed again. 'He's a fine boy, Ariana. A good man. He had the courage to come here to see me, to tell me the whole story. I respect that in a man.' And then he growled softly. 'It was more than Tamara had the decency to do. But the real issue here is not whether or not you and I were married, but what kind of people they are. Look at what he comes from, at his heritage. Look at your family, Ariana, what I know of it now. And we're Jewish. Can you really justify joining the two?'

'If they can. I don't think it really matters if I'm a German and you're a Jew. Maybe that only mattered so much then,

329

after the war. I'd like to think that now it doesn't matter quite so much.'

But Paul Liebman shook his head with determination. 'It still does. Those things will never change, Ariana. Long after you and I are gone, those things will go on.'

'Won't you at least give them a chance?'

'To do what? Convince me that I'm wrong? So that they can quickly have three children then come back five years from now to tell me they're getting a divorce because I was right and it didn't work out?'

'Do you really think you can prevent that?'

'Maybe.'

'And what of the next man? And the one after that? Don't you realise that she'll do what she wants anyway? No matter what. She'll marry whom she pleases, lead her life, go her own way. She's been living with Noel for a year now, no matter how you feel about it. The only one who will lose in the end is you, Paul. Maybe it's time you ended that war between us and took another look at this generation. My son doesn't even want to be a German. And maybe your daughter doesn't want to carry any more banners that proclaim her a Jew.'

'What does she want to be, then?'

'A person, a woman, a lawyer. They have ideas these days that I don't really understand. They're a lot more independent and free-thinking.' She smiled at him slowly. 'Maybe they're right. My son tells me that the war we talk about is our war, not theirs. To them, it's only history. I guess to us, sometimes, it's still real.'

'I looked at him, Ariana – ' his voice dropped painfully low – 'and I still saw those pictures that you held that day. I could imagine him in a uniform . . . A Nazi uniform like his father's . . .' He squeezed his eyes tightly shut, and then he looked at her bleakly. 'He looks just like him, doesn't he?'

She smiled gently and nodded. 'But Tamara doesn't look very much like you.' There was nothing else she could say to him, but at least he smiled.

'I know, she looks just like her mother. Her sister looks like

Julia though . . . and my boy . . .' He said it so proudly. '. . . he looks like me.'

'I'm glad.' And then after a long, empty silence, 'Have you been happy?'

He nodded slowly. 'And you? I wondered about you sometimes, what had happened, where you'd gone. I wanted to reach out and just let you know that I was thinking of you, but I was afraid to – '

'Why?'

'I was afraid to seem a fool. At first I was so hurt. I thought you'd just laughed at me all along. It was my mother who eventually understood it. She knew you'd done it for the baby, and she suspected that perhaps you loved me, too.' At the mention of his mother, Ariana's eyes filled slowly with tears.

'I did love you, Paul.'

He nodded slowly. 'After she thought it over, she knew.' And then they sat there for an instant, united after so long. 'What do we do now, Ariana, about our children?'

'We let them do what they have to. And we accept.'

She smiled and stood up hesitantly, holding out a hand. But he didn't take her hand, he walked slowly around his desk and for an instant took her in his arms.

'For what happened so long ago, I'm sorry. I'm sorry I wasn't big enough to understand it or let you explain.'

'It was the way it had to be, Paul.' He shrugged and nodded, and then she kissed his cheek and left him with his own thoughts, staring out at the Wall Street view.

Chapter 50

The wedding was scheduled for the following summer, after Tamara had duly finished law school, and the two looked around for an apartment, picked out what they wanted, and Tamara landed a job that was to begin in the fall. 'But first we're going to Europe!' She had announced it to Ariana and Max with a happy smile.

'Where to?' Max looked at her with interest.

'Paris, the Riviera, Italy, and then Noel wants to take me to Berlin.' But this time there was no shadow in Ariana's eyes.

'It's a beautiful city. At least it was.' But she had seen Noel's pictures from his trip two years before, and she cherished the photograph of the house in Grunewald – now she no longer had to strain to remember some fading detail. She could simply look at the photograph and see it all. He had even given her photographs of the schloss she'd heard about from Manfred and never seen. 'How long will you two be gone?'

'About a month.' Tammy sighed happily. 'This is my last free summer, and Noel really had to fight to get four weeks off.'

'What will you be doing on the Riviera?'

'Stopping by to see a girl I knew from school.' They had decided to visit Brigitte. 'But first – ' Tammy grinned at Ariana – 'we have to survive the wedding.'

'It's going to be lovely.' For months now Ariana had listened to the plans. At last Paul had softened, and he had to admit that he liked Noel, and they had begun to plan the wedding in February, for June.

When at last the day came, Tamara looked overwhelmingly beautiful in a dress made entirely of cream-coloured satin and covered by an overdress of priceless Chantilly lace. The cap she wore over her dark hair covered all but her chignon with the flawless lace, and the clouds of veil that floated around her created even more of an impression of ethereal splendour. Even Ariana was impressed.

'My God, Max, she looks gorgeous.'

'Of course she does.' He smiled at his own wife proudly. 'But so does Noel.' In his cutaway and striped trousers, he looked more elegant than ever, with the brilliant blue eyes and the shaft of blond hair. Ariana had to admit, as she smiled to herself, that he did look very German, but somehow even that didn't seem to matter any more. Paul Liebman was smiling at the young couple benignly, having disbursed fortunes on the wedding of his wife's somewhat extravagant dreams. Ariana had finally met her, a pleasant woman who had probably been a good wife to him over the years.

Debbie was married to a Hollywood producer. Julia was the loveliest and had the most spirit, and her children looked as though they were both intelligent and fun. But the two women only spoke to Ariana briefly. They had been too deeply wounded by the past. For all of them, Ariana had ceased existing the day that Paul had left her.

Paul glanced at her once or twice during the wedding, and once for a long moment, their eyes held, and for the first time in a long time she remembered him with love. And as she stood there, she felt a pang of sorrow over the loss of Ruth and Sam.

'Well, Mrs Tripp, we made it.' Noel grinned at Tammy and she nuzzled his neck with her soft lips. .

'I love you, Noel.'

'So do I, but if you do a lot of that here . . . I'm going to start our honeymoon right here on the plane.' She smiled coyly at her husband and retreated to her seat with a happy sigh. She glanced at the large, handsome diamond signet on her finger. She would never get over Ariana's giving it to her as her engagement ring. She had truly come to love Noel's mother, and she knew that Ariana loved her, too.

'I want to buy your mother something gorgeous in Paris, Noel.'

'Like what?' He smiled at her over his book. The nice thing about having lived together for almost two years was that it had taken the frenzy out of finally being married at last. They were comfortable with each other, and they both felt at home together wherever they were. 'So what do you want to buy her?'

'I don't know. Something exciting. Like a painting or a Dior dress.'

'Good God, that is exciting. How come?' She flashed her ring at him in answer and he smiled.

As a gift from Tammy's father, they stayed at the Plaza-Athénée in an elaborate suite. They went downstairs after their first candlelit honeymoon dinner in their rooms, to meet Brigitte at the famous bar. When they got there, the Relais Plaza was jammed with exotic-looking people, men in open shirts with chests covered with neck chains, and women in long slashes of red satin pants or little mink jackets with jeans.

Tammy barely recognised the girl she'd known at Radcliffe. Her face was white, her lips were rouged, and her blonde hair had been frizzed out wildly on either side; but the blue eyes still danced as mischievously as ever, and she was enchantingly tiny, and wearing a full tuxedo and a black satin top hat with only a red satin bra.

'My dear, I had no idea you'd gotten so conservative.' All three of them grinned. Brigitte Goddard had become even more outrageous than before.

'You know, Noel, you've gotten better looking too.' She grinned mischievously and Tammy laughed.

'Too late, you two, we're married, remember? Sorry, guys . . .' But Noel looked at her warmly and Brigitte only laughed.

'He's too tall for me anyway. Not my type.'

'Watch out, he's sensitive.' Tammy put her finger to her lips and the three laughed again. Together they enjoyed a pleasant evening, and for the next week Brigitte took them from one end of Paris to the other, from lunch at Fouquet's to dinner at the Brasserie Lipp in the Latin Quarter, to dancing at Castel's and Chez Regine, then on to the Halles for breakfast, and off to dinner at Maxim's the next day. And on and on and on it went, from bars to restaurants to parties, where everyone knew her and she knew everyone and men practically begged her for attention as she jumped from one crazy costume to another and Tammy and Noel stared in frank admiration.

'Isn't she divine?' Tammy whispered it to Noel as they

wandered through the boutique at Courrèges.

'Yes, and a little crazy. I think I like you better, kid.'

'That's good news.'

'I'm not looking forward to meeting her family.'

'Oh, they're all right.'

'I don't want to stay with them for ever. Two days and that's it, Tammy. I want to be alone with you for a while. This is our honeymoon, after all.' He looked at her petulantly and she kissed him and laughed.

'I'm sorry, darling.'

'Don't be. Just promise me, no more than two days with them on the Riviera and then we go on to Italy. Got that?'

'Yes, sir.' She saluted smartly, and Brigitte returned to them to drag them on to Balmain, Givenchy, and Dior.

At Dior, Tammy found exactly what she wanted for Ariana, a delicate mauve silk cocktail dress that she knew would look incredible with Ariana's huge blue eyes. It had a matching scarf, and Tammy threw in a pair of earrings. The whole shebang cost her over 400 dollars and Noel almost gasped. 'I'll be employed by September, Noel. Don't look like that.'

'You'd better be if you plan to buy those kinds of presents.' But they both knew that this was special. It was Tammy's way of saying thank you for the ring. Brigitte had noticed it almost immediately when she'd met them that first night at the Plaza; she had ogled it and then admitted to Tammy that she couldn't take her eyes off her hand. Apparently her father's gallery now had a section just for antique jewellery, but they had nothing as remarkable as Tamara's new ring.

On the last afternoon before they left Paris, Brigitte took them to the Galerie Gérard Goddard on the Faubourg-St-Honoré, and they wandered around it in wonder for more than an hour, admiring the Renoirs, the Picassos, the Fabergé boxes, the priceless antique diamond bracelets, the little busts and statues. It really was extraordinary. Noel looked at Brigitte with sheer delight and pleasure as they left.

335

'It's like a tiny museum, only better.'

She nodded proudly. 'Papa has some nice things.' It was rather a severe underestimation, and behind her Noel and Tammy smiled. It had been why her father had sent her to Radcliffe, hoping she would get a solid background in history and art, but Brigitte had other leanings, like football games and parties, med students, and grass. And at the end of two years of disaster, her father had brought her home to amuse herself more simply in France. At the moment she was talking vaguely about studying photography or making a film, but it was obvious that she had no burning ambitions, yet she was really a lot of fun. She was kind of a sprite that ran off madly in all directions, always amusing, but never lighting anywhere for very long. There was a restlessness about her that was rapidly becoming the *mal du siècle*.

'The odd thing about her is that she never seems to grow up,' Tammy mused about her as Noel shrugged.

'I know. But some people just don't. Is her brother like that?'

'Yeah. Only more so.'

'How come?' Noel looked puzzled.

'I don't know, spoiled, maybe unhappy. I don't know. You have to see the parents to understand better. Mama is kind of a nasty Lady Bountiful, and her father is just very withdrawn, as though he's haunted by ghosts.'

Chapter 51

The flight to Nice only took a little over an hour, and Bernard Goddard was waiting for them at the gate. He was as fair and beautiful as his sister as he stood there barefoot, wearing a silk shirt and silk slacks. He had an air of being totally absent, as though he had been deposited there without his knowledge. He seemed to come to when his sister threw her arms around his neck. The large silver box of

336

marijuana in the glove compartment of his Ferrari explained something about his vague aura.

But when pressed into conversation with Tammy and Noel, he seemed able to spring back to life.

'I'm planning to come to New York in November.' He smiled at them sweetly, and for an odd moment Noel had the feeling that he resembled photographs he'd seen somewhere a long time before. 'Will you be there then?'

'Yes, we will.' Tammy answered for Noel.

'You're going when?' Brigitte looked at her brother in surprise.

'November.'

'I thought that was when you were going to Brazil.'

'That's later, and I don't think I'll go to Brazil anyway; Mimi wants to go to Buenos Aires.' Brigitte nodded as though it all made sense, and Tammy and Noel exchanged a silent look of awe. Somehow Tammy hadn't remembered them as quite that racy, and suddenly she wished they hadn't planned to stop at St-Jean-Cap-Ferrat before driving on to Rome.

'Do you want to leave tomorrow morning?' Tammy whispered it to Noel as they followed the two into a huge French Provincial house.

'Perfect. I'll tell them I have to see a client of the firm on the way.' She nodded conspiratorially and they went on to their bedroom, a huge room with endless ceilings, an antique Italian bed, and a view that included a vast expanse of sea. The floor was a pale beige marble, and on the terrace was a wonderful antique sedan chair, in which Brigitte had conveniently left their phone.

Lunch was served downstairs in the garden, and despite their somewhat zany lives and plans, Brigitte and Bernard both managed to be fun. Knowing that they were leaving the next morning, Tammy and Noel felt better, less like prisoners in a strange science fiction colony, and more like guests.

But they felt a great deal more like guests that evening when they entered the formal dining room and Noel was

337

introduced to Brigitte and Bernard's parents for the first time. Before him stood a somewhat heavyset but still strikingly beautiful woman with enormous flashing green eyes. She had a dazzling smile and long, lovely legs, but there was also something very tough about her. As though she were used to commanding, as though she had always run her own show. She was not particularly amused by her children, but she seemed to find Tammy and Noel charming, and she made a great effort to be a good hostess, overseeing everything, including her husband, who was a tall, handsome blond man with quiet, but sad, blue eyes. Again and again through the evening, Noel found himself drawn to the older man. It was almost as though he knew him, or had seen him, and eventually he decided that it was only because he looked so much like his son.

When at one point Madame Goddard took Tammy out of the drawing room after dinner to show her a small Picasso, Gérard Goddard turned to Noel, and it was then that the American noticed his accent for the first time. It wasn't entirely like the others, not quite as rich or quite as French. For a moment Noel wondered if maybe he was Swiss or Belgian. He wasn't sure, but more than ever he was intrigued by the sorrow he could see amid the lines in the man's face.

When Tammy returned from her errand, the group began its aimless chatter once again, until Tammy put her hand on the table and the diamond signet ring sparkled in the candlelight. For an instant Gérard Goddard stared at it and simply stopped mid-sentence. And then, without asking for permission, he reached for her hand, held it, and stared.

'Pretty, isn't it, Papa?' Brigitte was quick to admire the ring again, and Madame Goddard looked disinterested as she made conversation with her son.

'It's lovely.' Monsieur Goddard still held Tammy's hand in his own. 'May I see it?' Slowly, she slipped it off and handed it to him with a smile.

'It's my engagement ring from Noel.'

'Is it really?' He stared at his young guest. 'Where did you get it? In America?' He seemed to have a thousand questions.

'From my mother. It was hers.'

'Really?' For an instant Gérard Goddard's eyes searched inwards.

'It has a long family history that she could tell you better than I could, if you ever come to New York.'

'Yes, yes . . .' He looked vague for a moment, and then smiled at his young friends. 'I do that sometimes – I'd like to call her.' And then, quickly, 'You know we've just opened a whole space for jewellery at the gallery. I'd be very interested in anything else she might have.'

Noel smiled at him gently. The man was so persistent. In a way so desperate, and so sad. 'I don't think she'd sell anything, Monsieur Goddard, but she does have another of my grandmother's rings.'

'Really?' His eyes were wide.

'Yes.' Tammy smiled at him. 'She has a fabulous emerald.' She showed him with her fingers. 'About this size.'

'You really must tell me how to reach her.'

'Of course.' Noel took out a pad and little silver pencil and began to write. He put down her address and phone number. 'I'm sure she'd be happy to hear from you whenever you're in New York.'

'Is she there this summer?'

Noel nodded, and the older man smiled.

The conversation then moved on to other subjects, and at last it was time to go to bed. Tammy and Noel wanted to retire early so that they would be fresh for their long drive the next day. They were going to rent a car in Cannes and leave from there. And Brigitte and Bernard had a party to go to, which they insisted wouldn't even start till twelve or one o'clock. So in a moment only Gérard and his wife were left in the salon, staring at each other and what remained of their life.

'You're not starting again with that nonsense, are you?' As she looked at him in the soft light from the candles, her

339

voice was harsh. 'I saw you with the ring the girl was wearing.'

'It would be a good piece for the gallery, if her mother-in-law has others. I have to be in New York anyway this week.'

'You do?' She looked at him with suspicion. 'What for? You hadn't mentioned it before.'

'There's a collector selling a very fine Renoir. I want to see him before he officially puts it up for sale.' At that she nodded wisely. Whatever his failings as a man, he had certainly done well for the gallery, better than her father had ever dreamed, which was why eventually she had let Gérard change the gallery's name to his own. But it had been an arrangement from the beginning, when they'd taken him in, given him a home, a job, and then an education in the world of art. It was when she and her father had escaped to Zurich during the war.

They had met him then, given him shelter, employment, and a home. And when they'd gone back to Paris when the war was over, they'd brought him along. And by then Giselle was pregnant and the old man had not given Gérard any choice. But in the end it was he who had prevailed over the two wily Parisians, he who had learned the métier so well that he had made the gallery a huge success. And as for Giselle, it didn't matter. For twenty-four years now, he'd played the part. They had given him what he wanted, a home, a life, success, money, and the means he needed for his search. But it was the search that had kept him going for all these years.

For twenty-seven years now he'd been looking for his father and his sister, and he had known long since that he would never find them. Still, he kept on looking, when he thought he had a lead to something, when someone thought they knew someone who . . . He had made over sixty trips to Berlin. And it was all fruitless. Useless. In his heart Gérard knew that they were gone. If they weren't, he would have found them or they would have found him. His name was not so different. From Gerhard von Gotthard, he had become Gérard Goddard. But to wear the name of a

German after the war in France had been to invite ridicule, assault, anger, beatings. After a while he had been unable to take it any more. It had been the old man's idea to change his name, and at the time it seemed a wise one. Now, after all these years, he was more French than German. And it didn't matter. Nothing did. His dreams were gone.

Sometimes he wondered what he would have done if he had found them. What, in reality, would it have changed? In his heart he knew that it would have changed everything for him. He would have had the courage finally to leave Giselle, and maybe even take his children more firmly in hand and maybe even sell the gallery and enjoy his money for a change. He smiled at the endless options, knowing secretly that to find them would be not the end, but the beginning of his whole life's dream.

The next morning Tammy and Noel said goodbye to Brigitte and her brother, and just before they left, Gérard Goddard came hurriedly downstairs. He looked deep into the eyes of Noel, wondering if . . . but that was crazy . . . he couldn't be . . . but maybe this Mrs Max Thomas would know . . . it was a kind of madness Gérard Goddard had lived with for almost thirty years.

'Thank you so much, Mr Goddard.'

'Not at all, Noel . . . Tamara . . . we hope to see you here again.' He said nothing of the address they had given him, but simply waved as they shouted their goodbyes again, and drove away.

'I like your friends from New York, Brigitte.' He smiled at his daughter warmly and for once she returned the smile. He had always been so vague, so distant, so unhappy. It had made him an absentee father all her life.

'I like them too, Papa. They're very nice.' She watched him then as he walked pensively back towards his bedroom, and later that morning she heard him on the phone to Air France. She wandered casually into his bedroom. Her mother was already out. 'Are you going somewhere, Papa?'

He nodded slowly. 'Yes, New York. Tonight.'

'Business?' He nodded. 'Could I come with you?' He was startled as he watched her. Suddenly she looked almost as lonely as he. But this was one trip he had to make without her. Maybe next time . . . if . . .

'How about if I take you with me next time? This is going to be a little rocky. Kind of a tight deal I'm making. And I don't think I'll be gone for long.'

She eyed him quietly from the bedroom door. 'Will you really take me next time, Papa?'

He nodded slowly, awed that she would ask him. 'Yes, I will.'

He was vague when he talked to Giselle later that morning. And then he went quietly back to his room and packed his bag. He didn't plan to be gone for more than a day or two, scarcely longer. After hastily kssing Giselle and the children, he hurried to the airport to make the flight. His long stride allowed him to reach the gate in time, and the flight went from Nice to Paris and then directly to New York. From Kennedy he took a taxi, and then with trembling hands he had the cab stop at a phone booth very near to her address.

'Mrs Thomas?'

'Yes.'

'I'm afraid you don't know me, but my daughter is a friend of Tammy's – '

'Is something wrong?' She was suddenly frightened but her voice held nothing familiar for the man who listened. It was probably another wild-goose chase. He had been on so many before.

'No, not at all.' He was quick to reassure her. 'They went to Italy this morning and everything was fine. I just thought . . . I had some business to do here . . . a Renoir . . . and I was impressed with your daughter-in-law's ring. She mentioned that you had another, an emerald, and I had a spare moment, I thought . . .' He faltered, wondering why he had come all this distance.

'My emerald ring is not for sale.'

'Of course, of course. I understand that.' Poor man. He

sounded so boyish and so shy. She realised then that this was probably the Gérard Goddard Tammy had mentioned and suddenly Ariana felt bad about so unwelcoming and unkind.

'But if you'd just like to see it, perhaps you'd like to come over in a little while?'

'I'd like that, very much, Mrs Thomas . . . Half an hour? That would be fine.' He didn't even have a hotel room; all he had was a taxi and a suitcase, and he still had to waste another half hour. He had the driver drive him around in circles, up Madison Avenue and down Fifth and finally into the park. And then at last it was time to meet her. With trembling knees, he got out of the cab.

'Do you want me to wait here?' the cabbie offered. The fare was already forty dollars. Hell, why not? But the Frenchman shook his head, handed the man a fifty-dollar bill he had changed at the airport, and took his briefcase and his bag. He rang the doorbell beside the brass knocker and waited for what seemed like a very long time. His well-cut grey suit hung well on his thin frame and he was wearing a dark blue Doir tie, his white shirt looked sadly crumpled from the trip, and his shoes were handmade in London, like his shirts. But for all the expensive trappings, Gérard felt like a very young boy again, waiting for a father who never would return.

'Yes? Mr Goddard?' Ariana swiftly pulled the door open and looked into his face with a gentle smile. The emerald ring was on her finger. Their eyes met – they had the same deep blue eyes. For a moment she did not know him and she did not understand, but as he stood there, the man who had been Gerhard von Gotthard knew that he had at least found one of them at last. He stood there crying softly, making not a single sound. She was the same girl who had haunted his memories . . . the same face . . . those same laughing blue eyes . . .

'Ariana?' It was a whisper, but it called to her mind the sounds of so long ago . . . the shouts in the stairwell . . . the shrieks from his laboratory . . . the games they had played outside . . . Ariana . . . she could still hear it . . . Ariana! . . . 'Ariana!' It was like an echo as a sob tore through her and she flew into his arms.

'My God . . . my God . . . it's you . . . oh, Gerhard . . .' She held him with the anguish of a lifetime, as in her arms the tall, handsome, blue-eyed man held her close and sobbed.

They stood there for endless moments, holding tightly to the present and the past, and when at last she brought her brother inside with her, she smiled up at him, and he smiled, too . . . two people who had carried lonely burdens for half a lifetime and who had finally found each other, and were free at last.

ZOYA

DANIELLE STEEL

One woman's odyssey through a century of turmoil
. . .

'St Petersburg: one famous night of violence in the
October Revolution ends the lavish life of the
Romanov court forever – shattering the dreams of
young Countess Zoya Ossupov.

Paris: under the shadow of the Great War, émigrés
struggle for survival as taxi drivers, seamstresses
and ballet dancers. Zoya flees there in poverty . . .
and leaves in glory.

America: a glittering world of flappers, fast cars
and furs in the Roaring Twenties; a world of
comfort and café society that would come crashing
down without warning.

Zoya – a true heroine of our time – emerges
triumphant from this panoramic web of history
into the 80s to face challenges and triumphs.

0 7221 8315 1   GENERAL FICTION

All Sphere Books are available at your bookshop or newsagent, or can be ordered from the following address: Sphere Books, Cash Sales Department, P.O. Box 11, Falmouth, Cornwall TR10 9EN

Please send cheque or postal order (no currency), and allow 60p for postage and packing for the first book plus 25p for the second book and 15p for each additional book ordered up to a maximum charge of £1.90 in U.K.

B.F.P.O. customers allow 60p for the first book, 25p for the second book plus 15p per copy for the next 7 books thereafter 9p per book.

Overseas customers, including Eire, please allow £1.25 for postage and packing for the first book, 75p for the second book and 28p for each subsequent title ordered.